The Disenchanted Widow

THE DISENCHANTED WIDOW

CHRISTINA McKENNA

amazonpublishing

Text copyright © 2013 Christina McKenna

Cover design and illustration by David M. Kiely.

Published by Amazon Publishing

PO Box 400818

Las Vegas, NV 89140

ISBN-13: 9781611099539

ISBN-10: 1611099536

Library of Congress Control Number: 2012922283

Also by Christina McKenna:

My Mother Wore a Yellow Dress (memoir)
The Dark Sacrament (nonfiction)
The Misremembered Man (fiction)
Ireland's Haunted Women (nonfiction)

*In
memory of
Mark*

"I saw an angel in the marble,
and carved until I set it free."

Michelangelo Buonarroti, 1475–1564

Chapter one

Bessie Lawless, recently widowed and routinely brazen, had reason to feel cheated.

Just days into a period of dry-eyed mourning (during which she'd buried her feckless husband, lost her job at My Lovely Buns bakery, and suffered palpitations when a plastic bullet, released by a paratrooper in riot-control mode on the Antrim Road, whizzed past her right ear while she was hanging out the Thursday wash), she thought—she really thought, and could have been forgiven for thinking—that things could not bloody well get any worse.

But alas, as is the way of woe, which bulks up on misery when given the chance, things did indeed get worse. And all it needed was a single phone call to North-Eastern Mutual to prove the adage correct.

Packie had taken out life insurance cover soon after they'd married, long before the drink had taken him over and the path of connubial bliss had wobbled way off course. As the torturous years passed, the thought of the maturing policy, realized in a Packie-free future, kept Bessie's hope alive and madness at bay.

She needed that money now. *She really, really needed it.* To free herself. To stall the Dentist. To buy herself more time.

The brute had given her a deadline—and that deadline was upon her.

She'd made the phone call the previous day, fingers slipping on the dial. Expectation unnerving her knees and making her head spin. How much money was due? Quite a bit, she'd reckoned.

A brisk, officious voice down the line.

"Patrick…Patrick who?"

"Lawless."

"Lawless…Patrick? Just a moment." The creak of a chair. A filing drawer pulled out and pushed home…shuffling papers… her hammering heart…Presently the voice back on the line. Gentler now. A small sigh launching words she could not bear to hear.

"I'm afraid…"

What?

"I'm afraid that…due to—" A polite cough. "Due to outstanding nonpayment of premiums, the account for Mr. Lawless was…was closed quite some time ago."

What? What was he saying? It can't be. *It can't be.* Bessie biting back tears. Sweat breaking. A scream rising. She'd been counting on this. She'd been bloody well counting on this. The nest egg. The money pot.

But the nest was eggless, the pot plundered, Packie's account as bare as a barn in winter.

That night, in a sleepless rage, she'd surveyed the wreckage of her life. What had she to show for her thirty-one years? A dead marriage and the miserable bequests left to her: a dodgy record player, a drawer full of unpaid bills, a wedding ring, and a barely roadworthy clunker. Yes, that was all.

The record player she'd keep, since it had given her more joy than the husband. The bills she'd ignore. The ring she'd pawn. The barely roadworthy clunker she'd use to do a runner. As for his use-less surname: in her head she'd ditched it already.

The rent was overdue, the gas meter on empty. There was noth-ing left to do but junk the old life and ship out—out of Belfast, she and the boy. Fast and free. Away from the Dentist, the debt col-lectors, and murderous bombs, the bad memories twisting in her head like rattlesnakes.

There was no time to waste.

Picture her now on the morning of departure: standing over her nine-year-old son, fag in gob, arms akimbo, impatience blazing in her troubled heart, while Hercules—named after a tattoo on his dead father's chest—crams clothes into a Dunnes Stores shopper, a bag that's already at bursting point.

"Now, get a move on, son! We have till get out of here quick."

"Och, Ma! This bag's too wee."

"Yer *head's* too wee, son."

She blew jets of smoke from her nostrils like a dragon in a fairy tale, crushed the fag in a prickly pear cactus on the windowsill, yanked the bag from him.

"Now, look here. What did I say, son? Essentials *only*." She pitched out a thick roll of comics, a headless Action Man, and a lumpy pouch of Stickle Bricks. "Clothes *only*."

"But I *want* them, Ma!" whined the boy. "*They're mi-i-i-ine! I wa-a-a-a-ant them!*" He stamped a tiny foot on the threadbare carpet as tears spouted out of his baby-blue eyes.

"Now, Herkie, none of yer oul' lip." She grasped him by the shoulders and shook him. "You've read all them comics, and what good's an Action Man with no head on him anyway? Mind you, yer bloody da had no head on him, neither, and that's why we're in this bloody mess. So think on."

"But me Action Man can still shoot, and I *wa-a-a-a-nt*—"

"He can't *see* till bloody shoot. Now, stop this nonsense or I'll slap ye." She raised her right hand in the manner of a traffic cop at a busy junction. "I don't wanna, Herkie luv, but…"

Herkie knew that his ma's threat was genuine, and stopped immediately.

"That's a good boy." She mopped his face with a cuff of her blouse. "I'll buy ye new toys as soon as we get on the road. A new life for me and new toys for you. How's that?"

"D'ye promise, Ma?"

"Promise, son." She hugged him briefly, grabbed up the bag, and made for the door.

Herkie, his mother's back turned, seized his chance. He stuck the headless Action Man down his pants.

"Hurry *up*, son!" She took his hand and they hurried downstairs.

The kitchen looked as though it had been done over by a burglar: drawers lay upended; cupboard doors gaped open; the sink, choked high with dirty dishes, was dripping water onto the floor.

"I'll check in here, son. You check the front room."

She snatched up her Seamus the Fireman ashtray, a pair of black tights, and a half bottle of Tullamore Dew from beneath a cushion on an armchair. Reapplied her lipstick at a wall mirror while stuffing the items into her shoulder bag.

Out back, the Morris Traveller—cracked seats, bald tires, and rotting timber frame—sat loaded up with all their worldly goods.

"Ma, we forgot the record player!"

The sound of a vehicle drawing up out front cut the breath from her.

Oh, my God! Could it be *him*? Jesus, it can't be. Not now.

She peered through the curtains and saw a shiny Austin Princess.

Jesus, it *is* him.

She had to think fast. Should she just leave the record player and dash out the back door? Was retrieving it worth the risk?

The bolted gate, the garden path, and the locked hall door lay between them and would buy her a couple of minutes at least.

She could do it.

"Is it the Dentist, Ma?"

"It bloody is, son." She threw Herkie the bag. "*Go on*, son. Go! I'll get it."

Herkie raced out the back, caught up in the drama of it all.

She slid the record player off the sideboard and staggered out through the back door, her arms aching, mock-croc stilettos skidding on the mossy path.

There was no time to shut the door. No time to bid farewell to the rented house on Valencia Terrace, and clearly no space in the car for the record player.

But Bessie Lawless was used to snap decisions. Life with a volatile husband had sharpened her wits, given her the reflexes of a championship boxer. She stowed the record player on the passenger seat and pushed Herkie in on top of it.

From within, the doorbell sounded.

"Hurry up, Ma! He's comin', he's comin'!"

In seconds she was behind the wheel.

She floored the accelerator.

Squeeeeeeee! The engine's high-pitched protest was alarming.

"What was that big noise, Ma?"

Bessie hadn't a notion. And had neither the time nor inclination to investigate. She hit the accelerator again. The car bucked—and they were away.

"Hi, come back here, ye fuckin' bitch, or I'll tear yer bloody—"

In the rearview mirror she caught sight of the furious Dentist standing in the middle of the road, his face the color of the wine-stain birthmark splashed across his bald head.

"Hopefully it's the last we'll see of *him*," she yelled at the windshield, her heart pounding, hands sweating on the wheel. She made a sharp right out of Dunville Avenue, cutting him clean from sight—and, with a bit of luck, clean out of her life for good.

It was April 1981, and Belfast was burning: a seething cauldron of hatred and division where down back alleys IRA gunmen performed impromptu knee surgery on informers, where no-warning bombs exploded in carrier bags and British soldiers kept eyes alert, Bullpup rifles at the ready. Margaret Thatcher was in Downing Street, Charles Haughey leading the Dáil. In the Maze prison H-Blocks, a succession of young men were starving themselves to death for the cause of Irish freedom.

The widow negotiated a warren of narrow streets, all decked out in tricolors and murals to the patriotic martyrs. Racing down Rossapena Street, she hit a ramp, causing Herkie's head to bounce off the ceiling, before turning right onto Cliftonville Road. She was glad to be avoiding the rush-hour traffic. With luck, they'd reach the border before nightfall.

"Where we goin', Ma?"

"As far away from this bloody place as possible. Who knows, son, if we can get the money together, maybe all the way till Amerikay till see the Statue of Liberry. But first—"

"I'd love till see the Statue of Liberry, Ma!"

"I know, son, but first we've got till earn us some money for the passage. Now, yer Auntie Joan in Sligo might help us out. Failing that, yer Uncle Bert in Hackney. But for now, son, light me a fag there like a good boy."

Herkie reached below the dashboard and picked up the Park Drives. He liked sitting on top of the record player (now that the ride was smoother) because it gave him a commanding view and made him feel as big as any adult.

Screechh-h-h.

She'd slammed on the brakes. At a zebra crossing—which she hadn't even noticed, her eyes being mostly on the rearview mirror for fear of the Dentist—an old lady was tottering out. Bessie fumed, annoyed at the delay, and pressed the horn.

The pensioner did a double take. On seeing Herkie with fag in hand, she waved her stick, appalled. The nine-year-old added to her dismay by dragging deeply on the cigarette and blowing the smoke out the window.

"Stop yer clownin', son." She snatched up the cigarette.

"Yer a disgrace!" the old lady called out. "I have the right o' way."

"Well, away on with ye then!" the mother shouted, revving the engine.

"Aye, away on with ye!" echoed the son.

Bessie shifted the car into first gear and roared off, causing Herkie to topple from his perch.

"Serves ye right for being a cheeky monkey. Now, make yerself useful and tell me if ye see any Brits from up there. This bloody thing isn't taxed."

"I think I see one," he said. He'd clambered back onto the record player and was holding on tight to the knobs.

"Don't be daft, son. The Brits are like friggin' blackheads. Ye never get one but a whole bloody rash—*and* when ye don't bloody want them...like *now*."

She slowed the car to a crawl and joined the queue as four members of the Queen's Own Highlander Regiment, in fatigues and tartan berets, sprang out of an army truck and began setting up a checkpoint.

"See, what did I tell ye? Now, you behave yerself, ye hear, and let yer ma do the talkin'."

"Aye, Ma."

The car in front was waved through, and Bessie moved forward, drawing even with a soldier. He'd an automatic weapon slung over his right shoulder, and its muzzle was now pointing menacingly close to her right ear. She instinctively raised a protective hand.

"Where's you off to then, luv?" the soldier inquired, chewing vigorously on a piece of gum and aiming the query at her bosom.

None of your bloody business. "Oh, just going out for the day… with my son."

He glanced into the back. "You take the whole 'ouse wiff you every time you goes out then?" He eyed Herkie. "What's that fing you're sittin' on, sonny?"

"What's a 'fing,' Ma?"

Bessie shot Herkie a baleful glance. The last thing she wanted was Soldier Boy going through her stuff. She'd have to nudge him off balance with a bit of the old girlie charm.

"It's my record player, sir. Helps me unwind in the evening… you know how it is." She was glad she'd reapplied her lipstick as she simpered up at him, fully aware that the three-quarter profile she was presenting was most alluring.

The soldier reddened, a vision of a *Playboy* centerfold rearing up at him—that was Bessie's idea, anyway, and she imagined she'd struck close enough to the mark.

The walkie-talkie in his breast pocket squawked, breaking the fantasy.

"Mind how you go then," he said, embarrassed, and waved them through.

No worries there, thought Bessie Lawless: she'd every intention of minding how she went.

She was in the driver's seat for the very first time in her life. She put the car in gear and sped off—away from the soldier, away from the bloody Dentist, her dead husband, and, with a bit of luck, the dreadful past.

Chapter two

Lorcan Strong was having no end of trouble with the bosom of Miss Theodosia Magill, Countess of Clanwilliam. She was showing far too much cleavage, for a start, which always made life difficult. He thought back to another lady he'd touched up only the year before: Harriet Anne Butler, a Belfast aristocrat. Miss Butler had been a joy to handle, she being more demure and less obviously endowed.

Flesh was always a problem for Lorcan. All that blending of zinc buffs, cadmium yellows, and canton roses made him giddy at times, and no more so than when he was dealing with an expanse of bosom. What you could get away with in a face or hand in a portrait you couldn't palm off so easily with a bosom. Everyone—male and female alike—was drawn, consciously or subconsciously, to that part of a painting more than any other.

Even though the air temperature and humidity levels in the restoration room were perfectly controlled, Lorcan found the atmosphere on that fine April day oppressive. This had nothing to do with climate and everything to do with the tension he was feeling. For these days he was a troubled man living in a very troubled city. People were being slain with a depressing regularity. The "wrong" name, workplace, or address was enough to condemn you.

In the general run of things, the conservator could remain on the periphery, an observer of events rather than a part of them. But all that had changed a month before when he, the idle spectator, had been dragged, through no fault of his own, into the fray.

His hand quivered and he drew back from the canvas. He'd never experienced such upset to his routine before, and he resented it. Repairing an Old Master and keeping true to the spirit of its creator was not the preserve of the cack-handed or faint of heart. But of late his heart and hand, steady and assured for so many years, were failing him.

He dipped a brush into a jar of thinner and stirred it, pondering his lot.

By rights you should not be here at all. You should be home fulfilling your duty to your dear old mother. He was addressing the unspoken to the equally silent Countess as she gazed serenely out at the cluttered workroom.

Yes, home: seeing to things in the family bar and on the land. You should have the malty whiff of stout in your nostrils, not the odor of linseed, and in your hand a dirt-grimed shovel instead of that very fine Siberian squirrel paintbrush. You're a fraud, Strong. And if you'd stayed at home and done as your mother wished, you wouldn't be in this mess now.

In disgust, he threw the brush down and got up to stand by the window.

Belfast was spewing its workers onto the streets. He could hear the muffled stamp of feet, the exhaling breath of air brakes, and the all-too-familiar strains of sirens wailing their way to yet another atrocity.

Perhaps he should return home. Escape. Save himself. Save his mother. After all, he owed her.

Oh, yes, he did owe his poor mother. He knew that all too well. His father, a farmer and publican, had died ten years earlier, and she'd been depending on her only son to come home and continue where her husband had left off. But Lorcan had let it be known that he was interested in neither the land nor the pub business.

"Mother, I'm not cut out for tramping fields and serving drunks." He'd meant "drinks" but hadn't bothered correcting himself. "I have an imagination." The young, defiant artist was unrepentant.

"Are you saying your poor father had no imagination?"

"Strictly speaking, only artists have imagination, and I can't afford to have mine stifled. This is not *me*." He'd swept an arm majestically with that last remark, to encompass not only the Crowing Cock pub and their outlying farm but the entire population of Tailorstown and the mountains beyond.

"I'm very disappointed in you, Lorcan. Just so long as you remember that your father's pub and the people of this town put food on our table and clothes on your back and funded your education."

But he'd won the day nonetheless, had rented out the land to local farmers, employed a bartender to assist his mother, and returned to Belfast. After graduation, he'd pursued a career as a painter and printer before finally fetching up in the conservation room of the Ulster Museum.

Now thirty-seven and considerably wiser, he winced at the arrogance of that younger self, turned away from the window, and sat down before the Countess once more. An act of justification, if nothing else.

These days, instead of toiling over his own canvases, he bent over the work of others. Not that he was bitter, for he was, quite literally, having a hand in the work of the great innovators. The Turners, the Reynoldses, the Laverys: all were revivified under his expert hand. One week in the Barbizon, the next in the Rococo, Lorcan moved between schools and periods and styles with the ease of a quick-change artist. It was fulfilling—and lucrative—work.

He considered the image on the canvas once again, flexed the fingers of his right hand several times, and took a deep breath. Sufficiently calmed to continue, he laid a speck of cadmium on a soupçon of white and blended the minute quantities to the required hue before taking the brush to the canvas again.

The Countess was a plain woman whom Reynolds had flattered as far as he dared, his brush more forgiving than a camera lens could ever be. There was little the great painter could have done about that nose, though: much too long. Each time Lorcan contemplated it, the perfectionist in him wanted to shorten it, to make her perfect.

That was his problem and he knew it: the quest for perfection, that unattainable moving target. But the chase brought excellence, and that realization was *his* prize.

Thump! Thump! Thump! His reverie was broken by a boisterous knocking on the door.

The insufferable Stanley from Fossils, no doubt.

"Are ye not finished with that oul' doll's hooters yet?" Stanley shouted, peering through the glass door-panel and trying the handle.

Lorcan did not flinch. Stanley was another good reason for keeping his door locked.

"I'm goin' for a drink. Wanna come?"

"No, I've no time. Away—back to your old crustaceans."

"Och, away with *you*. Ye're too involved with that woman. She's only been dead two hundred years."

"And your fossils have been dead fifty *million* years. See you tomorrow, Stanley."

"Ye can have more fun with a pair of the real ones, ye know... down the Empire."

"*Bye*, Stanley."

"Never know who ye'd meet..."

"Good*bye*, Stanley."

"Ah, right. Suit yerself. See ye the marra. But if ye change yer mind, ye know where I'll be."

"I won't change my mind!" He heard Stanley's footsteps retreating down the corridor, then hurrying back again.

For heaven's sake, what now?

"Hi, I forgot. Catherine gave me a note for ye. Said somebody left it in for ye at reception."

Lorcan tensed. He paused before answering, fearful that his voice might betray him. "Really?"

"Well, are ye gonna open the door so I can give it to ye?"

"Yes…I mean no. Just…just push it under the door, Stanley, please."

"God, you're a right queer one, Strong."

He waited for Stanley's departing footsteps, for the outer door to bang shut, before rising. He knew what the note contained. He knew who it was from.

Action was needed now. Yes, action. Anything to delay opening it. He checked his watch. Time to finish up for the day.

At the sink, he cleaned his brushes with turpentine. The remaining oils on the palette were sheathed in polythene and tightly secured to keep the air out.

He pulled on his green velvet jacket and positioned his Borsalino at just the right angle. Only then did he feel brave enough to bend down and pick up the wretched thing.

It was written in heavy, black pencil, as though by a child's hand. The import of the words, however, was far from childish.

Dont forget your wee dental appointment. Thursday 8 pm sharp. There'll be consawquences if you miss it Lorcan my oul son.

Chapter three

Being a city girl, Bessie Lawless was not used to reading road maps; never had much cause to. On leaving Belfast she'd headed northwest, toward the town of Ballymena, then followed a more westerly route because it looked more direct on the map. Since she was in a hurry to get away from Belfast, this seemed the sensible thing to do.

Her plan was to visit her sister, Joan, in Sligo and get a loan from her to help fund their passage to Uncle Bert in England. She'd already written to Bert, a former drains inspector from the Short Strand. Five years before, he'd come into unexpected wealth via the death of a maiden aunt. The windfall had enabled him to make flesh a long-cherished dream of owning a townhouse pub in Hackney.

If Joan loaned her the fare—and that was a big "if" indeed—Bessie's plan could work. But Joan had no idea that she was on her way, and Bessie had no intention of telling her. They didn't get on, and giving notice of her arrival would only mean offering Joan the excuse of being conveniently out when she called. Or hiding in a cupboard at the sound of the car drawing up. She knew her older sibling all too well.

But Bessie's unfamiliarity with maps ensured that, barely an hour into the journey, she found herself hopelessly lost on a series of rural roads without signposts. Herkie, still sitting regally atop the record player, was enjoying the novelty of it all. He'd never seen sheep or cattle up close and was paying more attention to them than to the map spread out on his knees—the map he was supposed to be following.

They drew up at a crossroads.

"Right, where to now, son?"

"Take a left, Ma," he said immediately, gazing in fascination at a goat tethered in a nearby field.

Bessie glanced over at him, irritated.

"How can ye be so sure, son?" She yanked the map away from him. "And is it any wonder we're friggin' lost: yer readin' that map *upside down*."

"But I see a signpost at the bottom, Ma. That'll tell us where till go."

"Right, if you send me the wrong way again, I'll put ye in a field with them bloody sheep, and *they* can take ye to yer Auntie Joan's."

The sign read TAILORSTOWN, but it wasn't marked on the map. Since they were in the middle of nowhere and heading nowhere, she decided to follow the sign and get a fill-up of petrol at least.

Some ten minutes later, they pulled into what appeared to be a filling station on the outskirts of the village.

God, she wondered, drawing the car to a halt, does anybody live here at all?

The filling station had an unsettling air about it. It looked by turns deserted and inhabited; smoke was curling up from what appeared to be a car-exhaust chimney pot set atop a dilapidated, two-room dwelling with a sagging roof tufted with weeds and patched here and there with flattened beer cans. At one window a set of lace curtains was half drawn. At another a piece of faded chipboard was doing duty as a windowpane.

In front stood two fuel pumps.

Farther down the yard, an open-fronted garage had a sign proclaiming Grant Auto Repairs in sun-bleached lettering. Several vehicles were scattered about in various stages of disassembly. A field to the rear was strewn with more bits of rusting car parts. A bomb might have exploded some years before and no one had bothered to clear up the mess.

Apart from a couple of hens pecking the ground, there was little sign of life.

The widow sounded the horn and waited.

"Can I get out and play with them birds, Ma?" asked Herkie, fascinated by the hens and thirsting for his freedom. Sitting on the record player for so long had given him pink welts on the back of his legs.

"No, you stay where you are, son. God knows what sort of lunatic lives here. Ye might end up in a pot o' Lurgan stew or something, and we wouldn't want that."

"Och, Ma, that's silly. Cannonballs do that." Herkie began bumping his head off the car ceiling to relieve his boredom.

"And how d'ye know a cannonball doesn't live here? I saw a film called *The Texas Chainsaw Masker* once, and these mountain men did that to a couple of city people who stopped to get petrol off them. Hauled them into the kitchen of a house just like that, and made a dinner out of the pair of them that fed them for a whole—"

"God, Ma, what's *that?*"

Bessie hoisted herself up in the seat. "What?"

"There!"

A small, fat animal was streaking toward the car, grunting and snorting.

"Jesus!"

"Is it a dog, Ma?"

"No, son. It's a bloody pig!"

She was just reaching for the ignition key when a middle-aged man emerged from the depths of the garage, wiping his hands on a dirty rag. He cut an odd figure as he loped up the yard: tall and rangy, clad in a set of outsize overalls that flapped about him like tenting in a gale. The piglet, sporting a black backside and matching face, raced to him.

He stooped down to stroke it.

"What did I tell you? Only a lunatic could live—"

"Didn't hear ye there," said the man, ducking close to the car window. "But Veronica here's got better ears than me."

Bessie recoiled from his unshaven jib and barn-owl eyes magnified behind thick lenses. "That's all right," she said. "Three pounds' worth of four-star, please."

"Ye're not from round these parts, are ye, 'cos I never seen ye afore. Then again, I don't get many comin' round here anyway."

How surprising! "No, we're just passing through."

"Headin' far, are ye?" He rubbernecked Herkie while waiting for the pause to be filled by explanation, but Bessie had no intention of disclosing too much to anyone—least of all this stranger.

"Just over the border."

"Ye've got a bit tae go then. Ye'll be wantin' yer oil and watter checked?"

The widow had never thought of checking those. That had been Packie's job.

"Well, if you wouldn't mind."

He filled the tank, then raised the bonnet.

"Ma, can I go to the toilet?" Herkie was clutching his crotch, face crumpled in pretend agony. He reckoned he'd be safe enough, she supposed, now that the ax murderer was fully occupied with the car.

"How bad d'ye need-a go, son?"

"I'm burstin', Ma!"

She stuck her head out the window. "Can my boy use your toilet?"

"Aye, just go behind the hedge there," came the reply. "That's the on'y toilet there is."

"Did ye hear that? No luxuries here, son. Watch that pig doesn't take a bite outta yer bum."

"Och, Ma!"

Herkie slunk off to the field. Veronica, in the inquisitive manner of piglets, trotted after him.

It was stifling in the car, and the raised bonnet was obscuring her view. Bessie pushed open the door.

"Everything all right?" she asked, sidestepping what appeared to be Veronica's poo—well, she hoped so, anyway—and coming round to the front of the vehicle.

The mechanic squinted up at her, looking decidedly worried.

"Well, now, ever'thing would be all right if ye weren't goin' far. Ye see, that fan belt's about tae go, and if ye broke down ye'd be stuck, 'cos there's not much 'tween here and the border. Ye can risk it if ye like, but if I were you I'd get it fixed right away."

That was all she needed to hear. The very thought of breaking down and being marooned in this Bally-go-Backward was unthinkable. At the same time, she wondered: How can I be sure this man is being straight with me? The old car, rarely off the road, had seldom given any trouble (apart from that time in 1978 she mistook the brake for the accelerator and plowed into the back of Mr. Yummy's ice-cream van, double-parked outside the Department of Health and Social Security office).

"Oh, that's news to me," she said, feigning calmness and composure. "The fan belt, eh? Are you sure about that?"

"Well, I'll show yeh."

He bent over the engine and ran a hand under the belt. "See that?" Bessie leaned in warily, affecting interest and expertise. "Far too much play. Too tight's bad enough, but too loose is even worse. Did ye notice her squealin' after ye started her?"

Damn. She had, right enough. She was recalling the high-pitched protest that kick-started her getaway from Valencia Terrace.

He knew what he was talking about.

Herkie returned from his comfort break, hitching up his jeans. The piglet, much to Bessie's relief, now had its snout stuck in a tractor tire and was busily occupied.

"What's wrong, Ma?"

"Never you mind, son. Can you fix it for me *now* then?" she asked the man, shielding her eyes from the sun and wondering how in God's name she was going to pay him.

"Could fix it for ye surely, if I had the part. But I don't have the part, ye see."

Bessie waited for more, but the mechanic simply adjusted his specs, rubbed his nose, inspected the toes of his size twelves.

"Could you get the part and fix it for me then?"

She had the feeling that she might take root and start growing chest hair if he didn't get a move on. She'd heard that country people were a bit slow, but this was ridiculous.

"Could get ye the part surely, but I'd have tae go into Killoran tae get it, and that's the thing."

Herkie, bored with the adult talk, had wandered over to Veronica and hunkered down beside her. He was deciding whether to pull her ears, tweak her tail, or poke her fat belly—in short, deciding which molestation might produce the most discomfort for the piglet and therefore the most entertainment for him.

"And could you do that?" Bessie asked patiently. "Go into Kill...Kill...whatever?"

"Killoran. Naw, 'cos Willie-Tom is closed the day. His ma's in the hospital, ye see…skidded on a mat when she was gettin' her hair done in Hilda Cahoon's hair saloon and broke her hip. Hilda had tae get the amb'lance, 'cos she couldn't get herself up."

"Well, I'm sorry to hear that, but—"

"Ye could try McMurty in the town but he'd charge ye an arm and a leg, 'cos he's got bigger overheads than me. He'd do a quicker job for ye, right enuff, but I'd put money on it that it wouldn't be as good a job as I'd do. I take me time, ye see, on account of havin' a bit more of it on me hands out here, not bein' in the town, like."

"Look, I'll tell you what: I'll just—"

"They're queuing up for McMurty in the town but that's only 'cos he's in the town and not out here in the cawntry like me…I couldn't guarantee that ye wouldn't have a wait on yer hands there, too. He could say he'd have it for yeh this evenin', then ye could go back this evenin' and he'd tell ye a different story altogether. He's like that, ye see. And at the end of the day he'd charge ye more, 'cos as I say, he's got bigger overheads than me…"

Bessie realized it was pointless trying to interrupt. She was put in mind of her old refrigerator. It, too, had a habit of droning on in similar fashion. A swift kick in the right spot usually sorted *it* out. However, in this case such a tactic might prove highly inadvisable. She'd simply have to endure it. Let the mechanic say his piece. He'd peter out eventually.

"…but it's a free cawntry and it's up tae *you*. As I say, I'll do it for ye as soon as Willie-Tom opens the morra…couldn't say fairer than that. I would of done it for ye today if Willie-Tom's mother hadn't skidded on that mat. But a body never knows from one day till the next what's gonna happen. So it's up tae you what ye want tae do."

"Look, I'll just risk it then," the widow said, not wanting to hear any more calendar entries for Willie-Tom's trials—past, present, and to come. She gave him the money for the petrol. "I've had no problems so far. What do I owe you for the—"

"*Squeeeeee!*"

They turned as one to see a frantic piglet hurtling down the yard toward the safety of the shed.

"Get back here, you little shit!" Bessie snarled at her son. Then, realizing her mask had slipped, she moved swiftly to repair the damage. "So sorry," she told the man. "He's not used to animals, I'm afraid. You know what city boys are like."

"Aye, a-do." The mechanic glared at Herkie as he sidled back to stand sheepishly beside his mother. "That wee pig does nobody no harm."

"Say sorry to Mister...eh..."

"Grant."

"Say sorry to Mr. Grant, son."

"Sorry, Mr. Grant," said a suitably chastened Herkie.

"Now, what do I owe you for the oil?"

"Oh, the oil's on me."

"Thank you very much, Mr. Grant."

"I'm Augustus." He held out a grubby hand. "But I get Gusty for short. And who would *you* be?"

"Halstone," she said at once, giving his hand the briefest of shakes, a smile flashing like a blade. "*Mrs.* Halstone." Had he looked even a teeny bit well-off, she'd have used her first name.

"Ma, that's not our—"

"Well, thank you, Mr. Grant," she said, a bit too loudly. Then, through gritted teeth. "*Herkie,* come on now. Let's go."

Herkie once again climbed aboard the record player. Bessie settled herself into the driver's seat.

She threw the car into reverse and drove out onto the main road.

The mechanic stood in the middle of his junkyard, tracking her every move. She rounded a bend. He slid from view. Her grip on the steering wheel tightened.

Please, God, let the bloody fan belt hold!

Chapter four

The road Bessie found herself on a few minutes out of Grant's garage was, like her past, a bumpy one. She raised dust and scattered crows as she roared along, trying not to think about the events that had brought her to this sorry remove.

For life had never been easy for the careworn blonde with eyes as sad as twilight. What with an alcoholic father and his foul-wafting rages, a harassed mother stretched out on Christ's suffering cross, and the grudging, green-eyed sister Joan, any happiness that might have been circling got turned away early from the gate.

If childhood had been difficult, then girlhood proved even more unpalatable. Cupid's arrow might have struck her heart, but the wound it left went deep. Packie Lawless—handsome once, attentive once, but all too soon mutating into a tattooed monster—had used the housekeeping money to fuel his binges and his fists to end disputes. He'd lit the wick of love, then snuffed the candle out, bringing mayhem into the home and the scourge of bloody IRA wrath into their lives.

At the mere thought of the terrorists, she raised a hand to her forehead and squeezed hard. They'd given her a headache that could last a lifetime—literally.

She pressed down on the accelerator, as if increased speed might zap the memory of it all.

And the reward for all that suffering? Well, was it this? Widowed, homeless, and penniless, barreling down a road to nowhere. Oh, the injustice! The sheer bloody injustice!

She braked suddenly for an unforeseen bend and unseated Herkie, who thumped down into the dashboard with some force.

"Och, Ma!"

He struggled back onto the record player, a ruby bruise forming on his forehead.

"Sorry, son."

At that, the loaded Morris Traveller began to slow. Bessie engaged the accelerator hard, but the vehicle wouldn't respond. Her temper rose with the red needle of the temperature gauge.

"Ma, look: There's smoke comin' outta the front!"

"*Jesus Christ*, I don't *bloody* believe it!"

But her expletive was lost in an ominous grumbling. The car began to buck. There came an ill-omened spluttering. The engine died.

She turned the ignition several times. Nothing. The engine was as dead as Packie and the Bogman of Aran.

"Will I run back and get Mr. Grant, Ma?"

"No, it's too far for you to go. Get me a cigarette there." She was trying to remain calm. "I'll take a wee look."

She got out, raised the bonnet—and was nearly blinded by blue-black smoke. Since the innards of a car were as alien to her as the abdominal viscera of a chimpanzee, she slammed the bonnet back down again in disgust.

Herkie came round the side of the car, puffing the cigarette into life. He handed it up to her. My God, what were they going to do now? She hadn't factored in a breakdown. A nervous breakdown, maybe, but not the bloody car.

She leaned back against the driver's door, her headache now in full throttle, dragged deeply on the cigarette, pulled the bottle of whiskey from her bag, and took a swig. By the hedgerow, Herkie amused himself by bursting the sepals of a foxglove. She stuffed the bottle into her bag just as he turned back to her.

"Ma, what's that called?"

"A flower, son."

"Aye, but what kinda flower?"

"A fox's glove, I think."

"Och, Ma, foxes don't wear gloves."

"Look, son, don't be silly. Yer ma needs till think."

Herkie, hot and bothered, left off his inspection of the foxglove and moved on to a gatepost.

The rush of the alcohol was having a steadying effect. A warm breeze fanned her face, curling the leaves on trees she'd never learn the names of. She shaded her eyes and gazed about. They were well and truly stranded. The pollution and clamor of the big city were a distant memory now, but the silence and the isolation of the countryside—which should have been welcome—were showing her another kind of woe.

"God, how can anybody live out here?"

Summer had come early for the farmers. All about lay pastures of rapeseed and barley, scorching under the sun. The sweet odors rising up through the steady heat threatened to nauseate her. An alien funk. Field upon field stretched away to the mountains, with not a house in sight.

"What are we gonna do, Ma?" Herkie was beside her, chewing on a piece of straw and gazing up at her.

"Don't know, son. Wait for someone to come, I suppose. And take that hay out of yer gob. One of them sheep back there prob'bly pissed on it."

"Yuk!" He spat it out. "But what if nobody comes, Ma, and it gets dark?"

"God, you're a real ray of sunshine, son." She threw down the spent cigarette and squashed it underfoot. "How should I know? We'll sleep in the bloody car then, and wait till somebody comes. We're not in the middle of Siberier, although we might as well be."

"Ma, why did you tell that man a diff'rent name?"

"Son, I've decided that's what we're called from now on. Till we get tae yer auntie's. You're not Herkie Lawless any more; you're Herkie Halstone."

"But *why*, Ma?"

"'Cos it's not safe using our own name with the bloody Dentist on our tail. Halstone's your granny's name, don't ye know, and my name before I married yer useless da. So, what's your name, son?"

"Herkie Law—Hilton."

"For pity's sake, Herkie *Halstone*!" She kicked a stone on the road. "See that? What is it?"

"A stone, Ma."

"Yes. And your name is Hal*stone*. Got it? Now, tell me again."

"H-Hal-stone. Herkie Halstone."

"Good boy!"

Herkie went over to a broken-down gate and began climbing it.

"You watch yourself, Herkie Halstone! I'm gonna sunbathe here. Might as well get meself a tan."

She took a cushion from the car and positioned it on the warm bonnet. Removed her blouse to reveal a flesh-colored slip with a lacy scalloped neckline. Hung the blouse on the open car door.

She settled herself on the bonnet and closed her eyes, offering her face up to the sun. She hoped the mishap with the car was just a blip on the radar of her plan. There was no way she was going back to Belfast. She'd suffered enough because of Packie, having been spouse, skivvy, and regular punching bag for far too long. And now, because of *his* shenanigans, she had the Dentist to contend with—a psycho who was threatening to drill holes in her shins if she didn't return the money Packie had made off with.

There was only one problem: Bessie hadn't got it. But would the Dentist believe that? Fat frigging chance of that...

She knew, of course, what Packie and his two "associates" had done. They'd concocted a plan to embezzle the money from the bank job the three had just pulled for the Dentist. She'd overheard them discussing it.

"Sure, of course the Dentist'll know," she'd heard Packie say. The three had drunk the best part of two bottles of whiskey, and consequently their voices were raised more than was good for them. "But we'll have tae get our story straight, so we will. The Dentist's a smart bastard. Any slipup an' he'll be on till us. Ye know what *that* means, don't ye?"

"The Nuttin' Squad," Donal Carmody had said, equally loudly.

"Aye, the Nuttin' Squad. And ye know what that bastard's like with a Black & Decker."

"I do," said Aidan Mahon, plumber by day and getaway driver by night. "Don't I have a pair of metal knees to prove it? So what's the plan then, Packie?"

"The plan is that we were stopped by the UDR. And they found the money. But they let us go."

"*What?*"

"Ye can't be serious, Packie," came the dismayed voice of Donal. "If we were stopped by the UDR we'd be in the clink now."

"We wouldn't," Packie said, "because the Ulster Defence Regiment is full of hoods, as you well know. What we'll say is that they pocketed the cash themselves. That way, it won't appear on a charge sheet, and no one but us will ever know it was recovered. So what d'ye say—split three ways or what?"

"Begod, it's a great plan altogether," Aidan said. "Let's split it now, Packie. No time like the present."

"No!" Packie had sounded vexed and a little concerned. "We don't split it yet. In fact, we don't so much as *touch* that money until all this has blowed over. I don't want your Maisie and Lil goin' mad and buyin' out half o' bloody Woolworths. It would draw attention to us. Nah, we have tae be one step ahead of that baldy fuck and them bastards in Special Branch."

"Aye, right enough," said Aidan. "So what do we do?"

"I'll hold on to it," Packie told him. "It's safe here. I couldn't do a runner with it even if I wanted to, 'cos I'd have you two as well as the Dentist on me tail. No, I've stashed it here in a safe place. Not even the missus would find it. We'll meet back here this day week, same time, and divvy it up."

"Bloody brilliant!" Donal said. "Ye're on, Packie."

"Right, now I'll run you home, Aidan. Then I'll go and break the bad news tae the oul' baldy. See you next week, Donal."

"Ye're on, Packie."

It hadn't worked out that way, Bessie thought bitterly now. Packie never got to tell his concocted tale to the Dentist. That had been left to the hapless Donal. That night, Packie and Aidan lost their lives in a head-on collision. Taken out by a Belgian nun, of all people, in a pair of built-up shoes, driving on the wrong side of the Belfast-to-Comber road.

Packie had never confided to her the hiding place of the £10,000.

Then the mayhem. Oh, the mayhem, gushing through the days and nights, swamping everything. She grimaced, her whole body tensing at the memory of it: the doorbell sounding in the early hours, a stern-faced cop, "Ye'd best sit down, Mrs. Lawless." Packie's mutilated face on a mortuary slab. The Dentist barging into the funeral home. "I'm givin' you a couple-a days tae bury yer useless husband, 'cos I'm considerate like that. Then I'll be back for *my* money."

She'd torn the house apart, combed the attic and every conceivable place of concealment.

Not a thing.

It was typical of Packie Lawless. In life he'd given her nothing but bother. And he was still tormenting her from beyond the grave.

"Ma!" Herkie was calling out from the top of the gatepost where he'd perched himself. "I think I see something comin'!"

Her eyes snapped open. She snatched up the blouse.

"Where, son?"

"Over there! It's comin' through a field. Maybe it's a tractor."

Quickly doing up her buttons, she went to the gate and hauled herself up next to the boy. He was right. She could just make out a vehicle turning onto the main road. It was headed in their direction.

"Thank God for that. Get down from there, son. Quick!"

Through the heat haze they watched as a smudge became a blob; grew into a shivering, jellylike mass; sprouted wing mirrors, a set of headlights, and a very grimy windshield. The windshield revealed what looked like a Martian wearing a cap and goggles; the vision finally mutated into an unshaven mug wearing thick glasses. Their most recent acquaintance, Mr. Grant, drew to a clattering halt alongside them in a battered green truck. He wound down the window.

"I kinda knowed ye were gonna have a bitta bother, Mrs. Hailstone. But I didn't think it'd be as soon. That's yer fan belt, I'd say."

"*Hal*stone," Bessie corrected him. "Yes, I suppose it is." She resented being dependent on this stranger. In her experience, a man never did a favor for a woman without expecting a return on his investment—usually of an unseemly nature—with added interest. She draped her arms about Herkie's shoulders and held him in front of her like a shield.

"As I say, I could fix it for ye when I get that part in Willie-Tom's."

"That would be great, Mr. Grant. I'm much obliged. Is there a B-and-B near here?"

"Naw, there's nuthin' about here—on account that nobody comes here."

You don't say. "Not even in Tailorstown?"

"Naw, nuthin' there, neither." He adjusted his glasses. Inspected a cloud formation. "But y'know, I maybe could help ye out."

"Oh, no, you've been too kind already, Mr. Grant." A picture of a shack with sagging sills and a warped door loomed up before her. Spending the night on a rubbish tip would be preferable. "I wouldn't dream of impo—"

"Now, it isn't the garage place. It's another house on the far side o' the town. It belonged to me Aunt Dora, but she died a couple-a months ago and it's been empty since." Bessie's ears pricked up. "Ye could stay there the night, if ye want, 'cos I wouldn't see a body stuck, so I wouldn't. An' sartainly not a woman like yerself, Mrs. Hailstone."

Now *that* was a different matter altogether. She hadn't reckoned on the scruffy mechanic having a second property. Besides, she was in no position to decline; she was effectively homeless. And he was offering to fix the car the next morning.

"That's very kind of you, Mr. Grant," she said, gifting him with a wide smile. She looked down at Herkie. "Isn't it, son?"

"D'you make Lurgan stew, Mr. Grant?"

"What's that ye're sayin'?"

Bessie pinched Herkie's arm. "Say *thank you* to Mr. Grant, son."

Herkie squirmed. "Thank you, Mr. Grant."

"Right ye be. Well, if ye want tae lock her up there, I'll run yis over tae the house. She'll be safe enuff tae I come back with me tow-rope."

"Okay...I'll...I'll just get a couple of things from the boot."
She turned away from him to cover her unease. "Come on, son.
Help me out here."

A scene from *The Texas Chainsaw Massacre* flashed into Bessie's
mind. Well, she'd have to take her chances. Augustus Grant, homi-
cidal maniac or improbable gift horse?

She'd soon be finding out.

Chapter five

Father Connor Cassidy paced the aisle of St. Timothy's parish church, one hand clenched behind his back, the other extended in front of him and gripping his breviary. At forty-five he was one of those fortunate men for whom the passage of time seemed to be having a beneficent effect. The lush, dark hair turning silver at the temples, as opposed to gray; the proud symmetry of a lean physique; the fine hands and gracious manner—all conspired to lend an elegance that he himself seemed unaware of. When ladies met him they wondered why he'd become a priest, and when men met him they felt grateful that he had.

He mumbled the prayers he knew so well, trying to instill some sincerity into the all-too-familiar words. But that afternoon his mind was on other things. Just six months into his tenure in Tailorstown, he was still smarting from the fact that he'd been plucked from his Derry City post to fill in for Father Billy Brady. Father Billy had tripped on the hem of his alb one Sunday morning while saying Mass and struck his head on the altar. Father Cassidy suspected that drink, not clumsiness, was the likely cause. On the few occasions he'd met Father Billy, the older man had smelled like a distillery in high summer, so who was to say when he'd be coming back? Between drying out and getting his head in order, he might well be leaving his stand-in, Father Cassidy, stuck in the backwoods parish of Tailorstown for the best part of a year. And that was being optimistic.

At the same time, Cassidy was discovering that there might well be an upside to being stationed in such an isolated little place. A priest running a one-man show in a small town was left pretty much to himself, to conduct himself very much as he pleased—behind closed doors, at least. He'd also had the good fortune to be blessed with a particularly unobservant housekeeper.

But his luck had not held. Miss Betty Beard, the dithering housekeeper, had announced she'd be taking a leave of absence. Her mother had been laid low by a Baker's cyst on her left leg, thus forcing Father Cassidy to look for a replacement. He'd already put an advertisement in the post office window, but so far the only respondent had been Rose McFadden, a woman who seemed to shadow his every move like some kind of Stasi spy. As a last resort he'd typed up a card advertising the vacancy, which the town's stores and eateries had put on display. And, just to be on the safe side, he'd commenced a "never known to fail" novena to St. Martha of Bethany, patron saint of cooks, cleaners, and domestic servants.

The priest came to a halt by the confessional at the back of the church and sighed deeply while gazing raptly at the solid oak box with its red velvet curtain and half door. He'd been a priest for fourteen years. The first ten had been spent serving parishes in Belfast and Derry—cutting his teeth on the raw, working-class housing estates of both cities.

How many confessionals have I sat in? he mused, as he stared at the box. *What truths and lies have been told to me?*

He was contemplating those questions when the rear door of the church creaked open. Who should appear, like an overweight bird of paradise in a blue frock, yellow cardigan, and pink tam-o'-shanter, but Mrs. McFadden herself?

The pest tiptoed inside, daubed her breast with a healthy splash of holy water, and squeaked up the aisle in her wide-fit Hush Puppies to claim her usual place in the pew. Father Cassidy's heart wobbled slightly as he acknowledged her with what he hoped was one of his most solemn don't-disturb-me-I'm-praying nods. He could tell by the way she eyed him that she was anxious to learn his housekeeper situation. He quickly transferred his attention back to the breviary, determining that nothing, or no one, would interrupt him.

It was almost time for his supper anyway, and Miss Beard was preparing his favorite: rib-eye steak with apple dumplings to follow.

He decided to cut his prayers short. One final turn up to the altar and a quick left into the sacristy, exiting by the rear, would be enough to foil the McFadden woman. At his approach, however, she got off her knees, joints popping, and with a heavy sigh sat back in the seat. Not a good sign. Father Cassidy could sense her looking up at him as he passed by, but he was determined to stick to his plan.

In the sacristy, he stowed his prayer book quickly in the book-case and made haste through the outer door.

"Father, would ye have a wee minute?"

He couldn't believe it. There she was, blocking his path as he came down the steps. How she could move with such speed, impeded as she was by two heavy shopping bags and chronic sciatica—an affliction that he and the entire parish never ceased hearing about—was a mystery.

Cassidy steeled himself. He knew what she wanted and was prepared to lie if he had to. There were times when the eighth commandment simply had to be circumvented.

"Yes, Mrs. McFadden, what seems to be the problem?"

"Well, I was wunderin', Father, if ye'd got any answers to your advert'mint for the housekeeper, like? For ye know, I'm good at the fries and the apple tarts and the sponges and what-have-ye. My Paddy said to me the other day, he sez: 'Isn't it terrible that Father Cassidy isn't gonna have nobody to do for him when Betty Beard goes away?' 'Do ye know, Paddy, you're right,' sez I. 'We can't have Father Cassidy sittin' there by himself in the parochial house, starvin' with the hunger and nobody tae ax him if he has a mouth on him or not—'"

"Yes, indeed, but—"

"Now, I do a couple-a days with me Uncle Ned, but I could work round that, Father. For I ast my Paddy would he mind if I helped ye out for a bit, 'cos it would mean that my Paddy would maybe have to make a drop o' tea for himself for a bit. And my Paddy said he wouldn't mind makin' the odd drop o' tea for himself because you, Father, are far more important than him, or any other man round here for that matter, so ye are." Rose halted to draw breath.

"Yes, quite, that was good of Paddy," the priest said, swooping on the precious pause like a hawk upon a field mouse. "And it's very good of you to offer, Mrs. McFadden. I'll certainly keep you in mind. But I'll be running the ad for another week." He checked his watch pointedly and made to move down the steps. But Rose stood her ground. "Now, I really must be going," he told her. Miss Beard would have to reheat his supper if he delayed further, and the rib eye steak would be fit only for shoe leather.

"Oh, Father, there was just another wee thing…"

He could hear her panting behind him like a dray horse.

"Yes?" He stopped and turned calmly to meet her.

She put down her cargo and rested a hand on her lower flank. "God, Father, the sicatical is killin' me, so it is." She gazed up at him.

"You're on your feet far too much, Mrs. McFadden. You should be at home resting." *And not out here bothering me.* He checked his watch again. "Now, what was the other thing?"

"The other thing was *The Comforter of the Affected* in the chapel, Father."

What on earth is she talking about? Oh, yes, the statue. "*The Comforter of the Afflicted*? Yes, what about it?"

"Well, I noticed she was a wee bit pale looking, Father. She'd need a bit of a touch-up, and I mentioned it to my Paddy, and he agreed with me, so he did. But then I got tae thinkin' who'd be able to do an important art job like that. My Paddy and meself wrecked our brains for tae see who we could come up with, and then it hit us, Father."

Rose paused for dramatic effect, and to heighten what she felt was the earth-shattering impact of what she was about to say. Father Cassidy, untutored in the ways of the country folk, waited also, wondering what he was supposed to say.

"Well, don't ye want to know who we came up with, Father?"

"Yes…yes indeed. How interesting! Whom did you come up with?"

"Lorcan Strong. *That's* who, Father. Now ye wouldn't know him yet, but he's Etta's boy from the Cock."

"You mean The Crowing Cock pub, I take it?"

"Aye, the Cock pub. Well, he's the greatest artist…could paint anything, so he could. If ye put him in a dark room with a bag over his head, and give him a brush and bitta paper, he'd still be able tae paint pitchers like a photo."

"My goodness. He sounds very talented indeed. I—"

"Now, I ast Etta tae ax him, 'cos he's due home for a wee break soon. He's got a grand job in Belfast, paintin' at a big place where they keep pitchers and the like. She said he'd do it and no bother since it's for the church—"

"Excellent!" Father Cassidy put a hand up. "Now I really must be going. Duty calls."

He strode off quickly.

"If ye can't get nobody for the housekeepin', Father, I'll be round next week tae help ye out!"

"Very good, Mrs. McFadden," he called over his shoulder, hoping it would never come to that. As he rushed away, he felt as helpless and distraught as a man trapped at the top of a burning staircase, with no option but to plunge through the deadly flames.

Chapter six

Mr. Grant's truck was filthy and smelly and looked like something that not only took him from A to B but provided board and lodgings as well. The floor was strewn with leaflets, shop flyers, and copies of *St. Timothy's Parish Bulletin* stamped with muddy boot prints. There were stray socks and skeins of baler twine. Flattened takeaway cartons and dead beer cans spoke of an unpartnered man who led a life of harmful habits. The stuffing stuck out of the seats. The dashboard had what appeared to be a bite taken out of it. Incongruously, a string vest was doing duty as a seat cover.

Herkie, with great reluctance and a sharp prod from his ma, clambered in first. There was nowhere to sit but on a piece of grubby foam rubber wedged between the two front seats. Bessie eased herself in beside him, disgusted that her good green skirt was making contact with the vile seat cover.

"That's the day, now!" Grant said breezily as the truck rattled off in second gear. "A bitta good weather makes all the differs tae a body, so it does."

He was bent over the steering wheel, nose almost touching the windshield, Mr. Magoo–style. Herkie, squeezed up against him with little room to maneuver, had a side-on view of his head. A great tuft of hair sprouting out of Grant's left ear merited close inspection.

"Yes, fine weather indeed," said Bessie, wrinkling her nose while she fanned herself with a parish bulletin she'd found on the dashboard.

They'd hardly traveled two hundred yards when she felt a coolness wafting up her legs. On looking down, she saw a hole the size of a saucer in the floor. Alarmed, she dropped the bulletin over it as the road flew past beneath them.

Before too long they entered a thirty-mile zone and a sign was bidding them WELCOME TO TAILORSTOWN.

"Here she is now," Mr. Grant announced grandly. With a grinding of gears—which set off a frenetic hammering under the bonnet—he slowed the truck to a crawl and proceeded down the main street. For a car mechanic, he wasn't showing much promise as a driver.

The town, little more than a glorified T-junction, was lined with the sort of shops and businesses one might see in any rural town: a grocery store, several pubs, a haberdasher's, a gent's outfitters, a newsagent's, Dan's Decorators, the Curl Up 'n' Dye hair salon, and the Cozy Corner Café. There were few signs of life. The widow imagined that most of the inhabitants probably hadn't bothered to rise from their beds. What would be the point?

Outside the Cozy Corner she saw a dog nosing at a carton of fries. It seemed to change its mind and moved on as they passed.

"Josie does a good fry-up, if ye's want tae ate later on," said Grant.

Bessie nodded, thinking, *Well, if a flea-ridden oul' mongrel turns its nose up at Josie's cuisine, I think I'll pass.* Moments later she saw the dog relieve itself on the takeout, confirming her suspicions.

Farther along, on the step of the Crowing Cock bar, a drunk was staggering about like a toddler. The ungracious sight brought

Packie to mind, and the memory of an overworked Indian doctor with bad English and curry on his breath summing it up for her.

"Well, if it be any comfort at all, madam, your husband he save himself much pain."

"How's that, doctor?"

"His liver, how you say, be size of the suitcase. So, only matter of time."

"So if the Belgian nun hadn't of—"

The doctor had shaken his head, and sighed. *"Oh, yes, madam, the cirrhosis it lie in wait very soon for him."*

She hadn't questioned the doctor's evaluation, not for one minute.

"I do a bitta work in the Cock there from time to time," Mr. Grant was saying, face still pressed to the windshield, big glasses slipping down his nose.

"Really!" she said, pretending to be interested.

"Aye, so if ye want a wee drink later on, I'll be there, and it'll be on me."

She did not like the way Grant's mind was working but sensed he was a harmless enough old critter. More bluster than action.

Meanwhile, Herkie, having lost interest in Mr. Grant's hairy earhole, was contemplating the mechanic's wallet. It was peeping tantalizingly from a back pocket, and Herkie was seeing the realization of a new Action Man within easy reach.

"What a lovely part of the world!" Bessie said. "How long have you lived here, Mr. Grant?"

"All me life…aye, all me life. Born here, an' I'll die here, too, I s'ppose. Ye're not from the cawntry yerself?"

"No, no, just passing through."

"Takin' a wee haul'day over the border, are ye?"

"Yes, something like that. Would you mind if I opened the window, Mr. Grant?" She was seizing on any ruse she could think of to deflect his nosiness.

"Well, ye know," he said, "I'm sorry tae say, but that windee beside ye doesn't open, on account of it bein' stuck. But we're nearly there, so we—"

He had to swerve sharply to avoid a horse-drawn cart coming at them on the wrong side of the road. Sitting atop the junk-laden vehicle was a disheveled man, clearly from the itinerant classes.

Grant braked suddenly. "That's Barkin' Bob for ye." He put the truck in reverse and drew level with the carter, who was singing merrily, oblivious to the head-on collision he'd nearly caused.

"Hi, Bob, did ye not see me there?"

"Jesus' blood never failed me yet!" sang Bob lustily. "Oh, Jesus' blood never—"

Grant sounded the horn.

Bob stopped singing and stared at Grant, plainly perplexed.

"Ye're on the wrong side of the road, so ye are."

The carter gazed up at the heavens. "Oh, Jesus' blood never failed me yet, never—"

"Aye, he'd need-a be on bloody full-time duty with the like of *you* about. Get over tae yer own side or you'll get somebody kilt."

Grant wound up the window and put the truck in gear. "Sorry about that, Mrs. Hailstone," he said, taking off again. "He's not right in the head. That's why they call him Barkin' Bob. Collects bits o' scrap and sells it."

"Why's the horse so wee, Ma?" asked Herkie, fascinated by the spectacle.

"It's not a horse. It's a mule. He calls it Brenda."

"There ye are, son," Bessie said. "You'd never see the like of that in Belfast, now would you?"

About a half mile out of town, the mechanic made a left turn down a narrow road and over a bridge. Soon, on the rise of a hill on the right, a small house hove into view.

"There she is now: Rosehip Cottage, me aunt's place. She called it that on account a them hip bushes at the side there."

Bessie had been half expecting a hovel and was pleasantly surprised by what she saw. It was a quaint whitewashed cottage, complete with dormers, window boxes, leaded panes, and a brick-tiled roof. There was even a garden out front, trimmed by thick box hedging, and a white wrought-iron gate.

The truck ground to a halt.

"How lovely!" Bessie exclaimed as they alighted. She brushed some hayseeds from her skirt. On consideration, it might be profitable to be nice to Mr. Grant after all. "Your aunt must have been very house-proud."

"Aye, she was right 'n' proud of her house right enough."

He opened the gate and led her up the garden path. A chorus of fragrances filled the air—freesias and slipper orchids. Bessie could identify them easily. Her mother had kept a little garden, not as healthy or well-tended as this one, but a garden nonetheless. And she knew her blooms. Was proud of them.

Meanwhile Herkie, glad to be out of the truck and excited by his new surroundings, dawdled behind. Out of sight of his mother and Mr. Grant he seized on the opportunity to twist the heads off some prize dahlias.

On the step, the mechanic produced a large key from the depths of his overalls and turned it in the lock.

Bessie stepped inside.

After the sun-filled yard, she was taken aback to find herself in murky darkness. She blinked, heard the swish of drapes, then suddenly, blessedly, daylight was flushing the gloom.

The doll-size living room, all blossoming pinks and chintzy coverings, was crammed. Aunt Dora had either been a house-proud hoarder or a miser who didn't believe in throwing anything out. Bessie's bemused eyes took in plump armchairs and embroidered cushions, trinkets and religious statues made of delft and molded glass. A glossy sideboard with porcelain knobs held a plaster replica of the grotto at Lourdes. In a corner: a spiky plant the height of a six-year-old. On the mantel: oil lamps of tulip-shaped crystal. Framed icons all but obscured the hunting-scene wallpaper.

It did not exactly chime with what the plucky widow aspired to, for, despite her humble background, she had a hankering after style and the finer things in life. In her book, life was too short to frill a cushion, crochet a doily, or stitch felt ducks on a satin pond and pass it off as a fire screen—activities which Aunt Dora had obviously engaged in. Terrible, she thought, what those old spinsters would do to compensate for the lack of a social life.

"I can see your aunt was very good with her hands," was all she could say.

"Aye, that's why I'd want all her stuff tae be kept just the way she left it, Mrs. Hailstone, if ye don't mind. She left it tae me in her will...the house. And she ast specially that nuthin' be touched."

As he spoke, he was eyeing young Herkie, who'd lifted an ornament from the windowsill and was earnestly attempting to liberate a purple gnome from its yellow toadstool. So much was there to see in the cramped room that the boy was growing excited, uncertain of what to vandalize first.

"I quite understand, Mr. Grant. Everything will be absolutely safe with me."

Bessie followed him upstairs, hauling Herkie after her.

Grant showed them the aunt's bedroom, their sleeping quarters for the night.

The small room was dwarfed by its outsize furniture. A brass bed with a candlewick coverlet took center stage. One wall was given over to a hulking great wardrobe and a chest of drawers.

Before the window: a dressing table embellished with curlicues, its oval mirror marred by a creeping efflorescence round the border.

"As I say, I wouldn't want any of me aunt's—"

"Of course not, Mr. Grant! I understand. Completely." She wished he'd just go and leave them to it.

"There's a couch bed in the corner there for the wee boy."

"Did ye kill your aunt in here?" Herkie asked, images of Grant the "cannonball" still very fresh in his mind's eye.

Grant stared at him.

Bessie gave Herkie a poke in the ribs. "Now, don't be saying silly things to Mr. Grant, son. I do apologize, Mr. Grant. It's his age. He reads far too many comics."

The mechanic adjusted his big glasses and stared sadly at the floor.

"I'm so sorry about your aunt," Bessie said. "You must have been very close to her."

"Aye, I was. But she didn't die up here. No. She tripped on the stairs and fell on her head."

Herkie was suddenly attentive. "Them stairs out there?"

Bessie coughed loudly. She gave Herkie a look that would curdle cream and pushed him out of the room.

"I'm very sorry to hear that. Must have been a shock for you."

She was beginning to warm to Mr. Grant and his kindness. If she played her cards right, goodness knew what might ensue from the little mishap with her car. The dark clouds were lifting, their silver linings agleam with fresh promise.

"Now, she was a big age, Mrs. Hailstone. Eighty-nine. So if the stairs hadn't of tooken her, something else would of. Now I'll show ye out the back."

The back door opened onto a sizable gravel yard flanked by rolling fields. An open shed at the side housed a stack of firewood. A stout nylon clothesline was secured to its eaves.

"What's that?" asked Herkie, pointing at a large stone atop a sheet of corrugated zinc.

"Oh, that's a well. That cover there has tae stay on it."

"Do you hear that, son?"

"Aye, Ma."

"Aye, if ye fell down that well," Mr. Grant warned, "ye might end up in China, begod, and would nivver be heard of again. So that's why that big stone's over the tap of it."

"You've been warned, son. You keep away from that."

Herkie nodded for appearance's sake. He was eyeing the big stone, already calculating the amount of effort needed to shift it.

"As I say, I'll get that fan belt for ye in Willie-Tom's and have her ready for ye as quick as I can."

"It's very kind of you, Mr. Grant. How can we thank you?"

"Oh, that's all right, Mrs. Hailstone. I wouldn't see nobody stuck—and me aunt wouldn't, neither, God rest her. She was a good, religious woman. Went tae Mass every day."

They followed him round to the front of the house and stood waving goodbye as his truck shuddered off again in the direction of the town.

"Look what I got, Ma," said Herkie. He was proudly holding a battered leather wallet.

"Where did you get that?"

"On the path, Ma. Maybe Mr. Grant dropped it."

"Well, whyn't you give it back to him then?" She snapped it up and began riffling through it.

"'Cos I didn't know if it was his, Ma."

"I hope you didn't steal it, son, for if you did you'll be gettin' a warm backside. We can't be drawing attention to ourselves."

Inside the wallet she found a novena to St. Anthony—patron saint of lost objects—two five-pound notes, a couple of stamps, and some hayseeds.

"Could I get me Action Man with that?"

"Now, son, are you gonna turn into your da, are you?"

Herkie kicked the ground and sighed. "No, Ma."

"Good. Next time we see Mr. Grant, I'll ask him if it's his. If it's not, then it means Saint Anthony threw it down from heaven to help us out, and you might—and I mean *just might*—get your Action Man."

"Och, Ma…" Herkie kicked a stone, grudgingly accepting her verdict. But he wasn't too disappointed. There was much to explore in this new playground.

After his ma had returned indoors, he made a beeline for the backyard. If China lay at the bottom of that well, he was determined to start at once on the removal of that big stone.

Chapter seven

Daylight gradually suffused Lorcan's room, making the ceiling tiles stand clear. He'd had a fitful night and was glad that morning had broken. Wednesday. It would not be an easy day. Wednesday afternoons were largely taken up by the weekly meeting with his superior, Sir Edward Fielding-Payne. Those meetings were generally fraught. And tomorrow evening he had that *other* appointment—the one he didn't even want to think about. To top it all, the previous evening he'd had a phone call from his ever-fretting mother to say her varicose veins were troubling her, a call that was calculated to make him feel guilty for his neglect of both her and the family business.

He eased himself into a sitting position and glanced at the easel in the corner. Would he ever be rid of the Countess? Her disquieting visage haunted his every waking minute. In the workplace he was retouching her and in his bedroom recreating her against his will. The thought of this dismayed him, as it always did, and he quickly switched his attention to the clock face. He saw it was six thirty. Time to get up. Already the day was rousing itself. The drone of buses was just about audible out on the Antrim Road. A muffled flushing sound from downstairs told him that Mrs. Mavis

Hipple, his landlady, had emerged from her cluttered nest on the ground floor, directly below.

Yes, mornings had become more stressful these days, and he resented that. A couple of weeks back, a new lodger had moved into the room opposite his: an earnest, hymn-singing, tea-drinking Presbyterian lady in hand-knits and sensible shoes who answered to the name of Miss Florence Finch. She was one of those ladies whom his mother might describe as having "missed her markets" in the marriage stakes.

Miss Finch had upset his bathroom routine; a new strategy had to be worked out in order to accommodate her. The difficulty lay in her rodent-like quietness. Lorcan could never tell when she was up and about. They shared a bathroom, off the landing, which as yet—despite his many entreaties to the landlady—had no lock. This deficiency made for a great deal of anxiety and reconnaissance before he could venture forth each morning. Only the previous week, he had, to their mutual embarrassment, surprised Miss Finch in there. The demure lady had beaten a hasty retreat, complete with her knitting and a Victoria Holt doorstop of a paperback pressed to her bosom. The memory of the meeting still had the power to scorch his sensibilities like a gaucho's branding iron. After much thought, however, he'd solved the problem: he'd invested in a transistor radio.

The radio, unlike a lock, fulfilled three separate functions. First: he could take it with him and listen to the news every time he used the bathroom. Second: the very sound of the radio would deter Miss Finch from entering at an inappropriate moment. Third: a quick twist of the volume knob would generate enough racket to drown out whatever lavatorial tumult he might set in motion.

It was a neat solution to a complex problem. He only wished he could tackle the rest of life's little difficulties with such aplomb. He thought of his mother and the pub in Tailorstown—and shuddered.

But first things first. He threw back the bedcovers, went to the closet, hauled out a long gray raincoat, and pulled it on over his pajamas. This, again, was done out of consideration for Miss Finch because he sensed that she was a prudish lady, for whom a man wearing pajamas might be as diabolical a sight as seeing Adam in the Garden minus his fig leaf. He gathered up his wash bag and towel and peered out into the corridor. All was quiet; he felt he was safe enough.

Once inside Mrs. Hipple's Lilliputian bathroom, fetchingly done up in shades of periwinkle blue and whorehouse pink, Lorcan switched on Radio Ulster and set about his ablutions.

The news items were mixed.

"Pope John Paul's private secretary will today visit the Maze Prison for a second time. It's understood that he will again try to persuade hunger striker Bobby Sands and his fellow protesters to call off the strike. President Ronald Reagan stated that the United States would not intervene in the situation, but said that he was deeply concerned at events. Bobby Sands has been on a hunger strike for a total of fifty-nine days, and his condition..."

Fifty-nine days, Lorcan thought. Fifty-nine days without food of any kind! He couldn't even begin to imagine how that must be. He'd read somewhere that after only ten days the body begins to eat itself for sustenance; after twenty days toxins have built up in the liver, kidneys, and brain, leading to dehydration, cracked skin, extreme cold intolerance, vital-organ shrinkage, blindness, bleeding joints...the list went on and on. And that was "only" the physical pain. What about the mental torture? Twenty days, thought Lorcan—and tomorrow Bobby Sands will have been on a hunger strike for *three times* that. The man was surely a goner.

He stared at himself in the mirror—lean face, high-domed forehead, Roman nose, eyes the color of ice chips, not unhandsome—and wondered briefly how he might look after fifty-nine days of starvation.

"...news just in of a security alert on Royal Avenue, Belfast. Police report an incendiary device, discovered in the changing rooms of a boutique close to the City Hall. The area has been cordoned off following a telephone warning, and army experts are examining a package."

Lorcan sighed and continued washing.

He pricked up his ears at the third news item. A man named Donal Carmody had been abducted from his home in West Belfast in the early hours of the morning. There was talk of IRA involvement. He thought of the ominous note he'd received yesterday and sighed deeply. The dreaded Thursday evening appointment was nearing. There was no way he could miss it. No way whatsoever. His hands shook as he pulled the plug on the washbasin and dried his face.

Back in the safety of his room, he dressed quickly. He favored a bohemian look: jade-colored pin-cord pants with matching velvet jacket, a white poplin shirt, a satin fleur-de-lis waistcoat in brandy tan twinned with a butterfly bow tie in a similar design. Choosing what to wear to the office was seldom a problem for Lorcan. He'd seven white poplin shirts, one for each working day and two spares for evenings and weekends. Mrs. Hipple very kindly laundered and ironed them, folded them, and placed them in his chest of drawers. He'd three velvet jackets: jade, russet, and black; seven pairs of socks in corresponding hues, and four pairs of black shoes. His main extravagances were his cravats and bow ties, handmade by Robinson & Cleaver. He'd more than twenty. He liked to wear a different one each day.

All thoughts of running into Miss Finch and the ghastly appointment were now being supplanted by snatches of his mother's phone call. They kept swirling about in his head like laundry on a slow spin.

Was he all right? It wasn't safe in Belfast: far too many bombs. What if he got caught in one and lost an arm, or a leg, or an eye—or worse still, both eyes? How would he work then? When was he coming home? Was he getting enough to eat? Did Mrs. Hipple change his bed regularly enough? And finally, the news guaranteed to make him feel guilty: Her legs were playing up. The Crowing Cock was busy at weekends especially, what with Hipster Fred and the Heartbeats doing the Golden Oldie Friday session and the Beardy Boys every other Saturday. Weekdays were manageable, but only just. Bunions *and* varicose veins. She couldn't be on her feet with those. A clot could go to the heart; Dr. Brewster had said so.

Henrietta Strong had given her son a bad night and a return of his chronic indigestion. Lorcan resented both; they affected his concentration. Concentration was paramount in a job such as his—in his day job *and* his "other" job here in his room. He doubted that Sir Joshua Reynolds ever had a lapse. But then Sir Joshua most likely didn't have a mother fretting about leg problems, or the threat of having to do stand-in as a bartender whenever family duty called.

He went downstairs.

"Would tha' be you, Lorcan?"

He found the landlady hard at work over the stove in the back kitchen.

"Good morning, Mavis."

"Hey up, Lorcan!" she said cheerfully. No sooner was he seated than she was bearing a fully loaded breakfast plate to the permanently set table: gingham cloth, cups turned bottoms-up, and a cruet set in the form of ceramic squirrels atop a log.

The landlady, a pensioner with maroon hair and no eyebrows, hailed from Yorkshire but had settled in Belfast thirty years earlier, having married a drywall plasterer from Ballymurphy.

"Tha tea's in 't pot. And there's more in 't oven, if you want 't."

"Thanks, Mavis. No, this is quite sufficient."

"Didn't hear yer come in yesterday, I didn't," she said. "Ye got me note then, from yer mam?"

"Oh, yes. Thanks for that, Mavis."

"Hope ever'thing's all right?" She brought her own fry to the table and sat down. "Yer mam must get lonely on her own, she must. Hope she's not poorly."

Mavis liked to pick and poke at her lodgers for news. The parlor bay window did not supply enough gossip for her needs. It was at such times that Lorcan realized his life would be infinitely less complicated were he to live alone. But then he'd never lived alone; there'd always been a woman conveniently disposed to do for him. First his mother, followed by Mrs. Campbell, who ran a boarding house for students from the art college. And latterly, Mrs. Hipple.

"My mum poorly?" he said. "Oh, no, not poorly—just the usual. She worries too much."

"Expect she'd like ye settled. A mam always likes a son to be settled afore she goes, like. You's a nice catch for a woman, Lorcan."

Don't *you* start, he thought. One middle-aged woman fussing over me is bad enough.

There came a creaking of floorboards from above. The landlady raised her missing eyebrows to the ceiling. "That'll be Miss Finch, it will," she said, as she always did.

Lorcan lost his appetite at once. But he knew he couldn't excuse himself until he'd made suitable inroads into the fry. Mrs. Hipple would otherwise be insulted.

"The tea's a wee bit strong, Mavis," he said. "Could I have some hot water, please?"

"Course you can, luv."

In the thirty seconds or so that it took Mavis to maneuver herself out of the chair and cross to the stove, Lorcan had deftly swept a slice of bacon, a sausage, and half a tomato into the napkin on his lap and stuffed the lot into his pocket.

"God, is that the time?" he said, getting up. "Really got to be going."

Mavis turned, kettle in hand, mouth open. "But—"

"Not to worry. I'll save myself for your lovely supper this evening."

He was down the hallway and out the front door before Miss Finch had time to place the square toe of her vinyl pumps on the first tread of the stairs.

He gave thanks to his gods for yet another escape.

Chapter eight

For all the misfortune and stress they'd encountered in the day, Bessie Halstone and her son slept soundly that night under the fusty covers and creaking timbers of Aunt Dora's cottage.

They awoke the next morning to the sound of a cock crowing and the drone of a tractor a few fields distant. Never before had they experienced tranquillity to match it.

"Can I go out and play, Ma?" asked Herkie, climbing out from under a tartan rug on his couch bed and pulling on his clothes.

Bessie yawned and threw back the covers.

"Canna, Ma?"

"Can ye *what*, son?"

"Go out and play!"

"All right," she said. She pointed to the ottoman at the foot of the bed where her clothing lay. "Hand me them things, there's a good boy. We have to get breakfast somewhere. You can't go farther than the garden, d'you hear? If you open that gate and go out on the road, there'll be no Action Man."

"Aye, Ma."

"And don't go near that well. D'ye hear?"

"Naw, Ma."

Herkie ran downstairs and Bessie got out of bed. She pulled on her blouse and skirt, then went immediately to the dressing table and sat down.

Whereas other women might start their morning with a cup of tea, Bessie started hers with her makeup routine. Appearances mattered most. Yes, the inner life might be a mess, but the outer packaging must be kept pretty. That's what people judged you on first. She believed this without question. So every morning without fail she set about the ritual of painting and powdering, yielding, like so many ladies with flimsy self-esteem, to the tyranny of the looking glass.

Her beauty might have coarsened in recent times, the stress and the smokes having done their baleful work. But she managed, through the application of cosmetics and the wearing of figure-hugging garments, to retain a certain kind of gaudy attraction, an attraction that frequently drew caustic looks from women and the glad eye of men—most usually those men of questionable reputation.

It was a bit unsettling to look into Aunt Dora's misty mirror, but Bessie reckoned her own reflection more pleasing. Oh, yes: more pleasing by far. Down in the living room there was a framed photo of a woman whom she took to be the aunt: a grim-lipped old lady with a frozen perm, sagging jowls, and wire spectacles. "Probably never laughed in her life," she said to the mirror, and immediately set to work on her face. Zsa Zsa Gabor was her role model. Every morning she'd plumb the depths of her battered makeup bag in an attempt to achieve Ms. Gabor's sultry look.

She could hear Herkie outside, swinging on the garden gate and imitating a birdcall. Would he ever be able to sit still? Maybe being in the country would settle him. Less distraction, for a start.

A sudden loud thwacking noise from outside made her put down her powder puff. She crossed to the window and looked out.

To her consternation, she saw Herkie methodically deadheading a line of pink and purple tulips with a stick.

"What the blazes d'ye think yer playin' at?" she roared.

Herkie did not look up. He dropped the stick and ran out of sight. She sighed and returned to her makeup. Some chance of him settling anytime soon, she thought. No surprise, given what the boy had been through following his father's death.

She blinked her mascaraed lashes, her makeup complete. Teased her bouffant hairdo into shape with a brush.

All the same, perhaps Packie's dying had done them both a favor. Now she could do what *she* wanted. Be what *she* wanted.

Why, she could even stay here.

The thought struck her as she rose from the dressing table. Yes, in this lovely little cottage, miles away from her old life. The Dentist would never find her in these backwoods. In fact she'd probably be safer hiding out here for a bit. But money was the problem. She had funds to last a month at most. And if she was being brutally realistic, her sister Joan would probably part with only enough to keep her in smokes for a week.

She continued to ponder her dire financial situation as she entered the kitchen. The modest space, with its varnished beauty board, was sparsely appointed: A rusty gas stove. A refrigerator. A Formica table with spindly legs. And on the table, an Oriental tea caddy and a pewter teapot. She lifted the tea caddy. An alarmed spider scurried across the table and vanished. It was bad luck to kill them, she knew. Given her present circumstances, it was better to let the creature be.

She pulled open cupboards and drawers, not really knowing what she was looking for. If the aunt had died two months ago it was unlikely there would be any food.

She crossed to the window. A row of healthy-looking potted plants lined the sill. Mr. Grant must water them. What dedication!

A job is what I need, she thought. Yes, a catering position like the one I left behind. I still have my glowing references. Why not?

The window looked down into a small valley of sorts. At the bottom she was surprised to see an imposing three-story house, painted white and set in its own grounds. It was obvious she was seeing it from the rear. Lines of stone stables skirted the extensive yard, and there was what looked like a well-tended vegetable garden.

Her nearest neighbor was clearly well-off.

Interesting.

"God, Ma, look what I found!"

She turned back from the window to see an agitated Herkie carrying in what looked like a filthy shinbone.

"Get that disgusting maggot outta the house this minute, son!"

"But, Ma, whose is it?"

"How the hell should I know, son? A horse's or a cow's maybe. Get it out."

He came and held it under her nose. To Bessie's horror, a fat red earthworm detached itself and plopped at her feet. "Throw that filthy thing away this minute! D'ye hear?"

"But, Ma, maybe it's the aunt, and maybe he cut her up and—"

"Son, I'll be cuttin' *you* up if ye don't get rid of that *now*!"

She chased him out the door and watched as he threw the bone over a nearby hedge.

"Now," she said, taking him by the ear and leading him back into the house. She pulled a tissue from her pocket. "You're gonna pick up that disgusting thing, throw it outside, and wash your hands. When you've done that, we're goin' into the town to get something to eat."

Twenty minutes later they were sitting at a claggy table in the only eatery in town: the Cozy Corner Café. The place was deserted save for an elderly woman nodding over a cup of tea and whispering animatedly to a bottle of HP Sauce.

"Ma, why's that oul' doll talkin' till the brown sauce?"

"'Cos she's dotin', son."

"What's dotin', Ma?" Herkie had started up a rhythmic kicking of the table leg, hungry for sustenance and some distraction.

"Talkin' till sauce bottles when ye're ninety, that's what dotin' is. Now, stop askin' silly questions, and *stop kickin' the table*!"

Herkie curled his lower lip in a sulk. "Canna have some ice cream?" The boy's taste buds were permanently in sugar-fix mode.

"Now, son, you'll be eating a fry, like normal people do this hour of the morning. That's if we ever get served in here." She looked about her. "Not as if they're run off their feet."

Finally the proprietor, Josie Mulhearn, a midlife crisis in a soiled overall, emerged through a beaded curtain behind the counter, wiping a dinner plate. Bessie, with half an eye still on the menu, was aware of the plate being slowly set down while she and the boy were scrutinized with almost palpable mistrust.

It was only when the widow looked at her pointedly, raising an eyebrow, that Josie finally decided to extricate herself from behind the counter and slap her way across the linoleum.

"What is it yis'll be wantin'?" she asked, a well-chewed blue ballpoint poised over a grubby note pad.

No "Good morning; how are yous today?" Bessie noted, feeling that her presence was already causing offense.

"Two fries, a cup of tea, and a glass of milk for the boy, please."

"Now, the fries might take a bit, for I've run outta gas, so I have. Had tae cook for a funeral yesterday evenin', and—"

"The fries are off then?" Bessie cut in. *What in heaven's name is wrong with these people? You asked a simple question and got a bloody life history.*

"Aye, the fries is off," said Josie, peeved. She was sizing Bessie up, wondering who this flashy stranger might be. "Are yis just passin' through, are yis?"

"In that case we'll just have the scones."

"Right ye be." Miffed, Josie headed back through the beaded curtain to fix their order.

There was a notice board near the door. Now, if only to pass the time, Bessie got up to take a closer look at it. Meanwhile, Herkie, bored beyond measure and annoyed that he wasn't getting his ice cream, pulled the sugar bowl toward him and began pouring salt into it.

The board played host to a collection of FOR SALE and WANTED notices.

Missing, spanneil dog brun with white ears and black paws
Reward oferred

Kittens FREE to good home.

Handie Man for higher to do wee odd jobs about the place. Can do plumming, tiling, painting and the like. Ring 226485

Get your fortune told by Madame Calinda as seen on the TV!!!
This Thursday one night only in Slope O'Sheas Bar!
No time waisters

The usual stuff, Bessie thought to herself, which was more than could be said for the spelling in these parts. But there was one advertisement, neatly typed, that stood out from the rest.

Wanted: Priest's Housekeeper
Temporary position for three months.

Must have pleasant manner and good catering skills.
Apply in writing to: Father Connor Cassidy,
St. Timothy's Parochial House, Tailorstown.

The widow found herself scribbling the details in her diary. At that moment, the seed of a plan that might bear fruit had dropped onto the fertile soil of her imagination, almost as though the sower in the parable had cast it, albeit unwittingly.

She returned to the table just as the tea and scones were arriving. She saw that Herkie had spilled most of the sugar and was busy graffitiing the tabletop with what looked suspiciously like life-size male genitalia, but which he earnestly claimed was the head of Dumbo the Elephant.

Josie, holding her tray poised above the table, glared at Herkie's artwork.

"That table was clean afore yis sat down at it," she said accusingly. "And look at the state of it now."

Bessie Halstone shook her head gravely, determined to humor Josie. "I *do* apologize," she said. "It's the artist in him, I'm afraid."

She took the tray from Josie.

"We'll just move to another table. Oh, by the way, would you know where I'd find St. Timothy's parochial house?"

"Ye might try lookin' for it beside St. Timothy's parish church, like a Christian wud."

Be gracious, be gracious, Bessie told herself.

"Thanks." She eyed the tray of tea and scones. "Oh, those look nice. Did you make them yourself?"

"Bake everything meself in here. It's me café, after all."

Oh dear! No time at all in the town and she'd made an enemy already.

Chapter nine

So, how are you faring with the Reynolds?"

Sir Edward Fielding-Payne croaked out the query from behind the vast desk in his antiquated, book-lined study. He'd been curator of the museum for so long he was beginning to resemble one of the exhibits, with his world-weary, watery gaze; the cloud of brittle gray hair riding a bony, waxlike visage; the knobbed knuckles like shot scallions. He would linger over words and was so deliberate in his manner that one could be forgiven for believing he was measuring the time left to him and savoring its bald scarcity. Seventy-four years on the planet had earned him that at least.

"The Reynolds, sir?" replied Lorcan. "Slow, but extremely well nonetheless."

"I take it you're still grappling with her intimates?" Sir Edward, a man of the old school—or, better said, the old-boy school—spoke a form of Victorian English that often made his communication stilted.

"Sorry, her whats?"

"Her…her embonpoint, man! Bosoms."

"Oh, yes, another week should do it, I'm happy to—"

"Sir Joshua," the curator interjected, bringing a crooked forefinger to his mouth to stifle a cough, "was a rather interesting fellow."

Being of solid Anglo-Irish stock, Sir Edward did not pay much attention to the opinions of those he considered to be from the "lower orders." Lorcan Strong fitted into that category—as did practically everyone else who crossed Sir Edward's path.

"Rather too largely and strongly limned," the curator continued, hauling Lorcan out of his reverie like a boatswain weighing anchor.

"I beg your pardon, sir?"

"Boswell said that of him."

"Ah. I see."

"Yes, a well-born and well-bred English gentleman. One must do right by his memory."

"Yes indeed, sir."

He hated these weekly meetings. Sir Edward, eccentric and a staunch stickler for protocol, could be willfully unpredictable. He'd ramble through thickets of verbiage and fire off arcane quotations simply to try and catch Lorcan out.

"A bachelor all his life," he waffled on. "It wasn't for the want of ladies, I dare say. He had enough of those to paint. A poof. What say you?"

All bachelors in their thirties—including Lorcan—were homosexuals in Sir Edward's opinion. He rarely missed an opportunity to vent his views on the subject.

"I couldn't really say, sir."

"He had all the hallmarks of a queer fellow-me-lad in my book."

Lorcan, not wishing to get himself entangled in a parley over the sexual proclivities of a pre-Victorian painter, tried to avoid commenting by feigning a sneeze. He drew a handkerchief from his inside pocket.

And wished he hadn't.

Onto Sir Edward's desk plopped the remains of Mavis Hipple's spurned Ulster fry: the charred sausage, the slice of bacon, and the half tomato. The items lay in a neat little group atop the highly polished wood. The artist saw at once an interesting still life worthy of Cézanne himself. Great art could be realized in the most absurd of situations. Was that not its genius?

The curator stared at the food offerings. His lips were pursed, causing the bristles of his mustache to extend outward. Lorcan was put in mind of a pig, Mrs. Hipple's favorite barnyard animal. Since becoming her lodger, it seemed he'd been served every part of the humble hog, bar the grunt.

"Sorry, sir," he said at last. "My landlady isn't the greatest of cooks, and one has to be polite."

The sausage, bacon, and tomato had come to rest by a framed photo of the formidable Lady Constance Fielding-Payne, the curator's wife, which took pride of place on the desk.

"Yes, a queer fellow, I'd say," Sir Edward continued, his gaze drifting toward a cut-glass decanter to his right. It was clear that the faux pas was being overlooked.

Lorcan, cheeks burning like a workman's brazier, seized the opportunity to raise himself discreetly off the chair and briskly brush the food items back into his hankie.

"Even so, fairy chappie or no, one must do right by his memory. I have no need to tell you how valuable the portrait is. A million pounds would not be an overestimation by any means. So, no fiddling about with bits of her that aren't there. No surplus rendering. Lady Constance was never one for surplus rendering. Frills belong on cabbages, not on necklines."

"I couldn't agree more, sir."

"Your foray with Lady Blessington was…how should one put it…"

"Too slow? Yes, I apolo—"

"Too *fulsome*. It was Lady Fielding-Payne who drew my attention to it."

"Oh, really?" said Lorcan, believing that his boss was about to wander off into one of his endless orations on the finer points of eighteenth-century portraiture. He slipped the food into his jacket pocket, prepared to be bored senseless, if only to save his own embarrassment.

"Lady Fielding-Payne has an eye for the abstruse," the curator was saying. Lorcan, half-listening, was unprepared for what came next. In his jaded mind's eye he'd been morphing Sir Edward's image into that of the victim in Blake's *Satan Smiting Job with Boils*. He'd been busy etching in a couple more nasty-looking furuncles on the cheeks when the boss's tone shifted up a gear.

"I say, my dear fellow, are you with me?"

"Yes, yes indeed, sir! Of course, sir."

"You seemed a little distant there. Now, what I'm saying is: Proponents of the Grand Style are not to be meddled with."

"Oh, yes, I couldn't agree more. The Grand Style…is what Reynolds is—I mean was—all about."

"Exactly! He made his sitters, the ladies especially, more elegant than they actually were. Hence his popularity. I dare say most of them looked like pigs' bladders, given what we know. Now you, my dear fellow, would appear to be 'improving' on his hard work."

"Well, thank—"

"It is meant," said Sir Edward, holding up a hand, "in the pejorative sense, my boy."

He donned his spectacles and checked his timepiece, an ornate fob watch, passed down the generations by his great-great-grandfather, who'd been an equerry to William IV.

"Almost time for my glass of claret. Will you join me?"

Never having shared such an intimacy with his employer, Lorcan assented with alacrity. He was still smarting from Sir Edward's phrase "the pejorative sense"; it had a nasty edge to it. Could the claret, he wondered, be a way of easing the pain for what was in store?

There was a tense little silence as Sir Edward moved to a side table and applied himself to the decanting process.

"Thank you, sir," Lorcan said, accepting a glass, "but I don't understand."

The curator harrumphed. "No, I dare say you don't." He raised his own glass briefly. "Chin-chin!" He resumed his seat.

"You're not pleased with my work, sir?"

"Mmmm…Château Tour du Videau. Splendid! I have it on good authority, my boy, that the uplift brassiere was not an undergarment with which ladies in the eighteenth century would have been acquainted. Lady Fielding-Payne knows about such things. We popped into your studio the other evening and she was most displeased by what she saw."

"But it's still a work in progress. I—"

"And progressing entirely in the wrong direction, it would seem."

He consulted his desk diary. "You need a holiday, my dear fellow. I see you haven't taken one in two years. The work becomes stale if you don't take a break from it now and then. Recharge the old batteries. Let the wind blow about your vitals."

"But I don't want a holiday. I don't *need* a—"

"Nonsense! Everybody needs a break. What d'you think you're made of, man? Galvanized tin? Pig iron?" He chortled at his little witticism.

"Well, no, but—"

"There'll be no well-no-buts about it. You'll take time off when I say so." He stabbed the diary with a finger. "And I say the day after tomorrow: the first of May. Is that understood? Back here at the end. Hopefully those wretched hunger strikers will start kicking the bucket any day now. And you can be sure that when they do, their Fenian supporters will run riot. You're best out of it. They tell me that Sands chappie is on his last legs, thank goodness." He raised his hands. "Imagine electing a ruffian like that to sit in the English Parliament! Worse than Caligula appointing his horse to the Senate of Rome. At least the blessed horse had breeding." He shook his head and fixed an eye on Lorcan. "So, are we agreed on the first of May? A little leave of absence?"

Lorcan found himself being bundled off on vacation without having much choice in the matter. He was reflecting on a rumor that was doing the rounds of the museum. Word had gone out that the curator's niece had just graduated from Cambridge, in archaeology and restoration. It didn't take an Einstein to figure out what was afoot.

"Yes sir," was all Lorcan could say. He was in no position to argue with his supervisor. He thought of his mother and the pub in Tailorstown, and of his dreaded appointment the following evening. Perhaps a month at home was what he needed. Perhaps the gods were trying to tell him something. "If you insist, sir."

"I jolly well *do* insist. Now, here's to it. Bottoms up!"

There was a pause while Sir Edward took another calming sip of wine. Lorcan set his glass down with care and stood up.

"Well, I'll be going, sir, if that's all."

"You haven't touched your claret."

"No, I'll pass on the claret if you don't mind." He moved to the door. "Bad for the concentration. One needs a clear eye and a steady hand for the work I do. It's more demanding than, say, being a trainee archaeologist."

"Breast flannels!" bellowed Sir Edward. There was a hint of triumph—perhaps smugness—in his voice.

Lorcan turned, nonplussed. "I *beg* your pardon, sir?"

"It's what the ladies wore before the brassiere was invented, according to my wife. The Countess of Clanwilliam had no uplift to speak of; therefore Reynolds wouldn't have given her one. Mind *you* don't, either."

Lorcan could hold his tongue no longer. How dare Sir Edward's snooty wife cast aspersions on his fine restorative work?

"Perhaps you'd inform your good wife, sir," Lorcan said slowly and evenly, "that wealthy ladies in those days, and especially those who were able to engage the services of Mr. Reynolds, could afford to wear corsets, which pushed their...their...assets up, as it were. Flannels were for the less well-off."

Sir Edward's mouth fell open. The sheer impertinence of it!

"I say, steady on, old—"

"Now, if that is all, I have a lot of work to do before I go. Good day!"

No one, not even his boss, had the right to show such disrespect.

Lorcan left the room, not slamming the door but shutting it quietly, as a gentleman would, on such blatant Anglo-Irish disparagement.

Chapter ten

As luck—or misfortune—would have it, the repair to Bessie's car was delayed. According to Mr. Grant, the unexpected death of Willie-Tom's mother had closed the shop in Killoran for three days, to "get him over the wake and funeral and the like."

Deep down, though, Bessie Halstone, with her newly revived surname and unexpected circumstances, was glad of this interlude. It gave her time to think. And the longer she dallied in the lovely, quaint cottage among Aunt Dora's things, the more she wanted to stay. After all, who would find her there? She was sure that the Dentist would not even have heard of a small place like Tailorstown.

A place to lay low was one thing. Finding money to live on was quite another. Not that Packie had provided her with much security at any time, but there'd always been something coming in, whether by fair means or foul—mostly foul—to keep the wolf from tearing down the door.

So, when finally the mechanic bumped down the lane in her Morris Traveller, its paintwork shining, its windows agleam, she'd a proposition to put to him. She invited him in for a cuppa.

"Have you ever thought of renting this house out?" she asked, pouring tea and turning on the charm like a floodlight. "So heavenly here after the bustle of the city, and such a lovely part of the world." She'd changed into her best frock—to oil the wheels— and applied generous dabs of Sweet Honesty scent to those all-important "pulse points": behind her ears and on her wrists.

"Rentin' the place? Well now, I never thought a that," said Gusty Grant, trying to ignore her creamy cleavage by concentrating hard on one of the open-billed storks his aunt had so painstakingly embroidered on the tablecloth. "Come tae think of it now, I nivver thought of it atall till ye mentioned it, like."

"Excellent!" Bessie said. "Shall we say a month to start with? Belfast is not safe, as you can imagine, given what these terrorists get up to. And now, with this hunger strike about to get worse, our lives would be in danger…no doubt about it." She proffered a plate of chocolate teacakes.

"God, aye, I know what yer sayin'. Must be wild there now with the hunger strike, as ye say. Ye're far safer in the cawntry right enough, so ye are. If them boys die—and Sands is gonna die any day now, by the looks of it—all hell's gonna break loose."

Bessie, quick as ever to reach for the low-hanging fruit, moved swiftly to clinch the deal. "So glad you see it that way, Augustus. How does five pounds for the month sound?"

"Aye, that'll be grand," he said, the words coming out and the cake going in on a tide of butter-melting surrender. Overwhelmed at hearing his first name from the lips of such a sophisticated city woman as Mrs. Hailstone, the mechanic-soon-to-be-landlord had agreed to the ridiculously low sum without a moment's hesitation.

"Excellent!" she said again, reaching into her handbag for one of Gusty's fivers from his "lost" wallet. She felt bad about the deceit, but desperate times meant desperate measures—for now, anyway. She slid the banknote across to him. "It's always better to have a house occupied, I feel. Deters thieves, don't you know. And I'll take very good care of your aunt's things. You'll have no worries on that score. How much do I owe you for the fan belt, by the way?"

"It would usually be the ten pound, but the five'll do it. I'll not charge ye for the time, 'cos I don't like tae see a wommin like yerself stuck, so-a don't."

"That's good of you, Augustus. How can I thank you?" She had a fair idea as to how the mechanic might like his generosity rewarded. She caught the flicker of hope behind his big glasses. What was it people said about eternal hope and the human breast?

"D'ye mind if I ask ye something, Mrs. Hailstone?"

"No, go ahead."

"Where would…where would *Mister* Hailstone be?"

"In heaven, I hope," said Bessie, adopting what she felt was a passable imitation of sadness: head tilted, eyes cast down.

"I'm very sorry tae hear that." The mechanic's heart fluttered in expectation, shifted up a gear. "What way—"

"Still, such is life," Bessie cut in, fetching his remaining fiver and handing it over. "As I say, it's terribly considerate of you to help us out."

That evening at supper, Bessie broke the news to Herkie.

"Och, Ma, I don't wanna stay here a month." He was sitting at one end of the kitchen table, slurping from a glass of milk and cramming a fairy cake into his gob.

Bessie sat opposite, one hand under her chin, the other resting on the stork-patterned tablecloth, holding the ever-present fag.

"Well, I've decided, son, and that's *that*. I've gotta get us some money for our passage to yer Uncle Bert in Hackney. Mr. Grant's givin' us this place for nothing—"

"Och, Ma, thought we were goin' tae Amerikay tae see the Statue of Liberry?"

"He doesn't know that he's givin' it for nothing, and he won't if we play our cards right. And ye can give over 'bout the Statue of bloody Liberry for now."

"But, Ma, it's *borin'* in this oul' place. I wanna go back till Belfast."

Herkie was missing the toys he'd had to leave behind and his friend Seanie McSwiney. He and Seanie would regularly clod stones at army jeeps. They dreamed of one day knocking a soldier out stone cold and making off with his automatic rifle.

He wanted to be a soldier when he grew up and often fantasized about lying in position on a rooftop, picking off unsuspecting pedestrians as they trod the city streets—especially men wearing donkey jackets and flat caps, and who talked with a fag in their mouth, because his father had worn a donkey jacket and a flat cap to cover his bald spot and kept a fag in his gob even when he was screaming at him and his ma.

"I know, son. I'm bored, too, but it's only for a wee while."

Through the cloud of cigarette smoke, Bessie eyed him dotingly: the only good thing that had come of her marriage. She loved her son dearly, in spite of everything, and hoped he wouldn't turn out like his da. But, for now, she fattened him up with her own insecurities—usually deep-fried, sugarcoated, and served up on a plate called "love."

Poor Herkie: so much like herself. Born with a tin shovel in his gob, as opposed to that fabled silver spoon. With a father not much better than her own. Where had it all gone wrong?

And oh, the dreams she'd had, the dreams! Kept alive through grim necessity from her earliest days.

Five years in secondary school had given her a pass in cookery and a fiery attitude leading to a succession of dead-end jobs: cleaning for the grand Mrs. Lesley Lloyd-Peacock on the Malone Road, cooking at a home for the mentally impaired, before legging it up a rung to the more refined surroundings of the Plaza hotel.

Ah, the Plaza. What days! Mixing with the upper classes. Well, ironing their percale sheets and dumping spurned food *was* mixing, in a way. Who might she not have met there if things had worked out differently? What rich gentleman might not have swept her off her feet if stand-in barman Packie Lawless hadn't got there first, making her pregnant and ending her brief career?

Her wedding day had been a fiasco, with Packie in a borrowed suit, still drunk from the night before, slurring his way through the vows, and she trying to hide her four-month bump under a cream two-piece from Mrs. McStay's Nu-to-You secondhand ladies' fashion store. The sheer misfortune of it all, pulling down the curtain on a Technicolor dream of mirrored ballrooms and glittering frocks, and being whisked away to foreign lands by a handsome millionaire.

She crushed out the cigarette in her Seamus the Fireman ashtray, and all at once a vision of Packie appeared, his brutal face contorted with rage, his fists raised in the waning light of evening. The alcohol had done that to him. It ran in the family genes as surely as young blood pumped through arteries.

But Herkie wouldn't suffer as she had. Packie had done them both a favor by checking out early.

"I'd luv another wan-a-them, Ma," Herkie said, pulling her out of her brown study.

"Now, Herkie, that's another thing I wanna say. You can't talk like a docker in a new place. It's not 'wan-a-them, Ma'; it's 'one-a-them, Ma, please.' You have to start practicing now in the house, d'ye hear me? No more of that unmannerly lip ye got away with in Belfast."

"Och, Ma, I wanna go back tae Belfast. I wanna play with Seanie McSwiney."

"Now, you listen tae me, son!" Bessie dropped her pose, finally losing her patience. "We're not going back tae Belfast. So get that into that wee curly head of yours. And forget about Sean McSwiney, too. There's plenty more wee boys ye can make friends with. We've a chance now tae start over. A couple of months here and we'll be on our feet and on a boat tae England. Nobody knows us round here, so we can be whoever we like. And the more posh we can be, the more the locals'll look up till us. And talking proper is where ye start. Them that talks proper get on better in this life. Just look at the Queen of England. D'ye think she'd be sittin' in a big gold coach with all them diamonds hangin' round her gizzer if she'd been comin' out with the likes of 'aye' and 'naw' and 'Canna have another wan-a-them, Ma?'"

"What's a 'gizzer,' Ma?" Herkie sat, blinking his innocent eyes, knowing he probably wouldn't get an answer, but using the tactic anyway, in the hope that he'd stall his ma, and she'd simply shut up and let him have the bun.

"Her gizzer isn't the point, son," the mother continued, clearly not about to stall anytime soon. "That grand lady I used to work for on the Malone Road knew how to talk." She'd had a fitful night and was in a snippy mood. "So I'm going to be talking like her from now on. Yes…Lesley Lloyd-Peacock didn't talk the way every eejit on the Shankill and the Falls talked, even though she had every right to, being born in the toilet of the Horn and Hound Arms to a ma barely fifteen, with a club foot and a hare's lip and a da nearly ninety if a day. No, she had the gumption to make something of herself. And d'you know how she did that, son?"

"What's a club fut, Ma?" Herkie had heard the story more often than he cared to remember. And always at times like this. Experience had taught him that his best ploy was to distract her when she was in full flight—as she was now. "When canna have me Action Man? Canna have another bun, Ma, *pleeeeease?*"

"Well, I'll tell you how she did it. She got the hell outta Belfast the minute she could walk in a pair-a high heels. And she never looked back, and only went back when she knew she could live in the richest part, and not among all the dog's arses she'd been reared with."

She drew another cigarette from the pack, afire with the image of the indomitable Mrs. Lloyd-Peacock. She recalled the fox fur slung over one shoulder, the little beady eyes of the beast peering down a smooth décolletage. The feathered hat cocked jauntily. The champagne flute clasped daintily between manicured fingers.

"Take another bun from that tin over there, son. And only one, mind."

Herkie breathed a sigh of relief and grinned. So she'd heard him after all. "Thanks, Ma!" He slid down off the chair and seized the tin from the dresser.

"I'll tell you when you'll get your Action Man: when we get a bitta money together, son. How d'ye think we're gonna manage that?"

"Take it from oul' Grant," said Herkie, not thinking.

Bessie slapped the table and Herkie nearly dropped the tin. "Are you gonna turn out like your thievin', good-for-nothin' da, are ye?"

"Naw, Ma. I mean no, Ma."

"Good! 'Cos you and me's gonna do what your da was allergic to: work! Now, here's the plan. I'm seeing the parish priest the morra about a job. He needs a cook, and we need money, and we need it badly. We'll never earn our passage if we don't work. So that's what I'm gonna do—besides other wee sidelines we can pick up."

"Ma, why did the banana go till the doctor?" The boy had a store of jokes memorized from the *Cheeky Weekly*. At times like this, when Bessie was in a bad mood, he'd trot one out to try and put her in better form.

"Pay attention, son! You'll drive *me* bananas, so you will. Now, here's one of the wee sidelines I've in mind for you. I've been watchin' the activity at that big house down the hill. I wanna know who lives there. There's a washin' out some days, so there might be a woman about, but I'm not sure. I never in me life knew an Irishman who did his own washin'. They'd wear the christening robe to the bloody grave if they could get away with it."

Herkie replaced the tin on the dresser and returned to the table with a chocolate éclair protruding from his gob like a Churchillian cigar. He struggled up onto the chair again, relishing the fact that his ma, too engrossed in her commentary and in the process of lighting her fag, hadn't noticed his naughtiness.

"We've got to start somewhere, so it might as well be with what's-his-name. You go down the morra and hide in the back field, and you see who lives there and what they get up to. If ye happen tae get the chance, slip in and see what the story is. Then bring a report back till me. D'ye unnerstan' me, son?"

"'Cos it wasn't *peeling* well, Ma!"

"What in God's name are ye sayin'?"

"The banana! It went tae the doctor 'cos it wasn't peeling well."

"Are you listenin' tae me atall, son?"

She stood up and leaned over the table. Herkie knew she meant business. She rapped her knuckles on the breadboard, making the supper things shiver.

"Now, the morra I want ye down there, to see what the story is in that big house. There's money about that place, if I'm any judge. So see who lives there and offer to run messages for them. D'ye hear me, son?"

"Och! When are we goin' away? Can I go out and play, Ma? When am I gettin' me Action Man, Ma? When will I be seein' Seanie McSwiney—"

"You'll be getting a warm ear if you don't do as I say, son. Now, get up them stairs and get yer parjamas on."

The timbers of the house creaked as Hercules, full of saturated fat and bad faith, trundled up the stairs to do her bidding.

Chapter eleven

Lorcan Strong dragged himself up the stairs of the dank house, his insides churning. Even though he'd been to the squalid place several times already, familiarity did not lessen his distaste. It was a house of horrors, where nightmares were real and death stalked the rooms.

No one who knew Lorcan the conservator would have recognized him as he mounted the stairs. He'd traded the bohemian garb for a brown gabardine overcoat and a dark cap. The uncustomary attire was necessary. Nansen Street, just off the Falls Road and within bawling distance of the Royal Belfast Hospital for Sick Children, was dangerous territory; he couldn't afford to draw attention to himself. He would willingly have done a deal with the Devil rather than make these visits to the appalling house and keep company with its odious occupants. But he had no choice in the matter, for his life depended on it.

On gaining the first floor, he heard voices: one low and deliberate, the other raised and pleading. They were coming from a room at the end of the corridor. He headed toward it with great reluctance. At the door he took a deep breath and gave his signal double-knock.

The voices in the room fell silent.

Lorcan waited.

"It's only the *fuckin'* artist," he heard a voice say. "Come in, Strong."

He warily turned the doorknob.

His entrance had mixed effects on the men gathered inside. It was a big room, and because it contained very little furniture, it seemed almost cavernous. It was actually two rooms of the original Georgian house, knocked into one.

The drapes on the tall windows were drawn so that no light intruded from the outside. The windows, Lorcan had been informed, enjoyed *triple* glazing. He soon discovered why such an extreme form of insulation was necessary. This was just one of several IRA torture chambers in West Belfast. A redoubt where "informers" screamed themselves to death in the dead of night while the street's other residents slept on, in blissful ignorance of the horrors being enacted in their midst.

There were three chairs in the room and two lights. Along the back wall sat a hostess trolley, incongruously laid out with a selection of surgical instruments and drill bits of varying sizes. Beer cans and cigarette ends littered the floor. A solitary low-wattage bulb hung from a ceiling fitting. In the normal run of things, its light would not have been sufficient.

But the second source of illumination was a huge arc light on a tripod. Lorcan reckoned it was emitting more than five hundred watts of electricity. Its beam was concentrated on a chair. It was a dentist's chair, not unlike those to be found in any dentist's surgery. The only difference was that it had built-in clamps for the wrists and feet. A man, naked save for his underpants, was seated in the chair and cruelly restrained by the clamps. In the harsh glare of the arc lamp he appeared white and terrified.

Two tough-looking men stood guard on either side of him. They were clad in jeans and sleeveless T-shirts that exposed sets of bulging biceps. One of the thugs had his face pressed close to that of the victim.

"Aw'right, Donal," he growled, his voice a gargle of rockery gravel. "Tell us again. Where did you and Lawless stash the readies?"

"I told ye! I told ye before and I'll tell ye again: I don't *know* where the bloody money is! Lawless took it all."

The victim's words had been aimed in Lorcan's general direction, even though in the glaring light the terrified man couldn't see who'd entered the room. Lorcan hung back in the shadows, wishing he could do something to help the wretch. He recalled the news item he'd heard the previous day concerning an IRA kidnapping. This Donal, most likely, was the hapless victim...yes, Donal Carmody: That was the kidnap victim's name. The harsh lamplight was picking out every rivulet of sweat running down the man's face.

Abruptly the door burst open.

The room fell silent again.

A powerfully built man strode in, allowing the door to crash shut behind him. His head was shaved nut-clean, and a portion of his pale scalp was disfigured by a burgundy birthmark. He was carrying an expensive briefcase, yet his clothing was not that of a gentleman. It was more suited to a tradesman or dockhand. Those acquainted with the Dentist in a former life knew that he had indeed worked for several years in the Belfast docks, helping to unload many cargoes—and not all of them of a legitimate nature.

The Dentist: Fionntann Blennerhassett, head of the Internal Security Unit for the Provisional IRA. Torturer-in-chief, he'd earned his stripes due to his dexterity with the rotary hammer drill.

Taking his time, the bald man hung up his biker jacket and opened his briefcase. He donned a white coat and buttoned it up.

It bulged in many places, giving him the look of an overstuffed bolster. He snapped the case shut and went directly to the man named Donal.

Donal cowered and tried to sink into the chair. The bald man adjusted the lamp slightly and lifted a wooden spatula from a tray beside the chair. Without a word, he inserted it between Donal's teeth and forced the unfortunate man's mouth open. He tut-tutted.

"Just as I thought," he said calmly. "Ye haven't taken care of them teeth atall, atall, have ye, Donal?" He tapped a brown specimen. "See that boy there, now? That'll have to come out. Nothin' else for it. Yer mammy would tell ye the same thing, so she would."

The victim gurgled, eyes wild with fright.

"Now that I see the rest of them," his tormentor said, "I'm inclined to think there's nothin' in there worth savin' atall."

Lorcan coughed politely.

The Dentist harrumphed and threw the spatula back onto the tray. He returned to his briefcase, drew out a set of keys. Lorcan followed him to a door at the far end of the room. He was conscious of Donal Carmody's terrified eyes following their every move, and the thuggish guards' unblinking vigilance.

The small room, which the Dentist referred to as "the office," was likewise sparsely furnished, a desk and chair taking up most of the space. On the desk stood a rod-stand lamp magnifier. Lined up neatly to the left of it were several dangerous-looking tools.

"So, how goes it, me old son?" He clapped Lorcan on the back with a meaty hand.

"I'm fine, thanks."

"Not you, ye bloody eejit. The *pitcher*. How far are ye?"

"Well, that's…that's what I wanted to talk to you about. I—"

"We're dependin' on ye, Lorcan. Ye wouldn't want anything tae happen tae them nice hands of yours."

"No…no, I wouldn't want that, sir." The artist's legs began to tremble, and he stood more rigidly in an attempt to calm himself. He could well have been the unfortunate Donal in the next room.

"I'll do the best I can," he assured the brute, trying very hard not to dwell on the wine-stain birthmark. He'd heard of men who'd suffered skull-numbing head butts and worse for having stared at it too long.

"'Course ye will. You'll do yer best. That's why we picked ye. Sure a man like you is wasted on all that nancy pitcher-work for that Brit-infested museum. See what them bastard Brits are doin' tae our boys in the Kesh?"

From the desk he picked up the May edition of *An Phoblacht*, the monthly newspaper of the Republican movement. Dominating the front page were black-and-white photographs of three young men—portraits that had acquired almost iconic status in Irish nationalist households. He shook his head and flung the paper down in fury.

"It's the fuckin' Famine again! Bobby's sixtieth day. Poor Bobby. What would you do in Bobby's position?"

Lorcan was in a quandary, sensing that whatever answer he gave would be the wrong one. "I'd…I'd do what I felt was right."

"And what would be right—in your educated opinion, now?" The Dentist's tone was grim.

"What…what I believed in."

"Ye'd die for Irish freedom then?"

"If I thought…if I thought it would achieve that aim." Lorcan rarely lied about anything. There'd been little need to. He'd been brought up to believe that such behavior was the default setting of lesser men.

The Dentist, calmer now, picked up the paper again and chuckled to himself. "That's a good 'un." He drew a finger gently round the emaciated features of Bobby Sands, a face with the hair and beard of a biblical ascetic. "Who would-a thunk it? Aye... who'd-a thunk it?"

"Sir...I'm taking...I mean I'm taking a month's leave of absence as of tomorr—"

"Are ye now? Who said ye could?"

The enforcer took a step toward him, bloodshot eyes like angry raspberries fixing on him. The artist took a step back.

"Well, my...my boss. H-he insisted on it. And my mother's not well. I—I'll be away for a...for a month."

"Now, let's get a coupla things straight, Lorcan, me boyo," the Dentist said, stabbing him in the chest with his trigger finger. It was a finger that had released bullets into the heads of an ill-fated cop and a squaddie before his promotion to Nutter-in-Chief. "First thing: ye have no boss tae answer till but *me*. Secondly, ye don't leave that pitcher for a month, 'cos I need it *last* month. Now, how d'ye suggest we get round this wee problem? I'm all ears, so I am."

He withdrew the finger and turned to ponder the display of instruments on the desk. Lorcan tensed. He could feel the perspiration in his armpits. He was deeply regretting having opened his mouth at all. Many men in his position had had similar regrets.

"I'm waitin', so I am." Blennerhassett had lifted a surgeon's scalpel and was running it along the inside of his palm. "Sharp wee bastard, that one. In the hands of the wrong man it could be lethal."

"I...I could take the painting home with me and f-fin...finish it at home...in Tailorstown."

The scalpel was placed back on the desk again—ever so daintily—as if it were a precious gem. The torturer straightened up, put his hands behind his back, rocked on his heels, and began whistling "A Nation Once Again" up at the ceiling light.

An imploring voice intruded from the other room. Donal's pleas were cut short by uncouth laughter.

The whistling stopped. The air quivered. Lorcan wanted to hightail it from the room. But the thought died as quickly as it had risen.

"See that bastard out there? Him and his mates did a wee job for me then took off with *my* money." He laughed at the floor, shaking his big head from side to side. "Ye'll never believe what he told me." He eyed the artist, who was still pressing himself rigid against the wall, hoping he might melt into it. It was clear the Dentist was demanding some kind of response to his rhetorical question.

"I-I wouldn't know, s-sir. I—"

"Said the fuckin' UDR took it. Can ye believe it, Lorcan? Aye, the fuckin' Ulster Defence Regiment took it and divvied it up between them...hmph! The other pair got themselves kilt in a car crash, which saved me the bother. But that boy out there?" He jerked a thumb at the door. "He'll be joinin' his mates very soon... ye see, that's what happens tae any fucks that mess up me plans. Now Lawless's whore of a wife has took off with my money. But, d'ye see, when I get me hands on her, I'll..."

At which point the brute seemed to suffer a psychotic fit. He crossed to the door and head-butted it several times.

Lorcan was appalled.

"And d'ye see this wee haul'day yer takin'? Well, it's messin' up me plans a fair bit. So tell me again how ye're gonna make me feel a wee bit better about things. Me ears are waitin' for some pleasant news, so they are."

A thought struck Lorcan. He'd blind him with science. Play up the importance of taking his time over the painting.

"I...I assure you, I'll have it completed within three weeks— four at the maximum. It'll take that time for each layer of paint to dry. Otherwise...otherwise the colors...well, the colors bleed into one another, ruining the effect. If that happened I'd have to abandon it and start all over again. Then it would take even longer.

It's the nature of oil painting, I'm afraid. You just can't rush it if you want the best result."

Blennerhassett glared. "Hmph!"

Lorcan knew he had him stymied. Feeling himself on firmer ground, he matched his stare, tempering it with a little shrug. "I'm sorry, but that's the way it is. Skill is important in a painter, but so is patience."

The floorboards creaked beneath the Dentist's heavy-duty boots. "Ye'd better be tellin' me the truth. Three weeks it is and not a fuckin' day more." He drew himself up to his full height and sneered. "Nice wee spot, Tailorstown, I believe. Would be a shame to spoil the peace and quiet—if ye folly me drift." He moved to the door. "And yer mammy not too well an' all. Sure where would we be without our mammies? Was that all ye wanted to discuss, Lorcan, me old son? Got a bitta surgery waitin' out here. Bad tae keep the patient waitin', isn't it, now?"

Lorcan simply nodded, unable to find his voice. He followed the torturer out, trying not to look in the terrified Donal's direction.

"Ah, Jesus, *no! Please, nooooooo!*"

The piercing pleas followed the conservator all the way down the stairs. When he finally gained the safety of the street and slammed the door on the horror, he stood panting under a murky moon and made himself a promise.

He promised himself that, no matter what the consequences, he'd never enter that dreaded house in Nansen Street again.

Chapter twelve

Kilfeckin Manor was a well-preserved Georgian mansion set in its own grounds a short distance to the north of Tailorstown. It was reached by a long and gracious graveled drive lined by ash and spruce trees. The lush rhododendrons that burst into life every summer, when the orchards were heavy with fruit, lent the place an opulence and sophistication much at odds with its present incumbent, the cantankerous octogenarian Ned Grant.

The house was big—one of the largest properties in the area—and built to last for centuries. It had two stories, groaning with antique furniture. The ground floor contained three generous reception rooms, a library, a kitchen, a scullery, and a pantry; the floor above it boasted six bedrooms and four dressing rooms (most of which had fallen out of use). A steep and narrow staircase led up to a third story that consisted largely of a single room at the rear. It was known as the Turret Room because of its circular shape and its commanding view of the trees and fields that surrounded it on three sides. It was rarely used.

Kilfeckin had a turbulent history. During the First World War it had been requisitioned by the military—two Nissen huts in the grounds still bore their Red Cross roundels, long faded to a ghostly pink—after which it had reverted to its rightful heir: Lord Sebastian Dinsford-Kilfeckin.

On His Lordship's death, however, things took a turn for the worse. The new heir, his only son, Viscount Lucien-Percy, a transvestite buffoon with no hair and a gambling habit, did not exactly value his inheritance. In no time at all, he'd frittered away his entire share portfolio at the gaming tables in Monte Carlo and Las Vegas, had sold off great swaths of the outlying land, and was just beginning to plunder the art collection when he decided to call it a day.

One fateful morning, his shocked gardener discovered his lifeless body, clad in nothing more than a bra and matching panties, dangling from the landing chandelier. The year was 1938.

The house was shut up after that. It lay vacant for several years. Rumors abounded that ill luck would befall anyone who dared enter through its linteled doors—until Ned Grant showed up. Joylessly wed and down on his luck, he saw the opportunity to take advantage of the silly rumor and bought the house for a pittance. The locals resented him for his fearlessness, and he disdained them for the pack of superstitious duffers they surely were.

"God, what's keepin' her the day?"

Ned's nephew, Gusty Grant, sat by the turret window in what had once been the ill-fated viscount's dressing room. The mechanic, in his oil-stained overalls and hobnail lace-ups, could have been a hog in a harem, so gloriously feminine and grand was the chamber.

Gilt-crested mirrors reflected what once had been an opulence of furnishings and fabrics, dusty and faded now. The theme was pink, the mood flirtatious—lavish drapes, frilled pelmets, and damask armchairs with heart-shaped cushions. There were satinwood closets and lacquered chests sporting swan-neck handles of ebony and glass. A chandelier dripped crystal from the ceiling. Two fat cherubs blowing fatly on trumpets flanked a three-mirrored dressing table raised on bun feet.

Gusty, backside sunk in an armchair, one foot resting on a velveteen gout stool, was training his binoculars on Rosehip Cottage. He was hoping to get a close-up of Mrs. Hailstone in her nightdress—or better still, out of it—but wasn't having very much luck so far.

At his feet lay his pet piglet, Veronica, snorting in porcine slumber.

He'd chosen this particular room, which he seldom ventured into, because it afforded the best view of the cottage.

From the moment Mrs. Hailstone drove into Gusty's life in her battered Morris Traveller, he knew he wanted to look at her for a wee while longer than the few minutes allowed for the fill-up of petrol. That worn fan belt was a godsend. Hadn't it all worked out so well? Because now she was caught in his sights, quite literally, and what a grand specimen she was!

On the armrest of the chair a copy of *Reader's Digest* lay open at an article about crop circles. Evidence of an alien invasion in East Surrey, or the Devil doing a spot of midnight mowing, who was to say? The mechanic was looking forward to getting stuck into his next article, a study of the eating habits of the twenty-two-tentacled star-nosed mole, but was loath to start it, in case he missed something on the hill.

He rotated the focus wheel on the binoculars and panned around the rear of the cottage. Her car was parked under the big ash, where she'd left it the day before. *But where was she?*

It hadn't taken him long to learn her routine. She'd go to bed around midnight and was usually up by eight thirty. She'd draw back the curtains in the bedroom at that hour. On three occasions, she'd come out the back in her nightdress to smoke a cigarette. She had two nightdresses: a pink frilly one and a red shiny one with a low-cut neckline. He liked the red one in particular and imagined her in Aunt Dora's bed thus attired, a fantasy that made his heart hammer and his knees shake.

Still no sign. Disappointed, he set the binoculars down on the floor beside him, knowing that any minute he'd be hearing a twin *thump* from the room below.

The thumper, his Uncle Ned, a onetime farmer who'd survived two world wars and served in one—flat feet and rickets having kept him out of the second—spent most of his time in bed with his bad legs and dodgy chest, nursing his war wounds and listening to the wireless. Gusty, the illicit fruit of a graceless encounter between Ned's late brother, Eustace, and a washerwoman, did double duty as caregiver and handyman. Along with his brief stints bartending at the Crowing Cock and sporadic work as an auto mechanic, he fell into that most superficial of categories, generally known as "Jack of all trades and master of none."

The young Gusty's arrival at Kilfeckin had been as unceremonious as one could imagine. He'd simply materialized one hot August morning with a change of socks and a note that read: *I rared him from scretch now its yew's turn.* His washerwoman mother had found better prospects—a used-car salesman with a mobile home set on two acres and a Triumph Toledo pickup that was "going places"—a couple of weeks after the errant Eustace had dropped dead of a hepatitic seizure outside a pub in Clonmany, County Donegal. In this new and unexpected state of affairs, the sixteen-year-old Gusty had become surplus to requirements and was thus unceremoniously sent back to his roots.

So Ned, a childless widower with more living space than was respectable, reluctantly accommodated the lad. Never quite accepting the fact that his "ward" was the issue of the wayward Eustace (even though Gusty carried the undeniable proof of the Grant progeny in his big feet and trophy-cup ears), Ned sought to advertise the falsity of such a claim by housing the boy in a lean-to attached to an old garage out the road.

Over the years, Kilfeckin Manor saw Gusty's constant coming and going as he both slaved for and befriended his crotchety uncle. The pair grew to like and loathe each other in equal measure, blowing hot and cold with the sureness and contrariness of the seasons. As time passed and Ned retreated more to the bedroom on the first floor, he became less aware that Gusty was even in the house. Raidió Teilifís Éireann's afternoon shows with their hourly news bulletins, coupled with encroaching deafness, would mute footfalls and creaking doorknobs and muffle the odd shouted salutation from the front hall door. These days even the roars and rattles of Gusty's truck were progressively going unheard.

Thump, thump.

"Hoi! Are ye up there?"

There it was: the all-too-familiar summons, made by the broom shaft the oul' boy kept by the bedside, sending tremors through the armchair. Veronica snorted and opened one piggy eye.

"Och, what d'ye want now?" Gusty muttered, half to himself and half to the uncaring universe.

With resignation he stood up, licked a grubby thumb to mark the page about the curious star-nosed moles, took another gape out the window, and kicked a trunk before lumbering down the stairs, piglet trotting behind him.

Old Ned was propped up as usual in his Elizabethan four-poster, sucking on a pipe and sending out great gouts of smoke that hung in the room like thunderheads over the Serengeti.

"Where's me tay?" he demanded.

"Rose is comin' today. Did ye forget, did ye? *She'll* make yer tea."

"She is, is she? Aye, Rose'll make me tay and not crab about it like *you*. Better take a piss afore she comes then. Help me up, will ye?" He hoisted himself up in the bed. "And get that bloody pig outta here. It ate one-a-me socks yesterday."

"She doesn't eat socks. Ye lost the sock yerself."

Gusty clumped over and helped haul his uncle out of bed. He knew that Ned was well able to get up unaided but assisted him anyway, if only to keep the peace.

"Now, open that windee for me."

"Och, ye don't need tae do it out the windee no more. That's why the commode's over there in the corner. That Mrs. Hailstone's up in Dora's now." In the past, he hadn't minded the old man using the yard as a toilet, but the arrival of Mrs. Hailstone had changed all that—hence the provision of Lord Kilfeckin's ancient commode.

"Aye, she'll not see nothin' she hasn't seen afore. The day I sit down on a chair tae piss is the day they kerry me out in a box."

"Ye didn't see me wallet, did ye?" Gusty was changing the subject, trying to forestall the repellent act while checking for activity on the hill.

"Naw, how would I see yer bloody wallet? Maybe ye give it tae that fancy wommin, seein' as ye give her my Dora's house."

"It's *my* house. Dora said she wanted me tae have it after she died."

"Aye, she did, did she? Well, she was dotin' and didn't know what she was sayin'. She told Barney Bap and Screw-loose John she was leavin' it tae them, too. She left that house tae half the bloody country afore she went."

"Well, she told me afore she went dotin', and Mrs. Hailstone paid me rent," said Gusty, his voice quick with annoyance. "And you're only pissin' out that windee tae embarrass me in front-a her!"

"I'll piss wherever I want."

"Och, you're nothing but a contrary oul' shite! Come on, Veronica."

Man and beast left the room while old Ned lurched in the direction of the window to water the bindweeds in the backyard.

Young Herkie, concealed in the field behind the Grant residence, was not much interested in what was happening beyond the hedge that shielded him from view. He lay surrounded by discarded sweet wrappers, engrossed in his *Cheeky Weekly* comic, bum-crack on show for all the birds to see.

Suddenly a noise alerted him. He looked up in time to see an upstairs window being thrust open. As he watched, an old man came into view, undid his flies, and let loose on a group of ducks leisurely grooming themselves below. He then stuck his head out the window and shouted something before banging the window shut again as the ducks ran squawking from the downpour.

Herkie, stifling a giggle, wondered what to do. His ma had instructed him to check out the big house to see if there was a woman about it. The man he'd seen at the window was definitely an oul' boy. Oul' boys were good news, because they were usually deaf and half blind, which would make his task a lot easier. Maybe he could make a beeline for the back door now. The Opal Fruits were all eaten anyway. There wasn't a blackbird in sight, so he had no use for his slingshot. Besides, he was bored and wanted some action.

But just as he was contemplating this, the back door opened and a man emerged carrying a bucket. He was surprised to see the mechanic-and-new-landlord, Mr. Grant. Grunting at his heels was Veronica, the piglet Herkie had tormented a few days before.

Crouching farther down behind the hedge, he watched intently as Mr. Grant lit up a cigarette, sat himself down on a crate, and began inspecting his reflection in a near window, elongating his neck, rubbing his stubble, and pulling faces. Herkie wondered what he was playing at. Maybe he was crazy—his ma had told him that most country people were a bit odd. All that living in the middle of fields and staring at animals gave them bumps in their brains and things like that.

By and by, Grant lost interest in his reflection. He stood up, grabbed a rake, raised it up to a first-floor window, and knocked on it a few times.

After about a minute, the window flew open and the oul' boy stuck his head out.

"Hi, I'm goin' tae the Cock," said Mr. Grant, "tae see Etta about the night. D'ye want anything, do ye?"

"Aye, right, Etta Strong's hard up tae want a boy like you. Get me a pouch-a that Peter's Flake and a quart of them Glassy-ear Mints."

With that, the window was pulled shut before Mr. Grant had time to reply.

In the silence that followed, all Herkie could hear was "Away with yeh, ye oul' shite!"

So Mr. Grant lived in the big house with an oul' boy. What would his ma say about that? Deciding that he'd had enough information for the time being, he gathered up his sweet wrappers, stuck the comic in his pocket, and slipped away up the field to report his findings.

Chapter thirteen

The phone rang as Father Connor Cassidy was firming up his Sunday sermon. He did not welcome the intrusion.

"Good morning, Saint Timothy's, Father Cassidy speaking."

"Hello, Father. It's Doris Crink here, at the post office."

Oh dear, thought the priest, why would the post office be calling? Could the price of stamps have jumped by a whole penny? A late delivery of the *Sacred Heart Messenger* perhaps?

Since coming to St. Timothy's he'd been besieged by a flock of bird-witted ladies, all wanting his ear on the most frivolous of pretexts.

"I hope I'm not interrupting you, Father."

"Not at all, Doris. How are you keeping?"

"Not too bad, Father. I just wanted to let ye know, Father, that I was talkin' to Josie Mulhearn. You know Josie from the café?"

"I do, of course." He had an idea what was coming.

"Now, Josie says there was a lady into her the day before yesterday and she was askin' after your position, Father."

"Excellent news, Doris! Is she a local lady?"

There was a slight hesitation from the postmistress. "Well... no. She's a stranger, so she is."

"Ah, yes. Well, that's splendid news."

In the brief silence that followed, Father Cassidy detected the wind of censure wafting down the line.

"Aye. But are you sure she'd be...well, *proper* for you, Father?"

"Well, Doris, since I've yet to meet the lady in question, I'm in no position to make such a judgment. Now, was there anything else?"

"Oh, no, Father. Just that...I thought...I thought I'd let you know, just to warn you in advance, like."

"Very kind of you, Doris. Thank you for taking the trouble. Bye now."

He put down the phone and smiled to himself. It was the second time that morning he'd been warned off. He'd barely finished breakfast when Rose McFadden, a woman whose very arteries seemed clogged with the minutiae of small-town life, had rung his doorbell.

"God, Father, I'm glad I got ye in time."

For a moment he thought there'd been an accident and he was being called upon to administer the last rites. But no, it was far more serious than that.

"Josie at the cafe tolt me," she'd blurted out breathlessly, "tolt me tae tell ye that there was a strange wommin in the café lookin' at your advertmint. And she ast where the parochial house was, so she did."

A wave of relief had swept over him at that point. A *stranger* wanting to work for him? How interesting! But of course she'd have to be the *right* type of stranger. Not too bright or intrusive. A capable sort. Yes, a capable sort who saw to her duties and left him alone. It was important that the newly formed Temperance Club not be disturbed.

"That's good, Mrs. McFadden. If she's suitable you won't have to desert your good husband or your uncle or worry about me. That way, we'll all be happy. Now I really must be going."

Rose, however, was not about to let him away so easily.

"But, Father, that's just it: Josie said she wouldn't be proper for a priest's house. That's why I thought I'd warn you. She just didn't look right."

"Oh. What do you mean exactly?"

"Well, now, Josie said she didn't look like a Cathlick."

He really hadn't wanted to encourage Mrs. McFadden, yet simply had to hear how Josie Mulhearn could discern someone's religion by appearance alone. "And how did Josie conclude that, I wonder?"

Rose had moved closer to him, pleased to have the Father's ear for another wee while.

"Well, ye know, Josie said she was cheeky to her and had what looked like a young son with her." Mrs. McFadden's voice dropped to a whisper. "But there was no sign of a waddin' ring on her, as far as Josie could see. The son, Father, was drawin' durty pitchers in Josie's sugar, what he'd spilt on the table. And as well as that, Josie said that the mother had a miniskirt, and yella hair all puffed up like Merlin Monroe's, and more paint on her face than would be in Dan's Decorators, or on them type of wimmin that do be taking up with sailors and the like."

"Well, thanks for warning me, Mrs. McFadden. But judge not, lest ye be judged, as the Good Book advises us. Now I really must be going."

Father Cassidy checked his watch. It had just gone eleven. The "Merlin Monroe" look-alike, which the Misses Crink, Mulhearn, and McFadden had so disapproved of, would be arriving for her interview in approximately three hours' time. Mrs. Halstone had telephoned the previous evening, and he'd found her most polite and genial. He was looking forward to meeting her; had thought it better not to divulge his plans to the gossip-hungry parish ladies, not wishing to bring on one of his migraines. No, best to keep it quiet. They'd find out soon enough.

Besides, he was tired of having his private affairs talked about behind his back. Since learning of the vacant housekeeper post, the rambling Rose had taken to haunting him like Marley's ghost. There was only one way to thwart her. Mrs. Halstone would, he hoped, save the day—and his sanity.

Yes, even if this "strange wommin" turned out to have webbed feet and a horn in the middle of her forehead, he felt sure he'd still be employing her.

Chapter fourteen

Bessie sat at Aunt Dora's dressing table and reached for her smokes. Today was an important day, one that would require a generous measure of restraint. An interview with a priest wasn't something she'd factored into her game plan. But urgent measures were called for, she reminded herself. She needed money—and fast. With last week's family allowance almost gone, the job would plug the gap, for now.

A masquerade was called for. A pretense to respectability. Good posture, a coordinated outfit, and a posh accent could carry the day and progress things considerably. Had it not done so for the formidable Mrs. Lloyd-Peacock?

She'd learned a lot from her glamorous former employer, a woman who, according to Bessie's dear-departed mother, hadn't had a brass farthing until Mr. Peacock, a wealthy accountant, showed up. On their honeymoon he'd done the decent thing: lost his balance on board a Cunard cruise liner and pitched face-first into the Atlantic swell. His widow had inherited half a million. Not bad going for a slapper from the Lower Falls. Who was to say she hadn't helped him over the side?

Father Cassidy had sounded like a real gent on the phone. Her interview was in a couple of hours' time. The problem was, he was requesting references from both My Lovely Buns bakery *and* the Plaza hotel, Belfast. The bakery was straightforward enough: Mabel McClarty, her colleague and friend, had written a reference a year earlier when Bessie, in desperation following yet another beating from Packie, thought she should move to another part of Belfast.

Yet in truth she'd never actually "cooked" at the elegant, five-star Plaza. Her brief tenure there, between skivvying for Mrs. Lloyd-Peacock and courting Packie, had included the most menial of kitchen duties: chopping vegetables and peeling potatoes if a member of staff fell ill. Still, what would a bumpkin priest know about anything, stuck in a parochial house half his life with nothing but a Bible and the parish accounts to keep him occupied?

She had, however, "befriended" a guest at the Plaza: a certain Colonel Padraig Redmond Murphy, who occupied a permanent suite on the third floor. She knew he was nothing but a dirty old man, but his tips were good. Bessie, always one for thinking ahead, had asked the colonel to write her a reference on the hotel's embossed stationery. It was her way of getting back at the German head chef, who'd rejected her pastry-cook application. Little did she know back then how serendipitous that move would prove to be.

She left the fag in the mouth of a china frog at her elbow and dipped into the bottom drawer of the bureau. Squashed on top of Aunt Dora's ancient underwear was Bessie's filing cabinet: a Walker's Shortbread tin in which she kept her confidential correspondence.

She flipped through the contents of the tin, delving down through her past, a paper trail of triumphs and tribulations—the latter, she reflected ruefully, massively outweighing the former.

A black-and-white snapshot fluttered onto the bed, and in an instant a gust of memory had her falling down a hole into the past.

A miniature bride with hands joined, white rosary beads entwined in her fingers, stared back up at her. Her First Communion.

"Ma, can I put me dress on now?"

"It's only half eight. Mass isn't till ten. You'll get it dirty. Eat yer porridge up."

"Ma, pleeasse!"

"Shut up, Bessie. Give my head some peace!"

"I'll put it on her." Da getting up from the sofa, newspaper sliding to the floor.

"No, Da! Ma, don't let him...please."

"I said I'll fuckin' put it on ye! Get into that bedroom now or I'll knock yer fuckin' head in."

Ma turning from the sink. "Leave her alone! Your hands are dirty, like yer bloody mind."

A fist flying out. Her mother falling. Blood spotting the floor tiles like crimson rain.

"Oh, Jesus. Ma!"

Bessie blinked away the tears before they had a chance to flow. She was good at that. A carapace of basalt, brilliant and hard against men and the world, had been laid down early. Layer upon sorry layer, ossifying down the years.

She returned the snapshot to the biscuit tin. Reaching for the cigarette again, hand quivering, she took a deep drag as she read through the colonel's reference.

When she'd first seen what Colonel Murphy—retired, confused, dementia galloping through his brain like pigweed on a dung heap—had written in his reference, she'd been a bit concerned by its lascivious connotations but was in no position to object or ask him to write it again.

To whom it may concern:

Miss Elizabeth Halstone has worked under me for the past year. She is an excellent hostess, committed to her work and very good with her hands. In fact, what has impressed me most about her is her willingness to go that extra mile just to please the customer. She is discreet, flexible, can work on her own initiative, and is able to apply herself with energy and enthusiasm to whatever is requested of her. I would highly recommend her for any future positions she may wish to apply for. All in all she is a magnificent hostess.

Yours Sincerely,
Padraig Redmond Murphy (Colonel)

P.S. Her puddings are particularly splendid.

The comment about the puddings she had asked him to add, believing, wisely, that it might be necessary to mention a bit about the cookery in order to clarify matters.

With a satisfied nod, she slipped the reference back into the envelope and put it in her handbag. She checked her watch. Herkie was away, monitoring activity at the big house, and would be up at any minute.

Time to get dressed.

She bent down to her underwear drawer and extracted a panty girdle and longline bra. She'd planned on wearing what she referred to as her tweed "interview" suit: a cast-off from Mrs. Lloyd-Peacock's winter wardrobe, circa 1968. However, it being a petite size 10 and Bessie being a healthy size 12, she needed all the help she could muster to achieve a pleasing yet voluptuous silhouette.

After slipping into the underwear and donning the suit, she stepped back from the mirror, squinting through a fog of cigarette smoke. She adjusted the jacket and appraised her bosom. Wisely, she decided that showing several inches of cleavage to Father Cassidy might not be *comme il faut*—not on a first meeting, anyway. She found a scarf and tucked it into place. A final squirt of Rapture cologne down her front and up her skirt, and Mrs. Elizabeth

Halstone was ready to face a rather late breakfast, the day, and whatever the good Father was likely to throw at her.

"Ma, Ma!" shouted Herkie, blundering through the door, breathless from the exertions of his reconnaissance mission. His yellow T-shirt had a big grass stain down the front and his bare knees were muddy.

His mother, smoking while stabbing at sausages in the frying pan, wetting tea, and laying the table to the yammering squawks of "I Will Survive" on the record player, was none too pleased at the interruption. Time was marching on, and she didn't need any annoyance.

"Look at the state of *you*, son. What were you doin' down there, havin' a fight with a bloody dunkey? Away up them stairs and change! I've an important day ahead of me the day, what with the parish priest, and I don't want no bother from *you*. Ye can tell me all about it when we're eating."

Five minutes later they were tucking into brunch—Bessie to her fry-up and Herkie to a bowl of cornflakes with a mountain of sugar on top, a chocolate éclair to follow.

"Now, what have you got for me, son? Who did you see?"

"Mr. Grant!"

Bessie stalled her fork. "What was *he* doing there?"

"I saw him coming outta the house, Ma. Then making faces at himself in a windee."

"Are ye sure it was him?"

"Aye, 'cos he had big, flappy trousers and big glasses on him, and the pig was with him."

Bessie chewed her food thoughtfully. What was Grant up to? Why hadn't he mentioned that he lived down the hill?

"But I saw an oul' boy as well. He lives upstairs and wears a cap."

"And how did ye see him?"

"'Cos he peed out the windee…down on the ducks."

"Well, that's not so surprisin' with bogmen, but don't use that durty word in front-a me, son. We have to speak proper in this place. Mind what I told you."

"Aye, Ma…sorry—yes, Ma."

"Anything else?"

"I saw the oul' boy pee—I mean going till the toilet—out the windee, and then Mr. Grant came with a bucket and fed the pig and started makin' faces at himself in another windee. After that he took a big, long fork and hit the oul' boy's windee with it, and the oul' boy put his head out and Mr. Grant shouted up at him, 'Am goin' tae see me cock about the night,' or something, d'ye—"

"*What* did I say about using durty words in front-a me?"

"What durty word, Ma?"

"Never you mind." She studied the tablecloth, trying to figure out what Gusty Grant might have meant. Then it dawned on her. "That'll be the Crowing Cock pub…he mentioned he did a bit of work there in the evenings. Then what happened?"

Herkie screwed up his eyes, thinking hard.

"Then the oul' boy shouted down, 'Get me a flake and some glassy-ear-mince' or something like that." He took a deep breath. "And then Mr. Grant went 'Och, away with yeh, ye oul' shite,' and drived—"

Whack! Bessie's hand smote the table. "If you come out with any more of that filth, son, I'll be taking off them shorts and beating yer bum so hard you'll not be sitting down for a week! D'ye hear me?"

Herkie lifted his glass of milk in both hands and took a long draft. He eyed his ma over the rim of the glass. Her next question would be whether he'd gone inside the house, and he was trying to predict how mad she'd be if he told her he had not. He decided to stall her by keeping outside in the yard of the big house and hoped she'd forget to ask.

"Did ye—"

"Oh, and outside there were some oul' stupid cows in a field and four ducks covered in pee because the oul' boy had peed—went tae the toilet on them—and—"

"Now, that's *enough*! I warned ye about that language. And a lotta good any of it is to me, son." Bessie was becoming irritated. A piece of bacon had dropped into her cleavage, and she was checking for a stain on her good silk scarf.

"So, ye went inside the house when Grant left. I hope ye did, son, for ye'll get the back a me hand if ye wasted time down there, lyin' in a field watchin' pigs and cows and some oul' boy peein' on ducks."

"I *did* go in the house, Ma." Herkie began mushing up his cornflakes with the back of his spoon, unable to meet his mother's eye. "It had big stairs goin' up, and a big lamp with four arms up in the roof."

"Aye, a likely story, son. I could-a told ye that meself, and I haven't put me toe near the place. Ye didn't go in the house, so don't lie timme, son. Ye can lie to strangers but not yer ma."

Herkie gazed into his cereal bowl, cheeks suffused with shame.

"Right, son, you're going down there again the morra when he goes to the pub, and you're gonna pay a visit tae that oul' boy. You're gonna knock the door first—to be mannerly—poke your head in and shout up 'Hello' when you're goin' up the stairs. That way, he'll know you're not a burglar. He's maybe in bed and can't get about, and that's good. For ye can be his friend and help him out. He'll slip ye a bob or two 'cos he'll be grateful for the company. And that's good for him, and you and me, too."

Herkie signaled his frustration with his usual kicking of the table leg.

"*Cut that out, son.* Now, if ye come back to me the morra with them pockets empty, I'll be lockin' that cupboard and ye'll get no sweets for a fortnight. D'ye hear me?" Bessie stood up and drained the last of her tea.

"Och, Ma!" Nothing dismayed Herkie more than the thought of going without his sweet treats.

"Right, I'm away now." She went to a mirror above the mantelshelf, unsheathed a lipstick tube, and reapplied a generous slash of Outrageous Red.

"Now, lock that door behind me and don't let nobody in, unless it's Mr. Grant. He said something about doing the garden. We have to keep on the right side of him until we get on our feet. So, if he comes, make him a drop of tea if he asks for it."

"Aye—yes, Ma."

"And another thing, son. Put out that washing on the back hedge for me."

"Yes, Ma."

She stood back from the mirror to admire herself, went to it again, teased at her hair, patted her lapels, then bent to the armchair for her handbag.

In the meantime, Herkie had picked up one of Dora's many ornaments crowding the windowsill—a leprechaun playing an accordion—and was figuring out how he might remove its head when his ma was out of the way.

"Now look, son!" She took hold of his wrist and gave his hand a sharp slap. "What did I tell ye about touchin' Dora Grant's things?"

Herkie sheepishly replaced the leprechaun. "Sorry, Ma."

"Now, mind to be polite to Mr. Grant if he calls, and remember what I said about being posh and speaking proper like Mrs. Peacock."

"Aye, Ma. I mean yes, Ma."

"What's your name, son?"

"Herkie."

"Oh, for *God's* sake! Herkie what?"

"Herkie Law—"

"*Ah!*"

"Herkie Halson."

"Now, Herkie, don't try my patience or I'll—"

"Sorry, Ma. Herkie Halstone."

"That's more like it. Where do we come from?"

"Belfast."

"*Where* in Belfast?"

"Mahone Road."

"Ma*lone* Road, son."

"Malone Road."

"What are we doin' here?"

"We're on haul'days."

"Good. I'm away now. Just remember, son, you and me's in this together. We're a team."

"Yes, Ma."

"Now, how do I look?"

"You look nice, Ma. Canna have another Curly Wurly, Ma, please?"

"You're just like your father." She playfully pinched his cheek and kissed the top of his head. "Wish me luck."

"Good luck, Ma."

"Just the *one* Curly Wurly then. I've everything in that tin counted. So no cheating. And another thing: Don't go near that well."

"Naw, Ma—I mean no, Ma."

On hearing her car move off, Herkie, Curly Wurly in hand, excitement frothing in him like shaken pop, made for the back door. He was intent on continuing his covert activity of shifting the big stone, bit by bit, off the well cover. China was nearly in sight: just a few more nudges to go.

Chapter fifteen

Half an hour later, the recently widowed Mrs. Halstone found herself sitting in an armchair, swinging an impatient foot, and staring up at a chandelier in the high-ceilinged parlor of the parochial house. She'd been there a good twenty minutes and wished the priest would get a bloody move on. It was stifling in the musty room, and her control briefs and long-line brassiere were causing her no end of discomfort. She wanted desperately to unbutton her jacket, throw her legs up on the coffee table, and have a smoke, but she knew that the move would be indecorous. After all, she'd put quite a bit of energy into this venture already and was determined to make a go of it.

She gazed about the room, trying to distract herself, but alas, there was nothing of much interest. The furniture was heavy and dark, the carpet sun-bleached and ancient, and taking up an entire wall was a series of glass-fronted cases full of useless old books.

A large, gilt-framed portrait of a jowly, bewigged individual in dark robes was obscuring most of the chimneypiece. She got up to read the brass nameplate: *Judge Cosgrove Carson*. Bet he put many the like of Packie behind bars in his time, she reflected.

Returning to the chair, she sighed, crossed her legs, wiggled a toe, examined her crimson nails, and checked her watch again. She was about to open her handbag and reapply her lipstick when she heard heavy footfalls in the corridor.

Presently the door creaked open and the housekeeper, a gray pillar wearing a scowl and elastic hose, waded into the room. Bessie knew she was face-to-face with the formidable Miss Beard.

"Father Cassidy will see ye now, Mrs. Hailstone," she announced grandly, casting a disapproving eye over Bessie's tight skirt, which had ridden up over her knees to expose a lacy frill of flesh-colored slip.

Bessie smiled demurely and rose. She followed the housekeeper as she galumphed out of the room and down a wide corridor.

Father Cassidy was seated behind a stout desk in what appeared to be his study.

"Mrs. Halstone, thank you for coming," he said, getting up and extending a pale, slender hand. "Please, take a seat."

"Pleased to meet you, Father," Bessie said, positioning herself in a bentwood chair. Then, realizing that the priest had a full view of her legs, she crossed them carefully at the ankle, in the manner of the matronly bench polishers he was no doubt used to seeing. Such decorum, she felt, would improve her chances.

Father Cassidy busied himself with the papers on his desk as Bessie looked on. Handsome, she thought: like Gregory Peck from the eyebrows up. She'd been besotted with Gregory from the age of ten and tended to see bits of him in all those men who were generally out of her league.

"I was very impressed with your credentials, Mrs. Halstone," the priest said, addressing her bosom for a fleeting instant before putting on his spectacles and glancing down at her letter. (Down in Hades, the Devil pushed his biggest pot onto a volcanic flame and began to sweat the ingredients for Priestly Lust over the intense heat.)

"Yes, you have considerable experience in the catering trade, I—" Abruptly, the priest was seized by a coughing fit. A sixty-a-day cough, she reckoned, noting the two packs of Rothmans King Size on his desk. "Oh, I *do* beg your pardon!"

"That's all right, Father...yes, cooking is my work as well as a hobby." She leaned forward in the chair and put a hand on her bosom. "My dear, late husband always used to say that the way to a man's heart is through his stomach." (More like through his breast pocket with a sharp kitchen knife, she thought—but Father Cassidy did not need to know her personal views.) The priest gave her an odd look, and Bessie quickly added a forlorn "God rest him!" just in case she'd given the wrong impression.

"Dear me. I *am* sorry, Mrs. Halstone. Taken suddenly, was he?"

"A road accident, Father." She gazed dolefully at the flickering red globe of a Sacred Heart picture above Father Cassidy's head. "Cut down in his prime." She crossed herself. "He was such a good man. But the Lord's ways are not our ways."

"No, indeed. I take it you are...hmm—"

"Catholic? Yes, of course, Father."

"It's just that I didn't see you at...crm..." Father Cassidy hesitated, trying to form the awkward inference as delicately as possible.

"Mass?" Bessie said helpfully, raising her Zsa Zsa eyebrows.

"Indeed. Mass."

"Yes, I'm sorry, but we—that is, me and my young son—we've only just arrived in these parts...Just settling in, you understand. You'll be seeing us at Mass without a doubt this Sunday, Father."

Bessie's visits to churches were as rare as a nun's to a strip joint, but Father Cassidy need not know that, either.

"Splendid! Now..." He glanced down at her letter again. "The Plaza hotel; very impressive—"

"Oh, just when you mention it, Father." She fished in her handbag for the colonel's letter, then stood. She was conscious of Father Cassidy's appraising eye as she leaned over the desk, just a whisper of cleavage on show beneath the scarf. "My reference from the Plaza."

(The Devil flicked his tail and did a little jig as the contents of his cauldron began bubbling and spitting, giving off an acrid smoke.)

Father Cassidy's hands trembled slightly as he studied the reference. He nodded and murmured his approval.

"Excellent. You are very experienced indeed, Mrs. Halstone." He glanced up from the page. "And Colonel Murphy's position?"

The missionary position if he'd ever got the chance. Filthy oul' goat. "Oh, he was a top man, Father! Terribly professional. I learned a great deal about the hospitality trade when I worked for him. Often, after a busy day, I would relieve him in the evenings. He trusted me completely, you see."

"Quite so. He must have thought a great deal of your puddings to have given them a special mention."

"Puddings are a specialty of mine." Bessie's confidence was growing. Who knew, if she played her cards right maybe she could earn enough dosh to take herself and Herkie all the way to her dream destination of Amerikay. Mrs. Lloyd-Peacock had done it on her wits. Why couldn't she? Sod Hackney and Uncle Bert. This country priest would be a pushover for a girl of her talents and resourcefulness. "My puddings? I've won prizes for them, Father."

"Really! D'you know, Mrs. Halstone"—the priest canted forward, threw a glance at the closed door, and lowered his voice—"I'm especially fond of puddings myself, but Miss Beard—that's my present housekeeper—tends to stick to the old jellies and tarts, I'm afraid, which can get rather tedious."

"Oh, jellies and tarts are terribly boring, I agree." She thought of Miss Beard and was not surprised by her limited scope. The woman had clearly never been "out." "I believe in experimenting, as opposed to the tried and trusted. One learns very little if one always plays safe. Nothing ventured nothing gained, I say."

Bessie was echoing the mantra of Mrs. Lloyd-Peacock. She could see that Father Cassidy was impressed.

She was beginning to warm to this personable priest and decided to cross her legs after all. "I would suggest something more adventurous. Pavlova, Baked Alaska, or syllabub perhaps. One needs to be daring in the kitchen, I believe."

"How extraordinary!" the priest said, gazing at Bessie's crossed legs. She was aware that a smidgen of thigh was on show, and most likely her slip, too. "Yes, splendid! Well, I can see, Mrs. Halstone, that you know the wood from the trees, so to speak."

"I've worked in the trade all my life, Father, and even though I say so myself, I've learned a great deal about the business over the years. Such knowledge is never wasted."

"Oh, I couldn't agree more." The priest touched his Roman collar as if checking to see if it was still in place. Bessie noted that his ears had turned a pleasing shade of cherry-blossom pink. He sat back in the chair again and removed his glasses.

"You know, the bishop calls once a month for an update, and we like to discuss things over a good lunch. He and I are alike in many ways. We appreciate an imaginative table. He has a rather delicate constitution, however, I'm afraid, and is very hard to please. Would you have any suggestions, I wonder?"

Bessie was caught off guard, but ever the trouper, she rose to the occasion.

"Olive oil is excellent for the digestion, Father," she said, smiling. "Pasta, perhaps tossed in a good virgin variety, and I would always serve it with a glass of full-bodied—"

"My goodness, you are very well informed." Bessie noted a mist of sweat breaking out on Father Cassidy's forehead. He took up the colonel's reference and began fanning himself. "But I was going to say that while the bishop and I might be epicures, we diverge somewhat when it comes to alcohol." *Epi-what? What the blazes is he saying?* "He likes a good cognac and a good cellar; I abstain completely. In fact, one of my new initiatives is the Temperance Club. A few of the young men from the village gather in my quarters every Thursday to discuss the virtues of abstinence. It's something I'm rather proud of, I have to say. It isn't referred to as the demon drink for nothing, you know. Would you partake—"

"Never touch a drop, Father," Bessie said immediately, aware that she was in dire need of another half bottle of Tullamore Dew, if the pennies would stretch.

"Excellent! 'Meekness, temperance: against such there is no law.'"

"Beg your pardon?"

"Galatians. Verse five, chapter twenty-three. Miss Beard and I wear the pioneer pin, as you—"

"I see you're a man of very refined tastes, Father."

"Oh, it's very gracious of you to say so, Mrs. Halstone." Father Cassidy, not being used to such forthrightness in a woman, tried to distract himself by faking interest in the papers on his desk. "Quite so! Well, I'd be…I'd be more than happy…er…Mrs. Halstone, if you filled the position."

"It would be a pleasure, Father."

"Excellent! Now, since you have a young son and have a duty of care as a mother, I would not expect you to be here all the time…just mornings and afternoons…six hours in total each day, for which you'll be paid thirty pounds a week. How does that sound?"

"Very good, Father," said Bessie, thinking, *Well, it isn't, really, but there'll be other little perks to the job. Other little ways to supplement that income.*

"Splendid. So, if I may, I'll just quickly run over your rota. I don't bother with breakfast—just lunch and supper really—so if you could come at, say, eleven, to prepare lunch. I eat at one o'clock. Feel free to go home in the afternoon if you wish. I eat supper at six o'clock and that's the height of your cooking duties. As for cleaning, I'll leave that up to you. Miss Beard cleans the whole house once a week, which I think is sufficient. I would of course prefer you to do the cleaning while I'm not around. I find the noise of a vacuum cleaner intolerable, I'm afraid. I keep the door to my bedroom locked at all times, simply because the safe is in there. It used to be downstairs in my study but not so long ago there was a break-in, so one can't risk it, you see. I will let you clean my quarters whenever it's necessary. It's not that I don't trust you, Mrs. Halstone; Miss Beard and I came to a similar arrangement. You *do* understand?"

"Absolutely, Father. One can't be too careful, I agree."

Presently Father Cassidy lifted a little bell on his desk and tinkled it a couple of times.

At the summons, the doorknob turned almost immediately and Miss Beard entered. So she's either been listening outside the door all along, thought Bessie, or she has a pair of bat's ears on her.

The housekeeper made her way ponderously to the priest's desk, the floorboards protesting with her every step.

"You'll be wantin' your tea now, Father," she announced, ignoring Bessie completely.

"Yes indeed, Miss Beard." Father Cassidy stood up. "But before that, I wonder would you be kind enough to show Mrs. Halstone here the ropes. She'll be filling in for you as from tomorrow."

At this news, Miss Beard turned her bullfrog eyes on Bessie. "If you say so, Father."

"Thank you, Father," said Bessie, getting up to proffer Father Cassidy her hand. "I'm sure you'll not be disappointed."

"I'm sure I won't, Mrs. Halstone," he agreed.

Bessie noted that his hand, which she held a beat longer than was necessary, had gone quite clammy. She smiled demurely and followed Miss Beard out of the office, aware that her departure was being observed with an intense degree of interest.

Chapter sixteen

Everything's well, Lorcan—except for the veins, of course."

Retired music teacher Etta Strong, a sprightly seventy-two, sat wedged in her old but comfortable armchair, looking as calm and contented as a roosting pigeon. It being Sunday, she was wearing a sober gray dress with a set of matinee pearls and matching earrings. Her legs, as solid and shapeless as stanchions, were snug in support stockings; her feet, jammed into a pair of fluffy slippers, were resting on an equally fluffy pouf.

"Oh, nobody knows the agony *that* man put me through," she continued with feeling. "I get weak just thinking about it."

Lorcan, sitting across from her in a club chair, a cup of fine Earl Grey tea to hand, was miles away. He'd just driven down from Belfast that morning and was tired. It had been a trying couple of days, extricating himself from his workplace and the clutches of his landlady. He couldn't decide which had been more fraught.

"Oh, Lorcan," Mrs. Hipple had said, face all frowny concern. "I'll 'ave to let out your room then, I will. You didn't give me any notice, you didn't, and I 'ave tae keep the rent comin' in, any road you look at it."

"I *will* be coming back, Mavis. I'm not leaving for good—only a month."

"That's as may be, Lorcan, but I've still got the heatin' and electric, I 'ave."

He soon realized that the only way to hold on to the room and get rid of Mavis was to wave some money in her face.

Unfortunately, at that point, Miss Finch had come down the stairs in a churchgoer's hat, bulky prayer book pressed to her bosom. Mavis, being Mavis, could not but draw her into the contretemps.

"Our Lorcan's leavin' us for a month, he is, Miss Finch."

"Oh dear," Miss Finch had said, her lovelorn eyes on Lorcan. "I hope there's nothing wrong, Mr. Strong?"

"Mother's a bit poorly—but it's nothing serious."

"Oh…I'll offer up a prayer for her at the service."

"Very kind of you, Miss Finch. Well, I won't detain you ladies further."

He thought now, as his mother rambled on, that at least Miss Finch would have the bathroom facilities to herself. Another benefit of having left Belfast was that there'd be no more visits to the ghastly house in Nansen Street. He planned on having the painting ready for the dreaded Dentist as soon as possible. That was the only way to get shut of him.

"I say, Lorcan?"

"Sorry…who—what, Mother?"

"Why, the surgeon, of course! 'I can cauterize those, Mrs. Strong,' he said, as if it were the simplest thing in the world. 'You won't feel a thing.'"

"It's your own fault, Mother. Didn't he tell you to stay off your feet as much as possible? But no, you had to go into the pub."

"Well, of *course* I had to go in, son. I'd nobody else to take care of things except Gusty. It's not that I'm ungrateful, for he's better than having nobody. And he's a good head for figures—not like your poor father when the derangement took hold of him, God rest his soul."

Lorcan could recall his father's unfortunate lapses all too well and wished his mother wouldn't keep alluding to them. Arthur Strong would be fondly remembered in Tailorstown for his inadvertent largesse during the summer of 1975 when, befuddled by medication and with senility taking hold, he gave away not only drink but money as well. The Crowing Cock's sudden popularity, especially on Saturday nights, was a mystery to other publicans in the area, who found themselves drumming fingers on idle bar counters while their booked-and-paid-for bands blared out the country hits of the day into empty rooms.

"You know, I only found out about how bad he was from Rose McFadden," Etta continued. "Hadn't a clue until Rose told me that her Paddy always came home drunker than usual and with more money in his pockets whenever your poor father was serving. The scandal of it, Lorcan! Oh, and just when I mention Rose, she asked if you'd touch up the Blessed Mother for Father Cassidy. I said of course you would. It's over there on the dresser."

Lorcan looked to the dresser and saw an odd collection of damaged artifacts. Incongruously, in among it sat a large, faded head of the Virgin Mary.

"That's not a problem, Mother. But where's the rest of her?"

"Now, Rose just brought her head to me yesterday, God bless her. The rest of her is coming today. It's a rather heavy object, you see, and poor Rose dropped it when taking it down off the plinth. She was so vexed—as you can imagine. She plans to do penance for it on Lough Derg with Paddy."

"Why does poor Paddy have to do penance as well?"

"Oh, you know how seriously Rose takes her faith."

He smiled. No matter how long he stayed away, he'd still be called upon to revive the religious objets d'art belonging to the locals. "Don't fret; I'll do what I can to reassemble the Virgin. And don't worry about Gusty, either. I'll keep an eye on him. He's a good head for figures, as you say, and he's honest. You don't give him enough credit."

Serving in the family bar was a specter that had haunted Lorcan from his teens, when he'd been coerced by his domineering father into lending a hand. More like two hands, two arms, and a boot on occasion. Many a legless and near-insensate patron he'd had to steer off the premises with pleas and cajoling, bundling them into waiting taxicabs while they protested like subarctic seals howling at the moon. And now, with his father in his grave and his mother in a pair of reinforced surgical stockings, the specter was looming again.

"Oh, I *do* give him credit. It's not that. Gusty's got odd ways, with that unhealthy interest of his in outlandish facts. All those strange things to do with nature. He took up a good half hour of my time yesterday, filling me in on the mating habits of African dwarfs and how they can eat frogs through their eyeballs or some such nonsense. I didn't know where to look. Such stories might scare people off."

Lorcan grinned. "Well, it's good to hear he has an interest outside the normal range of topics in these parts. There are more interesting things in life than speculating on the weather and cattle prices. And by the way, I think he might have been telling you about the African dwarf *frog*, which ingests its prey through its eyeballs."

"There's no need to mock, Lorcan Strong!" she shot back. "That's what comes of being a bachelor. A man gets set in his ways, becomes bitter and sarcastic."

"I'm not bitter, Mother." He knew what was coming next.

"You need to get yourself a wife, dear. You need a good woman to take care of you. I want to see you happy, son."

Mrs. Strong was as subtle as a sledgehammer when it came to her son's lack of a spouse. But Lorcan, expecting at least a couple of swipes in every conversation, was well able to duck and dive. His strategy was a simple one: he ignored her well-meant hints completely.

"How long will it be before you're all healed up?" he asked now. "You and the good folk of Tailorstown have the pleasure of my company for a month." Then he added, "But only the month, mind." In Lorcan's experience, Etta tended to malinger when he was around. It was her way of making him feel guilty for his prolonged absences from home.

He leaned across and placed his cup on the coffee table with the last remark, believing a physical gesture was necessary to soften what might be construed as harsh. He hoped also to get her off the subject of his private life. But the diversion was lost on Etta as she reached for the sledgehammer once more.

"You know, Nuala Crink—Doris's cousin—always asks about you, Lorcan. Now there's a very solid, hardworking girl. Can turn her hand to anything. Works in Mr. Harvey's underwear department, and if you ask me, she's lost there. She'd be very good behind the bar...very reliable, being used to customers."

He wondered how selling underwear to the good ladies of Tailorstown somehow qualified Nuala Crink to pull pints while exchanging bawdy banter with the patrons of the Crowing Cock. Wisely, he decided to keep these musings to himself.

A vision of Miss Crink sprang up at him out of the past: a dolorous, skinny girl—Veronese's Saint Helena—with a wan face and downcast eyes. "Hmm-hmm."

"I told her you were coming home," continued Etta, "and she said she was looking forward to seeing you. You should look in on her in the shop. Such an attentive girl. Keeps me well supplied with my Day-Long compression supports."

A fret of panic ran through Lorcan. He'd evaded the attentions of Miss Finch in Belfast only to be confronted by her doppelgänger in Tailorstown. He'd all but forgotten Nuala Crink. They'd journeyed through primary school in the same class. She'd been his comrade in battle, bullied in tandem—he for being too bright, and Nuala for being too skinny.

"I've taken work home with me, Mother, and—what with tending to you and keeping an eye on Gusty—I doubt I'll have the time for much socializing. Speaking of work, I must prepare my studio." He got up.

"It would do no harm to say hello to poor Nuala."

Lorcan took a deep breath. "Mother, I have no interest in Nuala Crink. None whatsoever." It was time to be forthright, or before he knew it, he could find himself exchanging wedding vows with the shop assistant at the altar rails and wondering how on earth he'd got there. "Neither do I have anything in common with her. I paint pictures; she sells underwear. I would be very disappointed if I thought you were putting ideas into Nuala's head. Very disappointed indeed."

He saw that she was gazing at a photograph of his father, which sat prominently on the mantelshelf. He knew that beatific look and sensed what was coming. "I do wish your poor father were still here. He could talk to anyone."

"Things change, Mother...sadly. Now, I'll check out my studio," he said as cheerfully as he could, "and unpack my things. And tomorrow I'll have a word with Gusty about his rota and see what's what." Etta was still staring at the photo of her late husband. He saw her eyes well up. He went to her and patted her shoulder reassuringly. "Don't worry. I'm here now, and I'll take care of things. Can I get you anything?"

"Thanks, Lorcan dear; you always were a good boy. No, I'll just have a read at the paper and then a little nap. You go on ahead and get yourself sorted."

His studio, not much of a room where space was concerned, had the advantage of two windows: one facing out onto the street, the other overlooking the backyard. It had been a struggle to get the studio. But that was a long time ago now, when he was at school. He was sixteen at the time.

"A *what?*" his father had asked irritably.

"A studio," Etta had repeated. "Lorcan needs a wee room for himself so he can paint his bits and pieces."

"Hasn't he got his bedroom? What's wrong with that?"

"He needs light, dear. All artists need light."

"Light! What'll it be next? I'm tellin ye, if ye don't stop mollycoddling him he'll turn into a nancy boy, and it'll be *your* fault."

Lorcan smiled at the memory. That had been his father's primary worry. He was from an era when men were men, and the field and pub were where you proved yourself. The creative urge was anathema to him, and therefore something suspect.

But Etta had won, as she generally did. Lorcan got his studio, and the people of Tailorstown got an artist on permanent call. One who could gild their chipped frames in gaudy gold, who could copy their photographs, touch up statues with putty and paint, even do a bit of signwriting for a tradesman when required.

The young Lorcan didn't mind. It earned him the pocket money he never got from his father, and it paid for the tubes of paint and canvases he needed for his real artistic endeavors.

Now he cast a glance at some of those early works, still hanging where he'd affixed them to the walls all those years ago. Crude though they seemed now to his sophisticated eye, he was still proud of the sheer enthusiasm displayed there.

He painted nature. The intricacies the untrained eye passed over, the things that went unnoticed amid the clamor and hurly-burly of everyday life. The sun glancing off a gannet's wing, a roil of cumulus preceding a thunderstorm, a sloughed-off chrysalis in the morning dew. The fleeting moment arrested.

The room was just the way he'd left it last time. His desks, swivel chair, canvases stacked against the back wall. There was a painting of the Slievegerrin Mountains in progress on the easel. It had been commissioned by the local bank. He'd hoped to finish it on this occasion, but for obvious reasons it would have to wait.

His artist's case sat on the desk. He opened it, drew out some fresh tubes of paint, and arranged them neatly by his palette. He replenished the jars of thinners and linseed oil and unwrapped a set of new brushes. Brushes were of the utmost importance. He treated his riggers and filberts, the rounds and mop-heads, with the utmost care. They were expensive, and he needed to get the most out of them. Besides, a portrait with the majesty and detail of the Countess demanded the best.

The mere thought of the portrait made him uneasy now. The Dentist's ugly face rushed at him. He heard the screams of a mana-cled man in a surgical chair. He cast a glance at the wrapped can-vas and couldn't bring himself to unwrap it just yet. Its unveiling would befoul the innocence of his little room. His creative niche. How could such an exceptional work of art come to represent something vile and reprehensible? The thought depressed him; he sighed and gazed out the window.

At that slack hour of a Sunday afternoon there was little to inspire him. Nothing stirred, save for a gathering of crows pecking at something in the gutter. Farther along, a car—a veteran Austin A40—sat puttering outside Plunket O'Brien's newsagents, its trembling tailpipe sending out little puffs of blue smoke.

As Lorcan watched, Master O'Hanlon, his old art teacher, emerged corpulently from the shop carrying a folded newspaper under one arm and what looked like a pack of Mr. Kipling Cherry Bakewells. With great ceremony he stowed both items in the boot of the parked vehicle. Retirement had made him fat. His plaid sport jacket and gray slacks looked way too small, giving the impression that having dressed that morning, he had hooked himself up to a compressed-air pump and inflated his body to twice its usual size.

The schoolmaster squeezed himself with obvious strain into the driver's seat; checked right, left, and right again as if he were on the busiest thoroughfare of a bustling metropolis; and then crept slowly out onto the street. He tootled off, his pudgy hands gripping the steering wheel with a Samsonesque zeal, his round face close to the windshield, shiny with hope and carbolic soap.

Lorcan found himself wondering how the master might fill his Sunday afternoons, and an image lumbered into his psyche. A very unwelcome image of the portly bachelor slumped in an armchair by the fire, crumbs dusting his front and the floor beneath him. He'd be reading the *Sunday Press*, a mug of tea and the sole survivor from the pack of Cherry Bakewells on a chipped plate at his elbow. Did a similar fate await Lorcan when his mother passed on?

It was at such moments that memories of his first and only love, Lucy, would ambush him. He'd met her at art college, but after a year of courtship had lost her to another.

That was thirteen years ago, and he'd gone off women after that. Too mercurial, too capricious. Better off without them. The two-dimensional kind were a safer bet. At least you could have a connection with them without committing yourself and suffering the pain of rejection.

Like every artist, Lorcan needed his fantasies. There were no starless night skies in his world. His paintbrush described reality on his own terms. Held the crudeness of the world at bay. Why spoil the illusion?

Why indeed?

The idea at once elated and disheartened him. He shook his head. Tailorstown was getting to him already—and he'd barely arrived back. He shuddered to think how he'd feel a week from now. Two weeks. A month. There was only one way to dispel the blues.

Work!

The sooner he got rid of the portrait, the sooner he'd be rid of the psychotic Dentist, too. His dear mother's well-being depended on it.

He went to the dreaded canvas and began unwrapping it.

Chapter seventeen

Bessie Halstone had settled well into her new job. Up until now she'd never given much thought to the priesthood. On the rare occasions when those befrocked, generally dour gentlemen had entered her life, it was to officiate at weddings, christenings, and funerals—"matches, hatches, and dispatches," in everyday parlance. No, the world of the rural priest was alien to her. And now she was discovering the awe in which such a gentleman was held by the country folk. She was also finding out that being a priest's housekeeper lent a woman a certain status.

She liked being in the grand parochial house, thinking herself more lady of the manor than skivvy for a priest.

Swift to establish her territory in the kitchen, she'd removed all traces of Miss Beard's unenterprising spirit by consigning the floral tablecloths and sturdy delft to the back of a cupboard, along with a couple of her dowdy aprons, a hand-knitted tea cozy, and a wad of *Sacred Heart Messenger*s.

Out with the old, in with the new, as Mrs Lloyd-Peacock was apt to say. It was a good motto, and Bessie intended using it to maximum effect.

So shelves of china and inverted glasses, cloistered in cabinets for yonks, were taken out and pressed into service. Drawers of linen—tablecloths and napkins that had never seen the light of day—were unearthed and aired on the clothesline. Scented blooms from the garden suddenly found their way indoors and flourished in pots or spilled elegantly from vases on tables and sills.

She'd seen Father Cassidy's eyes roam appreciatively about the place with the little changes she was making. Who knew, if she played her cards right he might end up employing her for a longer period, thereby guaranteeing her more money for her getaway. She did not know how this might sit with the locals but guessed they'd be none too pleased.

There was much to explore in the big house. Besides the kitchen there were two reception rooms, a library, and a study on the ground floor, and five bedrooms upstairs. Why, she wondered, do priests need such a spread? Just one man rattling about. All those acres of space going to waste.

The thought struck her most forcibly as she stood, duster in hand, in the front living room, which never seemed to be in use. Her mother-in-law—a harridan who'd taken an instant dislike to her—used to have a room just like it, also rarely used. Well, not as grand, but grand in Packie's mother's book. The "pawloor" she called it, and reserved it only for visitors and Christmas gatherings. When Bessie started dating Packie, she was allowed into the pawloor. That was, of course, before Molly Lawless decided she was "a bad influence" on her son.

But that was the past, the done and dusted past. Bessie shelved the thought, shut a door on the memory, flopped down on a velour sofa, kicked off her shoes, and threw her legs up on the armrest, just for the hell of it. She could not imagine her predecessor, old Miss Beard, disporting herself thus. There and then she decided that this room would be hers to relax in. Father Cassidy would hardly notice. He seemed permanently distracted by "affairs of the parish," whatever *they* were.

She wondered idly now what activities he engaged in, outside of the rectory. "Please don't wait around for me, Mrs. Halstone," he'd said the previous day. "I keep very irregular hours. It's the fate of all us parish priests, I fear." There was also the Temperance Club. Thursday afternoons and evenings were off-limits. The priest had made it clear that on Thursdays her services were required only in the morning.

She began to idly sketch circles with her toe on the rich velour fabric. *Perhaps he's got a secret woman somewhere. I wonder: Would he ever leave the priesthood for a woman?* She posed the question to her circling toe. He was too handsome to have a vocation. Yes, that was it. Men like him didn't join the priesthood out of choice. Maybe he was let down by a woman and was taking shelter from the lot of them under the cloth. Or—the more likely scenario—he was pushed into it by a domineering mother. Whatever the circumstances, she was determined to find out more about the mysterious Father.

Thud!

Her toe froze on the fabric.

She looked up. The noise had come from overhead. But she was alone in the house. Had Cassidy returned without her noticing?

She got up and tiptoed to the window. No sign of his car.

Thud…Scrape…Thud. Jesus, she thought, who *is* that? She slipped her shoes back on, edgy now.

Should she investigate?

She braved it into the hallway. "Hello. Anybody up there?"

Ding-dong-ding-dong!

The doorbell.

Bessie didn't hesitate but went at once and opened the door. A plump woman stood on the doorstep.

"Hello. Rose McFadden's me name," the woman said, proffering a hand. "And you must be the new housekeeper."

"Yes. Mrs. Halstone." Bessie shook her hand. "I'm afraid Father Cassidy isn't—"

"Oh, that's all right, Mrs. Hailstone. I just brought him along one of me wee fruit loaves, for I know he likes a bitta cake now and again." She dived into a shopping bag and presented the loaf, gift-wrapped in a tea towel.

Bessie accepted it with a grudging smile. *How insulting! This one thinks I can't bake. The cheek!* She cast an imperious eye over Mrs. McFadden's bloom-print frock with its crooked hem, her tree-stump legs stuck in a pair of brass-buckled flats, and said, "Thank you. I'll see that he gets it." Each word chipped from a glacier with an ice pick.

"How are ye likin' it round here, Mrs. Hailstone?" Rose asked. "Must be strange for ye, 'cos I heard ye were from the city."

Her eyes were roving over Bessie like a mop over a dirty floor.

"It's *Hal*stone, by the way. I'm liking it very well. Now, if you'll excuse me…"

"Well, ye know, I'm a good friend of Betty Beard's, and she worries about the Father, she does. She's too far away tae see if things is all right, so I tolt her I'd look in on him now and again, so tae keep her mind rested, if ye unnerstand me, Mrs. Hailstone. God, it's terrible hot." Rose looked up at the sky.

Angling for a cup of tea? Given her immediate circumstances— what with those mysterious and unsettling noises—Bessie could have used the company, but the cake was an insult too far.

"I'd love to offer you a cup of tea," she said, "but my shift is over now and I have to get on. I'll make sure Father Cassidy gets your loaf, Mrs. McFadden. Bye now." And with that she shut the door on Rose.

She stood in the hallway, clutching the loaf to her chest, gaping up the stairs. Should she go up there?

Through the glass door-panel she was aware of her affronted visitor hoisting herself onto the saddle of her bicycle and creaking off.

No, she wouldn't risk it.

She dashed down to the kitchen, stowed the fruit loaf in her bag—she and Herkie were more in need of it than the overly pampered Father—and left the house.

Down at Kilfeckin Manor, Herkie lay on his belly in the field, awaiting his chance. A whole week had gone by and he still hadn't made it past the back door. His ma was getting impatient and had warned that if he didn't return that evening with the spoils from an errand or two, she'd be locking away not only his sweet ration but his *Cheeky Weekly*s, too.

He'd brought along his coloring book and was busily giving the Loch Ness monster an extra set of fiery red eyes when he heard the back door opening. Through the hedge he observed Gusty Grant emerge, sucking on the last of a cigarette, his big glasses glinting in the sunlight. There was no sign of the pig.

True to form, Gusty stood for a while gazing up at Rosehip Cottage. Herkie hoped he wouldn't sit down and start playing with his face in the window again; he was hot and tired and simply wanted to get on with his mission. The sooner Gusty Grant made himself scarce, the better.

Just then the upstairs window was thrust open and the oul' boy stuck his head out.

"Hi! Are ye not away yet?"

"Nah, I'm still here."

"Stap lookin' up at that wommin. She's not lookin' at *you*. She'd be hard-up lookin' at a boy like you."

"Aye, *you'd* know, wouldn't ye...lyin' on yer arse all day, doin' bugger all."

"What's that yer sayin'?"

"Nuthin'!"

"Get me a bottle-a that Buckfast wine in the Cock...and a beg-a-them Epsom salts for me bowels."

With that, the window was banged shut. Herkie heard his landlord muttering, "Aye, ye oul' shite!"—or words to that effect. He then crossed to his truck and in seconds was gone.

The coast was finally clear.

Herkie made a beeline for the back door, quietly pushed it open, and tiptoed inside.

He immediately found himself in a large, untidy kitchen. There was a hearth fire burning; opposite it, an open archway led down a wide, flagged hallway to the front door.

He crept down the hallway and listened at the foot of the stairs. He needed to make sure that the oul' boy was still up there. He heard what sounded like a radio burbling overhead and reckoned the oul' boy was listening to the news—because that was what oul' boys usually did. There was no way he was going to go up there and introduce himself as his ma had instructed. He'd concoct some other story for her.

The sound of the radio was a bonus: even if Herkie did make some noise, he would not be heard.

There were three doors leading off the hallway, but he decided to return to the kitchen and reserve them for later. Kitchens were more interesting anyway: they meant food. And food in Herkie's world meant cake and sweets.

The fare laid out on the kitchen table, however—a half-eaten loaf, a pound of butter still in its wrapper, a bottle of milk, and the congealed remains of a fry—had him turning up his nose in dismay. He looked nervously at the big knife on the breadboard and wondered if it was the one Mr. Grant had used to carve up his aunt.

He was about to pull out one of the drawers in the dresser when the unthinkable happened. The front door opened and he heard a woman's voice.

"Cooeee, Uncle Ned! It's only me."

Where to run to? He couldn't make a dash for the back door, for the woman would have a clear view of him through the open archway. He cast about frantically for a place to hide. The cupboards and the dresser were too small.

"I'll just get us a wee drop o' tea!" he heard the woman call out. Her footsteps were getting closer.

He dived under the table.

From the concealment of the gingham tablecloth, his heart pounding, Herkie watched as a pair of stout legs wearing white slip-on shoes with big brass buckles clumped into the kitchen.

"Dearie, dearie me!" the woman sighed.

Her feet moved to the stove. He heard her strike a match, put the kettle on, turn, and approach the table. She started clearing away the breakfast things and piling dishes in the sink. The sound of a tap being turned on meant she was going to do the washing up. Herkie began to panic. What if she began sweeping the floor? She'd find him, and how would he explain himself?

He was trying to think up an excuse when a strange thumping sound came from overhead.

The woman stopped what she was doing, and Herkie saw water drip onto the floor.

"Yes, I'm comin' now, Uncle Ned!" she shouted. In a lower voice: "God, I better go up and see him, for he maybe thinks I'm a burglar."

To Herkie's relief, he heard the woman dry her hands and saw the white shoes clump out of the kitchen and echo back down the hallway.

He waited until she'd climbed the stairs before crawling out.

129

Feeling slightly braver now, he glanced about him.

Herkie was something of an expert at "spot the difference" puzzles. There was always one at the back of the *Dandy*, and they were his favorite game. Now, as he surveyed the kitchen, his little eyes locked on something that hadn't been there before.

A handbag.

A white handbag, sitting in an armchair. It must belong to the woman with the white shoes.

Handbags were good news because handbags usually had purses in them, and purses usually contained money. Although in his ma's case there sometimes wasn't even enough to buy himself a packet of Love Hearts.

He thought of his ma now, and her threat of no comics or sweets for a week if he returned empty-handed. No way could he risk that. He opened the bag and found a green purse. Inside was some loose change: a few coppers, ten-pence pieces, and a fifty-pence piece. He took the fifty pence.

But there was more. While putting the purse back carefully, he spotted a brown envelope. On the envelope was scrawled *Ned's Pension*. Herkie knew that the word *pension* meant money, because his grandma used to give him ten pence every Monday from her pension money.

He opened the envelope and found two ten-pound notes, one fiver, two pound coins, and ten pence. He pocketed the coins.

A squeaking sound above could only mean one thing: The woman with the white shoes was coming down again. Quickly he stuffed the envelope back in the bag, snapped it shut, and slipped out the back door.

The ducks set up a quacking at the sight of him, but in seconds Herkie was over the gate and up the field, richer by £2.60, with his sweet ration and comics assured for another week.

His ma would be pleased.

Chapter eighteen

Where were ye goin' when I saw ye comin' back yesterday?" asked Socrates O'Sullivan, shiftless loudmouth and regular patron of the Crowing Cock. "I shouted after ye but ye didn't turn round. I thought maybe ye didn't hear me and that's why ye went on...Jezsis, now that I come tae think about it, maybe ye thought I was shoutin' at somebody else, 'cos I shouted brave and loud...aye, I shouted brave and loud. Loud enough, begod, that a body could-a heard me in fuckin' Cork...so how come *you* couldn't hear me?"

Socrates had been sitting in the bar for well over an hour, bum cheek going numb on the vinyl stool; one foot asleep, the other on its way. On his fourth beer, his logic and capacity for rational discourse, never great at the best of times, were steadily diminishing.

"What time would that-a been?" Gusty Grant asked idly, well used to O'Sullivan's oath-laden rants and not in the least offended. Fulfilling his role as substitute bartender for Etta Strong, he was perched behind the counter, breaking the afternoon with a filched Guinness and a Woodbine cigarette. Above his head a TV set was tuned to horse racing at Down Royal.

"Wait tae we see now. I was only after me tea, so it must-a been around half five."

"Can't mind," Gusty said. "Whaddya wanna know where I was goin' for, anyway?"

"Don't know…just wundered."

There was an uncomfortable silence.

"*Yes!…Arrgh!*" The shouts from the back room came from youthful layabouts, Chuck Sproule and Kevin Flood, playing darts.

"D'ye know how long it takes the average man tae take an egg outta the fridge?" Gusty asked suddenly, recalling the interesting factoid from his latest reading, a 250-page compendium with the title *A Thousand Useless Things You Never Needed to Know.*

"Nah…how the fuck would-a know the like o' that?"

"Nought point seven nine two seconds—that's how long."

"Right." Socrates swigged from the pint and sucked on the last of his smoke.

"And d'ye know how many eggs the average man ates in a year?"

"Nah, but you're gonna tell me."

"Two hundred and eighty-six. That means he'll spend three minutes and forty-six point five seconds a year takin' eggs outta the fridge."

"I don't have a fridge, so I don't give a fuck," said Socrates, restless now.

"Aye, but if ye *had* a fridge, that's how long it would take ye, 'cos—"

At that point, much to Socrates's relief, the door opened and in stepped Lorcan Strong.

"All right, Lorcan?" Gusty said in greeting, getting up and try-ing to conceal his illicit half pint under the counter. "Yer mammy said ye'd be home."

"Yes indeed, Gusty." Lorcan's keen eyes scanned the place. They registered a fine powdering of dust on several liqueur bot-tles, a cloudy mirror that had rarely seen a cloth, and, on a shelf above it, two spiders busily weaving webs within the handles of his father's silver golf trophy. "Just arrived yesterday." He nodded at Socrates.

"How do, Lorcan? Keepin' all right?"

"The best, Socrates. Can't complain. Just thought I'd drop in to see how things are goin'." He might have grown up and gone away, but a few days back home and he was already cutting his language to suit the terrain, recasting himself as a publican's son. "Everything all right, is it?"

"Oh, grand, Lorcan, grand. Don't ye worry yerself too much about this place. You look after yer mammy. I'll take care of everything here, so I will."

"Thanks. That's good to hear."

At that moment the dart throwers emerged, bleary-eyed, from the back room. Kevin Flood: nineteen, tall and gangly, with acne-raked cheeks. Chuck Sproule: a reedy twenty-eight with the bravado and swagger of the ill-disposed and cocky.

"Be seein' ye, Gusty," said Kevin, rubbing his nose and leaving his empty glass on the counter.

"Hiya, Lorcan," said Chuck. "How's she cuttin'?" He banged his glass down in front of Socrates and elbowed him in the back. "Sock it to me, Socco. You still fuckin' here?"

"What's it tae you?" said Socrates. "Stay here as-long-as-a-want. If ye don't watch, I'll knock yer—"

"That's *enough*, lads," Lorcan told them. "Now, off you go, you two." He pulled the door open demonstratively.

Sproule straightened up and glared at Lorcan. "Keep yer arty-farty hair on. We were goin' anyway."

Lorcan shut the door on the pair, hoping it would be the last he'd see of the bold Chuck. The hoodlum had recently been released from Long Kesh Prison. The crime on this occasion: stealing a liter of white spirit and ten packets of Hot Rod condoms from a Protestant pharmacy in Killoran. He knew precisely what Sproule had stolen because Etta, unfortunately, had kept the newspaper cutting for his delectation.

"Aye, that's the thing," said Gusty. "Seen a big change in them since they joined the Temp'ance Club."

"The what?"

"Aye, it's not great news for you or your mammy, Lorcan," Socrates put in. "That Father Cassidy's vast against the drink, ye know."

"Sorry, am I missing something? If they're in a Temperance Club, what are they doing in a bar?"

"Oh, they come in for the darts," said Gusty. "That was lemonade and lime they were drinkin'. Aye, the darts and…"

There was an awkward pause, which Socrates felt moved to fill. "Isn't that the way of it, Lorcan? Give me another wee one there, Gusty."

"Well, I'll just check out the back. Don't mind me," Lorcan said, heading for the adjoining lounge.

He noted that the gloomy room was in need of a good scrubbing. Obviously Gusty's promise to "take care of everything here" didn't stretch to cleaning the place. No surprises there. The tables had not been cleared from the previous night, and the place smelled musty. He crossed to the windows to let in the light and some much-needed fresh air, then proceeded to empty ashtrays and collect glasses.

In the background he could hear Gusty doing what he was best at: sharing his seemingly endless store of useless and irrelevant knowledge.

"Then there's what's called the African Clawed and the African Dwarf…"

"Aye, so."

"Y'know the word that's used for that thing frogs do when they're matin' with themselves?"

"Nah, what's that?"

"Amplexin', that's what it's called. They usually do it in the watter, but the bufo frog, now, he would do it anywhere...in the watter, on the ground, even up trees, begod."

"Sounds like your oul' boy."

Gusty ignored the insult and took another swig of Guinness.

"What about this new wommin from Belfast that's in your aunt's house anyway? Are ye not lookin' tae do a bitta amplexin' with her? I hear she looks like a film star." Socrates's attitude to women was still in the larval stage.

At that point Lorcan decided to fetch a dishcloth, and his reappearance brought a halt to the conversation. He was intrigued but pretended he'd heard nothing. He wrung out the cloth and went back to the lounge.

"She's a well-lookin' wommin right enuff," Gusty continued. "But there's no Cathlick frogs left in Australia now, as far as I know, so they mustn't of went in for much of that amplexin' tomfoolery. Well, I suppose being Cathlick, they maybe wouldn't of anyway. Then there's a lizard in the Amazon called the Jesus Christ. Ye see, it's called that 'cos it can run like the Divil on the watter when..."

Lorcan smiled to himself as he wiped a table. A good-looking city woman "like a film star" choosing to live here, *in Tailorstown*. My, my, things had changed since his last visit. Lorcan now realized what his mother meant by Gusty Grant's liking for weird conversation. He was a walking encyclopedia of crazy facts.

Still, he would not be complaining. He was glad to have Grant manning the bar because it saved him the trouble. He had ample trouble upstairs. Between his mother and the portrait, life was complicated enough.

"Hi, turn that up, will ye?"

Lorcan halted the dishcloth midwipe. The serious tones of a newscaster were filling the room. He put his head round the doorframe as the cadaverous features of Bobby Sands flashed up on the screen.

"*We interrupt this broadcast to bring you some breaking news. The hunger striker Bobby Sands has died.*"

"Christ, he's gone," said Socrates.

"Shush!"

"*...just under an hour ago after sixty-six days of refusing food. The twenty-seven-year-old Republican spent the last days of his life on a water bed to protect his fragile bones.*

"*Mr. Humphrey Atkins, Secretary of State for Northern Ireland, issued a statement shortly after the death. He said: 'I regret this needless and pointless death. Too many have died by violence in Northern Ireland. In this case it was self-inflicted. We should not forget the many others who have died. It is my profound hope and prayer that the people of Northern Ireland will recognize the futility of violence and turn their faces away from it.'*"

"There'll be hell tae pay now," Gusty said.

Lorcan flung the cloth aside. He had to get away from the bar. He knew the regulars of the Crowing Cock. Could guess the prophecies of doom the martyr's death would let loose. A walk in the fresh air was called for. It was as good a time as any to reacquaint himself with the district.

In the hallway the artist donned his hat, picked up his sketchbook and his umbrella. It would double as a walking stick. A clear blue sky seen from the window promised a day that would remain dry.

He shut the front door and stepped out onto the street. The sun was strong, the day calm; there was nobody about and it was good to be free.

He shrugged, tipped the brim of his Borsalino against the sun, and set off in a southerly direction. He decided to head out the Killoran Road, knowing that a little way along lay a track to a stone circle. It was a favorite spot from boyhood, holding a charm that never failed to fire his artistic imagination. He tried to visit it whenever he returned home. Perhaps being in such a place would wash away the image of Sands and the prospect of what the man's death would bring.

On the outskirts of town, he passed the cemetery and struggled to keep the image of the hunger striker from his mind. Death was never easy, no matter who the victim might be. He thought of his Uncle Rupert. He lay somewhere in there among the silent majority; felled at sixty-two by a not inconsiderable heart attack, which had been spectacularly misdiagnosed by the local GP, Humphrey Brewster. Just a "little touch of indigestion," the good doctor had opined. Lorcan wondered now how many other poor souls lay there in the boneyard due to just a little touch of indigestion.

Soon the town was feeding into fields, as easy as dusk into night, and from then on it was open country and silence. The hedgerows hummed and the tarmac bubbled. The sky was vast and cloudless. The more he pushed into nature, the more Lorcan felt like a trespasser; the beat of his heels and umbrella point on the hard road caused cows to stir and sheep to stare.

He was glad he'd decided on the walk. The countryside he was striding through was raising his spirits. The artist in him valued nature above all else, the majesty of it. He recalled with a smile something Marc Chagall once said: "Art is the unceasing effort to compete with the beauty of flowers—and never succeeding." How true that is, he thought; how true.

He rounded a bend in the road and found himself on a gradual uphill pull under thrush-song. He paused, marveling at the sheer power of memory now drawing him back to his boyhood. A ten-year-old Lorcan in short pants and plastic sandals, dawdling on his way home from school. The hedgerows held him back then just as much as they did now: the loosestrife, the cockscomb, and round-leafed clover creating in his mind's eye the urge to remember. And he would carry those images with him, carefully, like a bowl of precious oil brimmed full, to spill out onto paper when he reached home.

Every farm, every dip and rise on the road, every tree, every rippling creek held a memory for him. Art, he mused, is the only way to run away without leaving home. He understood the truth of that statement every time he returned to the rural terrain.

He quickened his step, impatient to reach the stone circle. His sketch pad and pencils weighted his pocket but lifted his heart. If there was one great benefit to the whole practice of art, it was to focus him in the "now," where the ugly past and uncertain future could not touch him.

Or could they?

Chapter nineteen

At a loose end, his chores done, Gusty decided to head up to the Turret Room. If he got the timing right, maybe—just maybe—he'd catch a glimpse of Mrs. Hailstone getting ready for work.

The only obstacle: stealing past his uncle's room without being seen or heard. Gusty had never bought into the hard-of-hearing story. It was simply another ruse the oul' boy used to gain sympathy. And Ned was an erratic sleeper. Sometimes wide awake, making a nuisance of himself from six in the morning. At other times dead to the world until well after eleven.

The bedroom door, too, was a real threat. Ned was inclined to keep it open, not wanting to miss anything.

Gusty tiptoed up the stairs and peered into the room.

Luck was on his side. The oul' boy lay conked out, eyes shut, mouth agape, emitting rafter-rattling snores to the accompaniment of a monotonous news broadcast.

Reassured, Gusty turned and beckoned to Veronica. She was sitting at the bottom of the stairs, awaiting instruction.

Together, master and piglet bounded up the next three flights to Lucien's chamber.

Once through the door, Veronica made for her favorite spot, a Victorian daybed of watermarked silk, and settled down for a postprandial snooze.

The mechanic took up position in his usual armchair and raised the binoculars.

Good news. Mrs. Hailstone was in. Her car was parked under the big ash as usual. He trained the binoculars on her bedroom window. The crocus-print curtains were open. That was more good news. He panned over to the back door.

At that very moment, the door opened.

His pulse quickened.

But it was only young Herkie. Gusty saw the boy go over to the well cover and push at the stone weight with his toe. Watched as he hunkered down to inspect it, followed him as he sauntered down the yard and disappeared behind the woodshed.

Gusty made a mental note to warn the boy again about the dangers of the well.

He pulled back to the door once more and refocused.

He'd struck gold.

There she was, the object of his desires, filling the frame in a thigh-skimming nightdress: pink with satin bows.

Oh, God! He'd never seen so much of a woman's figure in his life. He tracked her legs as she walked—leisurely—in the direction of the clothesline, zooming in on her ankles, moving slowly up the shapely calves, to linger on her tantalizing derriere.

A small breeze was lifting the hem, ever so slightly.

She reached the clothesline and began unpinning pairs of tights.

She bent over.

Oh, holy God! The binocs began to shake in his hands.

She was wearing matching knickers, the frilly trim riding high on her smooth hips.

All too soon she stood up again and unfastened a couple of bath sheets. There was quite a lot on the line. More dipping down to the basket. More precious time to focus on those buttocks.

He was sweating now, blinking wildly so as not to miss a square inch of her loveliness. The lenses needed a wipe, but...

Abruptly she turned.

Damn!

The bosom he was so looking forward to ogling was concealed—hidden from his sight by the pile of laundry she carried.

She dropped a sock, bent down to retrieve it. Stood up, shielded her eyes from the sun—and looked in his direction.

Hell!

Instinctively, Gusty sank to his knees.

Veronica grunted.

What if she'd seen him? Impossible. A ray of sunlight glinting off the field glasses? Maybe.

When he dared peer out the window again, there was no sign of her. The back door was shut.

Undeterred, he swept the powerful lenses back to the bedroom window. She'd be getting dressed now. His heart was beating like a timpani drum, his knees aquiver.

She was entering the room. He saw her dump the washing on the bed. He blinked to get a clearer view.

Then...crocus print! Nothing but bloody crocus print. He lowered the binoculars. She'd drawn the curtains.

Ah, damn!

He collapsed back into the armchair, luxuriating in the brief pleasure Mrs. Hailstone had aroused. Had she spotted him? He didn't think so, not at that distance. Not that it mattered now. He'd hit the jackpot. Needed to get his breath back and was reluctant to vacate the room just yet.

Veronica slept on.

He plonked the binoculars down on the dressing table. A delicate scent bottle of ruby glass pitched forward, and before he could save it, it fell to the floor, breaking into little pieces. An ancient, musky fragrance suffused the room.

With resignation, he got down to pick up the pieces. Yet moments into the task, he wondered why he was bothering. Only he and the piglet would see the mess. On the other hand... what if Veronica injured herself? With that in mind, he hastily gathered up the glass fragments and threw them into a trinket drawer.

His hands were wet and sticky with the scent. He wiped them on the bib of his overalls and settled back into the chair.

His eyes drifted about the Turret Room. It had never really interested him much, but now he felt the stirrings of curiosity as his eye fell on a brass-bound trunk. There was something sticking out of it. A bit of material, not unlike the color of Mrs. Hailstone's nightdress.

That certainly merited investigation.

The hasps on the trunk, stiff with age, were hard to raise. He took out his Swiss Army knife, cocked an ear. Not a sound, apart from the chickens having a chinwag in the yard below. Hopefully the oul' boy would not wake up for another wee while.

He levered at the hasps, twisting and tugging. One by one they sprang free, each with a nerve-jolting *thwack*.

The heavy lid, once freed, creaked and groaned like the outer door to a pharaoh's tomb as he eased it up. The whiff of age-old camphor and stale scent had him reaching for his handkerchief to catch a sneeze. Having dried his eyes and with vision cleared, he peered into the trunk. He saw that a heavy velvet coverlet was protecting the contents.

He drew it back in amazement.

The pink material he'd seen protruding from the trunk was in fact the frill of a petticoat. He tugged. Out it came, flounce upon flounce of shiny satin, a tumbling rush of bows and braid and lace.

The softness of the fabric made his hands shake. He'd never touched the like of it before.

He held it to his cheek.

So this is what Mrs. Hailstone must feel like!

He caught his breath, looked again at the trunk. What else might be in there? Tenderly he set aside the petticoat and got down on his knees. He would delve deeper.

Sure enough, the gaudy undergarment was a mere foretaste of what was to come. The trunk was crammed with ladies' underwear. His grubby hands began plundering the secret hoard as he reveled in an orgy of newfound soft, downy, silken, yielding textures. He unearthed nightgowns and slips, corsets, girdles, stockings, suspender belts, garters, bloomers, knickers.

In a matter of minutes the floor around him was strewn with lingerie.

The mechanic sat back on his heels, marveling at the spectacle: a thrilling new world from a box in a room he'd never had much cause to visit. Hardly knew it existed until Mrs. Hailstone showed up.

But, oh…what could *that* be? Something else had caught his eye while he was hauling out the underwear. He peered into the trunk again.

Yes, there it was at the bottom: a large, rectangular box.

He lifted it out.

On the cover, Jean Harlow pouted up at him, her bosom thrusting out of a peach-tone brassiere. GIVE YOURSELF A LITTLE LIFT urged a speech bubble above her head. And across her midriff, the words THE ULTIMATE BREAST ADORNMENT.

He pulled open the box.

An extraordinary garment flubbered out onto the floor.

An elasticized contrivance in the style of a brassiere.

He turned it over and did a double take. Was he seeing things?

A pair of very ample rubber breasts, sporting maroon nipples, was staring back up at him.

He could not believe his eyes.

He reached down and gave each a squeeze. They felt not unlike the rubber bulb horn on his old bicycle but were a bigger handful by far, and for that reason much more rewarding to the touch.

He carried them over to a cheval mirror and held them up against his chest.

Thump, thump.

"Hoi! Are ye up there?"

His uncle's summons from below was startlingly loud.

The strange garment fell from his grasp and bounced into a corner.

He wheeled around, panic-stricken.

The floor! To Gusty it resembled what a stripper's changing room might look like after a night on the boards. If the oul' shite saw *this*, what would he think atall?

Frantically he began gathering up the scattered lingerie and piling it back in the trunk.

"Hoi! Are ye up there?"

The oul' boy again, sounding more impatient now.

Frantically he stuffed the last of the lingerie down and slammed the lid.

That was everything out of sight. Or so he thought.

"Come on, Veronica," he urged, going to the door.

Before dutifully joining her master, Veronica took a last wistful look at the fallen falsies in the corner. They most definitely merited further inspection...

Excited, she hopped down from the daybed.

"That's a good girl."

He bundled the piglet into his arms and dashed from the Turret Room, slamming the door behind him.

His secret was safe. Or was it?

The spirit of the decadent Viscount had been unleashed. Whether for good or ill, Lucien Percy would roam the corridors of Kilfeckin once more.

Chapter twenty

Rose McFadden was not having such a good time of it these days, and she put it all down to that new woman from Belfast. Not only had she got the job with Father Cassidy, but Gusty had given her Aunt Dora's house *as well*, when it wasn't even his to give. And God alone knew what that might lead to. Because once a woman got her toe in the door of a nice house, and her feet under the table, she could maybe squat there like a clocking hen for all eternity.

As she pedaled along the sun-dappled road that led to Kilfeckin Manor, Rose's mind was in a flurry. There was enough to be done without that Hailstone woman stirring up a storm.

Uncle Ned needed looking after since taking poorly and Gusty wasn't much help. A house with only men about it was not a normal house, anyway. A woman's hand was needed to keep things tidy and stop the roof falling in on the top of them. Sure if there were no women around, heavens above, what kind of state would the world be in?

Rose was cogitating on all of this as she pedaled up the driveway toward Kilfeckin Manor. She was out of practice—like the bike itself, which had been screaking in protest from the minute she'd left home.

Now I really must get my Paddy to oil them wheels, she thought as she dismounted in the yard and parked the bike under a gooseberry bush.

She noticed that Gusty's truck was not in the shed. But that was not unusual, for between the garage work and the barkeep stints for Etta Strong, she rarely saw him anyway.

Ned Grant had made Herkie Halstone rich by a whole £2 and 60p. His ma had been very impressed.

"God, son, what did ye do tae make all that?" she'd asked in surprise when he tipped the sum of money onto the table.

"Well, I went up and asked the oul' boy if he wanted anything done, and he said, 'Ye wouldn't empty me pot under the bed there, son?'"

"Thought ye said he peed out the windee."

He hadn't been expecting her to say that. "Aye—I mean yes—but...but at night when it's dark...aye, at night when it's dark...he...he can't see till piss, I mean pee, out the windee, so he doz it in the pot under the bed instead."

Herkie was proud of his quick thinking and fully intended using the same tactic again.

Lying in the rear field, musing on this recent success, he was alerted by the screeching of a bicycle coming into the yard.

His little heart lifted. The moneybags in the big white shoes had finally shown up.

He waited until the woman was safely through the front door before slipping out of hiding. He would peep in the kitchen window and seize his chance when she went upstairs with the oul' boy's tea.

Ned's face broadened into a toothless smile when he saw his favorite niece in the doorway.

"God, Rose, is it yerself? I didn't hear ye come in there." The old man's voice, normally all grinding gears and anger shifts for the nephew, was softer now, holding a cadence that only his niece and a few others could draw forth. "Ye can turn that wireless off, 'cos there's nothin' on it but things for nippers at this time-a day."

"Don't stir yourself, Uncle Ned," Rose said, setting her tray down. "And don't forget to put yer teeth in."

"Begod, I thought I had them in me already."

Ned took the dentures from a chipped mug on the locker, a mug that read TEETH, LIKE STARS, COME OUT AT NIGHT. The dentures had belonged to his dead brother, Silvester. Ned, a man who believed in letting nothing go to waste, had made sure to remove them from the still-fresh corpse—along with a pair of horn-rimmed spectacles—just as St. Peter was throwing open the pearly gates and Mr. Turtle, the undertaker, was en route to dress the body.

"So, how've ye been since I last seen ye, Uncle Ned?" Rose asked kindly, pulling up a Chippendale chair and settling herself. "How's that old chest?"

"Ah, now. Dr. Brewster was over yesterday and put the scope on me, and said it was nothin' but a wee touch of indigestion. He give me a bottle for the tickle of it."

"Well, y'know, Ned, my Paddy had that old tickle, too, and Dr. Brewster tolt him something the same. But he tolt him that it would be highly desirable if he give up the smokin'. Those were the very words he used: 'highly desirable.'"

Ned registered Rose's hint at his pipe smoking, but said nothing. His pipe was one of the few pleasures left to him, and he'd no intention of giving it up.

"So I got him a bottle of Mrs. Troutman's Chesty Solutions," continued Rose, "and d'ye know, he took a couple of sips and the cough went away. So I'll get you a bottle of it for you, too, next time I'm comin'."

She poured tea and proffered a plate of cake.

"Good enough," said Ned, his hand, now resembling a redemption claw in an arcade machine, grabbing up the cake.

"But there's something else I wanna tell ye. Something that'll cure ye completely of that chest of yours, as well as any other pain or ache a body might be suffering, and it doesn't involve a tablet or hospital or anything like that, 'cos it's a miracle."

Ned pushed himself up on the time-worn bolster, hope inflating like a birthday balloon. A miracle cure! Something that might render him virile and robust and full of pep once more. What could it be?

"Now...it concerns an Italian saint by the name of Padre Pio."

"Aw, I see," said Ned glumly, the balloon of hope shrinking miserably. He had little time for prayers and saints. He'd had enough of religion with his late wife, who'd been a wimple away from a convent when they met, and throughout most of their marriage had blamed him for parting her from her vocation.

"Now don't dismiss it just yet," said Rose. "A friend of mine, Amy Peebles, has a cousin who's a priest with the Passionate Fathers." (To be sure, Amy had told her it was Passionist Fathers, but Rose had a sow's ear for enunciation at the best of times.) "And she sez that he was in Rome last week and was give a glove of Padre Pio's, which cures the people. Amy said that, if ye like, the priest could call and give ye a rub with it. 'Cos he's very powerful, Padre Pio. Now, some would say ye suffer more when ye ask him for things—for just like them boxes of Milk Tray choclits, ye never know what ye're gonna get. There was a man down the country that Amy tolt me about. An Abraham Branny, suffered terrible with the palpitations. Got Ham for short. He would have been related to a..."

Ned switched off and just let Rose run on. There was no point in trying to stop her. For like most of the county councilors he heard on *Good Morning Ulster*, much of what she said slipped in through the ears without bothering the brain too much. So he faked attention, enjoying the sound of a woman's voice in the big empty house, and giving the odd nod now and again to let her know he hadn't fallen into a coma. When he checked back in, his niece was still on the subject of Padre Pio.

"...and the way I heard it, when Ham had finished up the novena to Padre Pio, on the ninth day, if he didn't go and drop dead havin' a sausage supper and a cuppa tea."

"God-oh," said Ned, not a little shocked at this unexpected outcome. "He got rid of the palpitations right enough."

"Yes indeed, he got ridda the palpitations and the novena was answered right enough, Uncle Ned, but not in the way Ham wanted. That's the wee risk ye run when ye ask Padre Pio for things. 'Cos maybe he thought it was better tae take Ham home tae the Lord and be done with it, than have him sufferin' on with the palpitations and him not gettin' no relief."

"God, I don't think I'd bother with that glove, Rose. I'd rather put up with the bad chest than be kerried outta here feet first."

"Just thought I'd mention it anyway," said Rose. "'Cos the Passionate Father doesn't get tae visit the North very often with the glove."

Ned sighed, not wishing to hear any more about passionate priests, or saints' gloves, or people dying.

"Any news from the town, Rose? Sure a hear nothin' from one end of the week tae the other, and since Gusty started doing turns for Etta Strong, he comes in here at night with drink on him...and it takes him so bloody long tae tell me things, I fall asleep afore he gets tae the end of it."

"Well, y'know, Gusty was never much good at the conversing unless it's about some of them odd things he doz be readin' about, like goblins or goats or whatever. But here's the thing, Uncle Ned:

All that drinkin's gonna stop. Etta's son, Lorcan, is home for a while."

"God, Gusty never tolt me that."

"Well, he wouldn't, Ned, would he? For Lorcan'll put him round the corners and he'll not be able tae drink as much when Lorcan's about." Rose cast a glance at the window. "Does he talk about that Mrs. Hailstone woman, does he?"

"Naw, sez only that she's rentin' Dora's. That's as far as I know. I haven't seen her meself, but Gusty says he sees her betimes in the mornin' out the back, smokin' in a night frock."

Rose was scandalized. "A *night* frock?"

"Aye, a short red boy he sez."

"Well, God save us all! And how did Gusty know it was a night frock and not a dress? 'Cos I know he'd never of seen a woman in the like of one of them. But at the same time, with the clothes they're makin' nowadays, there's not much of a difference between what they wear tae the bed and wear tae the shops anyway."

"He got himself a pair a them binoc'lars last week from some magazine so he could get closer up on her."

"What!"

"Oh, aye. A great pair-a things altogether, from what he tells me."

Rose was appalled. Gusty looking at Mrs. Hailstone's breasts!

"What? *What* great pair-a things?"

"The Vintage Towers. They're that big, ye could see Venus through them, begod! He'll not give them tae me…afeard of me drappin' them with these oul' shaky hands. But, ye know, I wouldn't mind seein' her close-up meself, Gusty sez she's very well-lookin'."

For one rare and remarkable minute, Rose was lost for words. Heavens above, who would have thought that a strange woman could arrive on the hill into old Dora's place out of nowhere and upset Gusty and Ned's way of going? Have them thinking about things that maybe a man shouldn't be thinking about.

Ned was worth quite a lot of money, what with Kilfeckin Manor full of antiques and a good seventy acres of land, which would naturally pass to Gusty.

It was time for Rose to speak her mind.

"Well, ye know, I met her the other day…called round to the priest's house tae give the Father a fruit loaf just like this one here. And if she didn't take it from me and shut the door in me face. Wouldn't let me in for a cuppa tea. I should hope that Gusty isn't getting no ideas about her."

"Well, ye know, when he was leanin' over tae straighten up the bed for me yesterday, I thought I got a whiff of perfume off him and—"

"See? What did I tell yeh? It's only a—"

"But Rose, I don't think it would be hers. Etta Strong was maybe sprayin' some on herself and he caught a bit of it in the pub. A wommin would need-a be bloody desperate to look at the like of Gusty. And that Mrs. Hailstone's too well-lookin' from what I hear, tae be that desp'rate."

"Well, that's where I disagree with you entirely," Rose shot back. She could have been a barrister at the bench pouncing on the perfume as that all-important "aggravating factor" to prove her case. "As you well know, a man could have a face on him like the back end of a Bilberry goat and the brains of a monkey, but if he's got a bitta money about him and a field or two under him, there's a type of wommin that'd still be after him. I believe they call them gold miners, and if I'm any judge, that Mrs. Hailstone's a gold miner."

She studied Ned's patchwork quilt, hoping it might give her some hints on solving the problem of Mrs. Hailstone, but all she got back was a dizzy head and sore eyes.

Then another snippet to bolster her defense. "Now that I mind, there was a wommin down the country Josie tolt me about. She was that plain-lookin' that not even the tide would take her out. But when her father died, leavin' her a farm of land, if the men weren't all buzzin' round her like midges on a Mullingar heifer's rump. So it works both ways, so it does."

She paused.

"God, Uncle Ned, before I forget: your pension money."

Ned trembled the teacup back unto the saucer, wondering how to phrase the next comment. "Did ye know, Rose, that last week there was a couple o' pound of it missin'?"

"Now, that couldn't be right."

"Well, I don't know. I thought maybe ye dropped it on the road somewhere. Then I thought maybe ye dropped it in the yard, but Gusty said he had a good look about and there was no sign of it. And God, now when I think of it, he sez he's lost his wallet, too."

"Well, that's the queerest thing." Rose studied Ned's quilt once more, hoping she might find the answer in a section of four-patch block. "Not unless, Ned...not unless Doris Crink didn't count it right. But that would be a first for Doris, 'cos she's never done that afore." Rose got up. "I'll just get me bag. Hold on a wee minute."

On her way down the stairs, Rose got a bad feeling. And it wasn't just a hangover from the beheading of the statue, unfortunate though that incident was. At breakfast that morning, she'd knocked over the saltcellar, and she remembered now that she maybe hadn't thrown a big enough pinch of it over her left shoulder, to dispel the bad luck that was sure to follow.

Then there was that lone magpie she'd seen on the way to Ned's. She'd taken a hand off the handlebar to wave away the bodement, only to nearly crash the bike into Bumper Grimes's bread van. No, something bad was in the air—and she had an idea who might be bringing it about.

Down in the kitchen she checked her bag. The pension envelope contained two fivers but the two pound coins and ten pence were missing. She emptied the contents of the handbag out onto the table. Maybe they'd slid down into the bottom of the bag with the jolting of the bike. Ned's long lane had many a bump in it.

But no. There was no sign of the missing coins.

She hurried outside and looked about, but all was quiet. The cows were in the field and Veronica in her pen. The ducks were swimming contentedly on the little pond at the far end of the yard, unruffled.

Something caught her eye, lying by the barn door. Something red. Couldn't be a sock, thought Rose. Gusty and Ned wear only brown or black. She bent down and picked it up.

"Oh, Jesus and his Blissed Mother!" She was holding a pair of lady's panties.

She looked back up the hill at Rosehip Cottage. There was no doubt in her mind who owned the scandalous bit of lingerie. But how, she thought, did they get from up there to down here? They didn't get to the barn door without a pair of hands—and she thought she could guess whom those hands belonged to. Affronted, she stuffed the offensive panties into her apron pocket and hurried back up the yard.

On the step, another surprise awaited her. She stooped and picked up the wrapper from a Milky Way bar. Neither Gusty nor Ned ate chocolate bars.

God-blissus-and-savus, what was going on? And how, oh how, was she going to tell Uncle Ned that part of his pension money—money *she* was in charge of—was missing for the second week in a row?

Chapter twenty-one

The stone circle was an extraordinary feature, set on a sheltered stretch of land that bordered two properties. Few people ventured there. The circle, an ancient relic from the Neolithic period, was held in superstitious awe and reverence by the locals, considered a sacred place that one disturbed at one's peril. It was reached by a small track that connected old Ned Grant's house with the Killoran Road.

Seated on his usual old tree stump, Lorcan inhaled deeply. On this, his second visit to the hideaway, he was savoring afresh the peace and tranquillity, marveling at the beauty shed by the trees surrounding him: a crackling rug of leaves and twiglets. This was a world away from Belfast.

He scanned the undergrowth, alive to the tonal shifts, the harmonizing hues that appeared so random to the untrained eye but which, to his artist's eye, were the very patterns of nature.

But what, he asked himself, was *this*? It clearly did not belong. He bent over and speared the offending piece of litter with his umbrella point. An empty Malteser bag. How singularly improper! And it wasn't alone. He found another pile of wrappers behind the stump, along with a spent roll of caps of the kind used in toy pistols. A trespasser was using his refuge. And from the evidence, it was an untidy young boy with a very sweet tooth.

He tut-tutted, resolving to pick up all the litter as soon as he completed his drawing.

Just then, as if prompting him to action, a thrush flitted down and settled on one of the lowest boughs of the nearest beech tree. It was a magnificent creature, all speckled brown and with eyes like tiny black pearls that seemed to miss nothing. Lorcan, with slow and easy movements, took his pencils from his breast pocket and opened the sketchbook. The thrush continued its business of preening its feathers.

Whack!

The bird flew away—and Lorcan jumped. He'd been struck in the left shoulder. It hurt.

An air gun, he thought at once. His fingers went to the place. But his jacket hadn't been holed. He looked behind him, wincing.

A boy stood on the track leading to the Grant house. He was chubby, with blond curly hair, and attired in jeans, a grubby T-shirt, and a pair of equally grubby trainers. In his right hand he held a slingshot.

"What the devil do you think you're playing at? You hit me with that thing!"

"Sorry, mister. I-I was tryin' till get the bird."

"And just why were you trying to get the bird, may I ask? What did the bird ever do to you?"

"Nothin', mister. It's just an oul' bird."

"I'll have you know it's a thrush, not 'an oul' bird,' and there aren't that many of them about. There'd be even fewer with lads like you, with nothing better to do than use them for target practice."

"Aye, mister—I mean yes, mister." Herkie stood gazing up at the odd-looking man in the funny hat. He'd never seen his like before and was intrigued. "Why are you talkin' all posh, mister?"

"Perhaps because I *am* posh! Where are your parents? Do they know you're killing off God's creatures?"

"I've only me ma. Me da's dead."

Lorcan bit his lip. He regarded the young boy with fresh eyes. There was something about his plump little face that reminded him of himself at that age. He picked up his sketch pad and umbrella and went to him.

"Well, I'm sorry to hear about your dad," he said. "I suppose that explains something about your errant behavior. But it doesn't excuse it, not for a minute. You mustn't go round shooting at birds, you know. They're lovely creatures. And they keep the pests down so they're useful into the bargain. Birds probably don't like the sight of *us* much, but they don't go round attacking us, now do they?"

Herkie gazed down at the toes of his trainers, his cheeks flushing with embarrassment.

"No, mister, but me ma doesn't like them, neither. They keep shittin' on the roof of the car. And one day they shit on her head and she was ragin', so she was."

Lorcan flinched at the boy's cavalier use of foul language.

"Well, they don't do that on purpose. Where do you live?"

"Up there."

"You're a Grant?"

"Nah. We live in an oul' doll's house up the hill. We're on haul'days, so we are."

"What, old Dora's place?"

"Aye—I mean yes."

He suddenly recalled Gusty's conversation with Socrates in the bar. So this must be the son of the "film star."

"I see," he said. "I'm Lorcan, by the way. What's your name?"

"Herkie."

"Well, pleased to meet you, Herkie. That's an unusual name. What's that the short for?"

"Herc'lees."

"Hmm. Hercules—the Greek strongman. Was that your father's name?"

"Nah—no, he was called Packie, but he'd a tattoo of Herc'lees on his belly."

"How very interesting." Lorcan thought of the body art of skinheads and sailors. He realized he was making a value judgment. Yet the belly was nonetheless a strange part of the anatomy to have decorated. Tattoos were usually displayed proudly on those areas more readily seen. Not unless this Packie person didn't believe in wearing a shirt. "D'you miss him?"

"Nah. He was always hittin' me...and me ma doesn't miss him either 'cos he was always hittin' her, too. She says he had no head on him anyway."

Lorcan had to smile at that, yet couldn't but agree with the ma's analysis. "That's a Belfast accent, isn't it?"

"Ehh...yes."

"What part of Belfast are you from?"

Herkie screwed up his face in consternation, trying to remember the name of the posh street his ma had coached him on.

Lorcan waited. And waited. Perhaps this Herkie was a bit slow—but he didn't think so. "You don't remember?"

"Ma...Ma-hone, Mahone Road," he said at last.

"Oh, right. I think you mean the Ma-*lone* Road."

It was a fib, of course. Herkie neither looked nor sounded like a child of the well-heeled class that resided in that part of the city.

"Mister, why are these oul' stones all in a big ring?"

"It's a stone circle, Herkie. When it gets dark, the fairies come out and dance inside it."

Herkie's eyes widened. "Real fairies? Could I see them?"

"Yes. But there's just one small problem." Lorcan bent down and put on his most serious face. "They only appear to the pure of heart."

The boy's brows knitted in puzzlement. He couldn't quite figure out this strange man. Had never met anyone like him before. He'd heard of fairies, though, and seen pictures of them. Miss Kerr, their teacher, had an old black-and-white photograph on the wall called *The Cottingley Fairies*. It showed a wee girl looking at fairies dancing around in a garden.

"It means, Herkie, that you have to be good before the fairies will reveal themselves to you. Which would explain—" Lorcan straightened up again and stared heavenward. "Which would explain why so few people have actually seen them. Alas, not enough good people in this cruel old world of ours, you see."

"Mister, why d'you wear a hat and have an umbreller when it's not rainin'?"

"Well, the hat shades my eyes from the sun, and the umbrella serves as a walking stick."

"But why d'ye need a walkin' stick when yer not an oul' boy?"

"I'm glad you think I'm not. You're an inquisitive little fellow—no bad thing in a boy. But I've another use for it: a litter-picker."

"What's that?"

"Come here. Let me demonstrate."

Herkie followed Lorcan gingerly round behind one of the stones. He watched with great interest as the strange man poked the umbrella point into the leaves and unearthed his stack of sweet wrappers.

"Now, I wonder how *they* got there."

"I-I dunno. Maybe the birds dropped them, sir."

Lorcan tilted his head to one side and studied the boy. Herkie looked down at his toes again. "Now, let me see. A bird that eats chocolate and," he speared the coil of used caps and held it up, "shoots a toy gun into the bargain. I'd also bet that this very dexterous bird wears jeans and tries to kill other birds with a catapult. Would I be right now?"

Herkie said nothing at first, merely toyed with the slingshot, wishing he could teleport like Mr. Spock to planet Vulcan.

"Och, mister, they're only oul' papers. You're like me ma. She's always shoutin' at me till lift papers, too. That's why I threw them there."

Lorcan tried not to smirk at the child's spirited defense of his bad habits. He admired the pluck the boy was showing and wished he'd been like that when he was that age.

"Tell you what: You put all those wrappers in your pockets, and I'll forgive you for trying to murder that poor thrush."

Herkie nodded solemnly and went to gather up his litter. Lorcan understood, or fancied he did. He tried to imagine how it must be for a Belfast boy—of what? Eight, nine?—suddenly finding himself in a cottage on the outskirts of Tailorstown. What would he do? How would he pass the time? No wonder Herkie was amusing himself by stalking thrushes with a slingshot.

"Right. You leave those birds alone, you hear? If I catch you taking potshots at them, I'll give you a clip round the ear. And I don't care what your mum thinks about that."

"I won't, mister."

"Lorcan."

"I won't, Mr. Lorcan."

"Just make certain you don't. Run along now. I'm sure your mother is wondering where you are."

Herkie turned to go, but stopped. Something had caught his attention. "What's that?" he asked, pointing.

"It's a sketch pad. I like to draw. Would you care to see some?"

The boy nodded eagerly.

Lorcan laid out the sketch pad on the stump and Herkie approached shyly to have a look. He watched in amazement as page upon page of perfectly executed birds and trees and flowers were revealed to him. He gazed up at the strange man with newfound admiration.

"They're class, Mr. Lorcan."

"Thank you, Herkie. You could do the same if you wanted to."

"Nah, I'm no good at drawin', but I love colorin'-in. Me teacher said I was good 'cos I keep inside the lines."

"Well, that's a good start. Tell you what: You pick out the ones you like best and you can take them home and color them in. Now, which ones d'you fancy?"

"Maybe...maybe that frog."

The bullfrog, with its spotty belly and bulging eyes, perched balefully on a riverbank boulder, was a very detailed study. In Herkie's imagination his coloring pencils were already busy, his sharpener at the ready.

"Good. You have your work cut out for you there. Now, another one?"

Herkie turned the pages clumsily. "And this rat sleepin' under the umbreller."

Lorcan smiled. "That's a dormouse, and he's hibernating under a toadstool. That means he goes to sleep for the winter months and only wakes up in the springtime."

He tore out the two sketches, rolled them into a baton, secured them with an elastic band, and presented them to a very pleased little boy.

"Thank you, sir—I mean Mr. Lorcan." Herkie was amazed. All the adults he'd known so far either treated him badly or ignored him completely, but this stranger with the long hair and funny hat was different.

"Now, you'd best run along, Herkie, or your mother will be worried."

"But when can I show them to ye?"

"Oh, don't worry. You'll see me here." He swept an arm around the clearing. "Here in nature's living room. Now, you've got a lot of coloring-in to do, and I've got a drawing to finish. Chop-chop."

With that, Herkie shot off. Lorcan sat down on the stump again, opened his sketchbook, and selected an interesting stand of bushes to his right.

As he began drawing, however, he could not help thinking about Herkie and his mother. He'd never heard of anyone coming all the way from Belfast to sojourn in the like of Tailorstown. There was an intriguing tale behind it all, which he reckoned, given the nature of small-town gossip, would emerge soon enough.

Chapter twenty-two

Ask and it will be given to you; seek and you will find; knock and the door will be opened to you. For everyone who asks receives; he who seeks finds; and to him who knocks, the door will be opened. Which of you, if his son asks for bread, will give him a stone? Or if he asks for a fish, will give him a snake? If you, then, though you are evil, know how to give good gifts to your children, how much more will your Father in heaven give good gifts to those who ask him! So in everything, do to others what you would have them do to you, for this sums up the Law and the Prophets."

Father Cassidy smoothed the ribbon in his heavy tome of scripture and gazed down upon his congregation. "Matthew, chapter seven, verses seven to twelve," he intoned in a grave voice as he shut the book.

Sunday, eleven fifteen, and he was saying his final Mass of the morning. Being the later service, it was the most popular, attracting a motley bunch of parishioners: harassed parents with young children; a few disheveled, hungover men holding up the back wall, yawning. And the usual half dozen or so pietistic old ladies who attended every Mass and looked as though they'd taken root over the years in the same pews and were now wilting before the priest's very eyes.

Father Cassidy had chosen those verses of scripture for a very good reason. The coffers were not healthy. Balancing the books had become of late a migraine-inducing chore rather than an agreeable task. Nonetheless, he regarded it as his bounden—if not sacred—duty to keep the ledger ink a deep and healthy shade of black.

Yes, he thought, isn't it all a question of balance? To balance the books on the one hand, and to balance one's duty to one's flock against a higher duty: the duty to God and country.

He moved to the lectern in front of the altar, drew a deep breath, and began.

"Which of you, if his son asks for bread, will give him a stone? Or if he asks for a fish, will give him a snake?" He repeated Matthew's words loudly as he surveyed the congregation. "Today I wish to talk about the importance of giving and about its opposite: the sin of greed and how it eats into the very core of the human heart, destroying all around it."

Halfway down the church sat his new housekeeper, Mrs. Halstone, dressed in a frock of unseemly scarlet, more suited to the cocktail banquette than the Sunday Mass pew. She stood out starkly against the other ladies, they in their sober costumes and sensible, churchgoing hats. Father Cassidy could not but notice her. He was finding her to be an unwarranted and gaudy distraction, and it was taking a Lenten resolve for him to focus elsewhere.

As for Bessie, it being her first Mass at St. Timothy's, she'd made a very special effort to impress the country folk. The jersey frock, another vintage cast-off from Mrs. Lloyd-Peacock's ever-changing wardrobe circa 1965, hugged her figure in all the right places. She'd accessorized it with a daring crepe rose pinned behind her left ear. She hoped Father Cassidy would appreciate the effort she'd made and gazed up at him now, God's inscrutable support act up there on the stage, wearing the green and gold vestments she'd ironed—steam knob turned to max—the previous day.

A fidgety Herkie sat beside her, tapping his foot against the seat in front and fiddling with a thread on the hem of his gray serge shorts. Bessie, aware that both she and the son were the focus of attention, would, from time to time, give him a sharp prod for appearances' sake. It was the third time in the course of ten minutes that she'd had to check him, so this time the prod was unapologetically forceful.

Herkie let out a small yelp, which caused Father Cassidy to halt briefly in his homily, and Rose McFadden, who was sitting in front with her husband, Paddy, to turn round and shush him to silence. Herkie immediately countered Rose's rebuke by sticking out his tongue when her back was turned again.

"It is all very well," Father Cassidy continued, "being generous to your own flesh and blood. Who, indeed, in this congregation would give his—or, indeed, her—child a stone if he asked for bread?" He scanned the expectant faces, and his eyes were drawn again to his housekeeper and her son.

Bessie smiled demurely, the wrong reaction entirely, and the priest shifted his gaze to another section of the gathering.

"But it is giving to others and not just ourselves which brings with it our heavenly reward. And giving freely, when your church requires it of you, should not have to be explained by me. But explain it I *must*!" Father Cassidy's voice rose on the last syllable and he hit the lectern an emphatic slap.

This uncharacteristic flourish visibly jolted the gathering. Small children began to whimper, mothers to fret, and a sizable proportion of the males—including the drunks loitering at the back—woke up to discover they were not in bed after all but actually at Mass. There was much embarrassed throat-clearing and shifting in seats.

"Now," the priest continued in a more even tone. "I do not have to remind you that the kneeling boards need reupholstering. This is for your own comfort, and especially for that of the more elderly members of the parish. The pain of arthritis and brittle bones is not something to be taken lightly in old age." The elderly ladies at the front nodded to each other and murmured approval. "Another very necessary outlay is the belfry. It's been worrying me for quite some time, so last week I had an engineer in for an assessment. I regret to say the news is not good. A great deal of strengthening work to the timber tower is required, since it is riddled with woodworm. As a result, the bell will have to be rehung with new fittings. God knows it could drop at any time."

Father Cassidy paused. Bessie recrossed her legs and examined her fingernails. She was bored and just wanted to be out in the fresh air. She glanced down at Herkie and saw that he was earnestly dismantling his new plastic rosary. He'd pulled the figurine from the cross and now Jesus was curled up on the pew ledge like a swimmer about to take a nosedive. She decided to simply let him get on with it.

Farther up the church sat a man Bessie hadn't noticed until then. He was wearing a black velvet jacket (maybe even a suit!) and she saw the glint of a gold cuff link as he turned a page of his missal. The older woman beside him, she assumed, was his mother. His proud posture and longish dark hair marked him out from the dandruffed humps and hair-oiled crops of the farming men around him. She wondered who he might be.

"These necessary improvements are rather urgent, and we need funds quickly," the priest continued, "for, alas, such refurbishment does not come cheap. Then," he leaned into the microphone, "I had an idea. An idea that will actually benefit all of *you*, while helping *me*."

A ripple of interest ran through the congregation. Heads bent toward each other in conference, and much speculative whispering ensued.

"*Bingo!*" Father Cassidy shouted.

The hubbub ceased, and all eyes were back on the priest.

"Yes, I've decided to increase the monthly jackpot from five hundred to one thousand pounds. As from next Saturday."

A cheer went up. There were beaming faces all round.

"Now, that's the good news. The bad news is that the entrance fee will increase from three pounds to five. But an extra two pounds won't hurt, given that there's so much to gain. And that extra will mean that the restoration of the belfry will be secure, and we'll all be safer for it. Can I assume that everyone is happy with this solution?"

There were audible gasps of excitement from the congregation. Bessie's mind, like all those around her, went into overdrive. A whole thousand pounds—and all her problems would be solved! The only thing she'd ever won in her life, though, was a stick of rock candy for coming second in the egg-and-spoon race when she was eight, but...

Father Cassidy adopted his serious, sacerdotal look once more and raised a hand.

"I knew I could depend on you, the faithful. As the good Gospel entreats, let me not see evidence of a heart that will give a stone instead of bread, a snake instead of a fish. A few paltry coins instead of a five-pound note. In other words, let me not see evidence of a selfish heart in your monthly stipend, either."

He paused for effect and was pleased to see so many heads bowed in shame before him. He consulted his notes.

"Well, I believe that is all for now. I will not detain you any further. Just remember to give generously in this week's collection and in subsequent ones." He shut his notebook and raised his hands. "All stand for the Prayer of the Faithful. Let us also pray for the hunger strikers in the Maze. Give them courage, Lord, in the face of their impending deaths."

There came the rustling of missal pages and the creaking of knee joints as the flock rose to do his bidding.

Half an hour later, Mass was over, and Father Cassidy was, as always, disappointed to see such an eager stampede toward the exits.

Bessie, ever ready to remain in the priest's good books—and much to Herkie's annoyance—continued kneeling for a polite few minutes, head bowed in an attitude of what she hoped was meaningful reverence.

Meanwhile, she was aware of Mrs. McFadden commencing the enactment of an elaborate final curtain call of devotion for *her* benefit. Rose got up, genuflected twice, struck her breast thrice, and crossed herself exuberantly before whispering in her husband's ear. At the prompt, Paddy obediently rose and shuffled out after her.

"Can we go now, Ma?" asked Herkie.

"Yes, son," said Bessie, getting up and seeing Father Cassidy had already exited the stage, thus negating any further pretense at worshipful respect. Herkie ran on ahead of her down the aisle.

Outside, a keen breeze was sending a bevy of behatted ladies hurrying for the shelter of their cars. Bessie held a protective hand to the rose in her hair, smoothed down the fluttering hem of her frock, and looked about her. Herkie was nowhere to be seen. She was about to call out his name when, to her disquiet, she spotted him over by the gates talking to the tall, long-haired stranger she'd spotted earlier. She saw, too, that the stranger was indeed wearing a beautifully tailored velvet suit, complete with starched white shirt and silk tie. What in God's name was Herkie doing, talking to *him*?

"Come along now, son!" she shouted, heading toward the Morris Traveller.

"That's me ma," she heard Herkie say, but he didn't move. Bessie, greatly irked, marched over to him.

"Ma, this is Mr. Lorcan," he said excitedly, grabbing at his mother's sleeve.

Bessie, caught between anger and politeness, and conscious of the stranger's scrutiny, managed a tight little smile.

"Well, I'm sure *Mister* Lorcan has more important things to be doing than—"

"Pleased to meet you, Mrs. Halstone." Lorcan smiled, extending a hand. "I'm Lorcan...Lorcan Strong."

Bessie faltered. She returned the handshake with a hesitance born of mistrust rather than shyness. "Elizabeth...Elizabeth Halstone."

He was appraising her. She shifted uneasily from one foot to another under the inspection.

"Mr. Lorcan draws pitchers, Ma."

"Does he now? I'm so sorry, you'll have to excuse us," she said, tugging Herkie away.

"Of course. I'm sure we'll meet again. Herkie is helping me with some artwork. He's very good, you know."

Herkie beamed up at his mother, the words of praise flooding him with a rare pride and happiness.

"If you say so, Mr. Strong," she said, faking a smile. Being a mother, albeit a flawed one, she was wary of strangers—and especially those who took an interest in children. "Bye now."

She took Herkie firmly by the hand and walked away.

Lorcan stood and watched their old car disappear through the gates. At close quarters he'd observed beauty on the wane: the dyed hair and dulled complexion. Read penury in the worn fabric of the scarlet dress, the dusty rose in her hair, the scuffed toes of the high-heeled shoes.

He sensed a life of desperation beneath the pretense and felt compassion for her—but in particular for the little boy unwittingly caught up in it all.

He found himself pondering the pair as he got back into his own car.

"I thought you'd forgotten all about me," Etta Strong said from the backseat, fingering her matinee pearls and peering at him through the spotted netting of a complicated hat. She preferred to sit in the rear, in case their neighbor, old Mr. Bagley, needed a lift. "I could see you were very taken with that Mrs. Halstone. And I have to warn you, Lorcan: she wouldn't be suitable, having a son and a past, and perhaps a reputation. Rose filled me in."

"We mustn't listen to gossip, Mother," he said, putting the car into reverse. "I wasn't 'very taken' with her, as you say. The boy, Herkie, is sweet. A bit lost, which isn't so surprising…I'd like to keep an eye on him. That's all."

"Yes, well, but what is *she* like?"

"Polite…enough." Lorcan guided the car out through the gates and onto the main road.

"I wonder why she's come to Tailorstown."

"Yes, you may well wonder."

Farther along, they caught sight of Mr. Bagley, laboring valiantly on his bad leg.

"Oh, sound the horn, will you, dear? I know he turns off his hearing aid during Mass."

"Well, who could blame him? That new priest of yours had me bored senseless."

Etta tut-tutted as Lorcan pulled up alongside the old man. He sounded the horn, but Mr. Bagley simply carried on heroically, oblivious to the car and the world around him.

The dutiful son got out and helped the enfeebled gentleman aboard. Why the poor fellow didn't just stay in bed of a Sunday morning was a mystery to him. But Lorcan had been away too long. Like a stage actor who'd left the set to stretch himself, there was no longer a part for him to play. By rights he should have been in a cameo role, but increasingly, with each return visit to Tailorstown, he felt relegated to the workaday duties of a stagehand.

Chapter twenty-three

Father Cassidy sighed with an air of splendid satisfaction and sat down in his armchair. He'd just finished another excellent lunch and was looking forward to a cigarette while he perused the newspapers.

Two o'clock on the Lord's Day, it being the busiest morning of the week—two Masses, two homilies, the ever-present possibility of a baptism—always brought with it a great sense of relief. Today, fortunately, there was no fresh addition to the flock and hence no claimant on his precious time. The day was his until devotions at six.

He lit a cigarette as his thoughts meandered back over his morning's work. The sermon had gone well, and it gave him great satisfaction that his new bingo plans had met such approbation. He congratulated himself again on having hit on such an excellent idea, the perfect way to bolster parish funds and take care of his private affairs without attracting unwelcome attention. He was also heartened to see Mrs. Halstone at Mass. She had not been to confession, however, nor had she received Communion. This was a trifle worrying. Receiving the sacraments was a given for any housekeeper of his. He made a mental note to have a quiet word.

That said, until her arrival his palate had never experienced such flavorsome cuisine; nor, indeed, had the kitchen Aga ever cooked up such a variety of dishes. Today she hadn't disappointed: coq au vin followed by Baked Alaska, a dessert that seemed to defy the laws of thermodynamics. Oven-baked ice cream. How ingenious. Who would have thought such a feat possible?

He must request a repeat for the following Sunday. Bishop Delahant would be calling for his fiscal appraisal of the parish books. Father Cassidy was not looking forward to that. Money was always a difficult subject for him. But who knew, after a fine meal and news of his plans for the bingo, things might not look so bleak.

He reflected that life was infinitely more relaxed with Mrs. Halstone about. Not only was she a wonderful cook, but also, with her living so near the village, there was no need for her to lodge at the parochial house. Such a situation suited him admirably. Miss Beard had been a real encumbrance in that respect. Her bedroom on the upper story, directly above his own, had proven rather unsettling to begin with. Often he'd been disturbed by her lumbering about in the early hours, his chandelier tinkling its dissent from the minute she rose. He'd been summoning the courage to ask her to move. After all, there were a number of other bedrooms to choose from. But hadn't Providence intervened at that crucial moment, laying her poor mother low and thereby solving the problem? God did indeed move in mysterious ways.

So her departure, while disruptive initially—thanks to Mrs. McFadden's daily pestering—had, in the end, brought a whole new set of possibilities into play: the stranger, Mrs. Halstone; a much-improved diet; and perhaps most important of all, blissfully muted mornings.

In the parochial kitchen, Bessie was tidying up. Since hearing the odd thumps upstairs a few days earlier, she had been putting off cleaning up there. Perhaps Father Cassidy could enlighten her. She'd mention it to him before leaving.

Now, though, as she set about her chores—drying dishes, binning leftovers, wiping surfaces clean—the stranger, Lorcan Strong, was stealing into her thoughts.

An artist! Herkie had mentioned meeting someone a few days earlier. He'd shown her a couple of drawings, but she'd barely paid them any heed. Now all was becoming clear.

Her immediate feeling on seeing him there with her son had been one of suspicion. Why would a man like that take an interest in a young boy? What was he after? She mistrusted men with good reason, tending, as she did, to see them all through the pernicious prism of her father and the dissolute Packie.

She opened a cupboard, pushed aside a soup tureen big enough to bathe a baby in, and began placing the dried china on a shelf.

The artist was well-off. That she could tell straightaway from the fine suit and spotless white shirt. And intelligent—those eyes scanning her like that. He wasn't doing that out of interest, though. It was more like taking the measure of her. Well, him being an artist, maybe he looked at everybody that way, viewing everybody as a possible sitter. She remembered Loose Lily from her secondary-school days. Lily had gone from being a part-time stripper to an artist's model without breaking a fingernail. Well, it was easier and much better paid, apparently, taking your clothes off for the sake of art instead of for a roomful of greasy builder's mates down the Brendan Behan Pub of a Saturday night. Maybe Lorcan Strong was sizing her up with just that in mind, deciding how to catch the best bits of her with his paintbrush.

She shut the cupboard door and unsheathed her hands from the clammy Marigold gloves. The nail polish on her right hand was chipped. He'd have seen that. Oh dear!

There was some Beaujolais left over from the coq au vin. That would cheer her up a bit. She fetched it from the refrigerator, poured some into a mug, and took a sip. She'd come up with an ingenious way of keeping herself irrigated with the odd tipple by opting mostly for those recipes that required a splash of alcohol in the mix. Father Cassidy had no idea he was footing her drinks bill. And that, she hoped, would be the way things would remain. Even if he did find out, she had the perfect explanation.

It was half past two. Time she was gone anyway.

She'd made enough lunch for four, so Father Cassidy's dinner was already taken care of. An added advantage of her new job was that Herkie and she could feed themselves well, at the priest's expense, which meant she didn't have to make many inroads into the paltry salary he paid her.

Scanning the immaculate kitchen, she felt smug with a job well done. She drained the last of the wine, ran the mug under the tap, and removed her apron. Then she took a sprig of parsley from a pot on the windowsill and chewed on it to banish any telltale whiffs.

At the mirror by the door she reapplied her lipstick, powdered her nose, patted her hair, drew on her cardigan, and picked up her bag of filched food. It was time to bid her employer good day.

But as she neared his study door she heard talking. He was obviously on the phone. His voice had a playful edge that she hadn't heard before. *Playful* and *Father Cassidy* did not normally belong in the same sentence. She wondered who he could be talking to and strained to hear a tidbit, but all she got back was an animated murmuring punctuated by the odd, suggestive snigger. In Bessie's world, only a woman could have that effect on a man, celibate or not.

Never one to stand on ceremony, she barged straight in.

"Well, I'm away now, Father. Was there anything more?"

He gave a start and quickly palmed the receiver.

"Mrs. Halstone!"

"Sorry, Father. Didn't know you were on the phone."

"Well, yes…just a moment." She'd rattled him. A rare thing, indeed. A first. Then: "Let me finish this call, Mrs. Halstone, if I may. I need a private word with you."

He indicated a chair, and spoke into the phone again. "I'll have to call you back. Sorry about that. Bye now." He hung up.

A bit abrupt with that caller, Bessie thought. The tension she'd created needed smoothing. "Was the lunch all right, Father?"

"Lunch was excellent…yes, excellent, as always."

"Thank you. Glad to hear it. Do you need me at six?"

"Yes indeed…Well, no…no, as a matter of fact. You don't need to come back." He was studying the carpet, distracted. "I have to go out. Yes, out…parish business. We priests are rarely off duty, alas."

She saw that he could not meet her eye. *Still thinking about the secret woman. Men!*

She wondered again about that "parish business." He could be away for hours at a time and could never say exactly when he'd be back for supper. He tended of late to disappear in the afternoon. Hence she found herself making meals in advance, for him to reheat on his return.

"Right," she said. "Well, if you're sure. It's no—"

"Yes, absolutely. You enjoy the rest of your Sunday." He turned his gaze to the window. Bessie studied the back of his neatly groomed head. "Lovely weather," he continued. "You should take a trip to the seaside. Portaluce. It's not far. I'm sure your boy would love it."

"Maybe I will." *He probably spends longer at the mirror on his hair than I do on mine. What's the point of that if he can't marry? But an affair on the sly?* "And the private word, Father?"

He turned to her, puzzled. "Private word?"

"Yes, you said you wanted a private word a minute ago, when you were on the phone."

"Oh, of course!" His voice took on a confidential tone. "It's a delicate matter, Mrs. Halstone, but one I feel a little uneasy about."

"Oh." Had he smelled the alcohol on her breath? Impossible. Not from that distance. *Not unless he's got the snout of a bloody Labrador. And even so, the parsley would have foiled him.* "Won't you sit down, Mrs. Halstone?"

"Well…no, Father, if you don't mind. My son, y'see. What was it about?"

"Yes indeed, how remiss of me. I'll come straight to the point then. It's just that, well…it's just that I haven't seen you, or indeed your son, receiving."

Bessie was flummoxed. *What in heaven's name is he on about? Receiving what? Stolen goods? Gentlemen callers?* "Sorry…receiving what, Father?"

"Oh, you don't understand the term. I see. Well, what I mean is that I haven't seen you receiving Holy Communion. It's an important part of the Mass. In fact, attending Mass and not receiving the sacrament is akin to—" Father Cassidy gazed heavenward and stirred the air in an effort to conjure up an appropriate comparison. "Akin to, shall we say…attending a banquet, suffering hunger pangs, and not partaking of the sumptuous feast laid on especially for you."

For a moment Bessie was lost for words, but she rallied, biting back impatience and affecting interest. "If…if you say so, Father."

"Yes, why go hungry when spiritual sustenance can be had right there at the altar?"

And why don't you give my head peace and let me get on? I cook and clean for you. Isn't that enough?

"You'll see us at the altar next Sunday, Father, that's for sure."

"Excellent. I hear confessions every Saturday morning and evening, as you know. Confession is an important prerequisite of repentance. Preparing the ground, as it were. Tilling the soil.

Rooting out the weeds." He checked himself. "But you must get on, Mrs. Halstone. I've delayed you quite long enough."

Too right ye have. "Oh, that's all right, Father." *Confession, indeed!* "If that's all?"

"Yes, yes…of course."

She made to leave, then wavered. "Oh, Father…"

"Yes?"

"We're alone here, aren't we?"

He arched a Gregory Peck eyebrow. "We? I don't follow you, Mrs. Halstone."

"Well, Father, what I mean to say is…you're…you're the only one that lives here?"

He stared. She felt her cheeks heating up; his coldness had her flustered.

"Well, it's…it's just that, the other day I thought I heard someone upstairs. But…but you were out."

"Oh." His face relaxed. "An old house like this." He scanned the ceiling. "It creaks, it groans. I expect we'll all be doing the same in our old age."

"R-right, but—"

"Now, Miss Beard would blame *him.*" He indicated the portrait over the mantelshelf. "Judge Cosgrove Carson, God rest him. He built this house in eighteen hundred and ten. Lived to the ripe old age of ninety-eight. A good man. Yes, a very good man. He bequeathed this house and its lands to the Church."

"Are you saying it's his ghost, Father?"

He smiled. "No, no. I said Miss Beard tends to believe in such things. The dead don't come back, Mrs. Halstone." He left off his inspection of Judge Cosgrove. "No, the dead do not return. So you either imagined the noises or simply heard creaking timbers." He plucked at imaginary lint on his sleeve, looked back at her, and smiled. "I'll hear your confession this Saturday. And the boy's, too, of course."

She was being dismissed. She wouldn't be getting a straight answer.

"Yes…well, I'll see you tomorrow then," she said.

As Bessie exited the room she felt uneasy. Father Cassidy was being less than truthful; she was certain of it. There was something not quite right about St. Timothy's parochial house and its handsome incumbent.

Disquiet tugged at her. She wondered what it was she'd let herself in for.

Chapter twenty-four

We're getting there, my dear Countess, and not before time. In fact—" Lorcan stayed his hand and shifted his gaze to the watch on his wrist. "In fact, another ten days at most should finish you. Yes, finish you and liberate me."

It was early morning in his studio. He sat in front of the easel, concentrating on the Countess's chin and jawline. Every morning since coming to Tailorstown he'd risen at six to spend three hours on the portrait. He needed the luminous clarity of the light in those precious hours. Flesh tones demanded a delicate touch, the keenest eye, the sharpest focus. Besides which, painting in oils was a painstaking process that could not be rushed, due to the various drying times required when layering pigments. The earlier the start, the better.

The silence of sunup aided his concentration, too.

With the aid of his loupe, he compared the photograph of Reynolds's original portrait with his own efforts. He nodded in satisfaction, set the instrument aside, and took up his brush again. As he blended paint, he was appreciating the harmonious chatter of birds in the trees beyond the square. Very soon, the churr of car engines would overwhelm such agreeable music, as man and his works intruded upon another day.

With this thought came the idea of escape, of finally casting off the Dentist's yoke and being free of the tyrant. Four long weeks of sustained effort were enough for any man. He was tired. He yearned to have his life back. But how, short of killing him, could he rid himself of the monster?

He stopped the brushwork. No, no, he could never kill a man. Even swatting a fly was difficult enough. Perhaps someone else would take him out. There were sure to be whole battalions of enemies simply waiting their chance, biding their time.

He dipped the brush into some linseed oil and brought it back to the canvas, moving now to shade in the hollow in the Countess's throat. But apart from the unlikely scenario of the Dentist's demise, what would ensure his freedom? Perhaps he could flee, go abroad. America? Yes, it was always a possibility. Aunt Bronagh, his mother's colorful sister, was forever inviting him.

In a sideboard drawer downstairs lay an accumulation of international money orders, sent by his aunt on successive birthdays. He recalled that the first little gift dated from the occasion of his twenty-first birthday. Year upon year the money orders would arrive, each one no great fortune in itself—$20 here, $50 there—but over time they amounted to quite a tidy sum, more than enough to cover his return airfare to Florida, with generous spending money. That, of course, was his aunt's intention.

But somehow he couldn't picture himself living under the same roof as Bronagh. She was so unlike his mother; she was a woman who believed in enjoying life to the full, having survived three husbands, four stepsons, a couple of heart attacks, and a botched face-lift. Retirement had not blunted her joie de vivre. Latterly the septuagenarian had found herself paid work as a fitness instructor in a Miami care home, where she'd recently put her back out while demonstrating the spine-stretcher resistance movement on a wonky Wunda Chair.

Yes, Aunt Bronagh was always a possibility, but only for the most extreme circumstance.

He smiled at the thought of her. Knew everything there was to know about her life through a frenetic correspondence of lavender-scented letters she kept up with his mother. Missives he was tasked to read aloud every time he returned home. With the passing of the years, Aunt Bronagh's handwriting had come to resemble a series of phonetic glyphs from an ancient scribe. Writing that was, of late, challenging even for his mother's lollipop magnifying glass.

How would he ever keep up with Bronagh's energetic life-style if he did decide to relocate stateside? He imagined there were no speed limits on the pace of life in Miami. The very thought exhausted him.

No, life was infinitely less complicated in Northern Ireland—for all its troubles. And nowhere less complicated or slower than in dear old Tailorstown.

He was amazed at how easily he'd fallen into a routine since coming home. He didn't really miss the museum, being under the yoke of the meddling curator or at the mercy of the chivvying Stanley. There was relief also in being free of his digs; no longer having to thwart Mrs. Hipple's fry-ups was doing his digestion a world of good.

Yes, banishment to Tailorstown had given him pause. Had forced upon him the need to stand back, take stock, evaluate his life and the direction it was heading in. Prior to this enforced break, he'd been seeing just as far into the future as a narrow beam might allow. Getting up. Going to work. Coming home to dine, read, reflect, before finally falling asleep under the eiderdown quilt of his rented bed. Now things had switched to full beam. There were matters that needed attending to. Decisions to be made. He could see all too clearly that only *he* could sort it all out: his mother, the business, his career.

Change was in the air. Life was demanding a different kind of action.

A couple of hours later, with the light altering and the demands of the day upon him, Lorcan stopped work, cleaned his brushes, and went to look in on his mother.

He found her in the living room as usual, cup of tea in hand, feet resting on the pouf, and the ever-present radio tuned to Radio Ulster.

"Morning, son," she said, her eyes going immediately to the headless statue on the dresser.

"Morning, Mother. Yes, I know. She'll be conjoined this very day."

"It's just that Rose said that Father Cassidy said...well, there's an ugly gap, you see, to the right of the altar, and it looks—"

"As though she's been assumed into heaven."

"Away with you! I was going to say it looks bad."

"Indeed! We can't have that."

He went through to the kitchen, helped himself to coffee, and carried it back into the living room.

"Father Cassidy is going to be raking in so much money from his new bingo initiative," he said, sitting down opposite her, "he could buy himself a new statue. I thought gambling was a sin, anyway."

"Yes, well...he's very thrifty, you know," said Etta, blinking rapidly—a surefire indication to Lorcan that she didn't approve of his criticism. "Raising money for church funds couldn't be classed as gambling. It's all in a good cause, you see."

"If you say so."

"Now, Rose said she'd call by this afternoon. She'll take the statue round to Father Cassidy if it's finished. She's very good like that, Rose."

Lorcan felt a small panic rising at the mention of Rose's name. In his experience the woman rarely gave her mouth a break. At their last encounter, she'd swamped him with a tsunami of information concerning the assorted ailments various people in the parish had suffered in his absence.

No, his time was precious. Rose was best avoided.

"Oh, no need for that! I'll deliver the statue myself. I would like to meet the good Father in person...get the measure of him."

"Just a minute, son," said Etta, raising the volume on the radio.

"The security alert follows a coded message to the Samaritans in the early morning. The green Renault was left outside Milligan's fashion shop in Canal Street. The area has now been made safe. Key holders have been asked to check their premises. This is the second bomb alert in Carngorm—"

"God, Lorcan, isn't it dreadful? That's just up the road from us."

"I know." Lorcan's grip on the coffee mug tightened. This rural outpost was a safe place, surely. Bombs and bullets were the language of the city he had left behind. The image of the decrepit house on Nansen Street rose in his mind like a dark cloud. It was as if the nastiness had followed him.

"What do those boys think they're about at all?"

"Don't worry, Mother. Nothing's going to happen *here.*" Lorcan was at a loss. "Milligan's must've been targeted because it's in a mixed community." Though he knew the real reason lay with the passing of Bobby Sands and the imminent death of hunger striker number two: local man, Francis Hughes.

Etta put a hand to her heart and sighed. "Now that you say it, son, you know I hadn't thought of that. Yes, Ivan Milligan married a Catholic, but he didn't turn himself. Although I believe that the children are being brought up in the faith."

He finished his coffee and got up. "Now don't waste your time worrying about those idiots. Nobody was hurt, and that's the main thing." He went to the dresser and picked up the statue. "The Blessed Mother needs to get her head in order. I'll fix her this very minute."

"Thank you, son. Father Cassidy will be pleased. Now, Rose will be calling and I'm sure she'd like to see you."

"Mother, I'm not in to anyone for the next two hours—and most especially not to Rose McFadden, d'you hear?"

"Yes, Lorcan dear. But y'know, Rose means well."

"That's as may be, but my ears need protecting from women like Rose, and I do not wish my day to be spoiled before it has properly begun."

At that same moment, the connecting door between the bar and the Strong home creaked open and the voice of Gusty was heard to say, "Aye, go on in there, Rose. Etta's in the sittin' room, so she is."

Lorcan made a dash down the hallway, the statue under one arm. He sprinted up the stairs and was in his studio with door secured before Mrs. McFadden had her first "Cooee" out in greeting.

Chapter twenty-five

I s'ppose ye heard about that new wommin gettin' the job with
the Father," said Rose, buttering a fruit scone with a generous
knob of Kerrygold. "I was very put out, Josie, and I don't mind
sayin' it. For I thought he'd take me, a member of the parish, afore
a stranger like that."

A slow noon in the Cozy Corner Café, and Rose, having left
Etta Strong's, was enjoying her thrice-weekly confab with the proprietor. They sat at a vinyl-clad table to the right of the counter:
Josie's table. It was within easy reach of kitchen and till—the two
most important things in Josie's life since her husband, Amos, had
been taken suddenly with hypertension and an enlarged heart into
St. Timothy's cemetery in 1975, barely six months into their tenure
at the Cozy Corner.

"Oh, no good'll come outta that, Rose," said Josie, warming to
the theme while replenishing the rock-fern teacups. "I knew that
her and that son were a pair-a bad ones when I first laid me eyes on
them. And her all done up like Murphy's mare. I believe that's a wig
she wears, 'cos the color of that hair could only come out of a bottle."

"God, Josie, d'ye think Father Cassidy could be led astray?
They're great wee scones. Was it the baking powder or the self-
raisin' ye used?"

"The self-raisin', Rose. Well, ye know, I'd put nothin' past her, but she's not livin' under the same roof as the Father, so the Father's safe enough. And besides that, the priest's a wise man. I'm sure it's not the first time he's seen the Divil in a pair-a high heels and a tight skirt."

Rose munched her scone, deep in thought. She needed to confide in someone; she couldn't keep her fears about Gusty to herself. Josie was a friend, even though she had a mouth on her the size of the Foyle Estuary. But Rose could live with that. She had to share her concerns.

"It's just that…well, it's just that I'd be terrible afeard for our Gusty."

"Och, Rose, I wouldn't think she'd look at the like of Gusty."

Rose dropped her voice to a confessional whisper and leaned over the table. "Maybe not, Josie. But that's not tae say Gusty might not have his own designs. Now, I wouldn't mention the like-a this tae nobody but yerself. Not even my Paddy. And what I'm gonna tell ye is for your ears only, but God forbid, Josie, the eyes nearly fell outta me head when I seen them."

Rose paused for breath, wondering how she was going to phrase the scandalous tidbit. Josie, eager to hear more, leaned closer.

"And what was it, Rose, that nearly made the eyes fall outta yer head?"

"Well, they could only be hers. Ye know I do a bitta tidyin' up for Ned once a week. Not that it makes much of a differs, truth be told, for him and Gusty are the durtiest pair-a men God put breath in."

"Aye, I know that," said Josie, having heard Rose's observations on her relatives' hygiene habits a hundred times before and eager for a slice of fresh gossip. There'd been a distinct lack of scandal in the town of late, and she was beginning to wonder if she shouldn't simply invent a bit herself to spice things up. There was only so much mileage in Screw-loose John's breakdown, Margie Mullard's weight gain, and Johnny Byrne watering Mrs. Tuft's hanging baskets three times in one day and her husband away at the plowing trials in Termonfeckin.

"But what was it that ye found?" Josie asked, exasperated.

"I was just comin' to that. I came across them in the backyard, no less. Lacy red things they were."

Josie's mouth was agape. *Lacy red things*. Her tiny eyes fixed on Rose. Seconds passed. *Lacy red things*. Her mind was a maelstrom of bawdy imaginings.

"Heaven's above, Rose. What were they?"

"Howyiz! Josie, me oul' fat hen! Long time no see."

The ladies turned.

Chuck Sproule had entered the premises and was sidling up to the counter.

"Ye're not wanted in here!" cried Josie, immediately on her feet and making for the protection of the counter.

"Now, what way's that to treat an oul' friend who hasn't had a bit of good grub since last Christmas?" Chuck stretched himself out over the counter, rested his elbows on the marbled Formica, cupped his chin, and studied Josie's chalkboard menu.

"Maybe," said Rose, getting up, "I should be going, Josie…"

"You sit yer ground there, Rose," Josie said, shooting Rose a don't-leave-me-alone-with-this-pup-what-if-he-groped-me look, and Rose sank reluctantly back into the chair with a gasp and a squeak. "Nobody's goin' nowhere but this boy, so they're not."

"Aye," said Chuck with a smirk, "you sit right where ye are, Rose, and finish yer tea. A burger and chip'll do me nicely, Josie. Plenty of onions on the bun."

"Ye're gettin' nothin' in here, ye unmannerly lout. Now, get out or I'll call Sergeant Ranfurley."

"Aye, right, and what law would I be brekkin', askin' ye for a burger and chip?"

Josie was caught on the hop. She looked to Rose for help.

"I think it might be called intrudement on a body's entry, Josie. And your mother wouldn't be very proud of you, Chuck, if she thought ye were breakin' the law again, and you only outta prison."

"Och, Rose. Now, I'd love tae see things from your point of view but, ye know, there's just one wee problem. I don't think I'd be able to get me head that far up yer arse."

"Oh, Jesus, Mary, and Joseph!" Josie cried. "Right. That's it. I'm gonna ring the sergeant this very second."

Rose, hot, bothered, and disgusted, grabbed up *The People's Friend* to fan her burning cheeks.

"There'll be no need for that," came a voice from the doorway.

The trio turned to see Father Cassidy. He glowered at young Sproule, who immediately unpeeled himself from the counter and stood up straight. He could have been a private in the presence of his commanding officer, so complete was the change in the young rascal.

"Thank God it's you, Father!" gasped Rose, dropping the magazine and rising up with a look that aped a visionary at Fatima.

"The Lord himself sent ye in the nick of time," added a relieved Josie. "This boy was goin' over some very durty talk, and—"

"Yes, the Devil makes light work for durty hands, Father," put in Rose.

Father Cassidy gave her a bemused look. "There's no need for explanation, ladies," he said. Then, turning to Chuck: "Now, apologize for your appalling behavior."

"I'm *sorry*, ladies," said Chuck, looking nervous.

"Good. Now, you're coming with me. You need work to do, and there are plenty of jobs that need doing at the parochial house."

Father Cassidy ordered Chuck out with a curt nod. A tense silence followed the ruffian's exit.

"Father, just one wee thing," said Rose, for whom lulls of any kind were a perversion. "Did ye get that wee fruit loaf I left round for ye?"

Father Cassidy had no recollection of having eaten a fruit loaf but knew better than to admit as much. "Yes indeed, Rose. It was lovely. Most kind of you. Now I need to be going."

At that point two hungry schoolboys entered. The priest used the diversion to make his escape. Rose gathered up her bags.

"God, Josie, I'd better be going, too. It's time for my Paddy's tea. Isn't it great that the Father enjoyed me wee fruit loaf?"

"But Rose," said Josie, ignoring the boys and following her to the door, "what about the lacy red things?"

"What lacy red things?"

"Ye were tellin' me about Gusty and a pair-a things that ye found in the yard."

"Oh, God save us, Josie, I'll call in the morra tae tell ye the rest of that. There's too much tae go over now, and I would need-a be sittin' down with a cuppa tea, so ye could get the full pitcher of the shock that I got."

"Right ye be, Rose."

Josie turned back inside, annoyed that her peek through the keyhole had been thwarted. She'd just have to wait. All the same, there was enough mileage in that phrase, "lacy red things," to kick-start a fresh bit of gossip without delay. Why wait until tomorrow?

Her next customer was in for a treat.

Chapter twenty-six

Lorcan ran an appraising eye over the reassembled Blessed Mother. In the space of two hours he'd not only attached the head with quick-drying plaster but brought her back to vibrant life with some acrylic paint. The original had been crude, and that fact made his retouching easier.

The Virgin now sported a pair of rouged cheeks that would not look out of place in the Folies Bergère. A bad-tempered serpent at her feet had been revivified with a startling coat of phthalo green, its terrifying fangs brought out with some brilliant white. He'd reserved the gilding of the inside of the cloak until last. With that final application, the lady shone.

Perfect.

Now all he need do was wrap her up in a suitable length of cotton and deliver her to Father Cassidy.

"Butter? Check. Caster sugar? Check. Ground almonds? Check. Lemon juice? Check." Bessie stood in the parochial kitchen, ticking off the ingredients on her recipe for lemon drizzle cake. It had been one of Mrs. Lloyd-Peacock's favorites. "When life gives you lemons, make lemon drizzle cake!" she used to say.

Father Cassidy was in his study working on the parish accounts. She felt safer when he was around. Since hearing the strange noises upstairs, she'd tried, as far as possible, not to be alone in the house. If his secret lady friend or the ghost of old Judge Carson was hanging around up there, she'd no desire to bump into either of them, even in the daylight hours. Her employer still hadn't requested that she clean his bedroom, which Bessie thought rather odd. But then, in the present circumstances, she wouldn't be in any hurry to ask him. He could do as he pleased, so long as he paid her on time and didn't ask too many questions. She smiled to herself; it was an amicable arrangement.

"Now, the flour...and..." She reached across the table and lifted a bottle of Bristol Cream sherry. "A nip of this to perk it up, and a wee sip to perk *me* up."

She cocked an ear. Father Cassidy had a very light footfall due to the soft soles of his suede shoes. She couldn't risk pouring herself a glass. He just might materialize in the doorway.

She listened, looked down at the bottle, decided she was safe enough, and sloshed some into a mug.

The sweet, syrupy taste hit the back of her throat, bringing back memories of half-forgotten Christmases. Her mother used to buy a bottle to carry her through those festive days—those inevitably stress-filled festive days. There were so many blighted Yuletides in Bessie's childhood.

She gripped the mug, knuckles whitening. Just another sip. The clouds were gathering again. The sagging, rain-fat clouds she never seemed fully able to outrun. But she would *not* be swamped. She was a woman now. A vulnerable child no more.

She plonked the mug back down. Stepped back from the table.

At that moment the doorbell sounded.

"*Damn!*" She tore off her apron. Dived on the parsley plant and stuffed a generous wad into her mouth.

In the hallway she checked herself in the mirror before opening the front door.

She was surprised to find Herkie's new friend, the weirdo artist, on the doorstep. He was holding a bulky object wrapped in cloth.

"Mrs. Halstone. Good afternoon."

"Good afternoon, Mister...eh..."

"Lorcan Strong. We met after Mass. Remember?"

"Yes, of course, Mr. Strong." Bessie patted her hair. She regretted not having taken the time to do her lipstick. Well, she'd thought it was probably Mrs. McFadden again with another piece of cookery for the priest.

"I need to give this to Father Cassidy," said Lorcan, sensing Mrs. Halstone's unease. He smiled. "It's a statue he needed retouching."

"I see. Well, I know nothing about any statue." She held the door wide. "But do come in, Mr. Strong."

"Thank you." Lorcan stepped into the hallway, taking in the mediocre portraits of long-dead celibates that lined the walls. They seemed to give the word *lifeless* a whole new meaning.

"The thing is, Mr. Strong, Father Cassidy is busy at the moment, and he left word that he wasn't to be disturbed."

"I see." Lorcan looked about him again. "I suppose, in that case, I'll come back another time. When it's more convenient."

"No, no, we couldn't have that. We can't have you going to all that trouble only to have to come back again." She was thinking fast. It was important to get the measure of this strange man. The ideal time was now. "Why don't you wait here in the living room, and I'll bring you a cup of tea. I'm sure I can persuade Father Cassidy to tear himself away from his work for a few minutes."

"Only if you're sure. I wouldn't like to put you to any trouble."

"No trouble at all."

She flung open a door with a flourish and ushered him through. Lorcan grimaced at the sight of a portrait depicting a judge, inexpertly rendered in neoclassical mode. He went to a prominent table. It was spread with a map of the locality and several sheets of foolscap paper scrawled with notes. He pushed them aside and set his burden down.

"Have a seat, won't you?"

"Very kind, Mrs. Halstone."

By the time she returned, some minutes later, the statue had been unveiled. The Virgin stood serene, the rich gold lining of her robe agleam.

"He'll be pleased with that, I'm sure," Bessie said. She set a tray on a side table and began to pour tea. "I told him he had a caller, and he'll be with you shortly. You're an artist then?"

"Yes. I work in Belfast, at the museum. Just home on a few weeks' leave."

"That's nice." She offered a plate of biscuits.

"No, thanks. My mother's a little unwell. She runs the pub over there on High Street. I came home to help her out for a bit."

"Sorry to hear about your mother. Will she be all right?"

"Oh, yes. It's nothing too serious."

Lorcan appreciated that he was telling Mrs. Halstone perhaps more than he should. At the same time, he was aware that he knew more about her than he ought to. And he felt a bit guilty about that. He was thinking of what young Herkie had confided. He saw a battered woman who'd recently buried an abusive husband, left the city and her home to get a job and make a fresh start in the back of beyond. He admired the undoubted courage and fortitude such a life-changing decision must have entailed. "You're from Belfast, too, I hear. I'm sorry for your loss."

Bessie rounded on him, the mask of composure slipping for a second. "How did you know that?"

"Oh, sorry…it was just that Herkie mentioned it," he said. Then, not wanting to get Herkie into trouble, added quickly, "But he didn't *mean* to tell me. It just came up in conversation."

"That son of mine! I don't know what I'm going to do with him at all." She turned her attention to the statue, inwardly cursing Herkie. "Looks lovely. You're very talented."

At that moment, the door opened; Father Cassidy came in. Lorcan rose to greet him. Bessie excused herself and made to leave.

"I'll bring another cup, Father."

"That's quite all right, Mrs. Halstone. Don't trouble yourself."

She withdrew, leaving Lorcan and Father Cassidy in each other's company. If a passerby had chosen to peep in the window, he might have detected a certain coolness between the two.

"Pleased to meet you, Father." He extended a hand. *He reminds me of that actor, what's his name? Gregory Peck. Younger, of course.*

"You must be Etta's son, the artist."

"Yes. Lorcan Strong. I came to deliver the statue." *A bit too handsome for the solemnity of the cloth.*

"It's very good of you…Lorcan? May I call you Lorcan?"

"Of course."

"I was glad to hear you were coming home to help her out." Father Cassidy went to an armchair. He gently tugged at the knees of his trousers, sat down, and flipped one lean thigh over the other. The move was not lost on Lorcan. Here was a man very conscious of appearances. "Staying long?"

"Until she gets her strength back."

"Excellent! Now, I'm glad you called, Lorcan, because…Well, I wonder if I might ask a favor of you."

"Yes…well, that would depend, Father." The artist was slightly discomforted. Please don't let it be another paint job. On his last visit to the church, he'd noticed that the Stations of the Cross were in sore need of a reviving lick of paint.

"I'm expecting rather a big crowd at the bingo next Saturday, you see, and I wondered would you mind helping out?"

Ah! Not as bad as I thought. "Be glad to."

"Perhaps collect the entrance fee on the door? I need someone honest, with a cool head." He fixed Lorcan with a look of pained sincerity. "Unflappable, I think, is the word I'm looking for. You strike me as someone who would be unflappable."

"I'm flattered that you should think so." Lorcan could see that Father Cassidy was a man used to getting what he wanted. He supposed that the movie-star looks, in tandem with the strictures of the Roman collar, gave him a power and confidence unique among men.

The priest got up and crossed to where the statue stood. "A fine job you've done with this, Lorcan. You have indeed returned the Blessed Mother to her former glory. God bless you. I'm much indebted."

Lorcan rose. He feared that if he lingered, another favor might be asked of him. "It was a pleasure to meet you, Father. But—"

"Oh, going already?"

"Alas, time and duty calls." He put his hat back on. "Very pleased to have made your acquaintance."

"The feeling is mutual, Lorcan," the priest said, opening the door. "I can count on you for Saturday then? Won't put you out in the pub, I hope?"

"No, not at all."

"Feel free to drop by any time."

"I will. Bye now."

The sun had disappeared by the time Lorcan emerged from the parochial house. He was disappointed, having penciled in an hour on the portrait before teatime. Never mind; as an artist one was at the mercy of the light.

He was just about to get into his car when a voice called out.

"Mr. Strong! Mr. Strong!"

He turned to see Mrs. Halstone coming toward him, clutching a folded fabric. "Your wrapping. You forgot it."

"Oh, so I did. Thank you." Lorcan held out a hand. "It was lovely to meet you again. Properly. Tell Herkie I'll be wanting to see those drawings finished very soon."

He was pleased to see Mrs. Halstone's wary face soften slightly. "I'll tell him. Nice to meet you, too, Mr. Strong."

She turned and hurried back to the house.

Lorcan climbed into the car and maneuvered it down the avenue. As he paused by the gates to allow a tractor to pass, he checked his rearview mirror and was amused to see that his departure was being closely monitored. At one window stood Father Cassidy; at another Mrs. Halstone.

"Well, well, well," he murmured, steering the car out onto the road. "I don't know if that's a good sign or a bad one."

Three paths had crossed. A nexus had been formed, a nexus whose consequences Lorcan, at that stage, could not even begin to imagine.

Chapter twenty-seven

Now, son, I have a crow to pluck with you." Bessie flopped down on the sofa, wrested the shoes from feet wrecked from a decade in four-inch heels, and sighed with relief. She'd stopped driving to work, deciding that the physical exercise would not only improve her figure but save on petrol as well. She hadn't reckoned, though, that such a laudable decision would result in corns the size of conkers.

"Och, Ma. I wanna finish this dormouse 'cos *Star Trek*'s comin' on!" From the moment his mother stormed through the door, he hadn't even looked her way, so intent was he on coloring Lorcan's drawing of the hibernating rodent.

"Dormouse, my foot! There'll be no TV till I hear what you've been up to!" Bessie hit her armrest an almighty slap. "And ye can stop that bloody drawin' this minute. For if ye don't I'll come over there and tear it into wee bits."

Herkie knew his mother meant business and put down the coloring pencil immediately.

"Now, I was talkin' till that Strong man today, that odd boy that give ye them drawings, and from what he said it was plain timme ye were blabbin' to him and tellin' him more than what ye let on till me."

Herkie twisted in his chair and pulled a curl of hair down over his nose. It was a defense tactic he used when cornered and feeling guilty. "I didn't tell him nothin', Ma."

"Right. How did he know yer da was dead then?"

"Don't know."

"Don't lie timme, son. Didn't I give ye strict instructions not to talk till strangers or tell anybody our business? We're on the run from the bloody Dentist, or did ye forget that already, ye wee dope? That man could be anybody. A Provo or a prevert or God knows what!"

"What's a pre-vert, Ma?"

"Never you mind. Now, what *else* did ye blab till him?"

"What ye told me till say…that I was Herkie Law—Hilton-Halstone, from the Malone Road. And…and that we were on haul'days for a bit. And I had till tell him Da was dead 'cos he asked me where he was and I wasn't gonna tell lies, Ma."

"Right, so long as that was all ye told him. Where did ye meet him anyway?"

"In the fairy's ring where they do magic things."

"*What!* Where in-under God is that?!"

"Och! It's only an oul' bunch of stones down a lane."

"Well, you're to stay away from that oul' bunch-a stones, ye hear?" She left off massaging a foot, retrieved a pair of fluffy mules from under the sofa, and slipped them on. "And ye're tae stay away from that Strong man, d'ye hear me? I don't know what sort of a character he is."

"Aye, Ma."

"I've enough on me plate without worrying about things like that. From now on ye're gonna come to the priest's house with me, so I can keep an eye on ye. I'm gonna ask Father Cassidy if ye can spend the afternoons with me when I'm workin'."

"Och, Ma. What'll I—"

"Now, none of yer oul' lip, Herkie Halstone. I've decided, and that's the end of it. Artists indeed!"

She got up and started clearing the table, collecting a melamine beaker and plate—Herkie was not trusted with anything breakable—along with her own cup and saucer. "What's the time there anyway?"

Herkie pulled back his sleeve—only to discover that his Snoopy wristwatch was missing. He wondered about that and decided, given the circumstances, not to disclose it to his ma. He was in enough trouble already.

"Can I have a Penguin, Ma?"

"Go in there and put the kettle on first. Ye have till work for yer keep."

With the tea made, and being in a clearer frame of mind, Bessie relaxed. Her feet were returning to normal. A much-needed cigarette was aglow in the ashtray. Dolly Parton was belting out "Baby I'm Burning" on the record player. And Herkie, on his second Penguin bar, was giving her head peace. Bliss!

She cut a generous slice of Mrs. McFadden's purloined fruitcake and sampled a bit. "Mmmm…" The cake was surprisingly good. "That Mrs. McFadden knows her raisins from her glassy cherries, I'll give her that!"

"What's glassy cherries?"

"Nothin', son. Just thinkin' outside meself."

Herkie was happy his ma was in better form now and hoped things would stay that way. He hated it when she was cross. Since leaving Belfast it seemed she was cross most of the time. Now, though, she was calmer, tapping her foot to the music. It was a good sign. He decided to try and prolong it by telling her a joke.

"Ma, why could the polo bear not eat the penguin?"

"I don't know, son. Why could the polo bear not eat the penguin?"

"'Cos he couldn't get the wrapper off."

Bessie chuckled. "Where did ye hear that, ye wee ruffian?"

"I read it in the *Cheeky Weekly*. Can I get another *Cheeky Weekly*, Ma?"

"Yes, son. Now, there's something I need-a talk to ye about. It's an important thing, so I want ye to listen. And if ye do it proper for me ye'll get yer *Cheeky Weekly*. All right?"

"Aye, Ma."

"Now, ye know what confession means, don't ye?"

Herkie screwed up his face, thinking hard. "Is it when ye go till the chapel and say bad things till the priest?"

"Well...more or less. It's *telling* the priest *about* all the bad things ye've done so he can give ye penance. In other words, the sins ye've committed. Now, I know ye haven't been till confession since ye were seven, but that's neither here nor there. Father Cassidy wants to hear our confessions this evening so we can get Holy Communion on Sunday."

"What's Holy Communion?"

"I was hopin' ye weren't gonna ask me that. Ye had it three years ago. It's a wee bitta wafer ye get at the end of Mass. But in order tae get that wee bitta wafer—"

"Aye, Miss Kerr used till give us bits of ice-cream wafer."

"Well, it's more or less the same, but it's the body of Christ as well as being a wafer. Anyway, ye have till tell Father Cassidy all the bad things ye've done in order tae get till ate it."

"Och, Ma. That's what cannonballs do."

"Don't be silly, son. Cannonballs might well do it, but we're not talkin' about a bunch o' bare people runnin' about the jungle. This is serious, holy stuff that Father Cassidy wants us till do. Now, what bad things have ye done this past month that ye can tell the priest? I'm sure there's plenty."

Herkie thought about:

- Stealing the wallet from Mr. Grant's back pocket.
- Stealing the money from Rose McFadden's purse and pretending the old man had paid him.
- Trying to kill a bird with his catapult and hitting Mr. Strong instead.
- Working the lid, bit by bit, off the well in the backyard.

Those were the big ones. Then there were the lesser crimes:

- Stealing chocolate bars from his mother's special Rover tin.
- Beheading the ballerina in one of Aunt Dora's jewelry boxes.
- Shooting the ears off the garden gnomes with his catapult on the first day in the cottage.

Herkie avoided his mother's accusatory eye as the great cauldron of misdeeds bubbled and spat in his small, ashamed head.

"Don't know, Ma."

"Well then, I'll tell ye. Ye broke the head off the fairy in that jewelry box. Ye stole two Taxis and a Bandit from my biscuit tin. Ye pulled that pig's tail belongin' tae Mr. Grant. Ye knocked the ears off them gnomes in the garden, not tae mention the flowers ye've destroyed. So ye see, son, ye're not short of sins tae tell Father Cassidy." She got up to fetch the kettle from the stove. "And another thing. He's gonna ask ye how long it's been since yer last confession. And for God's sake don't say two *years*. Say two *weeks*. Have ye got that?"

"Aye, Ma."

"Ye better mind that, son, for if ye don't, Father Cassidy'll think I'm bringin' up a heathen and—"

"What's a heevin?"

"Never you mind, son—and I could be outta me job. And if I'm outta me job we can't go till yer Uncle Bert in Hackney, or till see the Statue of Liberty, either, and we'll be stuck here, listenin' to the cabbages growin' and the butterflies flappin' their wings till the cows come home. D'ye understand me, son?"

"Aye—I mean yes, Ma."

The sudden clip-clopping of a horse had Herkie dashing out the door.

To his surprise, he saw Barkin' Bob, the traveler Mr. Grant had nearly collided with on their first trip to the cottage, making his way along the main road with his cartful of junk.

Old Bob raised a hand and Herkie naively waved back. He was not to know that in Bob-speak he'd just signaled an interest in buying his services or some of his merchandise. Before he knew it, the she-mule and her master were drawing to a halt in front of the cottage and Bob was launching into his well-practiced sales pitch.

"Wid yer mammy want to boy a bucket, a basin, a froyin'-pan tae froy her sausages of a marnin'. Some turf for de foyer ta keep her warm on de long winter noyt?"

Herkie looked in wonder at Barkin' Bob's cargo: kindling for an Eleventh Night bonfire. He saw an old radio, saucepans, a plastic Barbie with one arm, a teddy bear with no eyes, a bent shovel, rusty garden shears, an accordion with bellows ripped, a cot mattress with its stuffing hanging out, and a set of chipped mugs stamped with portraits of the Pope and the Queen. "Well, whaddya say, boy?" asked Bob, lunatic eyes blinking out of his ruined face.

"Would ye have a head for an Action Man, mister?" Herkie— ever the opportunist—asked.

"Nah, nuthin' loike that."

"Herkie, what's goin on out here?" Bessie stood in the doorway.

"How ya, missus," said Bob, raising his cowboy hat. "Wud ya like tae boy a froyin' pan tae froy yer sausages of a marnin', me lady?"

"I've got one already," Bessie said tartly, going over to inspect the cart.

"Some needles and t'read for tae sew a botton on a dhress... some pegs tae hang yer warshin' on the loin...some sunglasses ta keep de sun outta yer oyes?"

"Well..." Bessie guessed that she wouldn't get rid of him until she purchased something. "I'll have that packet of clothes pegs," she said, mindful of what Mabel McClarty had once told her concerning an aunt of hers who'd spurned a gypsy. In a matter of weeks she'd endured the palsy, the clap, and a myoclonic seizure, before finally collapsing on St. Patrick's Day with cardiac arrest while watching a flute band play "The Fields of Athenry" as they piped their way round Carlisle Circus.

"Dat'll be t'urty pence, and cheap at twoice de proice," said Bob. "Wud ya have a drap o' tea for a t'ursty traveler?" He unhooked a tin mug from Brenda's left flank and passed it to her.

"I've none made, but I'll get ye a drink of orange."

Herkie watched in amazement as Bob downed the drink in one gulp.

He raised the tin mug. "God bless ya, daughtur. God bless ya, son. Giddy-up there, Brenda!" He tugged at the reins and the mule did his bidding.

Mother and son stood and watched him go.

"Ma?"

"Yes, son."

"Ma, why does Gusty Grant call his pig Veronica and Barkin' Bob call his horse Brenda?"

"Because, son, it's the closest they'll ever get tae a wommin, dirty hellions. Let that be a warnin' tae ye."

Several hours later, mother and son were sitting grudgingly in a pew by the confessional. Bessie found the whole idea distasteful and passed the time examining her cuticles as opposed to her conscience. She knew that for appearances' sake she had to follow through. Father Cassidy needed to be assured that she was a bona fide member of the flock. This was a way to convince him. She still had enough of a grasp of the Ten Commandments to make a good fist of things and had already rehearsed a fairly innocuous list of sins, headed up with the obvious "sins of omission."

There were two rows of parishioners patiently waiting their turn. An evening sun, glancing in at the windows, threw pleasing patterns of color across the altar. Jesus flickered in a red globe. The chancel brasses gleamed. A dolorous St. Timothy surveyed the scene from a flower-choked plinth. Lorcan's revived Virgin stood proud.

The air, heavy with beeswax and varnish, was further deadened by the effort of so many consciences being scraped. A stifled cough, a sigh, the clack of rosary beads on polished wood relieved the doom-laden quiet by times. Confessing one's darkest deeds to a man in a black cassock behind a grille in the gloom was not an easy business.

At intervals the door of the confessional would creak open. A relieved parishioner would emerge, blinking, into the light, before stealing quietly up to the altar to parrot his penance. At this small spill of activity, the tension in the gathering would ease, heads would turn, and the row of backsides, as if obeying some unspoken command, would slide as one along the polished pew to fill the space left by the most recent victim.

Josie Mulhearn, seated next to Herkie, sniffing her way through a Divine Mercy novena, shifted herself at the sound of the confessional door opening. Bessie nudged Herkie into the vacated space and whispered in his ear. "You're next, son. Now, ye know what till say?"

"Yes, Ma." He suddenly needed to use the toilet but appreciated it was neither the time nor the place to ask.

"Good boy." She patted his knee.

By and by, there came a raised mumbling from inside the booth, a sure sign that Josie Mulhearn was being forgiven her sins. A minute later the door of the booth opened. Herkie shot up immediately and dashed into the box.

Disoriented by the darkness and dying for a wee, the boy resolved to get his confession over with as quickly as possible. He took a deep breath.

"Bless me, Father, for I've sinned. It's two years since me last confession. I—"

"Two *years*, eh?"

Herkie heard the priest making disapproving noises. He pressed on.

"I stole a Taxi and—"

"A taxi?" Father Cassidy was perplexed. "And where was this...er, taxi parked?"

"In me ma's biscuit tin. And I broke the head off a fairy and pulled Veronica's tail. That's all, Father."

"Her pigtails?"

"The pig's tail, aye."

"And why did you do that to another child, my child?"

"'Cos she was all durty and she was gruntin' in front of me and annoyin' me. Canna go now?"

Herkie didn't wait for an answer. Thirsting for freedom and the nearest lavatory, he bolted from the box and hightailed it from the church.

"Jesus *Christ*, son!" Bessie bawled after him, forgetting herself.

Two rows of horrified faces turned her way. A tide of embarrassment rushed up the widow's cheeks. All eyes were upon her. There was an appalled silence. "I'm sorry, I—"

The sound of a swishing curtain behind her had all heads pivoting further round. Bessie turned to see the bewildered face of Father Cassidy.

"What on earth is going on?"

"I'm sorry, Father. My son is…it's just that he's…" She struggled to find a plausible excuse. "Well, he's afraid of the dark, you see."

"Indeed. You'd better go and see to him then!" came the curt reply.

"Yes, Father."

"This is the house of God, not a barn dance céilí. Who's next there?"

As a new penitent entered the booth, Bessie, under intense scrutiny, gathered up her handbag and gloves. A show of piety was called for, to buy back some much-needed dignity.

She stepped out of the pew and into the aisle, halted, gazed raptly up at the altar, crossed herself, and with head bowed, genuflected deeply.

Only then did she feel sufficiently composed to turn, face her audience, and stride briskly out of the church.

Out of the church and into the sunlight—to find Herkie, take him by the ear, and *wring his bloody neck*!

Chapter twenty-eight

Now, Uncle Ned, I checked with Doris Crink," said Rose, handing the old man the first of many mugs of tea, "and she sez that she's definitely sure she give ye the right pension money. So maybe ye just forgot that ye'd got it. For as a body gets up in years, the mind can get a bit cloudy, can it not? God, me own mind's a bit cloudy betimes, and I don't have as many miles on the clock as yerself."

"Aye, maybe ye're right," said Ned, slurping the tea while reaching for a rocky road chocolate square. "It was only a couple-a pound anyway. Would-a been worse had it been a couple-a hundred, Rose."

"God, Ned, now you're talking. A couple-a hundred would-a meant callin' in Sergeant Ranfurley. And as you well know, Ned, nothing good ever came of a policeman having tae drive his car into a body's yard, whether it be night or day."

Rose and Ned had no idea, of course, that just a few yards away in the back field lay the culprit. Herkie Halstone was biding his time by coloring in Lorcan's bullfrog before making his next assault on the pension fund.

"That's why today I took the pre-conscience of keeping the handbag with me at all times, 'cos I understood it was when I'd left it downstairs in the kitchen outta sight of me eyes that the money went missing. Who knows, but maybe Veronica hoked it out and kerried it away tae a field. Them pigs can be very clever when they want tae be."

Rose reached for the handbag and took out the pension envelope. She counted out the money on the bedside locker. "See, Ned, there it all is. Yer two fivers and two pound coins."

"That's great. Just stick it in that drawer there."

"Well, she'll not get the chance tae put her snout in my bag again. Anyway, Uncle Ned, there's something important I wanna run past ye, concerning Gusty." She blew gently on her cup of hot tea before risking a sip. Ever since finding the underwear—Mrs. Hailstone's for sure—her thoughts had been fizzling and frothing like the hot oil in Josie Mulhearn's deep fat fryer. She could not tell Ned about the discovery, of course, but could try to solve the problem. Something had to be done, and done very quickly. A diversionary tactic was called for and Rose believed she'd come up with the ideal solution. First she needed her uncle's opinion. "Now, I wouldn't want him to be getting ideas about that Mrs. Hailstone," she began. "Ye know, I nivver thought he was interested in wimmin atall, tae she arrived."

Ned made some noncommittal noises, half-listening, more interested in his chocolate square than Gusty's love life.

"I think the best thing that could be done is for me to introduce Gusty to a more suitable woman, tae take his mind off that Mrs. Hailstone. And the one I think would be the right one for him is a far-out cousin of my Paddy's from down the country that goes by the name of Greta-Concepta Curley."

"Bit of a mouthful, that."

"Yes, she was a Greta-Concepta Curley tae her own name before she met Tommy Shortt."

Old Ned mulled over the unusual marriage of surnames. "Short and Curly! Like a haircut."

"Yes indeed. But that's neither here nor there. When I tell ye a bit about her background, ye'll see that her and Gusty would make a great match, haircut or not."

Ned settled into the bolster to commence his nodding dog routine. Mindful, nonetheless, that he must give his niece half an ear, lest she catch him out.

"Now, Tommy was a half-blind breadman from Buncrana. When I say breadman, Ned, I don't mean he baked the bread, not that any man would know how tae put a scone in the oven round these parts—or any part, if truth be told, my Paddy included. No, Tommy just driv' the van-a bread round the country."

"And how did he drive the van round the country if he couldn't see?"

"Oh, he kept running into people right enough, but never kilt nobody. And when people saw him coming they'd jump into the hedge, so tae get outta his way. The eyes had never been good. Clouded up with cattyracks they were. People said that it was a miracle that Greta-Concepta got any man tae take her, 'cos, well, tae put it this way, Ned, she'd be an occasion of sin for no man. But with Tommy not seeing much and her not looking like much, sure didn't it work out all right between the pair of them."

"God, doesn't the Lord move in wunderous ways?"

"Well, ye would think that, Ned, wouldn't ye? But y'know, this story doesn't have such a good end. It started with Sergeant Ranfurley having tae put Tommy off the road. 'Cos on this partickler day, didn't he knock the parish priest, Father Mehaffy, off his bike." Rose saw Ned's look of shock. "Oh, yes, knocked him clean off it, and him on his way tae expose the Blissed Sacrament at the evening devotions. Nobody knew a thing about it till wee Greta-Concepta went out for a walk with the dog, and didn't she find Father Mehaffy lying in the ditch with his feet up in the air."

"That musta been a shock for her!"

"Well, the light nearly left her eyes from all accounts. 'God, Father, what are ye doin' down there?' sez she. And Father Mehaffy sez, 'Your Tommy's only after knockin' me down, so he is.' And Greta-Concepta would-a had a heart attack had the heart been inclined that way. 'Cos ye know, if Tommy had-a kilt the priest it would-a been a terrible thing altogether."

"Terrible, right enough."

"Oh, terrible," Rose agreed. "Sure, you could be climbing Croak Patrick and hauling yourself round Lock Derg on pilgrimages with the blood running outta your bare knees from now tae the end of yer days, and ye still wouldn't make up for a sin like that. Anyway, wee Greta-Concepta helped the priest up and brought him back with her and give him a cup of tea, as a body would."

"And was Tommy still on Lock Derg?" asked Ned, concentration waning, eyelids beginning to droop.

"*What?* God, no. Tommy was nowhere near Lock Derg. He was out tootlin' about the yard. And when he came in, if he didn't walk right pass Father Mehaffy and out the back door, for that's how bad the eyes were."

"Didn't notice the Father?"

"No, didn't notice the Father. 'Did ye not see me out on the road there, Tommy?' sez the Father. 'For ye're only after knocking me off me bike, so ye are.' And Tommy sez, 'God, Father, was that you? I thought it was one of Mickey Boone's heifers that'd broke out, and I thought I'd give her a wee dunt tae get her back in the corner field.'"

"God! He thought the heifer was the Father?"

"Yes, indeed. Thought the heifer was the Father. Anyway, tae cut a long story short, Ned, Father Mehaffy tolt Sergeant Ranfurley, and the sergeant put Tommy off the road and tolt him he wouldn't get back on it again till he got himself a pair-a glasses up in Killoran from Mr. Millar. Ye know Mr. Mill—"

"That's a goodun," Ned cut in, throwing a lasso about Rose to haul her back to the point. "And diddy get the glasses, diddy?"

"Oh, he got the glasses, Ned—but here's the best of it. With the glasses he was able tae see wee Greta-Concepta proper for the first time, and it was only then he realized she wasn't as well-looking as he thought she was. So if he didn't run off with another woman down the country that used tae get two crusty baps and a jam sponge off him every Friday, and was neither seen nor heard of again."

"Boys-a-dear!"

"Oh, it took Greta-Concepta a while for tae get over it, Ned. And there was a time when the people thought she might-a had to go to the nervous hospital for tae get sorted out. But y'know, Father Mehaffy was terrible good to her. He blamed himself, ye see. For if he hadn't told Sergeant Ranfurley about Tommy knocking him off the bike, then Tommy wouldn't of got the glasses and wouldn't of seen how bad wee Greta-Concepta looked, and wouldn't of run off with that other woman that bought the crusty baps and jam sponge off him every Friday."

Ned nodded sagely, digesting this. "God, ye never know how things is gonna work out. And how is she now, Rose?"

"Oh, she's grand now. She had bother makin' hens meet in the beginning, but she had a wee bitta money put past in the credit union, and she moved tae Killoran and got herself a cooking job at the Kelly Arms." Rose took a long drink of thirst-quenching tea. "Now, wee Greta-Concepta mightn't be much to look at, but she's got hands for anything…a great wee worker. That's why I think she'd be ideal for our Gusty. Let's be honest, Ned, Gusty's not much tae look at, either."

A look of panic came into the old man's eyes. He thought of this strange women coming into his house, upsetting his routine. He had to speak his mind.

"I wouldn't want no stranger comin' in here, pullin' and haulin' at me in the bed, Rose."

"Now Greta's not like that, Ned," she assured him. "And a waddin' wouldn't be on the cards right away. What I'm proposing, Ned, is that I set up a meeting between the pair of them. Now, we wouldn't tell Gusty, of course. But what if you and me and him go for a wee day tae Killoran and we can call in at the Kelly Arms. That way, you'd get tae meet wee Greta-Concepta, too. What d'ye think?"

"S'ppose it wouldn't do any harm, Rose." Ned rubbed his chin, considering. "But I don't know about these oul' legs of mine."

"Now, I was just gonna say, Ned. Them legs need-a bitta exercise. Do ye no harm atall tae get outta the bed for a while. Will we say this Friday? That'll give ye enough time tae try out your legs, and give me time tae get a shirt washed and ironed for you and Gusty." Rose got up and lifted the tray. "Now, I'll just get us some more tea. We'll not say a word tae Gusty. I'll just say we're goin' intae Killoran to have a word with a friend of mine and it'll be a wee run out for the three of us."

"Good enough."

When Rose left the room, Ned stared out the window. He could see Rosehip Cottage from his bed. God, how things are changing, he thought to himself. Rose getting Gusty a woman because of another woman living in his sister's house, one he'd never even met.

What would Dora make of it all?

Suddenly he felt powerless, lying there in the big bed. Maybe Rose was right. It *was* time to get up.

It was time to take control of things, or before he knew it, Kilfeckin Manor might be taken from under his very nose, as he lay sleeping and oblivious to it all.

Chapter twenty-nine

Having spent an exhausting afternoon cleaning the parochial house, Bessie believed she'd earned a good slosh of whiskey in her afternoon cuppa, another slice of Rose McFadden's pilfered fruitcake, a cigarette, and Tammy Wynette's "D-I-V-O-R-C-E" on the asthmatic record player. She'd noticed it skipping and wheezing quite a bit since the move and wondered if Herkie's weight had done it harm.

"D, I, V-V-V-V…" Tammy stuttered.

Bessie sighed and went over to return the stylus to its groove. She settled herself on the settee, kicked off her shoes, and lit up. Aunt Dora's sunburst clock struck the hour of five. Herkie was still down at Kilfeckin Manor. She hoped he wouldn't delay too much longer. This being the evening of the big jackpot bingo, she intended to be first in the queue. But for now she'd relax.

Herkie was in no hurry to return home from his failed expedition to the Grant house. He was dreading his ma's reaction to his empty pockets. However, being a resourceful little chap, he'd already concocted an elaborate story for his ma by way of explanation.

Herkie was good at concocting plausible stories. It was a skill honed out of necessity: to keep the peace between his warring parents. Stories that often involved making excuses for his ma's absence to the father when he'd arrive home—roaring drunk in the back of a police car with his coat hanging off and shoes missing—demanding to know where that "whore of a mawer of yours" was. And Herkie's young brain would go into overdrive, rifling frantically through his memory file of plausible excuses as he stood, terrified, at the top of the stairs. By which time Bessie would already be out the back door and running down toward the garden shed in her nightdress.

"She's at Grandma's / Mabel McClarty's / Mrs. Ruff's down the street, Da...'cos...'cos she ran outta milk and...and...the shop was shut and Ma had tae bring her over some 'cos...she wanted till make cocoa."

"Makin' cocoa at this time-a the fuckin' night, son?"

"Aye, Da. I swear, Da!"

"I'll cocoa *her* when I get me fuckin' hands on her."

It was usually well into the early hours when the father would conduct these less than lucid exchanges with the son. Several minutes later, mercifully, he'd fall comatose on the settee. The monster asleep, the danger past, Herkie would scamper down to the garden shed to give his ma the all clear.

Now, as he dawdled up the back field, completed drawing under his arm, his little face puckered in consternation, Herkie was going over the story again, just to be sure he had it right.

When I was comin' in till the yard the ambulance came till the house and took the oul' boy out on a stretcher, 'cos he must-a been sick. His eyes were shut and his mouth was open and maybe he was dead. The woman with the big white shoes was crying and Veronica the pig was going mad. Gusty Grant came outta the house and locked the back door and put the pig in the pen. Then the woman with the big white shoes said: "You run on back tae your mother, Herkie, for there's no messages tae be run the day, for poor Ned'll maybe not last the night, the poor creature." Then Gusty and her got in the truck and went away.

He felt confident with the story, and with the oul' boy away in the hospital there would be no need for his ma to send him down to the big house again.

Not so eager to return home, Herkie decided to head for the fairy ring. Mr. Lorcan usually drew his pictures there in the afternoon, and he could show him the finished drawings.

Lorcan, seated on his tree stump, eyes closed under the warming breath of the sun, was relishing the peace and quiet in his favorite spot. He looked forward to these contemplative respites from the exertions—and, indeed, the people—of the day.

Sitting there in the woodland clearing among the sacred stones gave him entry to a sacred space, just as painting did. The stillness soothed the soul. What was it Picasso had said? "Art washes from the soul the dust of everyday life."

The scrunch of bracken underfoot broke in on his musings. An intruder approached. He tilted his hat—to see Herkie standing a few feet away.

"Ah, Mr. Herkie Halstone. I thought it might be you."

"Were you sleepin', Mr. Lorcan?"

Herkie had been observing him for a few minutes from behind a tree. The strange artist had been sitting there as still as one of the stones.

"Sleeping, Herkie? No, I shut my eyes in order to see. It's what we artists do."

"Huh?"

He removed his hat and swept an arm wide. "There is a pleasure in the pathless woods...There is society, where none intrudes."

"What?"

"Lord Byron. Don't mind me, Herkie. Come, sit." He patted the tree stump beside him and smiled. "I do believe I see a finished sketch under that arm."

Herkie sat down sheepishly and handed over the drawing. "The fur on the rat—I mean dormouse—was hard till do 'cos me sharp'ner was blunt."

Lorcan was studying the drawing. "Excellent work, Herkie! Excellent!" There was a large circular mark in the blue sky with yellow spokes emanating from it. "I like that Van Gogh sun. Why did you add it?"

"Nah, me ma set her tea down on it when I wasn't lookin', and so I made it into a sun."

"Very clever, that. Shows initiative. Not many artists could do that, you know."

He was glad to see the compliment lighting up Herkie's face. But not for long. Something was amiss.

"Would you like another sketch? Got plenty that need your master's touch."

The boy didn't answer. He bent down and rubbed the back of his leg. He'd taken six of the best on the backs of both legs for affronting his ma at confession.

"Did the nettles get you? Nasty things." On closer inspection, however, Lorcan saw that the welt marks were not stings. They'd been made by a rod. "How is your mother, by the way?"

"She's always mad at me. Said I wasn't to come here no more."

"Ah. Right."

There was a pause.

"Maybe you shouldn't then."

"She said you might be a Provo, or a prevert, or something."

"I think she meant *pervert*." He wasn't so surprised at Mrs. Halstone's poor opinion of him. He was guessing that her background predisposed her to be wary of all strangers, male strangers in particular. A thought occurred to him.

"Shouldn't you be in school, Herkie?"

"Me ma said it's all right. She sez I never larned much when I was in it anyway."

Lorcan was aghast.

"She sez I have to earn me keep and I can't do that in school. 'Cos Da didn't leave us a pot tae piss in. That's what she sez."

What a terrible burden to place on the poor child!

"She has a way with words, your mother, I'll give her that. But I don't thinks she means what she says. School is the best place for you to be right now, Herkie. You'll miss out on so much if you don't go."

He saw the boy chew over the words. He thought he might be getting through. Then: "Mr. Lorcan, what's a Peepin' Tom?"

Provos? Perverts? Peepin' Toms? What on earth was she filling the child's head with?

"Where did you pick up that name, Herkie?"

"Me ma sez there's one down in the big white house…and she sez he's a durty brute and she'll have tae buy nets for the windee."

Dear me, thought Lorcan. Well, it's hardly old Ned. That left Gusty. No great surprises there. Gusty would rarely come across the like of the glamorous Mrs. Halstone in the normal run of things.

"Well, a Peeping Tom is someone who looks through other people's windows when they shouldn't. But you mustn't be worrying about silly things like that, Herkie." He patted the boy's knee. "Great artists like you have more important things to think about. Isn't that right?"

Herkie smiled up at him, delighting in the praise.

"Tell you what. Here's another project for you. A more difficult one, mind, but I think you've proved yourself, Herkie."

Lorcan turned the pages of his sketchbook and found a drawing that would easily tax the painting capabilities of the great Henri

Rousseau. The beautiful pencil study of wildflowers had taken the best part of three hours: a mosaic of intricate clumps showing tufted vetch, cow parsley, marsh marigolds, and meadowsweet. He tore off the page.

"There you go. That should keep you busy for a while."

Herkie's face shone; he was marveling at the detail. Then he looked up at Lorcan, wonder losing ground to uncertainty. "What... what if I mess it up? Can't sharp me pencils no more."

"Nonsense. You're an expert now, Herkie." He reached into a pocket and produced a sharpener. "There. A gift for you."

"Th-thank you."

Knowing how much pressure the child was under to "earn his keep," he said, "Tell you what, Herkie, if you color that picture in really, really well, I'll give you a prize."

"What prize, Mr. Lorcan? Is it sweets?"

"Oh, no, far more important than sweets. Now, let's see. I'll have to put on my thinking cap and ask the fairies first. They're far wiser than I am."

Lorcan made a great show of pulling the hat over his eyes again, folding his arms and tilting his head skyward.

Herkie waited, watching closely.

After a couple of tense moments, he sighed deeply and removed the hat. He threw Herkie a suspicion-filled, sidelong glance. It did not bode well. Herkie's expectant face drooped and his shoulders slumped.

"What prize did the fairies say?"

"Well, it was very interesting. They said if you color the sketch well, you'll get third prize. That's fifty pence. If you color it in *very* well, you'll get second prize. That'll be a whole one pound."

Herkie's heart leaped at the thought of earning money for doing something he really enjoyed. He punched the air, unable to contain his excitement. "What's the first prize?"

"If it's brilliant," Lorcan continued, "and I mean really, really brilliant, you'll be in line for first prize of...drumroll...first prize of a whopping two pounds and fifty lovely pence!"

"Wheeee!" Herkie cried, jumping up and down. "I'm-gonna-get-first-prize. I'm-gonna-get-first-prize!"

"Well, you better go home and get started on it right away. The sooner you finish it, the sooner you'll have your prize money."

Needing no further encouragement, the boy shot off.

"Thanks, Mr. Lorcan!" he called over his shoulder. Then, halting, he turned back. "Oh, and Mr. Lorcan..."

"Yes?"

"Can ye say thanks till the fairies, too?"

Lorcan raised his hat. "They've heard you already, Herkie. They've heard you already."

Chapter thirty

So many showed up for Father Cassidy's big bingo event that in the end there weren't enough tickets and chairs, and people had to be turned away.

Lorcan sat behind a table in the lobby alongside sixteen-year-old Fergal O'Toole, a spindly, nervous boy whom Father Cassidy had drafted in at the last minute to assist him.

Judging from the moil of accents, the entire population of Ireland might have descended on Tailorstown. They'd come from all arts and parts, from up and down the country. Women mostly. Great gabbling, wagering hordes of them, flushed with the excitement of it all. Freed briefly from the drudgery of sink and stove, they were determined to make the most of it. They laughed. They joked. Their perfume sweetened the air and their fake jewelry glittered. They wore their Sunday best, clutched pencils and clipboards—the armory of the seasoned bingo player—ready to do battle.

In their wake trailed the husbands, reduced now to the role of mere drivers, cowed into silence by the sheer numbers of the female kind. Dotted throughout the swell of marrieds were other men, the plainly wifeless ones who, without the benefit of a hectoring spouse—"Clean yerself up a bit. Ye're not goin' out in that!"—or indeed a looking glass, appeared as though they'd garbed themselves up in the dark.

Many faces swam out of the past at Lorcan. Kindly faces lined by time and circumstance but still recognizable as the postmistress, the dinner lady, the school nurse from his childhood.

"Still paintin' the pitchers, are ye, Lorcan?" asked a little round woman worrying a purse out from the depths of a mighty alligator handbag—Lorcan had lost count of the number of times he'd been asked such a question—and immediately he was back in junior school, being handed a plate of boiled bacon and cabbage from the dimpled hand of Miss Alice Mulvany.

"Miss Mulvany…very good to see you," he said, accepting her fiver. "Oh, yes, still brandishing the brush for my sins."

"You were always great at the drawin' when ye were wee, so ye were." She dropped the purse into the jaws of the mighty bag and snapped it shut. "And isn't it grand ye've made a job of it in the city."

"God save us, Lorcan, ye made a great hand of the Virgin," cut in Rose McFadden. "Didn't he, Josie?"

"Oh, wonderful, Lorcan, so it was," Josie agreed. "Everybody's talkin' 'bout how well she looks."

Next up was Socrates O'Sullivan. "Gimme two-a them boys, will ye?" he said in the patois of the locale.

"They're the last two left, Mr. Strong," a voice broke in. It was Fergal. The boy had been so quiet that Lorcan, preoccupied with dealing with queries as to the state of his health, his mother, his job, et cetera, had forgotten he still sat next to him.

"Gosh! Are you sure?"

"Just as well I got here in time, so," said Socrates, smiling broadly while a line of expectant faces began to scowl and look askance.

"That's not fair, so it's not!" cried a woman whose bad perm and scalded cheeks hinted at many a suffering bout at the hairdressers. "Me and my Mickey came all the way from Muff, so we did."

Within seconds the relaxed jollity of the evening was on the turn.

"Aye, and *I* just walked three mile," a thickset man with an alkie nose protested. "Who's in charge here?"

All accusing eyes were on Lorcan. Not having factored in such a confrontation, he was at a loss. "Well, Father Cassidy's in charge. I don't suppose he expected such a big turnout." *Neither do I expect him to be able to conjure bingo cards out of thin air because you lot came late.* Wisely, he decided to keep that last thought to himself.

"Well, we're standin' our ground tae we get our cards," said the stick-wielding walker, his tiny eyes ablaze with a fundamentalist fervor.

"Aye, we're all standin' our ground," the sheep behind him bleated.

At that, the rear doors, which young Fergal had gone to shut, were pushed open again.

In breezed Bessie.

"Thank heavens I made it on time! Good evening, Mr. Strong."

"Hmmph!" the woman with the bad perm sniffed. "*Mister* Strong indeed! And you've wasted yer time, missus. There's no cards left, accordin' tae him!"

"I'm sorry, Mrs. Halstone," Lorcan said, trying to sound as genial as possible.

"But I'm the priest's housekeeper!" whinnied Bessie. "If anyone deserves a card, it's me."

"I know, but—"

"Aye, and why should that make you any better than the rest of us?" Bad Perm's cheeks were getting redder as she rounded on Bessie. There came murmurs of agreement from the assembly.

"I'm sure my employer, Father Cassidy—the man running this event—would beg to differ, madam." Bessie pouted.

Lorcan, sensing that something unpleasant might develop between the two ladies, moved quickly to quell matters.

"Look," he said. "I'll see if I can get Father Cassidy to come out here. Perhaps he can sort something out."

He opened the doors to the bingo hall. The place was packed, the noise level at an animated high. Father Cassidy was nowhere to be seen.

Suddenly, mercifully, a hush fell on the gathering. The reason? Fred McCrum, used-car salesman by day, emcee and resident bingo-caller by night, had clambered onto the stage. He tapped the microphone.

"Testin' one two, one two."

The mike squealed and shuddered.

"Evenin' tae yis all," said Fred. "Now, a few wee things tae mention afore we get started." He unfolded a piece of paper. "There's a blue Robin Riley, reg number en eye double-ye wan four-four five, blockin' the gate tae Scrunty Branny's back feel. Could the owner please move it, as Scrunty needs tae get his cows in for the milkin'."

Someone at the front approached the stage. Fred leaned over, unmooring his comb-over in an inelegant manner. There was a whispered exchange and an audible titter from those nearest the front. The emcee straightened up, red-faced. He returned to the microphone.

"Now, I've just been told that the blue Robin Riley belongs tae Deaf Mick. So cud somebody that knows deaf Mick go and get the keys aff him and move it, please? All eyes down for the first single line, a tenner."

Lorcan espied Father Cassidy stage left. He waved to him, but the priest's eyes were firmly fixed on Fred and the ball machine.

"Baker's bun…sixty-one. Young and keen…fifteen. Dirty Gertie, number thirty…"

"Check!" a voice shouted.

There was a ripple of dissent, and all heads turned to see Rose McFadden waving her bingo book in the air.

"Ye cudn't of checked," said Fred. "Ye have tae get the five numbers in a row, so ye have."

"Oh, God-blissus-and-savus!" cried Rose. "I thought it was the three, with the excitement of it. D'ye not get nothin' for the three?"

"Naw, ye get nothin' for the three, ye bloody eejit!" a man at the back called out. "Get on with it, Fred, or we'll be here all fuckin' night."

A round of applause had an embarrassed Rose sitting down again. Father Cassidy leaped onto the stage and grabbed the mike. Silence fell like a guillotine blade.

"That's enough! There'll be no bad language in this hall. Now, at the risk of repeating himself for a third time, Fred will run through the rules *again*."

He handed the mike back to Fred and got down off the stage.

Lorcan sighed.

"D'ye want me tae go and get Father Cassidy?" said young Fergal, joining him.

"If you wouldn't mind, Fergal."

Moments later the priest was making his way through a congested side aisle—a veritable Moses parting the Red Sea—to arrive, unruffled, in front of the disgruntled would-be bingo players.

Lorcan noted a distinct loosening in the air at the sight of the priest. The woman with the bad perm beamed broadly and nearly curtsied. Her husband removed his cap and crushed it apologetically between his big, hairy paws. The puce-nosed hiker dropped his pugnacious pose. He stood more erectly, in deference.

"Good evening, Father," said Bessie, simpering.

"Mrs. Halstone. Good evening." He smiled at the group, turning on the charm. "Now, what have we got here?"

"We've run out of cards, Father," Lorcan said pointedly. "And these people are none too happy."

"I do apologize. That, unfortunately, is the risk one runs when the stakes are high."

"I think at the very least *I* should get one," Bessie declared.

"Yes…well," Father Cassidy emitted a small sigh, waved a hand. "I do understand your disappointment, Mrs. Halstone, but one must be fair in this situation. These people came late, as did you, therefore all of you have missed out on this occasion. However, there is always next time. No one is saying the jackpot will be won tonight."

Bad Perm snickered.

Bessie breathed tersely through her nose. "Never mind," she said, not bothering with the "Father" honorific. She was seething at his total disregard for her position, but seizing the reins of propriety before Bad Perm could get there, said, "Gambling isn't really my thing anyway. See you tomorrow then."

She went out, not bothering to shut the door.

"We were just sayin' what a pity we didn't come earlier," Bad Perm said into the chilly pause.

"Aye, it's our own fault, Father," the husband agreed. "We'll know better the next time."

The rest of the group, unable to meet Father Cassidy's blessed gaze, shifted uneasily, surveyed the floor, and murmured assent.

"I *do* apologize," the priest said again. "Yes, well, you know what they say about the early bird. Better luck next time." He put a hand to his well-barbered hair and threw a glance back into the hall. "Now, if you'll excuse me, I really must get back."

The stragglers looked at one another and glowered at Lorcan before traipsing out, their dreams of being one thousand pounds richer wiped out for another month.

But the hiker hung back, eager to make a point, walking stick raised.

"If I come here next month and ye turn me away again, I'll shove this so far down yer throat ye'll be shittin' splinters for a week!" he warned.

Lorcan, drawing on his fine command of the English language, said nothing.

He shut the outer doors against further encroachment and closed his eyes in blessed relief. The only remaining task was to count the proceeds and deliver the money backstage.

Father Cassidy had provided a carpetbag for that purpose. A rather unusual bag, with a garish icon on the front. The image, Cassidy explained, was that of Our Lady of Guadalupe. He'd purchased the bag in Mexico. He'd been very specific regarding delivery of the proceeds.

"When you've got the money sorted," he'd said, "don't bring the bag through the hall. Too many strangers, a trifle risky." He'd handed him a key. "I think it would be safer all round if you used the side door to get backstage. It's usually locked, so you'll need that."

"Right, Fergal, let's get counting."

Lorcan pulled open the drawer. It contained a great deal of money. He heaped it onto the table.

Twenty minutes later, with more than £1,800 safely stowed in the carpetbag, Lorcan stepped outside and made his way round the side of the building. He was glad to be free of the stifling hall and stood for a while, eyes shut, savoring the fresh air and relative calm of the evening.

Suddenly, for no apparent reason, he got the feeling that he was being watched. He opened his eyes and looked about, but there was no one to be seen. From inside the hall came the monotonous calls of Fred McCrum and the low hubbub of voices. From the distant trees came the more pleasant-sounding calls of blackbirds.

He decided not to dally. It was safer all round to get the bag of money delivered into Cassidy's hands without delay, then return to the pub, Saturday evenings being rather busy. And this Saturday evening in particular. The bingo crowd would be filling the bars later on. From what his mother had said, the Beardy Boys were quite a draw.

He proceeded along the side of the building and, arriving by the stage door, fished the key from his pocket.

He went to insert it in the lock.

He didn't make it.

His hand froze.

He felt the touch of cold steel on his temple, heard labored breathing. Before he had time to react, a raspy voice—sandpaper on brick—close by his right ear said, "Just give us the bag and nobody'll get hurt."

"But I—I—" There were two of them, but Lorcan dared not look round.

"Are ye gonna argue with a gun, are ye?" The barrel was jammed against his temple, forcing his head against the door. He dropped the bag.

"That's more like it."

"Now, keep lookin' at that door," another voice commanded. A *woman's* voice. "Start countin' slowly to fifty and nathin' will happen ye."

Lorcan could not speak. The gun was now jammed against the back of his head.

"Start *fuckin' countin'!*" It was the man again.

"One...t-t-two, th-three...f-f-f-four—"

"That's more like it. If ye look round, ye're a dead man."

He heard something being dropped by his feet.

"A wee gift for ye, seein' ye've been a good boy."

All of a sudden, the thud of metal on bone.

The world reeling.

A stunning pain.

Father Cassidy pulling open the door.

Then, darkness.

Blessed darkness.

No more pain.

Chapter thirty-one

here...am...I? The words—weighty, cumbrous—took real effort to call forth. But he was able to voice them, if only in his head. A dervish was wheeling round and round in there, beating fiercely against his temples, hammering wildly on his skull. He could find no purchase in this alien world. What the blazes was happening?

"There wasn't much blood," a voice said, close to his right ear. "Just a bit of concussion. I've bandaged him up. He'll come round in a minute or two...be as right as rain."

"That's good to hear," another voice, a more familiar voice, said. "Must have been a terrible shock for the poor fellow."

Footsteps retreating.

A door closing.

Silence.

He opened his eyes. Tried to sit up. The blurry room looked familiar. He took in heavy furniture, brocade drapes, and portraits of dour clerics.

Dour clerics? He'd been here before. In this room. Slowly, fragments of the jigsaw were locking into place. Father Cassidy. Parochial house. This room. Father Cassidy...yes...sitting there

in the armchair. *"I wonder if you'd do me a favor."* Money...collect...
something about bingo...yes, bingo.

Something terrible must have happened.

The tightness in his head was fierce. He raised a hand to his
scalp and was startled to discover a bandage there. Then it came
back to him. He'd been struck on the head. Yes. He was remember-
ing now.

Voices...gun...Guadalupe...Guadalupe Virgin bag...money.
Falling down. Blacking out. He shut his eyes again. It seemed such
an effort to keep them open. There were voices in the hallway. He
kept his eyes shut. It seemed safer that way.

Father Cassidy, as calm as a toad in summer despite the shock, and
always thinking ahead, had decided to keep the mugging of Lorcan
to himself. Best not to cause too much alarm. He'd announced to
the gathering that a suspect package had been found by the stage
door, "most likely a hoax," and urged them to vacate the community hall in an orderly fashion. Yet his cautionary words had had
little effect. At the utterance of "suspect package" a stampede had
erupted akin to the bull run of Pamplona.

Now, back in the parochial house, having just seen out Dr.
Brewster and with Lorcan recovering in the living room, Cassidy
paced the hallway, awaiting the arrival of the constabulary. He eyed
the telephone, and it suddenly occurred to him that he needed to
alert Mrs. Strong.

A sudden rapping on the front door put paid to that. He
turned to see the ruby cheeks of Rose McFadden at the frosted
side panel.

That insufferable woman! What on earth is she *doing here?*

He pulled open the door.

"God, Father, was it a real bomb or one-a-them old hoaxes?"

"The police are investigating, Mrs. McFadden. That's all I know. Now, if you'll excuse me…"

"Och, I know, Father. Most of them bombs is hoaxes anyway. But what I was gonna say is that the very minute ye made the announcemint, if I didn't have the five numbers."

Rose waited for the priest to fill in the blanks, but all she got back was a steely glare and a terse "*And?*"

"Well, Father, and I shouted 'check' and 'yo-ho,' but nobody could hear me in the din, like."

"Really, Mrs. McFadden, this is neither the time nor the place. Now, *if* you don't mind."

"But Father, I won the twenty pounds!"

"Yes…yes, if you say so. I'll see about that later. Now, I'm awaiting the arrival of the police. So if you'd be kind enough to—"

"Right-ye-be. I'll call round the morra tae collect it. For ye know, the floribundas in the grotto are startin' tae droop and I thought I'd buy some fresh ones with the money, like. 'Cos—"

Mercifully, the phone rang at that moment, affording the priest the perfect exit. He shut the door on Rose.

It was Etta Strong, wondering what was detaining her son.

"I'm terribly sorry, Mrs. Strong. I was just about to call you. I'm afraid Lorcan's had a small mishap…"

There was an audible gasp at the other end of the line.

"Now, there's nothing at all to worry about. He's simply had a fall. The doctor's given him the all clear and he's recovering here at the parochial house." He did not want to frighten the elderly lady by mentioning the police. She'd find that out soon enough. "I'll drive him home myself in about half an hour."

No sooner had he replaced the receiver than he heard a car in the driveway. The Royal Ulster Constabulary had arrived.

Soon enough came the sound of two car doors being opened and banged shut, followed by the crunch of regulation boots on gravel.

Cassidy checked his appearance in the hat-stand mirror. Smoothed his hair, adjusted his collar, and called on the stoicism of St. Paul to sustain him. This was turning out to be a very stressful evening indeed.

He took a few steadying lungfuls of air before opening the door.

"Thank you for coming so soon, officers." He enunciated the words carefully and calmly. "It's very good of you."

The policemen removed their peaked green caps. "All part of the job, sir," said Sergeant Ranfurley, entering first.

He was a bulky man, his girth boosted by a duty belt. From it dangled an array of accoutrements for the apprehension of the wayward: handcuffs, a baton, a holstered Ruger Speed Six pistol, ammunition. His assistant, the much younger Constable Johnston, similarly attired, seemed puny by comparison. He shuffled self-consciously in his superior's wake.

"Has the bomb been—"

"Made safe?" the sergeant harrumphed. "A brick in a shopping bag, Father. It's called 'wasting police time.' But we're used to it, aren't we, Constable?"

"Yes sir."

There was a strained pause. "Etta Strong's lad, ye say? Where would he be now?"

"Yes, Lorcan Strong. He's in the living room. Allow me."

Lorcan was sitting upright and nursing a glass of water when the door opened. He recognized Ranfurley immediately. His mother had had a few run-ins with the sergeant regarding after-hours drinking. He was an overbearing man by all accounts. One who enjoyed exerting his power within the small nationalist community.

"Took a wee bit of a fall, Lorcan," he said now, leading the way into the room. "How's the mammy?"

"Fine, thank you, Sergeant." Lorcan did not care for the smirk that accompanied the word *mammy*. The constable, following behind, nodded briefly, his face stern.

Father Cassidy offered chairs. Constable Johnston sat down immediately, but a look from the sergeant had him springing to his feet again.

"Oh, I don't think it's a time to be sittin'," Ranfurley grunted. He clasped his hands behind his big back and began a tour of the room. "No, I don't think we should be sittin' atall, in the circumstances. Wouldn't be the first time you've had money stole, eh, Father?"

"That is correct. We had a break-in here last month."

"Are ye takin' notes there, Constable?"

Constable Johnston stood awkwardly, pen hovering over a notebook while Father Cassidy tracked Ranfurley's inspection of the room with bemusement.

"We're busy men," the sergeant continued, pausing by a bookcase to run a pudgy forefinger down the spine of *Fundamentals of Catholic Dogma*. "Very stretched we are, Father, given the times that's in it these days."

I doubt that, thought Lorcan, still dazed but alert. The RUC of Tailorstown was probably the most underworked unit in the region. The predominantly Catholic village was rarely bothered by the constabulary's attentions. Their duties amounting to little more than settling the occasional brawl outside O'Shea's of a Saturday night, alerting the absentminded Paddy McFadden that he'd forgotten to turn his headlights on, *again*, and steering a rather "refreshed" Jamie McCloone away from his tractor on Market Day, he having celebrated the sale of a heifer a trifle too extravagantly. Such was the extent of the district's lawbreaking—if one could call it that.

But all that could change, the artist thought ruefully. The startled face of his mother hove into his mind's eye. God, he needed to call her. His head began to throb again, and he pressed down firmly on the bandage. Perhaps he should not be too judgmental of Ranfurley and Johnston. They risked their lives every day simply by donning those dark green uniforms. That aside, he hoped they'd be quick.

"I fully appreciate that these are very difficult times, Sergeant," Father Cassidy was saying with a note of impatience. He had his sermon to prepare for early Mass. A bath to take. His altar shoes to polish. Valuable time was being squandered. He turned to Lorcan. "Perhaps you'd like to give the gentlemen some details. Your mother rang earlier and will be expecting you shortly."

"What did you tell her? I wouldn't want—"

The priest raised his hand in a gesture of appeasement. In the midst of his pain Lorcan saw *The Saviour of the World*, an El Greco masterpiece, bar the robes and globe. "Now, I assured her you were fine, Lorcan, and that I'd run you home within—"

"We'll ask the questions, Father," Ranfurley interjected. "If ye don't mind, that is." No Taig was going to tell *him* how to do his job—least of all one in a frock with a girl's hands and wearing women's shoes. *What sort of man wears suede slip-ons anyway?*

"Why, of course, Sergeant."

Constable Johnston hovered nervously, pen still cocked above the blank note page.

"Now." Ranfurley eyed Lorcan. "The Father says here that ye were mugged. Would that be right?"

"Yes, that's a fair assessment. I was walking round the side of the building with the bag of money and—"

"What kinda bag was it?"

"It was rather distinctive, in fact. A kind of carpetbag with an emblem of the Blessed Mother on it."

Ranfurley raised an eyebrow at the priest. "A funny sort of bag to put the spoils of gamblin' in, if ye don't mind me sayin' so, Father."

"It was the only one I could find big enough. The jackpot being rather substantial, I expected the takings to be equally so."

"Right." He turned his attention to Lorcan again. "And what color was this bag with the Blissed Mother on it?"

Father Cassidy gave a tactful cough. "May I just explain, that it wasn't *our* Blessed Mother—"

"Well, whose Blissed Mother was she, then?"

"Our Lady of Guadalupe. The Mexican one."

"Didn't know ye had different types. Thought there was just the one."

Cassidy did not care for the note of mockery. "There *is* just the one. But Our Lady has appeared in many places and in many guises across the globe."

"If ye say. So, this bag with the Lady of Guady-loopy-whatever—"

"Guadalu*pay*. It's a mountain in Mexico. The image is, as Lorcan says, quite distinctive."

"Guadalu*pay*...begging your pardon. Would ye have a pitcher of her?"

Father Cassidy crossed to the glass-fronted bookcase and scanned an upper shelf. "Yes, here we are: *The Life of Juan Diego*. He was the visionary whom she appeared to." He handed the book to the sergeant.

The depiction was of a crowned Virgin of dusky complexion clad in green-and-pink robes studded with golden stars. She was being held aloft by a banner-waving angel sporting red, white, and green wings, echoing the colors of the Mexican flag. From the figure there emanated an amber-tinged ethereal glow. Ranfurley studied the illustration. "Aye, unusual indeed. Wouldn't be too many of these around."

"No indeed," Father Cassidy said. "It was given to me by the Bishop of Monterrey when I had the good fortune to be invited to the Synod Conference on Latin-American Interfaith Relations in nineteen seven—"

"Aye…right, I'm gettin' the pitcher," said Ranfurley bluntly. "We'll need tae be holding on to this."

Father Cassidy removed the dust jacket and handed it to him.

"Now, Lorcan. What time would this of been that ye left the hall with the beg of money?"

"Hmm, let's see." Lorcan did a quick calculation. "It took us about fifteen, twenty minutes to count the money…so ten to eight."

"You said 'us.'"

"Fergal O'Toole and I."

"Are ye gettin' this, Constable?" Johnston was scribbling in the notebook. A seam of perspiration was forming on his upper lip. Lorcan reckoned the poor constable's uniform to be as stifling for him as his bullying boss. "Young Fergal is Molly's son. We'll be needin' his version of events, too."

"Yes sir."

"Yes, it would have been ten to," Lorcan said.

"Ten to what?"

"Why, eight, of course."

Over the sergeant's shoulder, Lorcan saw Father Cassidy roll his eyes heavenward.

"Ten to eight then. See anything unusual in the vicinity, did ye?"

"No…nothing really."

"And when ye got to the stage door, then what happened?"

"Well, that's when I was attacked. I was pushed into the door from behind. I felt the point of a gun in the back of my head. I was ordered to drop the bag and was struck from behind. That's all I remember."

"And there were two of them?"

"Yes. A man and—"

"What kinda accent did this man have?"

"Oh, just ordinary. Regional. A bit guttural."

"Gutter-what?"

"Deep. Throaty. The kind of voice that comes from drinking and smoking too much."

"Hmph!" said the sergeant, pondering an ornately gilded portrait of Pope John Paul II. "That would account for most men round these parts, wouldn't it, Constable?"

"Yes sir." Constable Johnston looked up from his notepad and seized the opportunity to wipe the sweat from his lip.

"And the other boy's accent, what was it like?"

"It wasn't male, Sergeant. It was a woman's voice."

"A *wommin*?"

"Yes."

Sergeant Ranfurley scoffed. "Dearie me! These Fenian vermin are really scrapin' the saucepan now, gettin' the missus tae share their durty work. And what kinda accent did this wommin have?"

"Belfast."

"Belfast. Are ye sure about that?"

"Most definitely."

"Not somebody from these parts, then?"

"Wouldn't think so, Sergeant."

Father Cassidy, still standing in front of his desk, shifted uneasily in his suede slip-ons. "Well, I'm bound to tell you, Sergeant, that that's not strictly true. You see, I recently employed a new housekeeper from Belfast, a Mrs. Elizabeth Halstone."

Lorcan bit his lip. He did not like the direction the interview was taking.

"Is that so?" said the sergeant, swaying back on his heels and sucking air through his dentures. "Elizabeth Halstone. I can't say I've heard of her."

"Well, you probably wouldn't. I engaged her a few weeks ago. Miss Beard, the usual housekeeper, is indisposed."

"Now that's interesting," said the sergeant.

He has a look in his eye, thought Lorcan; a look that's putting two and two together and coming up with ninety-nine. He felt moved to quell the suspicion immediately.

"It wasn't Mrs. Halstone." Immediately, three sets of eyes were on the artist. "Well, it wasn't her. I've spoken to her on two occasions. I know what she sounds like."

"Do ye now?"

"Yes."

"How well do you know this Mrs. Halstone, Father?" the sergeant asked, eyes still on Lorcan. "Her background. I imagine she came with references?"

"She did. And I have to say she gave me no reason to question her honesty and integrity."

"Does she live here with you?"

"Oh, no. She's renting the late Dora Grant's cottage."

"In that case, Johnston, we'll not waste any more time here." Ranfurley repositioned his peaked cap, and Johnston followed suit. "I'll be wantin' tae speak with you again," he said, throwing Lorcan an inculpatory look. "Ye haven't seen the last of us."

Lorcan did not doubt it for a moment.

Chapter thirty-two

The holding cell was an airless box with one tiny window latticed by iron bars. Bessie stood looking up at it now, wondering what had brought her to this sorry pass and idly speculating on why iron bars were needed on a window so tiny. Maybe if a leprechaun got arrested—a very strong one—he could wrestle his way through it. But she hadn't seen many of those little green men running about the locality.

She gazed down at the wooden bench that doubled as a bed and, even though her head was throbbing and her feet ached, resisted the urge to sit down. Sitting down would mean giving in to the smarmy bastard who'd arrested her. The cheek of him! Interrupting her bath of Yardley bubbles and tumbler of Erin Go Bragh single malt—an extra-large one at that. Compensation for having been refused entry to the bingo and missing out on a possible grand. What she couldn't have done with *that*.

She'd worked up an elaborate fantasy as she lay soaking, eyes closed against the steam, face caked in a mudpack mask. A thousand pounds could have taken her all the way to Amerikay. Sod having to earn it from Cassidy and Uncle Bert. No begging from Joan, either, come to that.

New York. The Waldorf Astoria. She'd read a feature on it once, in *Woman's Own*. A job there not only would make her pots of money but would improve her chances of netting some rich old codger just a breath away from Satan's junkyard. Then she really could do a Mrs. Lesley Lloyd-Peacock. Swan home in her finery, a mink stole draped casually over one shoulder, diamond choker agleam, stilettos as thin as crochet hooks. Oh, the sheer, sweet joy of it all!

She'd just been summoning forth the envious look on her sister's face when there came three thunderous knocks on the front door. Seconds later, a breathless Herkie announcing, "Two peelers at the door, Ma!"

At first she thought he was joking. But a gruff cough from downstairs disabused her of that notion. Several minutes later—irked by the intrusion and not a little disconcerted—she found herself confronting Oliver Hardy and his sidekick in her nightgown and slippers, with an air of phony confidence and a painted-on smile.

They wouldn't tell her anything until she produced identification. That's when reality kicked in. She remembered that Elizabeth Halstone was not the name on her passport and driver's license.

They waited while she went upstairs and feigned a search.

"I'm really sorry; I just can't find it now. Moving house…you know how it is."

"In that case, you'll need to get dressed and come down the station, Mrs. Hailstone," the fat officer said with a conceited smirk. "We have reason to believe ye might-a been party to a robbery this evenin'."

"That's ridiculous!"

"Even so, we'll need a full statement of your movements earlier on. And the only way that can be done is down the station. So, get yerself dressed. And you, too, sonny."

Now here she was in the bloody cell. They'd put Herkie in another room with a pile of tarnished building blocks and a can of Fanta. She worried how he was doing and hoped he hadn't pitched the blocks out the window from boredom. It would only give Fatso and his pal more ammunition to view her as a scarlet woman—and unfit mother.

Then it dawned on her. *Jesus, what if they search my handbag?* Her precious passport and driver's license—she kept the one inside the other—were in an inner pocket. Why hadn't she tossed them out in the bedroom before leaving? Why-o-why-o-why? God! What now? She fumbled in the bag. There was only one way out of it. She'd slip them into her girdle. As far as she could see there were no policewomen in the small station. That meant they wouldn't be able to do a body search.

She found the inner pocket and fumbled in it.

What!

The documents were not in the bag.

She paced the floor. *Think! Think!* The last time she'd seen the documents was the morning they left Belfast. She'd checked her handbag before the Dentist showed up, to make sure. They were definitely *in the bag.*

She'd taken only the one handbag. The roomiest one she owned. She pulled out the inner lining of the pocket. A year's accumulation of lint fluttered out onto the floor.

Her mind started churning a riot of frightful outcomes. What if she'd dropped them at the parochial house? If Father Cassidy were to find them, he'd see she'd been lying about her identity and shop her to the cops. Then he really would think she was guilty.

She tried not to panic. Decided to sit down after all. It was essential not to show these bastards how scared she was. An innocent person would not be scared. And she *was* innocent. She hadn't stolen the bloody bingo money.

The thought reassured her a bit. She needed another cigarette. She was about to light one when footsteps in the corridor and the jingle-jangle of keys changed her mind. Stan Laurel stood in the doorway.

"If you'd like to come this way, Mrs. Hal-Halstone. We need to interview you now."

He led her down a corridor and into a sparsely furnished room. Sergeant Ranfurley was already seated at the table, his pudgy fingers wrestling with the keys on a tape recorder. The room reeked of mildew and stale sweat.

"Would ye mind sittin' down, Mrs. Hailstone," the sergeant said, looking Bessie over as a chef would a juicy joint, carving knife at the ready.

Bessie remained standing, defiant.

"Now, the sooner ye sit down and cooperate, the sooner you and that wee boy of yours will get home tae your beds." She found his sinister, flat South-Derry accent unnerving. "Not unless ye'd prefer to spend the night in that wee cell ye've just come outta. Now, what's it tae be?"

Ranfurley nodded to Johnston. The constable dutifully pulled out a chair for the widow before taking up position by the door.

With a pained reluctance Bessie sat. The tape recorder was switched on.

"Saturday, May the nineteenth. Time..." Ranfurley shot a cuff to reveal a watch face the size of a frying pan. "Ten-o-five p.m. Sergeant Ranfurley and Constable Johnston. Suspect's name: Elizabeth Hailstone."

"*Hal*stone," Bessie corrected.

"Beggin' yer pardon. Suspect's name: Elizabeth Hal-stone. Now, Mrs. *H-a-a-l*-stone, what brings you tae these parts, and when exactly did ye arrive here?"

"Work! Three weeks ago."

"No work for ye in Belfast?"

"No."

"What sort of work d'ye do?"

"I'm a qualified cook." She had an unimpressive O-level pass in what was grandly referred to as Home Economics. Writing your name correctly at the top of the exam paper was usually enough to guarantee a pass. Still, her proud mother had framed it, since it was the only qualification ever gained in four generations of dunderhead Halstones.

"Place of work?"

Bessie faltered, about to say, "My Lovely Buns," but checked herself in time. "Just a bread shop," she said, "on the Antrim Road."

"Address?"

"Number forty-six," she lied.

"Are ye gettin' this, Constable?" Ranfurley turned his head in Johnston's direction. On seeing his assistant standing with hands by his sides and staring blankly, he let out a roar that made the filing cabinets rattle. "What the blazes are ye doin' there? Where's yer notebook, man?"

"But we're taping it, sarge."

A pause. The sergeant looked from Johnston to the purring recorder. He reddened. "So we are." He shifted his eyes to Bessie's bosom. "Good at the floury baps, are ye?"

"There's a lot more to cooking than baking baps, officer."

"If ye say so." Vexed. "Now: your last address."

Bessie hesitated.

"No point in givin' us a false one, Mrs. Halstone; we'll be runnin' a check. Givin' false information to the police is an offense under section four of the—"

"Ten Brookvale, Antrim Road," she said, giving a false one anyway.

"Husband's name?"

Bessie hesitated. There was a picture of the chief constable, Sir John Hermon, on the wall opposite.

"Jack Hyman." She had it out before realizing she should have used her own surname.

Ranfurley's Neanderthal brows puckered in surprise.

"My husband was killed in a car accident a month ago. Halstone is my maiden name."

That bit was true.

"I see." The sergeant sat back on his chair. It groaned alarmingly. He stuck his thumbs in his lapels, his fat neck ballooning toadlike above the tight-fitting collar. "Sorry to hear about the husband," he said, with all the sincerity of a politician on polling day, "but gettin' rid of his name so quick after the event would indicate to me that there was no love lost between the pair of ye."

"He was an alcoholic. I wanted to make a fresh start."

The sergeant released the thumbs from his lapels and sat forward. The chair let out a squeak of relief. His big hands thumped heavily on the table. "A fresh start!" His small eyes bulged with menace. He twisted the wedding ring on his left hand.

Bessie tried to imagine his wife; she'd be a nervous wreck and have mousy hair, and not speak unless spoken to.

"Now, what I'm wonderin' is why would a recently widowed wommin from the big city of Belfast leave her home—a home that's now free of the dhrink-sodden oul' boy and, for that very reason, a more peaceful place than ever before—leave her friends, assumin' that you've made a few in yer life so far, and relatives, not forgetting paid employment, to dhrive all the way to the wee village of Tailorstown, which, in a city wommin's eyes like yours, is in the back end of nowhere—"

Bessie thought of the unpaid bills, the overdue rent, the untaxed car. Of Packie's IRA connections, the robbery, and the psychopathic Dentist. She took a hankie from her bag and dabbed at her nose.

"—a place she's never visited before," Ranfurley continued, "and apply for a job with yer man the priest, and decide tae stay?"

"It's hardly a crime to want to start over."

"Aye, but maybe now it was a crime that made ye *want* till start over in the first place! A crime that ye're runnin' away from." A sneer tugged at the corners of his mouth. His scathing gaze held her fast. Bessie's fear mounted. But she knew her rights.

"I want a solicitor," she ventured, with an evenness that masked her panic. Her eyes were on his big, meaty fists. She saw them raised above his cowering wife.

Snap!

Ranfurley had hit the recorder button. Things were on the turn. The air crackled. He thrust back the chair and stood up.

"Now, you listen tae me, ye Taig trollop." His stance was menacing, hands splayed on the tabletop. "You'll not 'solicitor' *me*. Who d'ye think you're talkin' to? Eh?"

Bessie wanted to tell him exactly what she thought of him and make a run for it. Her eyes flicked to the door. Constable Johnston looked anxious. But she knew Ranfurley's game. He was trying to provoke her. Insulting a police officer was a punishable offense. One that no doubt would land her back in the slammer for the night. She had no intention of letting that happen. No intention of giving this bully the satisfaction.

"Eh? I'm waitin', ye lyin' trollop."

Bessie looked down at the table as rage and calm fought for mastery in her. Ranfurley was the Dentist in another guise. A dangerous bastard. She visualized Herkie, tired and bored in the waiting room, itching to go home.

"I'm waitin', bitch. Who d'ye think you're talkin' to?" His fist knocked the tape recorder to the floor. "And *look* at me when I'm bloody speakin' tae you."

She took a deep breath. "I'm talking to a member of the RUC."

"Sir!"

"Sir."

"That's more like it. You're all the same, you goddamned Taigs, gettin' above yerselves. Damned right: I'm an officer of the Royal Ulster Constabulary, and you better start showin' some respect or I'll have ye banged up. Solicitor, indeed." He kicked the tape recorder in Johnston's direction and the constable jumped. "So much for recordin' this whore's lies, eh, Johnston?"

"Y-y-yes sir."

Ranfurley sat down again and leaned chummily toward her.

"Now here's the thing, Mrs. Hyman, Halston, or whatever ye call yourself. Mr. Lorcan Strong was robbed this evening. He was carrying a bag with the takings from the bingo. A substantial sum of money, I might add. Some IRA bastard and his doxy mugged him. But here's the best bit. The doxy had a Belfast accent—just like yours. And he would know, a clever man like him. Said he's spoken with ye on two occasions."

He leaned back in the chair again, waiting for a response.

Bessie sat twisting a tissue in her lap, trying not to cry. She'd cried enough at the hands of lesser men: her father, the husband, the Dentist. Now Ranfurley was stepping up to join that ignoble company.

The silence in the room mocked her thoughts. In the corridor a door clanged shut. She thought again of Herkie, bored and helpless behind the door of the dayroom. A fat tear—a solitary, fat, faithless tear—began a traitorous journey down her cheek.

"Ye don't deny ye were speakin' to him on two occasions then?"

"No."

"Sounds like an admission of guilt tae me. I hear you went tae the bingo and were a bit miffed when ye couldn't get a ticket. Puttin' two and two together, it doesn't take a Sherlock Holmes tae figure out what you and yer fancy man did next—"

"I lost my husband a few weeks ago, sir."

"So ye did. But something tells me that it wouldn't take long for a doxy like you to get herself hitched again to some unfortunate scoundrel." He laughed, moving his big head from side to side like a tethered bull in a market stall.

"Now, 'cos I'm a reasonable man"—the chummy tone again—"I'm gonna let you go home now. And ye may thank that wee boy of yours. 'Cos it's him I'm thinking of. We'll be keepin' a very close eye on you. Ye haven't seen the last of us—oh, no, not by a long shot, missus. And if ye don't watch your step, I'll be alertin' Social Services. From where I'm sittin', that wee boy should be in school, would be better off in a foster home than livin' with the likes of you." She just about found the strength to walk from the room. The thought of losing Herkie was intolerable. No one had ever threatened her with that before. Not throughout all the years of heartache with Packie. Not even when he'd put her in hospital with two black eyes and a broken jaw. Tears welled up again.

"Are you all right?" The voice belonged to Constable Johnston. She made no reply.

"I'm sorry," the constable whispered, casting his eyes at the now-closed door of the interrogation room. "He scares me, too… sometimes. I'll get your son."

Herkie burst from a door farther along. He ran into her open arms. "Ma, Ma, can we go home now? I'm tired."

"Yes, son," she said, hugging him to her. She took his hand and fled the building.

The game was up.

It was time to get the hell out of Tailorstown.

Chapter thirty-three

From the many rooms in Kilfeckin Manor—the majority unused, furniture under dust sheets, windows tightly shut—Lucien-Percy's Turret Room was coming in for a great deal of attention these days.

Since he'd stumbled upon the lingerie trunk, Gusty's trips upstairs had become more and more frequent. The desire to spy on Mrs. Hailstone, while still a lure, was giving way to a new obsession: the urge to become the woman herself. He couldn't explain it—didn't think he wished to try and explain it. He knew only one thing: It was exciting, in so many different and wonderful ways.

To assuage any suspicions Ned might have regarding his lengthy dalliances up above, Gusty had invented a plausible story. He claimed to have discovered some dry rot in the ceiling beams. If left untreated, he said, it could spread to the rest of the house. Better see to it right away.

It had proved the perfect ruse. His uncle, grateful for once that Gusty was usefully employed doing important work on the house, did not nosy into his business as much, thus giving his nephew the freedom to come and go as he pleased. Also, the room's location, at the apex of four knee-testing flights of stairs, made it unlikely that

Rose—always a clear and present threat—would risk worsening her sciatica by climbing them to check up on him.

He'd also thought of another excellent way to thwart her. On her days in attendance, like the present one, he'd leave the truck at Grant Auto Repairs and take his bicycle instead. That way she'd have no idea that he was even in the house.

Late afternoon, two hours before his evening stint at the Crowing Cock, and Gusty was standing, sweating and gasping, before a gilded cheval mirror, trussed like a festive roast. It had taken him a good ten minutes of squishing and squashing to get the two-way stretch panty girdle on. A further ten minutes had gone into positioning the falsies—since finding the first pair, he'd uncovered two more sets of different shapes and sizes—under the strap-adjusting nightmare that was the conical cup bra. Jezsis! This wommin business was harder work than stripping a bloody engine.

Leaving that aside, however, he was well-pleased with the astonishing transformation the hosiery had wrought. He ran his hands over his curvaceous silhouette—hairy chest and extremities notwithstanding—and delighted in the sheer, tightening feel of the fabric that gripped him in all the right places. He pranced and capered in his reflected glory, turning and twisting to get the most fetching views of his rear and legs.

In a corner, gathering dust, lay a pile of discarded copies of *Reader's Digest* and *National Geographic.* His longtime hunger for arcane facts about life and the universe had of late been supplanted by urges of an entirely different order.

Veronica, installed on her usual couch, was not a concern. She was fully occupied with a pair of gold-mesh harem slippers, worrying the laces free and sinking her snout into the soft, silky linings for a quick snooze whenever the task grew tiresome. Occasionally she'd turn one piggy eye on her master and give a small, satisfied grunt, which Gusty interpreted as a sign of approval.

Pleased with his choice of underwear, he sashayed over to one of Lucien-Percy's satinwood closets.

There were three, and they took up most of the back wall. Each held a mesmerizing collection of day and evening apparel, which had hung there undisturbed since their owner's demise all those years before. One closet was stuffed with cocktail dresses and ball gowns; another held flirty casual wear, punctuated by a mink stole or two. The third was given over to shoes and handbags.

As well as all that, he had chanced upon an ebonized ottoman, which, to his joy, had revealed a variety of wigs—both blonde and brunette—three large jewelry boxes brimming with baubles, and several beaded pouches of cosmetics.

He began to rummage through the ball gowns, marveling at the extraordinary range of fabrics. He'd yet to put names to the textiles but in time would learn to distinguish his taffetas and chiffons from his crinolines and tulles. The styles were just as varied: strapless, backless, halter-necked, low-cut, high-cut, long, short, flapper, sheath, gathered, full-skirted, and plain.

A geranium-pink shift with a plunging neckline of Battenburg lace, gold lamé trim glinting at cuff and hem, caught his eye. He released it from the row of tightly packed garments and set it to one side.

Now: shoes. There was a bewildering array of calf-straining stilettos in metallic and suede. He reached for a fetching pair of peep-toe slingbacks in burnt orange with diamanté bows and gold spike heels. A shimmering rhinestone handbag completed the ensemble.

Time to dress.

So engrossed had Gusty been in his wardrobe that Rose's arrival had escaped his notice. This was all the more remarkable because

Rose, already an hour in the house, had been making quite a bit of noise. Not only had she washed the dishes and mopped the floors, but she'd also helped Ned to get up, got him dressed, and settled him into a lawn chair in the back garden.

The planned meet between Greta-Concepta and Gusty would be coming round soon, and it was important to Rose that Ned, her ally and support in the venture, should "get the legs out and about and workin' proper" before the great event. God forbid that he should be unsteady on his feet on such an important day. A day that Gusty had no idea was in the offing.

"Now, they say the whole lot was took, Uncle Ned," Rose said, filling her uncle in on the latest news regarding the theft of the bingo money. She was sitting beside him at a wrought-iron table with lion-paw legs, which had stood bogged in the soil of the back garden since Lord Kilfeckin's day. On the table sat a jug of lemon cordial, a plate of meringue nests, and a folded copy of *The Mid-Ulster Vindicator.* "And poor Lorcan, heavens above, nearly got shot."

"That's the worst I ever heard," said Ned. He sat with a herringbone rug over his knees, a frayed Panama hat shielding his eyes from the sun. "Just as well they didn't shoot Father Cassidy."

"Oh, they would never shoot a priest." Rose dipped her chin at the very utterance of such a sacrilege. "But between you and me, Uncle Ned, they say it was a wommin that did the robbin'. And not any wommin, either, but one with a Belfast accent." She threw a glance up at Rosehip Cottage. "Have you seen that Mrs. Hailstone yet through them spyglasses o' Gusty's?"

"Nah, he won't lend them to me...I don't see much of him anyway since he started tae work on the roof up above."

"Now, from what Josie tolt me, Mrs. Hailstone didn't get into the bingo on account of being late and not gettin' no ticket. So maybe she took it badly and grabbed the bag when she got the chance. Another wee nest, Ned?" Rose proffered the plate.

The old man selected a meringue and bit into it, flakes showering the herringbone rug. He took a swig of lemonade to help the confectionery on its way. When he considered Rose's theory regarding the bingo robbery, he saw more holes in it than the tea-leaf strainer on a plate in front of him.

"God, I don't think a wommin would do the like-a that, all the same," he said. "How could she knock a man clean out?"

"Well, in the ordinary run of things, Uncle Ned, I'd maybe be inclined tae agree with you. But ye know, when I see what she puts on tae go tae holy Mass, it's not a modest wommin in a sensible dhress I'm looking at, but a brazen hussy in a frock so tight it'd make a blind man blush...maybe even give him a seizure."

A grand mal seizure might have been in store for Rose had she seen what was going on just three floors above her head.

Gusty, fully attired now in the shift dress, big feet wedged into the frail slingbacks, was clopping about the room, admiring his stunning transformation. The girdle sucked him in, the bra pushed him out, creating an hourglass figure to rival that of a Hollywood siren. Rhinestone chandelier clips swung from his earlobes; an expandable timepiece gripped his wrist. And, to complete the look, an eight-strand pearl choker was doing its best to mask that unsightly Adam's apple.

It was hot in the room. He decided to throw caution to the wind and open a few windows before starting on the pièce de résistance: his face.

At the dressing table several cosmetic bags lay upended. A seduction of lipstick tubes, powder compacts, and makeup pots glittered and winked for his attention.

He couldn't wait to try them all out.

Installing himself on the bay stool, he turned his back on the piglet, removed his big glasses, and blindly set to work.

"What color was the dhress, Rose?" asked Ned, rheumy eyes suddenly agleam. He was trying to conjure up an image of the comely Mrs. Hailstone. Her name had rarely left the lips of his nephew and niece, and he was growing more curious by the day.

"What does it matter about the color?" Rose sniffed. She swept crumbs from her pristine apron. Poured more of the cordial into the frosty pause.

Ned rubbed his chin, conscious that he'd spoken out of turn, and tracked the progress of one of the Muscovy ducks as it waddled across the yard.

"It was the sort of article," Rose continued, "which a particular kind-a woman would wear tae bed, not in the church. And that's all you need tae know."

"Aye…What about that *Vindicator* there?"

Ned had heard enough about the Belfast woman for the time being and was becoming irritated by Rose's ramblings.

"Yes, Uncle Ned, I was just comin' to it." She drew a pair of spectacles from her apron pocket and picked up the newspaper. "I s'ppose it's the 'Round the County Roundup' you'll be wantin' tae hear first?"

Up in the Turret Room, Gusty was dipping his garage-stained fingers into a dainty pot of Helena Rubinstein rouge. Totally absorbed now in the application of his makeup, he'd forgotten all about Veronica. Didn't really care what she got up to, as long as she left him alone.

Unnoticed, the piglet had left the sofa and was snuffling about the room, intent on mischief. She discovered the set of falsies that her flustered master had let fall. They still lay in the corner where they'd come to rest.

She trailed them across to the window seat.

"Now, the weekly darts championship in O'Shea's pub last Sa'rday night," read Rose, "was won by Jamie McCloone. Jamie received a plague for his efforts from county councilor John Madden."

"That'll be a plack, I'd say," Ned grunted.

"God, but ye know, ye're right! Jamie received a *plack* for his efforts from John Madden," quoth Rose, newspaper held two inches from her nose. "I must get an eye test with Mr. Millar in Killoran one-a these days."

"What *about* Jamie, Rose?" Ned tilted the mouse-nibbled brim of his Panama. "Never see him about much. But then I wouldn't see much with these oul' legs of mine being the way they are."

"Well, them oul' legs is outta the bed now, Uncle Ned, and you'll be able tae see as much as you like. Oh, doin' the best is Jamie. He takes regular haul'days with his sister, Lydeea, down in Cork. She married Dr. O'Connor, don't ye know."

"That's a fair bit tae go on a tractor tae see somebody."

"Oh, no, he doesn't take the tractor. He gets the bus. I make him a packed lunch, some rock buns, and a jam tart for the journey. Would be too long a journey for a man tae go without a bun or biscuit inside him. Anyway, here's the best of it, Ned. If he didn't become an uncle last year, tae twins, no less."

"Ye don't say!"

"Yes, indeed. A wee boy and a wee girl: Becky and Colm. Jamie calls them Bec and Col for short. Did I mention them before, did I?"

This was the umpteenth time in the course of a year that Ned had heard about Jamie and the twins. But Ned's memory loss was Rose's gossip-mongering gain.

"Aye, maybe ye did, Rose."

She consulted the *Vindicator* once more. "Now where was I, afore I went down the side road with Bec and Col? Oh, yes: here we are. 'Madame Calinda will be reading fortunes at the Royal Neptune Hotel for one night only this coming Friday. A half-hour consolation with the famous physic will cost three pound and fippence.'"

"That'll be psychic," corrected Ned. "You'd wunder why she needs the fippence."

"Well, ye know, if she got ten customers and—"

Whump!

With a flash of pink rubber, a set of falsies struck the table.

Their speed and trajectory caused them to bounce three feet into the air. They landed in the grass—nipples up—close to where Ned was seated.

The old man leaned over, peering in astonishment. "Jezsis boys!" was all he could manage.

Rose got slowly to her feet. The blood had drained from her face. She beheld the strange object. A look of fright and disgust had taken hold of her features, making her eyes stand on end. She could have been Father Merrin of *The Exorcist* confronting the demoniac Regan for the first time.

"Oh, Jesus and the holy martyrs!"

"What kinda things are they, Rose, atall, atall?" Ned was easing himself out of his chair with the aid of his blackthorn stick. He tilted back the Panama hat and squinted to take a better look.

"Stay away from them, Uncle Ned!" She was frantic. "Them's durty things."

But Ned's curiosity was aroused, and there was no stopping him. He went to the fallen falsies and, with one deft motion, slipped the blackthorn stick under the band that joined the rubber hemispheres. He lifted them up out of the grass and swung the stick in Rose's direction.

"Oh, Lord-blissus-and-savus! Get them durty things away from me this minute, Uncle Ned!"

Rose was thinking on her feet. She snatched up the copy of the *Vindicator* with both hands, wrapped it hurriedly about the falsies, effectively relieving Ned of the burden. Her heart was pounding. She held the paper-wrapped bundle at arm's length, as though its contagion might infect her, and let it fall in the grass.

Where had the disgusting things come from? Had a bird dropped them? Unlikely. She looked up at the top story.

And spied Veronica.

The piglet's head was jutting out over the window ledge of the Turret Room. As Rose watched in dismay, the animal moved its head from side to side, ears flapping. Its piggy eyes were searching for something down below. Rose guessed what that something might be. She was appalled.

"*Gusty, are you up there?*" she roared.

There was no answer. Veronica stared down at her, blinking rapidly in the sunlight.

"Where is he?" She looked back at Ned.

To her disgust, the old man had lifted off the newspaper and was down on his knees. "I think it's one-a them brassy ears but with a—"

"Don't you dare touch them things!" She snatched up the rubber boobs and wrapped them more tightly in the *Vindicator*. "They're goin' on the hearth fire this very minute."

Up above, a window was banged shut.

"Whyn't ye say Gusty was up there?"

"I thought I tolt ye he was fixin' the roof."

Rose glanced down the yard. "Where's his truck then?"

Ned searched for the answer in the garden grass.

"I don't know what's goin' on in this house atall, atall!" She thrust the scandalous parcel under her arm. "But the Divil himself is in it. Father Cassidy will have tae come and bless the place. The people were right tae say this was a bad house. There's no religion about it. Brassy ears indeed!"

Mrs. McFadden turned on her heel and marched inside to incinerate the breasts and have it out with her errant cousin.

Chapter thirty-four

The piglet, ears flat, curly tail held high, bolted from the Turret Room and down the stairs, squealing like the Banshee of Beara at a Hallows' Eve moon.

"I wanna word with you, Gusty. And I want it now." Rose's voice rising up from the stairwell, words slicing the air like scimitar blades.

Ah, Jezsis!

He tore off the jewelry, peeled off the dress, threw the bra and falsies into the closet. No time to lose the girdle and finicky suspender belt. They'd have to stay put. The boots and baggy boiler suit would cover all.

He hauled them on.

"Gusty, do I have tae climb these stairs with me bad legs or what?" Rose's voice more shrill now, querulous, stabbing into his ears.

Christ! What if she *did* climb up?

He dashed to the door. "I'm comin' now!" he shouted, stalling her, buying precious time.

He scoped wildly about the room.

The cosmetics!

Open pots of rouge and tubes of lipstick littered the dressing table. He lunged toward it, tripping over the gout stool, wrenched open the top drawer, and swept the lot into it. As he slammed it shut, a tacky pantomime dame—rouged cheeks, croquet-hoop brows raised in painted surprise—stared back from the mirror.

Bloody hell! The makeup.

No soap or water in the room. He seized a fistful of brocade drape and used it to rub it off.

He dashed down the stairs.

"Now, Gusty, you come in here this minute." Rose stood in the mouth of the kitchen door, feet planted firmly, arms folded tightly across her chest. "I need a private word with you."

He followed her meekly. Slid into a chair by the scrub-washed table, adjusted his big spectacles, uncertainty holding sway. *Christ, what if she notices some of the makeup? Maybe the curtain didn't get it all off. How the blazes am I gonna explain that?*

The odor of burning rubber hung on the air. A spluttering and spitting from the coal-banked hearth told him that Lucien-Percy's funbags were being unceremoniously cremated.

No big deal. He had a couple of spare sets upstairs.

"Now, that pig o' yours just dropped a pair-a things on top of Ned and me. Things that only the Divil himself would have about him. You're up tae something up there, and it's got nothin' tae do with fixin' a roof, if truth be told."

Gusty, face burning, feeling as frantic as a ferret in a foot-locker, tried to remain calm. He gazed past her out the window to see a neighbor, Dan McCloskey, chopping wood in a far field. The *thuck, thuck* of his ax reached into the room. God, if he could just be out there, like him. He concentrated on Dan, bent like a birch branch over the labor, and tried to summon forth a plausible explanation.

"Well, it's like this," he began, "Veronica found them pair-a things up in—up in the roof space, and—and when I went tae grab them, begod if she didn't shoot past me intae…intae one-a the rooms, and—and threw them out the windee. They musta been lyin' up there from Kilfeckin's day 'cos I never seen them afore."

"I hope ye're tellin' me the truth, Gusty, 'cos if you're not, I'll have tae get Father Cassidy tae come and put the holy watter on ye here and say a Mass."

"No call for that, Rose. Swear tae God! I'll soon be finished up with the roof anyway." He saw Dan straighten, chuck the split wood onto a trailer, swing up into the tractor seat. Gusty placed his palms on the table. "Needa be gettin' ready for the Cock this evenin'. Time's goin' on, so it is."

"You just sit your ground there, Gusty." Rose was grim-faced. "I'm not finished with you, not by a long sock." The image of Mrs. Hailstone's briefs was flapping wildly in her head, like a flag atop a tyrant's palace. "That's not the only thing I have tae discuss with ye."

She rooted in her handbag. Since finding the unmentionables on the barn step, she'd carried them round with her, wrapped in brown paper for modesty's sake. Heaven forbid that Paddy should come across them.

She placed the package on the table.

"Now, don't ask me what they are. 'Cos I think ye know only too well what they are. It's a piece of that Mrs. Hailstone's underwear, if I'm any judge. I found them out there on the step the other day. And don't tell me that ye don't know how they got there, for they didn't get there without a pair of hands. And don't blame Veronica this time, for she doesn't have hands. Your Uncle Ned doesn't have the legs to climb up that hill to Dora's. Not that he'd ever feel inclined tae do such a thing, even if the legs were working proper. So that only leaves *you*, Gusty."

He twisted in the chair. The tight girdle was hot, the suspenders digging into flesh unaccustomed to feminine restraints.

"W-well, I can explain how that pair-a things got there, Rose." A small popping sound from the grate, a spew of sparks, and the last of the Jean Harlow contraption was roaring its way up the chimney. "I—I was clippin' the hedge round Dora's rosebush when I found them lyin' in the field. They must-a blowed off the hedge when she put out the washin', like."

"And whyn't ye put them back on the hedge then?"

"Well, I was gonna, only...only..." Gusty struggled, saw Dan McCloskey firing up his tractor, ripping out of the field. "Well, I was gonna, as I say...but then...but then the rain came on. Aye, the rain came on...and...and..." He stuck a finger in his ear and rotated it wildly, as if the action might trip the switch in his brain marked Ready Excuses. "And they would of got wet...aye, they would of got wet. Her car wasn't about, so I knew she wasn't in. So I put them in me pocket and I was gonna put them back on the hedge today. They must-a fell out of me pocket and I didn't see them, like."

Rose was shaking her head slowly. "This is a terrible business, Gusty. For if you started consortin' with the like of that Mrs. Hailstone, you'd be a laughin' stock."

"There's no fear of that, Rose. She wouldn't look at the like of me anyway."

"Well, ye better let it stay that way. Uncle Ned doesn't need no annoyance at his time of life."

Rose got up, satisfied she'd had her say. "Now, this comin' Thursday ye're takin' me and Ned tae Killoran. A friend of mine's got a new job at the Kelly Arms in the kitchen. Do Ned good tae get outta the house for a glass of stout."

"I'm in the Cock on Thursday afternoon," Gusty lied, factoring his latest diversion, the Turret Room, into his hamster-wheel routine.

"I'll have a wee word with Etta then. Lorcan can fill in for—"

"No, that's all right, Rose." It was best to agree with her and end his agony. "I'll take yis tae the Kelly Arms, no bother." He shot up quickly from the chair, his bum, paralyzed in the elasticized girdle, itching for relief.

"And as for that Mrs. Hailstone's underwear," Rose continued, "I'm gonna have tae give them back to her meself."

"Aye, I better go up and get meself ready," Gusty said, backing painfully out the door, sweat flying off him.

He gripped the banister—an iguanodon with the palsy—letting out oath-freighted sighs as he climbed.

Unbeknown to him, Rose had padded into the hallway and was tracking his progress. There was something funny about Gusty, and she was concerned. What was that black stuff under his eyes? Was he not sleeping? Or maybe it was the oil from the dryrot can. And them cheeks were far too red to be sunburned. Was it the blood pressure? And he couldn't sit still in the chair. Could it be the piles that were tormenting him and he was too embarrassed to say?

"Are you all right, Gusty?"

Startled, he turned.

"Naw...aye." Then, in a flash, the perfect excuse: "It's that oul' bicycle of mine. I'm not used tae her yet."

Chapter thirty-five

Bessie hung up the phone, having informed Father Cassidy that she wouldn't be in until late afternoon. She couldn't face him. Not yet, anyway. The risks were too great. It's just a headache, she'd told him, and assured him she'd be fine. He'd been most sympathetic. "Take the whole day, Elizabeth," he'd said. "I'll manage." Naturally she hadn't mentioned the real reason—the aftereffects of having spent most of the previous night at the police station. He'd find out about that soon enough.

She'd sent Herkie to the shop on the pretext of buying milk. She needed to be on her own, to think things through.

She crossed to the record player. A bit of music might soothe her nerves. She unsheathed Tammy Wynette's *20 Greatest Hits* and lowered the stylus onto the vinyl. In moments the crackling static was giving way to one of the country star's plaintive laments.

In the kitchen she tried to calm herself by making tea. The familiar ritual might clear her head, because she had to think—and think fast. The unexpected spiral of events had wrong-footed her completely.

When she and Herkie got home from the station, she'd turned the house upside down, looking for the passport and license. In the early hours she'd scoured the car, too. Nothing. The only place left was the parochial house. She'd have to go there when Father Cassidy was out of the way and do a thorough search. At three in the afternoon on Fridays he did his visits to the sick. That took him a couple of hours.

She loaded a misshapen raffia tray with the tea things. The tray had sentimental value, having belonged to her mother. Poor, long-suffering Hilda. She'd tried her best, had battled through against the odds, but her heart had given out in the end.

Strains of "I Don't Wanna Play House" were drifting in from the living room. Bessie felt tears well up at the poignancy of the lyrics and the thought of her poor mother. She'd cooked and cleaned for most of her life. The raffia tray, which she'd made herself, held the promise that perhaps, given half a chance, she could have put more of herself out into the world.

She carried the tray through to the living room and sat down. I need a whiskey, she thought, pouring the tea. In the past, Dr. Montgomery had given her sedatives to get her through the rough patches. But there was no Dr. Montgomery now. There was no support whatsoever now. All the props had been kicked away with Packie's death and her decision to do a runner.

She could phone Mabel McClarty at the bakery, of course; Mabel was also "bad with her nerves" at times and would maybe have a tranquilizer or two. But the thought brought another set of problems into play. Mabel didn't drive, and there was no way Bessie could visit her. The raging face of the Dentist flashed before her. No, Belfast was no longer home. It was a bitter memory. A wound that had yet to heal.

The past held no solutions. Deep down she knew that. Going there only threw up the usual snarl of misery and regret. As for the present, well, who in this village could she turn to? The only woman she'd spoken to at length was Mrs. McFadden, and Bessie

had ended up insulting her when she'd come a-calling to the parochial house with the fruit loaf.

She'd virtually no female friends. In truth, there wasn't much
for other women to like in Bessie. Her looks made her a threat on
sight. She knew that. Gusty Grant? Not the brightest bulb in the
chandelier. How could she trust him? Besides, the price would be
having to sit through a drink or a meal with him. The very idea was
too unattractive to contemplate.

The only option left was to pack up the car right there and
then and get the hell out. But without a driver's license or passport, and only sixty pounds—the amount she'd managed to save
to date—she would not get far.

She drew deeply on the cigarette as her gaze roamed the
room. Out of necessity she'd not been able to take many of her
own things from Valencia Terrace. The only bit of furniture, if
you could call it that, was the record player. Dead Dora's abun-
dance of dusty old effects reminded her of her own lack. She
couldn't decide which state was the more desirable: too many pos-
sessions or too few.

The song ended.

A hissing pause.

Then a melody she didn't much care for: "Run, Woman, Run."
Apprehension gripped her. The song title was urging her to action.
She drained the teacup, crushed out the cigarette. Went to the
record player and silenced Tammy. The cops knew where she lived.
They could come and arrest her at any—

A gentle knock on the door slammed a brake on that thought.
She stiffened. They're here, *now*. Oh, dear God! She should have
got up early and simply left. Why hadn't she done that? *Why?*

She moved cautiously into the hallway and put a hand on the
banister. She'd slip back upstairs and lock herself in the bedroom.

"Mrs. Halstone? Are you in? It's Lorcan, Lorcan Strong."

She sighed with relief, but it was with anger that she pulled open the door. Was it not Lorcan Strong who'd identified the woman's Belfast accent to the police, effectively putting *her* in the frame?

"What the hell are you doing here? How dare you come here!"

"Excuse me?" A shocked Lorcan held up Herkie's Snoopy watch. "I found this...and just thought I'd—"

"Oh, you just thought, did you? Well, I've just spent the best part of the night in a prison cell because of you and your bloody thoughts."

Lorcan stared. He saw that she'd been weeping. Her face was without makeup, the blonde hair awry. It was as though she'd aged by several years overnight.

"May I come in? I need to know what I'm being accused of. I'm sure there's been a mistake, unless it's your form to go around accusing innocent people without hearing their side of things."

Bessie faltered. He had a point. And it was clear that he wouldn't be going anywhere until he got answers. Hard on the heels of this thought came the notion that it might be best not to make an enemy of this man. Since her arrival in Tailorstown, he was the only person who'd genuinely tried to befriend her and the boy. All at once she felt uncomfortable and regretted her rudeness. Her hand relaxed on the door handle. She stood back to let him in.

"I've just made tea. Would you like some?"

"Yes...please. Thank you."

She fetched a cup and saucer.

Lorcan sat down in one of the armchairs. He removed his hat and laid the Snoopy watch carefully on the coffee table. He noticed her hands trembling with the teapot, the spout joggling on the cup rim. He thought of Ranfurley, knew something of what she must have endured at the police station. To spare her further unease, and to break the pained silence, he looked away from her, his eyes taking in the cluttered room, and asked, "You like it here?"

She made no reply.

"I have an idea what Sergeant Ranfurley told you," he ventured, taking the cup and saucer from her. "Did he claim that I'd said the woman who robbed me had an accent like yours?"

"Too right he did."

"Well, let me assure you that I said nothing of the sort. He inferred that himself."

"It doesn't matter." She could not meet his eye. Wanted desperately to light another cigarette but knew her unsteady hands would betray her nervousness. Her disheveled appearance was making her feel vulnerable. No makeup. Nothing to hide behind. *Why on earth did I let him in?*

"I believe you," she said, "but the truth isn't important to the RUC in times like these, is it?" Her eyes were on her mother's misshapen serving tray. "They see a woman on her own with a child, and…" She trailed off, not knowing what she was saying. Part of her wanted him to leave, but another part was saying *Trust this man; he's on your side.*

Lorcan took a sip of tea. It was too strong. Builder's tea. The kind his father used to favor. He put the cup down gently on the saucer. "And?"

"And…and…a woman on her own…well, she's an easy target, isn't she?"

She fumbled a cigarette from the pack. It dropped onto the coffee table. Lorcan retrieved it and handed it to her. His fingers brushed hers. Embarrassment flared in him as he struck a match.

"Here, let me," he said.

"Thanks."

There was another awkward pause. "Sorry, I forgot to offer you one."

"No, it's all right. I don't smoke. Tried a few times but… hmm…" He noted her hands, the fingers flat, square-tipped. The skin abraded. Dishpan hands. "Where did you go when you left the bingo hall?"

"Why are you asking me *that*?" The words plucked from the air, harsh and defensive.

"Sorry, I—I only ask because if someone saw you, they could provide an alibi or something."

"I walked back here. I didn't talk to anyone. I didn't see anyone."

"Look, I'm only trying to help." He was studying her face in profile. The nose was definitely Modigliani. The clean jawline just a hint of Kauffman. Mixed media on paper probably more flattering than paint. There was little color to work with, though. "It can't be easy, losing your husband and having to—"

"No, it wasn't—isn't." She didn't like where the conversation was heading. "You shouldn't believe all Herkie tells you. He's just a boy."

"But your husband is—"

"Dead, yes. That bit's true."

"I'm sorry."

"Don't be. It wasn't a happy marriage, if you must know. I doubt if many of them are. People pretend. *Women* pretend."

Lorcan was lost for words. He watched her stub out the cigarette with a studied diligence. She might have been stubbing out the memory of the husband. The cuff of her blue sweater was frayed. The beige skirt had seen better days. A section of hem had come loose and been crudely sewn with black thread. The poise he'd observed in the church grounds was gone. She sat there staring blankly at the tea things. There was a great deal of repressed emotion packed into that look. He thought of what Herkie had told him about his father. "*He was always hittin' me, and me ma, too.*"

A great wave of pity swept over him.

"You're young...you can marry again." He let loose the words, then quickly wished he could take them back.

"Why in God's name would I want to?"

It was best to change the subject. "Do you...do you miss Belfast?"

"No."

"Can't say I miss it, either."

A car passed by on its way into town. They heard the note of its engine change as it rounded the bend. Lorcan thought of other lives being led; Bessie thought of escape.

"Can I trust you?" she blurted out, taking him by surprise.

"Trust me? Well...well, of course you can."

"How can I if I don't know you?"

"Well, the only way you'll find out *is* by trusting me. That's the paradox."

She did not know what the big word meant.

"I can't," she began. "I can't..." She looked away from him, unable to meet his eye. "It's just that...I've lost my passport and my driving license."

"That's easily remedied. Just put in applications for new ones. You can pick up the forms at the post office."

Bessie didn't know how to phrase what she wished to say next. Instead she broke down and began to sob.

Lorcan, discomforted, drew a silk handkerchief from his breast pocket and reached it across to her. "Here," he said gently.

She took it and dabbed her tears.

"Look, Mrs. Halstone, I promise you that whatever you have to say will remain with me. Things are never as bad as they seem if you talk them over."

She looked up at him. He smiled at her reassuringly.

"I want to help you and Herkie. Now what's the matter?"

"I'm...I'm not who I say I am...I mean my name isn't really Elizabeth Halstone. My name's Bessie Lawless and I'm...I'm on the run from the IRA. They think...they think I've got money my husband stole."

Lorcan was gobsmacked. *Lawless.* The name had opened a door in his memory.

Suddenly he was back in Nansen Street, a witless man's screams in his ears, the Dentist head-butting a door with rage. *"Now Lawless's whore of a wife has took off with my money. But, d'ye see, when I get me hands on her, I'll..."*

"Go on," he said carefully.

"He—Packie—he did a bank job for them and hid the money in our old house...in Belfast. Then...then he was killed in a car accident before...before he could tell them where he'd stashed it... They were comin', ye see, to the house to get it and I had to run for my life with Herkie."

Lorcan nodded, hoping she wouldn't sense his own alarm. "And the money? Do you...do you know what became of it?"

"No. I looked everywhere in the house 'cos I wanted them to have it. When I couldn't find it, I had to leave, 'cos I knew they wouldn't believe me and I...and I couldn't take..." She reached for the teacup. The tea was stone cold, but she gulped some anyway.

"You couldn't take...?"

"Another visit from *him.*" In her imagination she felt again the rough hands about her throat. Gusts of whiskey-breath on her averted face. *"I'm givin' ye two days tae mourn yer useless husband, 'cos I'm considerate like that. Then I'll be back for my money."*

"Him?"

"The enforcer, Fionntann Blennerhassett. Or the Dentist, as he's called."

"Ma...I'm back," came a voice from outside.

"Herkie!" Bessie sat up quickly and dried her eyes.

"Well, if it isn't the artist himself," said Lorcan, already on his feet.

"Mr. Lorcan!"

"Look what I found." Lorcan held up the watch.

Herkie's face lit up. He made a grab for it. "Gee, me watch."

"No, no. What do you say to Mr. Strong, son?"

"Sorry. Thank you, Mr. Strong."

Lorcan took the boy's wrist and fastened the watch in place. "There you go!"

"I'm nearly finished the drawin', Mr. Lorcan."

"Excellent, Herkie. The fairies are waiting with the prize money."

Bessie managed a smile. "I don't know what any of this men's talk is about."

"Well, I'd best be off." He ruffled Herkie's curls. "You take care of your mum, you hear?"

"Aye—I mean yes, Mr. Lorcan. Ma, can I watch the TV?"

"Go on then."

On the doorstep Lorcan turned to her. "I want to help you, you and Herkie. Don't worry about Ranfurley. They have more important things to deal with these days. Your passport would be the least of his worries."

"I *have* to find it. The only place I haven't looked is the parochial house."

"There you are."

"But…but what if Father Cassidy finds it? He'll know I'm not who I say I am and…oh, God!" Bessie clasped her face in her hands, the tears welling up again. "They'll lock me up and take Herkie away."

Laughter from a sitcom filtered through the door, as if mocking her. Lorcan quietly pulled the door to.

"Look, that's not going to happen. Go to the parochial house and check. Father Cassidy wouldn't do that. He's a priest, after all."

Bessie grasped his arm. "Will you take care of Herkie if anything happens to me? Please…please, Mr. Strong. I—I need to know. There's nobody else I can…"

Lorcan felt her grip tighten. He looked into her desperate, frightened eyes, astonished at the earnestness of her pleading.

"Of course I will," he reassured her, "but that's *not* going to happen." He reached into an inside pocket and took out a card. "My number at the pub. Just ring me."

Bessie withdrew her hand from his arm, suddenly self-conscious. She studied the card. "Thank you, Mr. Strong."

"Lorcan."

"Lorcan." She looked up at him. "I'm sorry…sorry for…but I don't know anyone round here. I—"

"It's all right. Thank you for the tea, Elizabeth—I mean Bessie."

She stood, not looking at him, her hand covering her mouth.

"Call me later on," he said. "I'll be at the pub all evening. Let me know if you find the passport. We'll figure something out, all right?"

He was glad to see her smile as he turned to go.

Chapter thirty-six

Having left Rosehip Cottage, Lorcan strode along the road leading back to Tailorstown, deep in thought. Nature's beauty might have been unfurling around him, rogue clouds playing catch-up with the sun, but the artist in him, normally alert to these subtle shifts, was off duty on this occasion.

Elizabeth Halstone—or, rather, Bessie Lawless—and their recent conversation were laying siege to his thoughts. A problem shared might indeed be a problem halved in the normal run of things, but not in this instance it wasn't. Blennerhassett was no problem halved. He was a curse, a pestilence that blighted the lives of those who had the misfortune to stray into his path. How could Lorcan confide to Bessie that he, too, was a victim, that his fears were just as visceral as hers? Why burden her? She was suffering enough. Had enough to carry on her own.

In his mind's eye he saw her sitting in the drab cottage, frail and alone, kneading the handkerchief. He thought of little Herkie, naive and blameless, with his catapult and coloring pencils; a boy already damaged, but young enough not to be beyond salvation, and deserving of a better future than the one welling viciously out of the mother's past. What would become of him if the mother were to meet with a mishap? He had to do something to help them.

To help the mother. For, deep down, he sensed there was another Bessie, a caring, lovable one that had never received the nurturing. He reflected now that perhaps, with the right attention and sufficient time on a sun-facing slope, maybe—just maybe—she could blossom.

On the edge of town he stood into the hedge. The itinerant Barkin' Bob was approaching, his junk cart bouncing precariously over the stones.

Bob, a regular on the road since Lorcan's school days, had served in the Irish Army. A rejected man. Spurned, looked down upon by his fellow countrymen because he'd switched uniforms to fight for the British against Hitler in World War II.

Lorcan reflected on the courage such an act must have demanded—to fight the evil of fascism for the greater good. Bob had taken part in the D-Day landings. Had helped liberate the German death camp at Bergen-Belsen.

Man and beast trundled past, Bob acknowledging Lorcan's gesture by giving his own tattered greeting.

The horrors he'd witnessed and the brutal treatment he'd faced on his return home—dismissed from the army and stripped of everything—had left him a broken man. Out of desperation he'd sought and found Jesus. Now he traveled the roads, spreading the word and selling his wares.

Lorcan was still thinking of Bob as he entered the town and made his way along the High Street. Must be amazing to live so freely with no ties whatsoever. The lines of a poem by W. B. Yeats came to him:

An aged man is but a paltry thing,
A tattered coat upon a stick, unless
Soul clap its hands and sing, and louder sing
For every tatter in its mortal dress.

The poet could have been describing Bob.

He'd planned on using the bar entrance, to see what Gusty might be up to, but changed his mind.

In the hallway he slid his umbrella into the brass bucket by the hallstand mirror and hung up his hat. He sniffed the air. Cigar smoke. Odd. Not unless Gusty Grant had started to smoke the vile things.

He overheard voices in the living room. His mother had a visitor. She sounded quite animated.

He listened. It was a man's voice. Dread seized him as he laid a hand on the doorknob. He knew that voice. He *knew* before he opened the door on the terrible tableau.

There, seated on the sofa—cup and saucer in hand, pinkie extended, a plump cigar burning in an ashtray—was the Dentist.

"Lorcan, there you are at last," his mother said. "You never told me about your friend Mr. Blennerhassett."

The Dentist winked at Lorcan. "Just passing through, Lorcan, as I was tellin' your lovely mammy here. Thought I'd drop in and see how you were gettin' on with that wee commission ye're doing for me."

Lorcan's voice splintered. "R-r-right."

"You never mentioned you were doing a painting for Mr. Blennerhassett, dear. I was telling him about that awful business with the bingo money—"

"Terrible business altogether," the Dentist said, nodding his bald pate in mock concern. "And how are ye now, Lorcan? Is the head still sore?"

"I'm fine." Lorcan's shock was morphing into anger. He backed out of the room. "The picture's upstairs if you want to see it. I'll be with you shortly, Mother."

The artist waited until they'd mounted the stairs and he'd shut the studio door.

"What in God's name do you think you're playing at?"

"Oooh, very nice," the Dentist cooed, going immediately to the portrait of the Countess on the easel. "Ye're nearly finished, if I'm any judge. But you're the expert, so ye are."

"You haven't answered my question."

The Dentist swung round and caught Lorcan's cravat, twisting viciously as he shoved him up against the wall.

"Is that a good enough answer for yeh? Now, I don't like yer attitude one wee bit, me boy. Nothing like yer lovely mammy down there. A real lady."

Lorcan stared into the murderous eyes, courage deserting him.

"Fine wee place ye've got here. Pity if it all went up in smoke with yer mammy inside. But sure wouldn't ye get it back on the insurance...the price of this place, I mean. It's not all bad news. See that Mervyn Campbell's clothes shop in Carngorm? We gave him a fifteen-minute warning. We're considerate like that. Time for him and the missus tae get out. That's 'cos Mervyn always give us what we wanted. No backchat. No questions ast. But see *you*, that disrespect ye've just showed—tut-tut-tut. I might now be inclined tae give no warnin' atall. Be a pity, wouldn't it? For no way could ye claim back that nice mammy of yours on the insurance. 'Cos she's priceless, if ye get me drift. Isn't that right?"

Lorcan was gasping for air. Blood pounded in his eardrums. The room was beginning to spin.

"*Answer me.*"

"N-no, I—I wouldn't—w-w-want that," he spluttered. "I'm sorry, really sorry. I—I didn't know what I was saying."

The Dentist eased his grip.

"That's better. Now, ye have a week from today tae finish that pitcher. If it's not ready when I come callin' again, you'll be sorry. Is that understood?" He shot his cuffs and smoothed down the outsize jacket of his chalk-stripe suit. "Need tae be on me way. I'll say cheerio tae yer mammy on the way out. Thank her for the brew and the nice wee fruit scone." At the door he turned. "Aren't you the lucky boy now, with a mammy like that."

He opened the door.

Lorcan, still struggling to get his breath back, was fighting the urge to pick up the nearest chair and break it over the monster's back.

He fought the urge—and won. The Dentist left, shutting the door softly behind him.

From downstairs came the sound of his mother's voice. He stumbled across to the door, opening it a crack to listen.

"Well, were you pleased with Lorcan's work, Mr. Blennerhassett?"

"As pleased as punch, Mrs. Strong, but he's got a wee bit more tae do."

"He's a perfectionist, you know. He gets that from me, I'm afraid."

"Never a bad quality in an artist, Mrs. Strong. That's why I chose him. Well, I'll be off. Thank you for the tea. You make a lovely wee fruit scone, if I may say so."

"Why, thank you, Mr. Blennerhassett! Hopefully we'll meet again."

"We certainly will, Mrs. Strong. We certainly will. Good day to ye now."

Lorcan heard the front door close.

"Lorcan!" Etta called up the stairs. "There's still some tea in the pot. Would you like some?"

"Yes, I'll be down in a minute."

He went immediately to his bedroom at the front of the house and peered through the curtains. Blennerhassett was getting into a green Ford Cortina, not his usual Austin Princess. He watched as he swung the car onto the main thoroughfare. Would he take the

Killoran road heading back to Belfast or the road to Carngorm? The Carngorm road would take him past Bessie's cottage. What if he spotted her little car? It was distinctive enough, and it would be parked out front. Worse still, what if he saw her and Herkie out walking? The consequences were too horrific to contemplate.

"Lorcan, what are you doing up there?" His mother was in the hallway again.

"Coming...just changing my shoes."

The Ford Cortina sat idling at the T-junction.

"Please, God, let him go—" Before he'd got to the end of the sentence, Blennerhassett was turning, mercifully, onto the Killoran road. The road that would take him back to Belfast.

Bessie and Herkie were safe.

The danger had passed, quite literally, for now at least.

Chapter thirty-seven

Bessie sat on the edge of the bed, having woken from a brief nap. Exhaustion was overtaking her, but she had to stay focused.

Lorcan's visit had unsettled her—yet galvanized her, too. She held fast to the idea that she'd done the right thing by confiding in him. He was a respectable man. She hadn't met many of those in her life. It was fortunate that Herkie had happened across him in the stone circle. She thought back to all the vile judgments she'd made about him and felt ashamed. The tears were brewing again. God, why could she not simply trust people? Why was everyone an enemy on sight?

Suddenly vexed, and conscious of the repetitive frustration of her life, she picked up a hairbrush and flung it at the far wall.

Glass shattered.

"Oh, Christ!"

She'd struck one of Aunt Dora's holy pictures—*St. Clare, Patron Saint of Embroidery*. Aunt Dora had painstakingly sewn the caption in neat letters of purple cross-stitch.

The sound of the shattering glass had brought Herkie to the top of the stairs.

"What'd ye brek, Ma?"

She went and retrieved the hairbrush, returned it to the dressing table.

"Nothin', son. The brush just flew out of me hand. Is *Star Trek* over?"

"Aye. I'm hungry, Ma."

"Well, you'll have tae go without your tea for a bit, son. You're comin' with me till the priest's house."

"Och, Ma!"

"We have to find me passport, son." She bent down and gripped his shoulders. "It's very important, 'cos if I don't find it we can't go to England, or Amerikay, or anywhere. We'll be stuck here, and ye don't want that."

Herkie shook his head. "Why were you cryin', Ma?"

"I wasn't cryin', son…just one of me heads. Tell ye what: After we're finished we'll go into Killoran for fish an' chips. How's that?"

Herkie's cheeks dimpled with delight. "Can I have red sauce on me chips?"

She hugged him to her, the thought of separation, of losing him, triggering a newfound intimacy. "Course ye can, son. Brown as well, if ye like. Now, change into your blue T-shirt—I washed it yesterday—and we'll go."

She kissed him.

"Och, *Ma!*" He rubbed his cheek vigorously, as though to rid himself of the contagion.

He dashed from the room, the thought of the fish supper muting all notions of protest about having to change. Bessie got to her feet. The broken picture and Gusty Grant's reaction would have to keep. Laying her hands on the passport was now the priority. Father Cassidy would be away until six. It was nearing four. She had plenty of time to do a thorough search.

Twenty minutes later she was parking the Morris Traveller at the rear of the priest's house. Better not to alert undue attention by parking at the front.

"Now, Herkie," she said, turning the key in the back door and entering the kitchen, "don't touch anything, d'ye hear me?"

Herkie, clutching his headless Action Man, was already scanning the worktops for things of interest to "play" with.

She plopped her bag on the table. "I need ye to help me. And the first thing I want ye to do is get down on your knees and look under them cupboards for me. I don't want tae split me good skirt."

She found a torch on the windowsill.

"And here, use that. It'll be dark under there. There's a good boy."

Herkie took the flashlight and fell to the task with relish. Heaven knew what he might find under the ancient furniture. The corpse of a small animal, perhaps, or even better, some lost coins.

Meanwhile, Bessie made a search of the drawers in the glass case. She rooted through the top two, the ones she would normally have used. She upended cutlery and linen, a set of gaudy Antrim Coast place mats and coasters. Nothing. The drawers underneath likewise held few surprises: crumpled prayer leaflets, receipts and bills, bits of string.

She sighed. It was a pointless exercise. There was little chance of finding the passport in a drawer anyhow. Why would she have taken it from her bag in the first place?

"Yuk! It's all dirty down here, Ma."

"Is that all ye can tell me?"

"I think I see a dead mouse."

"Well for God's sake leave it there!"

"Or maybe it's a—"

"Shush!" She thought she'd heard something upstairs.

She tiptoed to the kitchen door, opening it a fraction.

Herkie, still kneeling, looked up at her. Bessie put a finger to her lips.

Footsteps were moving across the landing.

If it was Father Cassidy, she had a story already planned: She'd forgotten her purse and only discovered it missing when she went to buy more headache pills. But how could it be him? His car was *not* outside.

A feeling of dread seized her. Who else would be upstairs in the house? The judge's ghost? Father Cassidy's secret woman? She'd always had her suspicions—a handsome man like him. Hardly, though, in this close-knit community. The risk would be too great. If he *were* having an affair, it would be conducted far away from the parish.

A burglar? *Oh, my God, what if it's a burglar?* But at this time of day?

She reached across and slid a knife from the block on the bench.

"Ma!" whispered Herkie, attempting to get up.

She turned her head and threw him a warning look. He sat back down again.

Heavy footsteps were coming down the stairs.

She had the best vantage point. The kitchen's location at the rear of the hallway meant she'd have sight of the intruder's back before he became aware of her.

A tattooed forearm appeared on the banister. That ruled out Father Cassidy, Betty Beard, or a secret mistress. A T-shirt above belted denims, dark hair, slim build. The man reached the bottom of the stairs, lingered for a moment, then moved with a casual air toward the front door—as if *he knew the place well.*

A burglar wouldn't behave like that. He wouldn't exit by the front door, either.

Bessie's grip tightened on the knife handle. She stepped into the hallway, shutting the door on Herkie.

"Excuse me!"

The man turned.

Young, late twenties, fit-looking; she wouldn't like to mess with him. His narrow face had a crafty look she didn't care for.

"What are you doing here?" she demanded.

He grinned. "Well, well—the housemaid, I presume. I wondered when our paths would cross. You're an improvement on oul' Beardie Drawers, I'll give ye that." He stuck his hands into his pockets and made to slink down the hall toward her.

"Stay where you are! I've got a knife and I'll use it if I have to." Fear was pulling moisture from her mouth, trying to knock the legs from under her.

"Oh, nice way to treat a fellow worker. You city wimmin— a hard lot ye are." He made an exaggerated curtsy. "Charles H. Sproule, but ye can call me Chuck."

"Father Cassidy never mentioned you. I've been here nearly a month and I've never seen you working here."

"Ah, he must-a forgot. I'm his handyman: wee jobs here and there, bitt-a this, bitt-a that." His eyes roved over her. She knew that look. It disgusted her. She wanted to smack him very hard.

"I doubt if he needed anything done upstairs. He would have told me."

"Got a lot on his mind, the Father. Aye, a lot on his mind." He spun on his heel and pulled open the front door. "Must-a forgot." The sun threw a wedge of welcome light into the hallway. He turned again to her, his face in shadow now, unreadable. "Well... be seein' ye, Mrs. Lawless. Hope ye find what ye're lookin' for."

She tried to speak, but before she knew it he'd slammed the door, taking the sun with him and leaving her stunned in the murky silence of the hall.

"Who was that, Ma?" Herkie tugging at her sleeve. "What'd he want? Did ye not use the knife on him?"

She was speechless.

Mrs. Lawless. He knew her real name. *And he knew she was looking for something.*

"Ma!" Herkie was tugging her sleeve. "Ma!"

"Somebody...somebody who works for the priest." She suddenly felt faint. "I need to...I need to sit down, son."

Herkie pulled out a chair at the kitchen table. She eased herself into it, hardly aware of what she was doing. Her head throbbed. Her hand ached from having gripped the knife so tightly. The words—*Be seein' ye, Mrs. Lawless. Hope ye find what ye're lookin' for—*rang in her head.

How in God's name did he know?

"Some water, son."

Herkie, seeing his mother's distress, went into action mode. Making as little noise as possible, he lifted a chair over to the sink and climbed up to pour water into a glass. He carried the water carefully to the table.

"Thanks, son."

He settled himself opposite and watched her gulp down the water. Wondered how he might cheer her up. Remembered that a cigarette might help. Wordlessly he rooted in her handbag, found a pack of Park Drives, lit one, puffed it into life in his practiced way, and handed it to her.

"Thanks, son. I'll be all right in a wee minute."

"Can I play on the stairs, Ma?"

"Yes, son, but don't make too much noise. I'm gonna put me head down for a bit."

With his mother resting, Herkie slipped into the hallway. He'd been itching to climb the stairs, since glimpsing them from the kitchen doorway.

He gazed up the wide staircase, suddenly afraid. The line of dour clerics staring down upon him from their golden frames seemed to be sending him a warning. *Do not trespass, boy. You have no business here.*

He placed his hand on the banister. He knew they were only a bunch of oul' boys someone had painted. He stuck out his tongue.

Planting a trainer on the first tread, he began his ascent. His feet made not a sound as, step by step, they sank into the plush crimson carpet runner, taking him higher and higher into the strange, dark house.

When he reached the landing, he was delighted to see that there was another flight, and yet another: so much to explore. Maybe his ma would fall asleep at the table and he could simply roam.

In fact his mother had done just that.

One minute she was in the parochial kitchen, the next she was drifting toward a pebble-dashed semi and stopping by a green-painted door.

The face of her sister, Joan, never pleasant at the best of times, appears in the frame. Her look is one of self-righteous displeasure. She is not aging well, thinks Bessie. That job at the launderette isn't doing much for the complexion. A bit of makeup would not go amiss...

"What are *you* doin' here?" Joan demands, eyes narrowing. Hard voice scything into her.

"Can I come in?"

"I s'ppose so. Ye want something, don't ye? I never see ye unless ye want something."

"Look, he left me with nothin'. I was dependin' on the life insurance, but..." She breaks down as she sits down on the sofa. "Just to tide us over till we get on our feet. I'll pay ye back, I promise, Joan."

"If I had a pound for every time ye told me that, I'd be a millionairess. I told ye: Packie Lawless was useless from the start.

From the minute I saw him I knew. But would ye listen? And why is it ye always expect *me* tae bail ye out? D'ye think—"

"Oh, go on, make me really feel it. Don't you think I've come through enough? Haven't ye any charity? Or is it all for show, just like our silly mother? Prayin' till she wore her knees out. And where did it get *her*? And where is it gettin' *you*?"

"A bloody lot further than it's got *you*. I've got a job and a roof over me head."

"Call that a job, cleanin' other people's shite?"

"Get outta my house!"

"Don't worry, I'm goin'. Charity starts with yer own. Fat lotta good all that bloody prayin' is doin' you. Eatin' the altar rails. Ye're a bloody fraud, Joan Halstone!"

Joan slams the door...

Bessie woke up with a start. She looked about her, confused.

A cigarette was smoldering in the ashtray. Herkie's Action Man lay at the far end of the table. She was in the parochial kitchen. He was upstairs, and she was here to find the passport. She *had* to find it. Find it before Cassidy returned. But what if he'd come home already and was now in his study, totally oblivious to the fact that they were even in the house?

She tiptoed into the hallway and peered through the paneled glass of the front door. No sign of his car. She turned to shout for Herkie but was relieved to see him already at the top of the stairs, a hand raised. He was holding something he wanted her to see. "Look what I found, Ma!"

"What's that, son?"

Herkie blew up a balloon and released it. It sputtered loudly like a cheeky raspberry, flew down the stairs, and dropped, deflated, at his ma's feet.

"*Jesus!*" She jumped back. It was most definitely not a balloon. It was a condom.

Herkie descended, and she grabbed him roughly by the arm. He was clutching a small, flat packet. The brand name was familiar to her—as it was to every adult north and south of the border. "Give me *that* this minute! Where in God's name did ye get that, son?"

"Ma, you're hurtin' me arm!"

"I'll be hurtin' yer backside if ye don't tell me where ye got that thing."

"Up there."

"Where up there? Show me."

She fetched a handkerchief, scooped up the deflated condom, and stuffed it into a pocket of her skirt. That done, she frog-marched Herkie up the stairs.

He led her down the passage to Father Cassidy's room.

"It was lyin' there."

Herkie was pointing at a spot just outside the bedroom door. Bessie was horrified. She thought of young Sproule, who'd just left the premises. What in God's name was Cassidy playing at? And right under the noses of his parishioners. The thought of him having a mistress was bad enough, but a *boyfriend*? It didn't bear thinking about.

"Och, Ma, it's only an oul' balloon." Herkie tried to squirm free.

Bessie stared at the doorknob. "Wait, son." She put out her hand and tried it. To her astonishment, the door opened freely.

"Whose room is this, Ma?"

Her appalled eyes took in the scene. The room was in disarray. Two wastepaper baskets were overflowing with take-away food cartons and crisp packets. Several empty beer cans and an ashtray chock-full of fag ends littered a nearby desk. There were the distinctive odors of sweat and alcohol. In the adjoining alcove the bed was unmade.

Temperance Club indeed! Snippets of her job interview came back to her: "*I abstain completely…it isn't referred to as the demon drink for nothing, you know.*"

Her housekeeper instinct getting the better of her, she crossed immediately to open a window—but stopped herself.

"God, I'm not even supposed to *be* here! Herkie, you stand there and keep a lookout. If ye see a big black car, let me know."

She tried the drawers in the desk first, but both were locked. The wardrobe was also locked. There was the safe, but no point in even trying. The bedside lockers? Neither drawer nor the cupboard door of the one on the right would give way. Annoyed, she looked across at its twin and then at Herkie. He was standing with elbows on the windowsill, face pressed against the glass, plain for the outside world to see.

"For pity's sake, son, ye're meant to be on spy duty for me. We're not s'pposed to be in this bloody room, remember?" She repositioned him behind the curtain.

"Och, Ma, I'm bored. When am I gettin' me fish an' chips?"

"As soon as I get me passport."

She went quickly to the remaining bedside locker. Since everything else in the room was locked she didn't hold out much hope. But, to her delight, the drawer opened, if a little stiffly.

She rummaged through prayer leaflets, various blister packs of pills, and—not so surprising, given Herkie's find—two packs of Durex. If that wasn't a sacrilege, well…Since the aged drawer couldn't be extended fully, she put her hand in and groped about. Way at the back her fingers made contact with the hard surface of what could be, just might be—

Her heart did a somersault

She drew out her passport.

"Ma, I see a car."

"*What?*" The last thing she needed was for the priest to know she'd been snooping in his room. And she was surely holding the evidence of her snooping. Her hand was shaking as she stared at the passport. No, she couldn't risk it. She dropped it back in the drawer. "Quick. Let's go."

They were in the downstairs hallway, Herkie clutching his Action Man, Bessie with shoulder bag in place, just as Father Cassidy opened the door.

"Elizabeth!" he said with surprise. "I didn't expect to see you here."

"My purse, Father." She saw him throw a nervous glance upstairs—as well he might. "I forgot it yesterday, ye see...left it in the kitchen. Only missed it when I went to buy more pills for my headache."

Father Cassidy's face took on a look of pained concern. "And how are you now, Elizabeth?"

"Getting there, Father—"

The priest broke out in a sudden fit of coughing.

"Maybe you'd like a glass of water," she said, trying to keep fear and disgust out of her voice.

He recovered himself. Took a deep breath. "No, no, don't even think of it. You go on, and take this fine boy with you." He pinched Herkie's cheek. "I'm sure he'd prefer to be out playing in that lovely sunshine than hanging around a gloomy old priest's house."

"Yes, Father," said Herkie, looking up at the strange man in black who'd heard his hurried confession.

The priest gave an indulgent smile, the one he reserved for children, idiots, and people he deemed less intelligent than himself—which covered most of his parishioners. "Oh, the honesty of children!"

You'd know all about honesty, Bessie thought bitterly, conscious of the condom packet in her pocket.

"Well, see you tomorrow, Father," she said, tugging Herkie down the hallway.

As she pulled the kitchen door behind her, she heard Father Cassidy slowly mount the stairs.

"Aye," she said to herself, so softly that not even Herkie could hear. "Oh, aye, Father: *'An old house like this. It creaks...it groans. I expect we'll all be doing the same in our old age.'*"

The downright cheek! "He must think I came down with the last shower!"

Chapter thirty-eight

Rose proudly led the way into the Kelly Arms hotel in Killoran, trailed by Uncle Ned and Gusty. She'd insisted that both men don their Sunday best. A good impression had to be made for the sake of Greta-Concepta, the jobbing cook she'd picked out as a suitable squeeze for Gusty. It wasn't every day she was called upon to shunt the tracklines of a body's destiny so that they veered in what she believed to be a more agreeable direction than the one leading directly to Mrs. Hailstone's door.

"Terrible grand place," old Ned said, his carpenter's eye taking in the spacious lounge, a mossy-carpeted expanse of shiny wood paneling, teak tables, and leatherette chairs; sash windows swagged in velvet drapes; light fixtures thrusting out of walls like cupped hands.

He looked quite the gentleman, in a black suit that reeked of mildew and turf smoke, a woolen scarf tucked into place against possible chills. He'd refused Rose's offer of a supporting arm and leaned instead on his blackthorn stick. His frail hand gripped it with a determination only oldsters can muster when within gasping distance of the wooden overcoat.

"Oh, it's terrible grand," agreed Rose. "Mr. Kelly got blowed up last year, don't ye know, so this is all new-furbished."

"Aye, the IRA's makin' many a eejit rich in these parts."

"God, Ned, keep yer voice down. Mr. Kelly might hear ye. We'll take that wee seat over there by the windee, in that nice wee alcove where nobody'll see us, for a bitta privacy. Come on, Gusty."

As usual Rose was stepping out in her own handiwork: a frock of buttery yellow, which she'd accessorized with a necklace of gemstones the size of gull's eggs. From one arm swung a cream-colored handbag; from the other a shopping bag containing a sticky-toffee tipsy Irish whiskey layer cake with crushed nuts and touch-o'-mint, a gift for Greta-Concepta. It was her own version of a confection she'd had at the wedding of erstwhile friend Biddy Maryanne Mulgrew, in the way back when. An event Rose was still talking about, all of a decade later.

Gusty followed her like an obedient hound. He was in the outfit he hated most, the one reserved for Mass and funerals. The jacket was a tweed cast-off with suede elbow patches, purchased at tremendous discount from a Pakistani trader on a fair day in Killoran. It was teamed with a pair of ill-fitting Trevira trousers, sitting high on the waist and secured by a cowboy belt with a tin buckle the size of a cake tin.

Rose helped Ned into one of the chairs. "Maybe a wee drink first, Uncle Ned?"

"Aye, so," said Ned, sinking his stick into a copious potted cheese plant with the ease of a man not much bothered about appearances or the fripperies of etiquette. "A half-a...a half-a that black boy and a drop-a that Paddy'll do me."

"Did ye get that, Gusty?" said Rose, confused. "For I don't know what the Divil any of it means."

"He wants a Guinness and a whiskey," Gusty translated. "What about yerself, Rose?"

"Oh, just a fizzy orange. None of that old drink for me."

Gusty traipsed up to the bar and Rose ensconced herself in one of the club chairs, settling down like a Scots Dumpy on a nest. She placed her bags on the floor beside her and peeled off a pair of lacy gloves.

There were not many patrons in the lounge: a couple with a toddler, a lone pensioner staring dolefully into a pint of lager, and, seated at the bar counter, a traveling salesman type in a shiny suit, reading a newspaper.

Old Ned looked about him, awestruck. "Wunder how much all this cost?"

"A fair bit I'd say, Uncle Ned."

"Good strong legs on that boy there, Rose."

Rose looked round at the salesman, mortified. Uncle Ned could be unpredictable at the best of times. What in God's name was he doing admiring another man's legs? A thumping on the table had her turning back again. The couple with the toddler stared over at the commotion, as did the traveling salesman. The child started to whimper.

"God-blissus, Ned, what are ye at anyway?"

"That's the hunched mortises for yeh." He gave the table a good shake. "Take a lot tae break the legs of that boy."

Rose breathed a sigh of relief. So it was the *table* legs that had caught his attention, not the salesman's. Thank heavens for that. She relaxed, sank back into her chair and surveyed the room. The couple were busy now with plates of food: meat, veg, mounds of mashed potato rising up like Macgillycuddy's Reeks. Absorbed in eating, the parents had let their toddler roam free. The boy staggered up the lounge. A few feet from Rose, he stopped suddenly— as if hit by a stun gun—and stared.

"Och, would ye look at the wee one, Ned," cooed Rose, reaching out a hand. "C'mere, ye wee darlin'."

The child, a vein pulsating fatly in a pink brow, swayed, emitted a gurgle, and then, suddenly, extravagantly, discharged his most recent feed into his diaper.

An unpleasant smell spread quickly. Rose flapped a hand under her nose.

"Oh, dearie me!"

She freed a handkerchief from her sleeve while the toddler, mission accomplished, wobbled back to his unmindful parents.

"God, look at the size of them," Ned observed. "Great pair-a dropped hips. Take a brave lot tae tumble *her*." A waitress, passing with a tray of drinks, halted, turned, and shot him a look that said: Act-yer-age-you-durty-old-brute. But the insult was lost on the old man, who'd merely been admiring the hip joints in Mr. Kelly's vaulted ceiling.

Rose pretended she hadn't heard any of it. "Look, there's Gusty coming now."

Ned sniffed the air. "Christ, what's that bad smell?"

"Well, it's not me," protested Rose. "That wee baby musta dirtied himself."

"Somebody's gonna bring them over," Gusty said. He sat down again.

Minutes later a plump girl with a pink face arrived with the tray, panting with the effort of having made the two-yard journey from bar counter to table. "Will yis—will yis be wantin' anything tae eat?" she gasped out, straightening up.

"Eat what?" asked Ned.

"Maybe in a wee minute," said Rose, fanning herself with the menu in an effort to repel a hot flash. She hadn't counted on this expedition being so fraught. "Is Greta-Concepta about, is she?"

"Who *is* this nice wee fat girl?" asked Ned. "Is she Gretti-Conceptee, is she, for if she is—"

"No!" Rose cut in loudly, fearful old Ned was about to give the game away. "This isn't Greta-Concepta."

Gusty shifted uneasily, reached for his pint of Guinness, and eyed Ned accusingly. He resented being inveigled into this trip by Rose. Could have been propping up the bar at the Crowing Cock, chatting to Socrates O'Sullivan about the finer points of overhead camshafts and catalytic converters. Or better still, up in the Turret Room. There was a lot to get through up there. An unopened box labeled Witchy Wilhelmina promised plenty more thrills to come.

"Greta-Concepta's in the kitchen," said the abashed waitress, "gettin' ready for this evenin's teas, she is."

"Could ye tell her that Rose is here? Now, she knows I'm comin', so she doz." And Rose was off like a greyhound out of the trap. "Me and Greta goes back a long way. She used to be married to Tommy Shortt, the breadman. He would-a been a second cousin of me husband's late sister's uncle's mother twice removed, who married one of the Bap McDonalds, don't ye know." Rose could trace ancestries back to the Lower Jurassic if time and a pair of captive ears would allow.

"R-right," said the waitress, trying to keep up. "I'll tell her ye're here." She hugged the tray to her chest by way of repelling old Ned, who was now openly ogling her.

"Chicken sambiches will do me, and a pot-a-tay ye could do a jig on!" he shouted after her.

"Yes, Ned, we'll get ye tea in a wee minute." Rose got up. She needed to freshen up. "Now, I'm just gonna go to the ladies, and I'll take me bag." She grabbed the shopping bag, "'Cos I wouldn't like nothing tae happen tae Greta-Concepta's cake afore she even had a chance tae see it, so I wouldn't."

Bessie negotiated the Morris Traveller into a parking space outside the Kelly Arms and cut the engine.

"Och, I thought we were goin' till the chippie." In Herkie's world the grand exterior meant boring food and too many posh big people.

"Ye can have your fish an' chips in here," his ma said bluntly. "I need a bloody drink after the day I've had. And I'll not get that in a chippie. This looks like a respectable place. Nobody'll know us in here."

She had a lot to think about. A Tullamore Dew would calm her down. Maybe clear her head, for she didn't have a clue what to do next.

She checked her face in the rearview mirror, daubed some powder over her T-zone, and snapped the handbag shut.

"Right, son, now you behave yourself in here. D'ye hear me?"

"Aye, Ma."

"Where are ye, Rose?" a voice called from the far reaches of the lounge.

Rose, fizzy orange suspended in midair, turned to see Greta-Concepta Curley at the far end of the lounge. Wearing a butcher's apron and a chef's white beanie, she was laboring across the floor on swollen ankles. Her glasses, steamed up from her exertions at the stove, had her heading toward the couple with the toddler.

"Cooee!" cried Rose, getting up. "We're over here, Greta-Concepta, so we are." She went to her, grabbed her by the arm, and steered Ms. Curley back on course to their table.

"Wee Carmel tolt me ye'd come in," said Greta, pushing her condensation-fogged spectacles up on her nose and coming to a breathless halt. Gusty attempted to stand up. "Now don't stir yerselves on my account."

Old Ned, loosened by the whiskey, was showing the flustered cook his full set of tawny dentures, a sight that was, mercifully, lost on her.

"I'll just sit down here," she said, and to Ned's unexpected delight she very nearly sat down on his lap.

"Oh, God-blissus, not there!" cried Rose, appalled, pulling her out of harm's way. "Uncle Ned's on that chair. You sit here." She guided her into a seat beside him.

"That nice young lady can sit on my knee if she likes," said Ned.

The cook beamed in the old man's general direction. "Oh, heavens above," she said, taking off her glasses, "I need to give these a wipe."

"This is me friend Greta-Concepta," said Rose, stating the obvious. "The one I was telling ye about, Ned. This here is me Uncle Ned. And this here's me cousin, Gusty."

"Pleased tae meet yeh," said the cook, extending a flour-dusted hand first to Gusty, then to Ned. Ned held on to her hand for longer than was necessary, and Rose had to pry it off.

Greta, unused to the attention being lavished upon her—even if only from a pensioner thirty-five years her senior—was breaking out in a sweat. "I'll not stay long, Rose. I'm in the middle of the evenin' teas and we just finished with the carvery lunch."

"Can I get ye a drink or whatever, Greta?" asked Gusty, getting to his feet, embarrassed by the oul' boy's antics and itching to get away. There was a poolroom at the rear of the lounge, and he thought he might spend his time more productively knocking colored balls about, instead of sitting there listening to wimmin's talk and having to look at his crusty uncle.

"No, thank you, Gusty. Can't take anything when I'm on duty, 'cos—"

"Ye're a cook, not a policeman," Ned cut in.

"A wee mineral maybe," said Rose.

Ned clapped a hand on Greta's knee and squeezed it. "Och, ye'll take a wee sherry, won't ye, for the day that's in it?"

A butterfly flapped its wings in Kathmandu and Rose's heart nearly missed a beat. "Now, Ned!" she cried, realizing with a jolt that her matchmaking venture was in danger of veering wildly off course. "Greta-Concepta is on duty in the kitchen. She just came out tae say hello."

She'd forgotten how drink affected her uncle. Thought old age might have withered his enthusiasm for the ladies. At her sister Martha's wedding, he'd danced with every woman in the room before collapsing, inebriated, in an armchair and snoring his head off for the rest of the evening. But that was twenty-five years before, and he'd been more vital then, with a full head of hair and his own teeth.

"I'll get ye an orange then," Gusty said, backing away.

"And another one-a them black boys for me," said Ned, draining the last of the Guinness. Finally free from the confines of his bed, he was determined to enjoy himself.

Gusty knew better than to refuse the old man's request. If he didn't get his way he was liable to start gushing swearwords like a burst pipe. Gusty couldn't risk that in a fancy hotel among strangers.

Bessie and Herkie settled themselves at a table farther up the lounge. She was glad to see that business was slow. Just a scattering of customers, all so engrossed in their own worlds that their entrance had barely registered.

She handed a menu to Herkie. "Now pick something from this that's under a pound, and be quick."

Herkie studied the glossy pictures on the menu card in a daze of delight. The last time he'd seen a menu like this was back in Belfast at the Lido. His ma would take him there on the very rare occasions when she was in a good mood, had money to spend and something special to celebrate, like a birthday.

Overcome by the many pictures of delicious desserts on offer, he decided to ditch the fish and chips, and plump for a knickerbocker glory, a trifle, and a Coke.

Bessie lit up and nodded at the waitress who was leaning against the bar, eyeing the torpid hands of the clock on the back wall.

"I'll have a whiskey and soda," she said. "Herkie, what's it to be?"

"D'ye want ice with that?" asked the waitress.

"No thanks. Just neat...Herkie, hurry up!"

"Ah...ahh...a Nicky Bocker's glory, a trifle, and a Coke."

"Hold yer horses, son. I didn't say you could order everything on the menu. Who d'ye think I am, Rocky-feller?"

"Och, Ma, ye said tae keep it under a pound and it comes tae... it comes tae seventy-two pee."

"A likely story. And since when did ye become a mathymatician? Give that over here." She snatched the menu from him.

Herkie curled his lower lip, staring up sadly at the waitress. She smiled down at him.

"Accordin' to my calculations, ye're out by—"

"I'll not charge ye for the Coke," the waitress said, taking pity on the sweet little boy with the cherubic cheeks and blond curls.

Bessie softened. "Well, that's very nice of you. Say 'thank you' to this kind lady, Herkie."

"Thank you, miss," Herkie said, smiling. Then, seeing he might be on to a good thing: "Can I have plenty of choclit sauce on me Nicky—"

"Don't push it, son."

"It's all right," said the waitress. "It comes with choclit sauce, but I'll put a wee bit extra on for ye." She winked at Herkie, scooped up the menu, and headed off.

"You're an oul' charmer, Herkie Halstone." She reached across and pinched his cheek.

He beamed. "Ma, can I go tae the toilet?"

She scanned the room. The businessman at the bar gave her the glad eye. Bessie simpered. Touched her hair. For a moment allowed herself to forget the real fix she was in. "Go on then. And be quick."

Herkie climbed down off his chair.

"And don't talk tae any strange men, d'ye hear me?"

"Aye, Ma—I mean yes, Ma."

A few minutes later, Herkie returned from the toilet.

"I saw Mr. Grant down there."

"Nonsense. You'd never see him in a fancy place like this."

"But I *did*."

"Be quiet now, son."

He was smiling broadly as he clambered back onto the chair. Bessie eyed him with suspicion. "What is it *now*, son?"

"There was this pome on the door of the toilet, Ma."

"If it was on a toilet door then it wasn't a pome."

"But it was funny. Canna say it?"

"Only if it's clean."

Herkie took a deep breath. "Here I sit, broken-hearted. Tried till shit, but only farted."

The businessman looked over and smirked.

"Shush! Wash out yer—"

She didn't get to finish. Her words were drowned out by an ear-splitting siren. Its wailing seemed to fill the entire building and the street beyond. "Christ! I hope ye didn't touch anything in that toilet."

"Didn't, Ma! I—"

"Bomb scare! Everyone out *now*!" a man roared. It was Mr. Kelly, the proprietor, charging into the middle of the lounge. "Everyone out! Out now!"

The businessman sprinted out, followed by the couple with the now-screaming toddler. The waitress, halfway to Bessie's table bearing the whiskey and knickerbocker glory, did a U-turn.

"Oh, no you don't!" cried Bessie. She dashed after the waitress and, in the blink of an eye, scooped up the drink and downed it.

"God save us, is it you, Mrs. Hailstone?" a female voice called out.

Bessie turned to see Mrs. McFadden, Gusty Grant, and an elderly man staring at her.

"Is *that* Mrs. Hailstone?" the old man said. "Fine lookin' wommin."

"*Jesus!*" She caught Herkie by the sleeve and made a dash for the exit.

"Ma, what about me Nicky Bocker?"

"Hi, ye haven't paid for that drink!" cried the waitress.

Outside, army personnel were hastily erecting barriers and ushering people down the street to the town square. Bessie and Herkie joined the jostling throng. She held tight to the boy's straining hand.

"Ma, what about me Nicky Bocker?"

"Now, son!" She bent down to hammer home the point. "Would you shut up about yer bloody knickeebucker. There could be a bomb in that hotel. And we could be blew into wee bits any minute."

Not far behind them followed a well-lubricated Ned on the supporting arms of Rose and Gusty. At some point in the commotion they had shed Greta-Concepta, but Rose didn't much care. She was beginning to dearly regret the venture.

A befuddled Ned, now blinking into the light, was not a little rankled that he'd been torn away from his drink. A staunch supporter of the Republican cause all his life, he had a raging hatred toward all things British. Had been known to chuck his slippers at the TV whenever the Secretary of State, Sir Humphrey Atkins, appeared.

Picture him now catching sight of a platoon of British soldiers erecting barricades and barking orders at the disorderly crowd.

"Feckin' murderin' scum!" he roared, waving his stick at a squaddie in a maroon beret. The maroon beret marked the soldier out as a member of the much-reviled Parachute Regiment, fiercely unpopular with the nationalist community since their gunning down of fourteen unarmed civil-rights marchers in Londonderry nine years before.

"Put a sock in it, granddad," said the squaddie, turning his juvenile, pasty face on the trio.

"God, Ned, don't say anything more." Rose tightened her grip on his arm. "You'll get us all arrested."

"Aye, shut the fuck up," Gusty added helpfully, more interested now in Mrs. Hailstone sashaying up ahead. She was wearing a green bias-cut dress that moved nicely about her hips. Lucien-Percy had one similar, but with braiding round the hem.

Rose crossed herself. "There's no need for that language, Gusty."

Ned ignored the pair of them and launched into a boisterous rendition of a ballad from the IRA hit parade: a paean to the doomed Republican martyr Roddy McCorley.

"Oh, see the fit-hoof hosts-a men who march with faces on—"

"Jesus, Ned, don't sing that here!" The sweat was pouring off Rose.

"For young Roddee McCurlee goes tae die on the bridge-a Toome the day." On a bawling endnote he broke free of Rose's and Gusty's grasp and headed toward the nearest army jeep. "I need-a piss."

"Ye can't piss here." Gusty plunged after him.

"I'll piss anywhere I want in me own yard."

"This isn't yer own yard, Uncle Ned," Rose cried. "Gusty, quick! He's gonna do it."

"I said get back in line, granddad!" The young paratrooper, fingers drumming on the stock of his self-loading rifle, was growing impatient with the old man's antics. He had more pressing concerns. His gaze alternated between the crowd and the rooftops. The threat of sniper fire was an ever-present danger. Wouldn't be the first time the IRA had used a bomb scare to lure them out, only to pick them off like ducks in a shooting gallery.

Gusty nodded sheepishly at the soldier while steering Ned toward the public toilets.

On finally gaining the square, Bessie sat down on a sunseat and lit up. The quick shot of whiskey had done her a power of good. She felt calm and happy; didn't much care how long she'd be detained. She'd been caught up in so many bomb scares in Belfast that she considered them to be a part of everyday city life.

Herkie, still smarting from the knickerbocker glory that never was, stood staring up at a soldier's gun, wondering what it would be like to hold it and peer down the barrel.

Rose, in the meantime, exhausted from old Ned's antics and the unexpected nature of the evening's events, needed urgently to sit down and get her breath back. She spotted a vacant space on one of the sunseats and made a beeline for it. It was only when she'd settled herself and the person next to her turned round that she realized it was her nemesis.

"God, Mrs. Hailstone, is it you?"

"Oh, Mrs. Mc..."

"Fadden. I'll just sit down here beside you tae get me breath back." Rose's fingers fluttered at her necklace, face red as a radish.

Bessie smiled and made more room for her. Her sudden change in circumstances, her recent turmoil, was inclining her to kindness rather than her usual knee-jerk hostility.

"Is Mr. Grant all right?" she asked, having seen Gusty frog-march the elderly man out of the square moments earlier.

"Oh, Gusty just took him to the toilet over there. Ye know what these old men are like. They're like cars, truth be told. The more miles on the clock, the more chance that sartin things don't work proper, or God-blissus-and-savus, stop workin' alto-gether."

Bessie, unaware of Rose's propensity for verbosity, didn't know what to say. Then, recalling what Herkie had told her about seeing Ned Grant being stretchered out to the ambulance, she said, "But he's out of hospital now. That's good. It was very good of him to give Herkie a bit of work. Keeps him out of mischief. You know what young boys are like."

Rose mopped her brow with a hankie, looking puzzled. "Oh, but he was never in the hospital, Mrs. Hailstone. Ye could hardly get him tae go tae a doctor's surgery, never mind a hospital."

Snatches of a shortwave radio exchange could be heard in the background. *"Roger, over…suspect package…location…ladies' Kelly… arms…backup…"*

Bessie looked over at Herkie. A soldier was hunkering down beside him, showing him his machine gun.

"That's a lovely wee boy ye have there."

All at once, the mystery of Ned's missing pension money and the telltale evidence of the Milky Way wrapper she'd found on the doorstep was becoming clear to Rose. But tactfully she decided to spare Herkie's embarrassment—for the time being anyway—and his mother's certain blushes.

"He must miss Belfast," she went on. "Big change for him, coming here. But I suppose it's better for him to be away from all that bother in the city. Must be hard for him without his father… hard for you, too, Mrs. Hailstone, truth be told. Taken sudd—"

"Y'know, I had a slice of that lovely fruit loaf you made Father Cassidy," said Bessie, slamming shut the closet door that Rose was trying to pry open. Those skeletons were not for her to see. "It was very good. You're an excellent cook."

The trick worked a treat. Rose blossomed. "God, d'ye think so, Mrs. Hailstone? Well, d'ye know I must show ye something I made this morning." She reached down for the bag. "It's a sticky-toffee layer cake I made—"

Her hand grasped empty air.

She quested about, shock and disbelief tensing her normally jolly features.

"What is it, Mrs. McFadden?"

Herkie ran over to them. "Can I hold the soldier's gun, Ma?"

Normally she would have said no, but Mrs. McFadden appeared very distressed. Bessie glanced over at the soldier. He smiled and nodded.

"Go on, son. But be careful, you hear?"

"Aye, Ma."

Bessie turned, to find a horror-stricken Rose clasping her face in her hands.

"What *is* it, Mrs. McFadden? Are you ill?"

Rose's mouth moved, but the words would not come.

"I'll get you some water," said Bessie, getting up, "You'll be all right in a minute. It's the heat and this crowd. I feel faint meself."

Rose caught Bessie's arm.

"Oh, God, don't go, Mrs. Hailstone," she pleaded, finally recovering speech.

Bessie sat down again.

Rose held on to her arm, gazing unhappily about her: at the Lynx helicopter circling ominously, at the disgruntled crowd eager to be home, at the irate motorists being diverted, the army bomb disposal teams and siren-wailing cop cars.

"I...I caused...I caused all this," she croaked.

"What? Don't be silly, Mrs. McFadden. The bloody IRA caused all—"

"Me...me...me sticky-toffee..."

"Yes, what about it? You were gonna show me it."

"Me sticky-toffee...tipsy..." Rose was hyperventilating now. "Irish...Irish whiskey—"

"Yes, I know. Could be using another glass meself."

Rose shook her head emphatically. "No, me Irish whiskey... layer...layer cake with...with...crushed nuts...and touch-o'-mint. Me cake for Greta-Concepta. I...I left it in the ladies'."

Bessie had to think about that for some moments. At last, comprehension dawned.

"You mean the suspect package is...?"

Rose nodded, in tears now.

"Oh dear!" Bessie glanced back at Herkie. He and the soldier were chatting animatedly.

"I can't...I can't. God, how am I gonna..." Rose found a handkerchief and mopped her tears.

Bessie knew she had to act. If she didn't, God knows how long they could be stuck in Killoran. The sooner the army knew they were dealing with a hoax, the sooner everyone could go home.

"Look," she said. "I'll go and tell that soldier, the one that's talkin' till Herkie there. I'll say...I'll say ye weren't feelin' too well and forgot ye'd left the cake in the ladies'."

Rose caught Bessie's arm. "God, would ye do that for me, Mrs. Hailstone? Will I be arrested?"

"Oh, I wouldn't think so. Now, the sooner he knows, the better."

Bessie got up, prepared to turn on the old girlie charm for the soldier. Well, it had worked before, when she was making her escape from Belfast. Meanwhile, Rose found a rosary in her cardigan pocket and launched into a decade of the Sorrowful Mysteries. She was going to need all the help she could get.

Chapter thirty-nine

Lorcan sat at the dining table trying to work up an appetite for his late dinner. It had been a singularly unsettling day. Bessie's confession, along with the Dentist's violation of his home, was robbing him of the quality he valued most in himself: his equanimity. He tried to focus on the Steak Diane in order to clear his mind. His mother was a much better cook than Mavis Hipple, and he appreciated the effort that must have gone into his meal. One thing at a time, he thought. For now, just eat and concentrate on the moment.

He could hear Etta moving about in the kitchen and knew that soon he'd be probed about his new "friend," Blennerhassett. She'd been quite taken by the brute. If she only knew the reality! He could still sniff him in the pretty room: the pong of cigar smoke, even though he'd opened all the windows.

"How is it, dear?" Etta said, coming in with a pot of tea.

"Splendid, Mother. Really splendid."

"It was your father's favorite, you know." She pulled out a chair at the table and sat down stiffly.

"Oh, sit in the armchair. Please. Put your feet up. I don't mind eating alone."

"That's all right, son. I saw Dr. Brewster yesterday. He was pleased with my progress…said my legs were well on the mend and that I should walk about more. Better for the circulation. Now that nice Mr.—"

"That's good news. How is the good doc?"

"Just the same. He was asking about you. Wondered had you met any nice ladies in Belfast."

"Did he now? The patter never changes, does it? Is he still touching up Gladys Millman at the Ocean Spray, I wonder."

"Now, son, that was just a rumor."

He saw Etta gazing dreamily out the window. Knew what was coming next.

"Son, that nice Mr. Blennerhassett—"

"Yes, what about him? Is there any more by the way?"

"Yes. I'll get it."

"No, no, sit."

Lorcan went into the kitchen, hoping his diversion tactic would derail her. He spooned some of the remaining sauce onto his plate.

"He said I had beautiful hair. Wasn't that nice of him? Your friend, I mean."

What a bloody liberty! Well, since he's got none of his own, the bald so-and-so! He gripped the spoon handle, wondering how to respond. He couldn't show his mother how incensed he was. Control, that's what was needed. Calm. Blennerhassett was not going to take away his composure.

"Did you hear me, dear?"

He relaxed his grip on the spoon. Set it down gently and took a deep breath.

"Well, he was only stating the obvious," he said, coming back to the table and faking a smile. "You *do* have beautiful hair."

Etta beamed, patting her coiffure. "You know, your father never paid me many compliments. City men are different. I suppose it comes from mixing with all kinds of people."

You can say that again. He had a mental image of the Dentist's two henchmen, jaws clenched, muscles ballooning.

He pushed the plate away, the unwelcome image making him nauseous.

"Your father was never a good mixer, God rest him. Very set in his ways. Your friend Mr. Blennerhassett said he was in the security business."

Oh, the barefaced cheek of him!

"Mother, he is *not* my friend. I barely know him. He is a business associate, a client, and he had no right to impose himself on you and pretend he was otherwise." At that moment his eye fell on an airmail letter propped up on the mantelshelf. The perfect distraction. "I expect that's from Aunt Bronagh. Would you like me to read it?"

"Oh, yes, I forgot to say. Time enough, son, when you're finished."

"You know, I think I've had enough. Doesn't do to overindulge." He fetched the letter and sat down in an armchair. Etta took her cue and did the same.

He opened it and an international money order fluttered out.

"Not another one! She's doesn't give up easily, does she?"

"Well, you should go and visit her, son. You're her favorite."

"All in good time." He crossed to the sideboard, pulled out a drawer, and added the money order to the others Bronagh had sent him.

He began reading, imitating his aunt's Yankee drawl.

Dear Etta, honey,

I hope life's treatin you mighty fine these days. I'm a writin this on my patio with a Naked Waiter cause the sun's so darn hot I reckon I've earned it. I'm all tuckered out from the—

"What on earth is she talking about? She's just trying to shock me."

"It's the name of a cocktail, Mother."

"But how do you know, son?"

"Well, for a start it's written with a capital *N* and a capital *W*. She says it's hot and believes she's earned *it*, not *him*. The last time she visited, she had me make her one. Pernod and pineapple juice, if I recall. Shall I continue?"

"Then why not say, 'I'm having a cocktail on the patio'?"

"She's only teasing. You know what she's like." He resumed reading.

How's ma favorite nephew and when's he a-comin ovah to see me? I enclose a little something to help toward his trip.

Lorcan sighed. "You know, Mother, I'm not ungrateful. But she forgets I'm in full-time employment and no longer the bohemian, carefree artist she imagines me to be."

I'm all tuckered out from my fitness class. I've stopped givin em and started takin em again. The new instructor guy has a great bod and can sure kick ass. He may be thirty-five but he ain't as flexible as me—

"Still as coarse as ever," Etta sniffed. "What happened to dignity in old age? She *is* seventy-six, after all. No spring chicken."

Have had the most Gad-awful month. My poor Bubba came down with a virus. Had to take him to the Woof Woof sanctuary out on Twenty Seven till he got himself better. I'm sure glad he did get himself better, otherwise I might a been fixin to get him a plot at the pet sematary. It's all down to Pastor Cooperman. He came and said a prior over him.

"Said a *what* over him?"

"I think she means 'prayer.' She writes the way she speaks sometimes."

Then if that gaddamned Cuban broad of a cook Rosalia I hired last month didn't go get herself banged up on solicitation charges. Didn't know a cotton pickin thing about it till the darn law enforcement shows up with an arrest warrant. Transpires she was dealin drugs and turnin tricks at Betty Mae's Cat House out on Forty Nine 'tween doin shifts for me and old man Chamberlain at Number Eight. I tell ya this, Etta, if I could get me a decent live in maid I'd be happy.

"My goodness," Etta said in bewilderment, teacup halfway to her lips, "what *is* she talking about? Why was the cook playing tricks?"

Mercifully, the phone rang at that moment.

"I'll get it." Lorcan went out into the hall.

A couple of minutes later he was back in the room.

"Sorry, have to go out for half an hour."

"Who was that?"

"Er…umm…It was Father Cassidy's housekeeper, Mrs. Halstone."

"Oh, I didn't know you knew her."

"I don't…not really."

"Is she in trouble, son?"

"Trouble? No, nothing like that."

But Lorcan had a feeling, judging from the tone of Bessie's voice, that a great deal of trouble was just about to come his way.

Chapter forty

Thanks for coming over," Bessie said, showing Lorcan in, "but I couldn't tell you on the phone."

"Don't worry. It's sometimes a relief to get away from my mother for a bit. May I?" He took off his hat and motioned to an armchair.

Bessie felt awkward, not used to this level of politeness in a man. "Oh, sorry...yes, please sit."

He handed her a brown paper bag. "For you. I bet you could use some, given what you've been through."

Bessie opened the bag and, to her surprise, drew out a bottle of fine Hennessy brandy. She rarely received gifts and was so overcome she didn't know what to say. She turned her back on him and mumbled her thanks.

Then: "Maybe...maybe you'd like some?"

"Yes, but only if you'll join me."

Bessie needed little persuading. She found two tumblers and poured a generous measure into each.

"Where's Herkie?" He accepted the rather full glass wondering how he was going to manage it.

"I sent him to bed. He was misbehaving."

Herkie had been reprimanded for fibbing about Ned Grant's hospitalization.

"I'm not surprised. He must be bored silly here."

Bessie sat down on the sofa. She had tried to make herself presentable. Had put on makeup. Changed into her brightest dress: the red one. But the stress of recent events showed all too readily in her face. Insomnia and worry had done their wicked work, dimming the light within.

Lorcan raised his glass, trying to keep the atmosphere light. "Well, here's to better times."

"Yes, better times," she said halfheartedly.

He took a discreet sip. "Did you find your passport?"

"Yes."

"That's great news!"

"Yes, but you see, I couldn't take it. I—"

"You couldn't?"

"No, I couldn't—because I found it in Father Cassidy's bedside locker."

"Oh…I see."

"I panicked, for if I'd took it he…he'd know I'd been in there. He keeps his bedroom locked, ye see. I—I only went in because… well, because Herkie found a…found a…" He saw her predicament. Wondered what was coming next. "I mean something lying outside the bedroom door, and…and when I tried the door handle, it opened." She took a large gulp of brandy to help with the next embarrassing revelation.

"R-right." Lorcan was mystified.

She opened her handbag and rummaged in it. He saw her draw something out, then promptly thrust the item back in again. "I just can't believe he's like that!"

"Like what?"

"And him a priest…it's just unbelievable!"

There was a disquieting pause. Bessie coughed politely, trying to fill it. But not Lorcan. He was a man rarely daunted by silences, who could fully inhabit the lull in a conversation with a therapist's ease. While others babbled he sat and listened, absorbing everything. So he waited now for Bessie to entrust him with this nugget of information about Father Cassidy. She would tell him eventually, and he was in no hurry.

Finally, she made up her mind and decided to get it over with. She dipped into the handbag again and dropped the packet of condoms onto the coffee table.

"*They* were in his bedroom. What do you make of that?"

Lorcan studied the Durex. There was another long pause.

"It's disgusting!" She gulped more brandy, aware that Lorcan had barely touched his, but she didn't care. The cognac was giving her some much-needed courage.

"What d'you think it means?" he said finally.

"Well, I think it's bloody obvious, don't you?" *This Lorcan must lead a very sheltered existence.* "He's having an affair with somebody... and not just anybody, either. I mean I wouldn't mind if it was a woman, but it's a...it's a..."

"A man?"

Why does he not look shocked? Oh, God, maybe he's that way inclined, too. Christ, what have I got myself into?

"Some ruffian called Chuck something. I only met him today. Didn't even know he was in the house until—"

"Chuck Sproule."

"That's him. Do you know him?"

"Local bad boy. His bark's bigger than his bite, as they say." He swirled the brandy in his glass. "Why does Father Cassidy lock his room?"

"The safe is in there. Also, he holds the Temperance Club meetings there."

"Ah, the famous Temperance Club! In his *bedroom*, though?"

"Well, not exactly. His bed is in a smaller room off it. The main area is a kind of sitting-room-office kind of thing.

"I need to have a look in there."

"Why?"

Lorcan got up and stood by the window facing onto the backyard. "God, this takes me back. That old well...I used to play there as a child. Dora Grant used to warn me if I fell down there I'd end up in China."

"Funny, Gusty Grant said the same thing to Herkie."

"Bit dangerous having it exposed like that. D'you want me to replace the cover?"

Bessie got up, feeling quite light-headed, and looked out.

"Damn, Herkie's always doin' that. No matter how many times I tell him to leave it alone."

"Shall I?" Lorcan gestured toward the back door.

"No, no, don't bother yourself with it. I'll do it when I'm bringing in the washing." She went back to the sofa.

"Can I ask you a personal question, Lorcan?"

He resumed his seat. "Of course."

"Well, I wondered if you'd...if you'd ever been—"

"Ever been married? No."

She waited for more, but Lorcan simply sat there, being his calm, unreadable self. "Sorry, I shouldn't be nosy," Bessie said, plugging the awkward pause again.

"Would you recommend it?"

"What?"

"Marriage."

"No." She shook her head vehemently. "Marriage was a prison sentence for me." She drained the brandy glass. Felt the tingle of threatening tears. Excused herself and went into the kitchen. At the sink she poured herself a glass of water. Held it to her flaming cheek.

"All right?" Lorcan asked from the kitchen doorway.

"No, I'm far from all right! I've no money and my job's as good as gone. My uncle in England said he'd give me a job, but I wrote to him ages ago and he didn't have the manners to answer my letter. The police are accusing me of I-don't-know-what. If the Dentist finds me he'll kill me. I've nowhere left to go. Oh, God, what's the use?" She broke down and wept into the sink.

Lorcan went to her, took her gently by the arm. "Look, Bessie," he said. "I'm going to help you out of this. I—"

"God, I had such plans for Herkie and me." She allowed herself to be led back to the sofa. "I thought we could go away—somewhere, anywhere. God, I even dreamed of us going to Amerikay. Can you believe that?"

"And you can still do that, Bessie. Dreams come true, if you hold on to them."

"Well, a fat lot of good that's done me so far! I've been holdin' on to useless dreams since I was ten!"

Into the silence came a bee, zizzing at the window.

"Don't give up. You've shown nothing but courage so far. You left Belfast, your home, and you made a new start here. You will go far. I *know* you will. Trust me."

No one had ever talked to her like that before. Offered words of praise. Acknowledged her efforts. Lorcan Strong could have been the last spectator in the theater, the one who stood applauding her when all the rest had given up and gone.

She leaked a tear. Dropped her gaze.

"Now, it was good that you didn't take the passport. It means Cassidy won't have suspected anything—yet. As I say, I need to have a look in that room."

"But now he knows that I'm not who I say I am! Sproule called me Mrs. Lawless...if *he* knows, then Cassidy knows. Who's to say he hasn't reported me to the police already? Then they really will think I stole the bingo money."

"He won't report you, believe me. I have a feeling that the RUC are the last people he wants to get involved with. Now, it's very important that I have a look in that room. There's something not right about this." He threw a glance at the packet of Durex. "And those...they're not what you think they're for. But, first, I need to make sure that my suspicions are correct and you need to get your passport. Can you get me in there tomorrow morning?"

She nodded. "He says Mass at half eight, according to his timetable."

"Right. So what time would he leave the house?"

"No later than a quarter past. He's very punctual when it comes to Mass times."

Lorcan got up. "Good. I'll be there at twenty past eight, on the dot. I'll knock on the back door."

"But I don't have a key for his bedroom."

"Don't worry about that."

"But you haven't finished your drink," she said, not wanting him to leave.

He sensed her unease, leaned over and took a swig, just to please her, for solidarity.

"Now, you get some rest. I'll see you tomorrow morning, twenty past eight, sharp."

After another sleepless night, Bessie was up with the Kilfeckin Manor rooster, and at the parochial house by the appointed time. She let herself in through the back, just as Father Cassidy was exiting by the front.

Lorcan, sitting in his car within sight of the parochial house and idly scanning the newspaper, was alerted by the sound of a gate opening. He lowered the paper and watched as the priest stepped onto the curb, busied himself with the latch, and strode purposefully toward St. Timothy's, cassock flapping in the breeze.

"Now what are you up to?" He checked his pocket for the paper clips, put on his gloves, and left the car.

The house was eerily quiet when Bessie let him in. Wordlessly they climbed the stairs and proceeded down a long corridor to the last door on the right.

She tried the handle. "Locked. What now?"

"No worries." Lorcan dropped to his knees and removed his gloves. He drew two paper clips from a pocket and began unbending them. "A little trick I learned as a necessity in my digs. My landlady, a rather absentminded lady, would sometimes lock me out."

She watched in fascination as he raked the lock a few times before pushing in the second paper clip. Seconds later an audible clicking sound.

"Now, that's what I like to hear."

The door opened.

"It's just like it was yesterday," Bessie said, going in first. "But the door of that was shut," she added, pointing at the safe.

"Not very tidy, our good Father, is he now?" Lorcan sniffed the air. "That smell?"

"It's drink, isn't it?"

"Yes, but there's something else."

He scanned the room. Went to the safe and peered in. Empty.

"Keep a watch by the window. Just in case."

He went to the closet and jiggled the central knob back and forth. It wouldn't budge.

"Aha, there's something in here he doesn't want us to see, and it's not his ceremonial robes." He looked about. "Now, the key. Where would that be, I wonder."

"Maybe in his bedside locker. I thought I saw a key in it yesterday. Will I get it?"

"No, you stay there. How's the time?"

Bessie checked her watch. "Nearly half past."

Lorcan rummaged through the locker drawer. "My passport, can you—"

"Have it, already." He found the key.

After several tries the key turned in the closet lock. With difficulty he pulled the doors open.

Bessie, looking out the window, noted that Lorcan had gone quiet. She turned to see him staring down at something in the wardrobe.

"What is it?"

"Come here."

She followed his pointing finger. In the bottom of the closet sat a large carpetbag. And not just any old carpetbag. No, this bag was a one-off. The garish emblem of the Virgin of Guadalupe was unmistakable. He took it out and unzipped it.

Empty.

"I don't understand," she said. "It's just a bag."

"Perhaps, but even empty, it puts Cassidy in the frame. It's the one I put the bingo money in."

He shut the closet doors and turned the key. He crossed to the desk and tried the drawer.

"No, everything's locked. It was—"

"It isn't locked. Just old." He yanked the drawer open. A glance inside confirmed his worst suspicions. There were several timer switches, a bottle of colorless liquid, and packs of condoms.

"I was right! Come here."

Bessie looked in the drawer. "I don't understand."

He carefully uncapped the bottle and sniffed. "Sulfuric acid."

"What's it for?"

"These," he held up one of the condom packets, "are used to determine fuse delay. The time it takes the acid to dissolve through several layers of those is regulated by"—he lifted one of the timers—"one of these, which gives our terrorists an idea of how long it will take to ignite an incendiary device."

"You mean a bomb."

"Afraid so. Our parish priest isn't running a Temperance Club in here. He's running a bomb factory."

Chapter forty-one

Early Monday morning and Sergeant Ranfurley was, for the first time in twelve long hours, feeling calmer and somewhat more confident. From the moment he received the anonymous call on Sunday afternoon—followed by the seemingly endless consultations for clearance from Divisional Command (not to speak of the administrative difficulties involved in securing a search warrant from Justice Robert Jenkins)—Ranfurley's mind had been in a state of fever.

To say he'd been shocked by the revelations confided to him in the course of that phone call would be putting it mildly—very mildly indeed. For in all his born days, and most of those as a serving officer, he had never heard the like of it. Father Connor Cassidy, parish priest of Tailorstown, exemplar of virtue, absolver of sins, spreader of the Sacred Word; he of the fine manner, pious air, and seemingly equanimous nature, was running a *bomb factory*. And not from any dank old basement or derelict shed in the middle of some woebegone bog, as was customary with the skulking scumbags bent on destruction. No, he was planning and executing his nefarious deeds right under the very noses of the constabulary—in his own bedroom at St. Timothy's parochial house, no less.

Ranfurley shifted uneasily in the passenger seat of the bullet-proof Ford Cortina as it sped along the Killoran Road. A shrouding mist, rolling down off the Slievegerrin Mountains, was settling eerily over the fields and hedgerows like a cerement over a corpse. It was another grim morning in the life of the two officers. The previous day had claimed not one but two more IRA hunger strikers: Raymond McCreesh and Patsy O'Hara. You didn't need to be a bloody psychic, thought Ranfurley, to predict that those deaths would lead to the murder of more innocents. He knew that he and his fellow law enforcers would have to be *extra* vigilant from now on. There'd be reprisals from the Fenians; that was a certainty. Even in the backwater that was Tailorstown they'd have to expect the unexpected, and check for explosives planted under their cars. Not just first thing in the morning—as was routine—but before each and *every* bloomin' trip. No, their lives weren't about to get any easier.

Constable Johnston, in the driver's seat, was a nervous wreck already: biting his lower lip, hands sweating on the wheel, wondering how the morning would unfold.

They'd taken the unmarked vehicle on the orders of their superior, Chief Superintendent Ross. "Bad enough, your having to arrest the Devil's disciple on his own doorstep, but it'll have to be done discreetly," Ross had warned. "If these allegations turn out to be unfounded—and bear in mind it wouldn't be the first time we'd been wrong-footed by some cretinous half-wit—it'll be my head on a platter, your station up in flames, and every Holy Joe and Josephine queuing up to genuflect at the bloody IRA's altar."

Johnston glanced now at Ranfurley's stern profile. "How d'you think he's gonna respond, Sarge?"

"Oh, he'll not bat a godly eyelid, if I'm any judge. The unscrupulous are well practiced in the art of deception, Constable."

They rounded a bend and the parochial house loomed up out of the mist.

Johnston slowed, threw the indicator switch, and eased the car through the gates.

The moment of reckoning had arrived.

"Ma, can I go out down the back field?"

Bessie heard the question through a fog of crazy and confused dream sequences. They involved:

1. Rose McFadden,
2. a machine gun,
3. Ned Grant singing his lungs out,
4. the Virgin Mary rising up out of a carpetbag, and
5. a toffee tipsy whiskey layer cake being blown to bits by an army bomb disposal team in the foyer of the Kelly Arms hotel.

She threw back the bedcovers and sat up.

"Jesus, son, what is it? Why are ye shoutin' at me?"

Herkie stood at the foot of the bed, a half-eaten Curly Wurly in one hand, his slingshot and what looked like a letter in the other.

"I'm not shoutin', Ma. Canna—"

"What time is it?"

"A quarter by eight—"

"And what d'ye want to be goin' down a back field at this hour of the mornin' for, son?"

"Mr. Grant said there was a fox chasin' his chickens, and if I kilt it with me catapult he'd give me a pound."

"All right," she said. "No farther than that back field, d'ye hear? I'll be watchin' from the windee."

"Thanks, Ma."

Herkie rushed to the door.

"Not so *fast*, son! What's that ye've got there?"

"Aye—I mean yes, I forgot. A letter came for ye." He threw it on the bed, and off he ran.

The Hackney postmark and the childlike backhand, underscored by ruled pencil lines, meant it could be from only one person. Uncle Bert.

"About bloody time, too," she said, reaching for her first cigarette of the day.

Ranfurley banged loudly on the door of the parochial house and waited. After a moment or two it was opened by Father Cassidy. His expression was unreadable.

"Good morning, gentlemen," he said. "And what—"

"Morning tae you, too, Father," Ranfurley interrupted. No time for poncy small talk on this occasion. "I'll come straight to the point. We've come about a rather serious accusation that's been made against you."

He surged past the priest and into the hallway, Johnston in tow. Father Cassidy was immediately outraged.

"Excuse me, what on earth d'you think you're—"

Ranfurley held up the search warrant. "We've come to search the premises."

He and the constable began to mount the stairs.

"How dare you! On what grounds?" Cassidy, hard on their heels, shooting words like bullets. "You just can't come in here and…"

But the officers were already at the top of the stairs. Following the anonymous caller's instructions to the letter, they made straight for the third door on the right.

It was locked.

"Open it, please, Father," Ranfurley ordered.

"This is preposterous! On what grounds?"

"If ye don't unlock it, we'll have no choice but to force it. Now, what's it gonna be?"

Father Cassidy, judging that to argue further was futile, took a key from his pocket and did their bidding.

"Go ahead," he said, pushing open the door. "I've got nothing to hide."

"That's for *us* to decide."

The officers entered the room. It was exactly as the caller had described it: a mess. They took in the unmade bed, the overflowing wastepaper baskets, the stench of stale beer, a poster on the back wall proclaiming that ALCOHOL IS THE ROOT OF ALL EVIL.

"Temperance Club indeed!"

Ranfurley went directly to the desk and pulled open the drawer. No wrong-footing this time. He'd hit the jackpot!

Revealed were the unmistakable paraphernalia of the seasoned terrorist: a collection of condoms, acid vials, and timer switches. In and of themselves, they were harmless. But when combined, they constituted the deadly improvised explosive devices that had brought many of his colleagues' lives to an abrupt and gruesome close.

"Well, well, well," he said, turning to face Cassidy. In his mind's eye, the sergeant was on his last beat on the streets of Londonderry; he was stooping to collect the remains of two officers blown to pieces. Their charred limbs hardly filled a single body bag, so little was left of them. Their life's blood trickling away down a drain grid in the driving rain. The image, seared in his memory, would never let him go.

Rage welled up in him, but he held it in check. There would be plenty of time for that down at the station.

"There's also this, Sarge." Constable Johnston was holding up the carpetbag. The garish image of the Virgin Mary seemed very much at odds with the grim contents of the drawer. "Same one used in the so-called robbery, I'd say."

Ranfurley looked from the bag to the priest.

"Nothing to hide, ye say? Constable Johnston, read him his legal rights."

Bessie settled herself back on the pillows and tore open Uncle Bert's letter.

The Blarney Stone Tavern
Mare Street
Hackney
London
18 May 1981

Dear Bessie,

Sorry tae hear about Packie and sorry I couldn't make it till the funerill. It is good that yiz got outta that hole Belfast. Tailorston sounds like a grand wee spot. I no I said you could come any time and work for me in the kitchen, but things is changed from the time I writ that till you.

"Oh, yes, here we go!"

I met Babs three month ago and we're gettin married at Christmas. She came into the Stone one night for a Bloody Mary and a Rusty Nail and didn't leave till morning for it was love at first sight. She's a great cook. Doz the best sausage supper a man could hope for.

"Aye, it takes a real brain box to make a sausage supper, ye oul' fool."

She's a grate cleaner too. Could scour a floor and a sink in the time it'd take me till lift a mop.

"Ye never lifted a mop in yer bloody life...aye, a cook, a cleaner, a whore, and a wife, all rolled into one. Ye've got yer hands full, Babs. Damn you, Bert Halstone, ye durty oul' divil!"

Anyway what I'm tryin till tell ye is that with Babs bein such a gret cook and cleaner and what have ye she's gonna take over in the kitchen, so when I'm out at the front she'll be in at the back. It'll work out well for the pair of us. I nivver thought I'd meet anybody at my age.

"Aye, you're seventy-two—no young buck. She must be a desperate slapper on the skids to take on the likes of you."

What it means is that I don't need yiz comin over for tae help me out now that I've got Babs to do for me in the kitchen. I wouldn't be able to pay ye even if ye wor comin over, anyway for now with the waddin things is tight.

Hope you and Herkie can come over till the waddin. If you write back and tell me yer plans I'll send yiz a invite.

All the best,

Your Uncle Bert

"Bloody cheek! Who does he think he is? They'll be ice-skatin' in hell the day I stoop as low as tae go till his stupid waddin'."

She stuffed the letter back in the envelope. Stubbed out the cigarette in disgust. Got out of bed and went to stand by the window, which looked down on the backyard.

"What now for the pair of us?" Herkie was lurking at the far end of the field, slingshot at the ready. "And what am I going to tell him? He was looking forward to going away."

She raked a hand through her hair, suddenly tearful. God, could things get any worse? Uncle Bert was an escape route she'd been counting on, but a couple of scrawled jotter pages had put paid to that idea. She tried not to cry.

A blackbird swept down, landed close to the open well. She thought of Lorcan. He'd offered to put the cover back on. Said it was dangerous. She'd get dressed and do it right away. If Herkie tripped and fell in there, she'd never forgive herself.

Spurred into action, she snatched up her dress from the ottoman.

Creak.

She tensed.

The noise had come from downstairs. Was it the back door?

"Herkie, is that you?"

Silence.

She was about to call out his name a second time but turned instead to check the window.

He was still there in the field.

Fear fluttered. Her pulse quickened. Clutching her dress, she tiptoed to the top of the stairs.

"Hello? Is anyone there?"

No answer.

Aunt Dora putting in an appearance? Well, so long as she showed up in daylight and not at night, it was okay with Bessie. Gusty Grant up to his Peeping Tom tricks?

"Is that you, Gusty?"

Still no answer.

You imagined it, Bessie. And any bloody wonder, given the last couple of days. Yer nerves are in shreds.

Back in the bedroom, she pulled on her dress. She'd just go out and put the cap back on the well. No time like the present.

She went down to the kitchen and reached for the back door knob.

She didn't get to turn it.

Out of nowhere an arm appeared and clasped her waist, knocking the breath from her.

A knife flashed before her eyes. A blade edge was pressed to her throat.

"So ye thought I wouldn't find ye, ye thievin' whore! Time for us tae have some fun, Bessie luv. I've missed the smell of ye. This wee meetin's long overdue."

The Dentist, Fionntann Blennerhassett, IRA enforcer and boss to Packie—evil incarnate—had crashed from the past into the terrifying here and now.

Chapter forty-two

Lorcan sat within the fairy ring, savoring the birdsong, the sibilating beeches, the clean, untrammeled air.

Eyes shut, senses alert, he was identifying the various birdcalls as a way of clearing his mind. The sweet raspings of a corncrake. The melodious fluting of blackbirds. And somewhere in there was a valiant little robin, piping its distinctive trilling notes. Tuning in to nature's music was a way of reminding himself that it was indeed a beautiful world, despite recent indications to the contrary.

Breathe, he told himself, when the inevitable thoughts of the previous day threatened to tug him back into darkness.

Breathe! Forget! Dwell in the present! You've done your bit. You made that all-important phone call. By now Cassidy will be in police custody, the bomb factory dismantled, innocent lives saved.

Half an hour had passed, and Herkie Halstone was becoming restless. Mr. Fox had not put in an appearance—only a floppy-eared rabbit he'd missed by a whisker and a gray squirrel too swift for his aim.

He was sweaty from having lain on the grass. His back was hot from the glaring sun. The Curly Wurly was long gone. He needed to pee. On top of all that, he was thirsty.

There was a can of Creamola Foam in the kitchen cupboard. He'd go home and mix himself a big glass.

He got to his feet, holstered the slingshot, and wandered back up the field. Maybe he'd meet the fox on the way.

Bessie struggled, her heels skidding on the linoleum floor. She yelled. She cursed. But her efforts were as nothing against the brute's strength.

"If ye yell again, ye'll get this knife across yer fuckin' juggler. D'ye hear me?"

Her teeth chattered as she tried to clamp her lips tight. Her eyes bulged in terror. She felt the force of his forearm solid against her rib cage, fought in vain to pry it loose.

He dragged her backward. "Now, yer gonna sit down on this fuckin' chair for our wee chat, civil-like."

She found herself being forced down onto one of the chairs by the table. She kicked wildly. A stiletto came down on his instep. Hard.

The Dentist roared like a stuck buffalo. He grabbed her by the throat, thrust her head back. "Try that again and ye're dead!"

His grip was getting tighter.

She was gasping for her life. Her head growing light. Her grip on consciousness ebbing.

He released her. Her head lolled, flopped forward.

There was no fight left in her. She drifted further into blackness…

She came to, gagged and bound. Hands behind her back, each ankle tethered painfully to a chair leg.

She couldn't move.

She couldn't speak.

The Dentist sat before her, arms folded high on his stevedore's chest, cruel, bloodshot eyes steady on her.

On the table—Aunt Dora's table with its beautifully embroidered storks—sat a bizarre and gruesome display. Neatly laid out on a canvas roll were pliers, a hammer, a drill, a set of drill bits, and a surgeon's scalpel. They were unmistakably instruments of torture.

"Ready for a bitta foreplay, Mrs. Lawless? Ye haven't been gettin' much of it since Packie passed away. Shapely woman like yerself."

He set down his switchblade and considered the table display, rubbing his hands in anticipation. "Now, which one of these lovely wee bastards tae get the party started?"

Bessie tried to wrench her hands free, but he'd used cable wire as restraints. Every time she moved, the pain was agonizing.

He picked up the scalpel and traced a line from the base of her throat down her breastbone, slicing through the fabric of her dress.

Tears sprang up in her eyes. She felt the blade prick into her skin.

"Now, when ye're ready tae tell me where my fuckin' money is, just nod."

Bessie nodded, terrified.

"That's more like it...a wee bitta progress...always nice tae see."

He leaned closer. She caught the whiff of Old Spice, commingled with Cuban tobacco. Smells she knew only too well.

His disgusting hand was on her thigh. She froze.

"Ye see, 'cos I'm a reasonable man, I'm gonna remove this gag so ye can tell me where exactly my money is. If there's as much as a squeak out of yeh, ye'll be doing the tango in hell along with yer fuckin' husband. Understand that, Bessie luv?"

Herkie pushed open the gate at the end of the yard.

He halted, cocked an ear.

He'd heard something. Something terrible.

He waited.

Suddenly, into the silence, a yell. Unmistakable. Blood-curdling. His ma!

He raced up the yard—but stopped short of the door. He heard a man's voice raised in anger. He thought he knew that voice. He crept up to the partly open window and peeped in.

The Dentist! The wide back and bullet head were unmistakable.

Herkie shut his mouth tight on a scream as his eyes met those of his mother—his terrified mother, blood trickling down her chest, face wet with tears.

The Dentist, firing up his drill, was oblivious to the new observer and the degree of fear and loathing his hulking frame was stirring.

Herkie heard his mother's beseeching cries. *"Please…oh, God, please…let me…let me get…get me breath back…then I'll tell…"*

He was seized by rage, and by a courage that went beyond his tender years. He felt for the biggest stone in his pocket. The one he'd been reserving for the fox.

"Ye've had enough fuckin' time, ye bitch."

"Oh, please, God, please don't…"

Herkie raised the slingshot. His hands were shaking but his resolve was firm.

The Dentist lifted the drill. Its whine was the soundtrack of nightmares.

"Them lovely eyes-a yours first," he said in a voice that would chill a desert sun.

Herkie pulled back the sling with all his might. His mother's screams were pitiful. The drill moved ever closer to her eyes.

He let fly.

Thwack!

The stone found its target. It ricocheted off the Dentist's bald head and struck Aunt Dora's table lamp.

The torturer let out a roar and dropped the drill. He spun round and caught sight of Herkie.

"Ye snivelin' fuckin' maggot! When I get me hands on ye, I'll wring..."

He flung back the chair.

Herkie took to his heels, running for his life. The Dentist crashed through the back door in hot pursuit.

Herkie flew down the yard, the Dentist's oaths thundering in his ears.

"Come back here, ye fuckin'—"

A crash!

A crack!

"*Aaaarrghhhh!*"

Silence.

The boy stopped running. He looked round.

There was no sign of the Dentist.

He was confused. Had the ogre decided to return to the house and finish off his ma? He raced back.

He was overjoyed to find her alone in the kitchen, still tied to the chair.

"Jesus, Herkie, get me outta here, quick!"

Herkie seized the Dentist's switchblade and sliced through the cable wires.

"Where is he, son?"

"Don't know, Ma."

Bessie gasped with relief and buried her face in Herkie's abundant curls, hugging her to him.

"God, son, you're a wee hero! Ye saved me life."

"Aye, Ma, I got him in the bonce. Ma, can I have a new Action Man and a Nicky Bocker glory later on?"

"Ye can have a *hundred*, son. Now, help me up quick before he comes back."

"But ye're bleedin', Ma."

"It's only a wee cut, son." She went to the set of torture weapons. "He'll not be so funny when I get me friggin' hands on him—the fat, ugly bastard."

In the fairy ring Lorcan had been jolted out of his meditation by an almighty roar cutting across the mellow birdsong. His eyes snapped open.

It had come from the direction of Rosehip Cottage; he was certain of it. He left the woods quickly and took a shortcut across a field. The rutted ground was a challenge for his city shoes and he nearly fell over twice, but he kept going.

Bessie, holding tight to Herkie, crept out of the kitchen and into the yard. They'd armed themselves well from the Dentist's torture kit. Herkie had the drill in one hand, the hammer and pliers in the pockets of his shorts. Bessie was clutching the deadly switchblade that had nearly done for her.

There was no sight of the enemy in the yard.

"Ma, I think he ran a—"

"Shush, son...what was that?"

They heard a low moaning. It was coming from close by.

"It's the gate, Ma," he said, pointing down the yard. "I forgot to close it."

The moaning came again. Louder.

"That's not the gate, son. It's coming from the bloody well!"

When Lorcan finally reached Aunt Dora's backyard, he was confronted with an extraordinary spectacle. Mother and son were bent over the open well, swear words shooting from them like forked lightning.

"Not so funny now, ye fat, baldy bastard," Bessie shouted. "Now ye know what it feels like, ye fuckin' psycho—"

"Aye, now ye know what it feels like, ye fuckin' psycho," echoed the boy, entering into the spirit of things.

"That's *enough*, son!"

"What on earth is going on?"

They turned to see Lorcan coming up the yard.

"Aye, *that's* what's goin' on!" Bessie cried, pointing down.

Lorcan, shielding his eyes from the sun, peered over the lip of the well.

He couldn't believe what he was seeing. Looking back up at him: a pair of bloodshot, affrighted eyes that could only belong to one man. There was no mistaking the bald head, the wine-stain birthmark. Fionntann Blennerhassett was clinging on for dear life several yards down the deep well shaft, immersed in dark water up to his neck.

"Please...please...*please!*" he moaned. "Please help me...*help meeeee!*"

"Oh...my...God!" was all Lorcan could manage to say.

"Feckin' Satan, more like."

"Aye, feckin' Satan—"

"Now, Herkie, I warned you..."

Lorcan looked from mother to son, astounded. He could barely get the words out. "H-how...how...did he...?"

"He was about to slit my throat with *this*." The widow was brandishing the switchblade. Lorcan took a step back. "Only Herkie—"

"Only I got him right in the bonce with me cata-puller and—"

"*Please...get...me...out...Lorcan!*"

"Oh, my God!" Bessie turned pale; her jaw went slack. Her eyes moved from Lorcan to the Dentist, and back to Lorcan again. She backed away, holding the knife high.

"H-h-he *knows you!* Oh, my God. You're one of them. Oh, Jesus, you're—"

"No, Bessie. I'm on your side. He made my life hell as well. Trust me. I'll explain later."

She lowered the knife slowly, uncertain of what to believe.

Lorcan peered down at the Dentist's beseeching face, the eyes wild with fright, the knuckles straining, white. He thought of the victims the monster had tortured. The men he'd murdered. The devastation he'd visited on so many lives and families. He thought of how his own life had been blighted. Of how he'd never known terror until that day, barely a year before, when he'd been bundled into a car, gun pressed to his back, after stepping off a bus on the Antrim Road.

In spite of it all, he couldn't let the wretch die.

"*Lorcan, please...get...me...OUT...*"

"Herkie, get a rope."

"You'll do no such thing, Herkie! Come here, son. Have you any bloody idea of what this bastard put us through?"

"Yes, I have some idea, believe me, but we can't let him die. We have to try. I couldn't live with myself if—"

"Well, *I* could."

"That's the difference between you and me then."

"No. The difference is that you don't bloody well know what sufferin' is—you with yer posh life and everything handed to you on a friggin' plate!"

Lorcan sighed. "It's not the time for this. Herkie, is there a rope somewhere?"

Herkie glanced down the yard. "Aye, there's one in—" He tried to twist free of his mother's grip, but she held him fast.

"You're not goin' nowhere, son."

Lorcan shook his head and ran to the clothesline. He took his pocketknife and sliced through the stout nylon cord.

The Dentist was sobbing like a child when Lorcan returned. Great, whimpering, desperate sounds were echoing up out of the well shaft. The final refrain of the doomed man mere breaths away from extinction.

Lorcan looped the severed cord around a wooden post and began feeding the remainder down the well shaft.

"I can't bloody *believe* you!" cried Bessie, snatching up the rope. "Let the fecker drown!"

"Aye, let the fecker drown!" Herkie agreed.

This time his mother didn't rebuke him. For Bessie, the rules had changed. Lorcan Strong was no longer on their side.

"Give me the rope, Bessie." He held out his hand. "I've never killed anyone in my life and I'm not going to start now. And you're not, either. I don't think you have it in you."

She stared at him. "Try me. Some people deserve to die, and that bastard's one of them. I'd be doing the world a favor."

The cries of torment were getting louder.

"Think of Herkie," Lorcan said. "He needs you. He's suffered enough. Don't...don't have something like this on your conscience."

"Ma!" Herkie backed away from her, to stand by Lorcan's side. He started to cry. "Give him the rope, Ma. Please, Ma."

She was outnumbered. Her heart broke. She let go of the rope.

The Dentist made a grab for the lifeline. His right hand closed about it. He grasped it with his other hand. It held.

The wooden post creaked.

The trio bent over to track his progress.

Bit by bit, gasp by agonizing gasp, Blennerhassett hauled himself up. Slowly, achingly, inch by hard-won inch, second by tortuous second, until his shoulders were clear of the water. But he was still a long way down the shaft.

"Come on," urged Lorcan. "You can do it."

"Feck off!" shouted Bessie. "I hope it bloody well breaks!"

Cra-a-ck!

It wasn't the rope. The worm-eaten post, hammered into the soil decades earlier, splintered and split in two.

The free end rushed toward Lorcan, drawn by the hapless Dentist's weight.

Lorcan tried to grab it, but it flew from his grasp.

A scream.

A splash.

Gurgling and thrashing.

Silence.

An empty, deathly silence, into which a lone magpie chackered.

As one, the three looked down into the well—just in time to see Blennerhassett's wine-stain birthmark sink beneath the surface. Air bubbles appeared, many and frantic at first. Before too long, their number decreased. And died.

It was over.

Bessie lifted Herkie and swung him round.

Lorcan turned away.

A chill wind blew. The back gate clanged.

The Dentist was no more.

Chapter forty-three

So ye don't deny it, Father: That was *your* bedroom we just inspected?"

Ranfurley sat facing Father Cassidy in the interrogation room of Tailorstown's police station. On the table between them lay the bomb paraphernalia recovered from the desk drawer in the parochial house.

Constable Johnston stood to one side, manning the door as usual.

The sergeant couldn't believe he'd landed such a big fish. What would the chief superintendent have to say? A Provo priest—an IRA man in a cassock. A first. Who could credit it? He saw the double-star insignia on the pressed sleeve of his inspector's shirt, the glitter of a gong in the not-too-distant future.

"No, I don't deny it, Sergeant," Father Cassidy said, sitting as still as a lizard, eyeballing the officer. He had his elbows on the table, hands clasped under his chin, in ruminative mode. "It's *my* bedroom in the sense that it is *my* house. Therefore all the bedrooms, strictly speaking, are mine. I used it as my private sleeping quarters at one time. That is, until I started to hold the Temperance Club meetings there. It was the ideal place: quiet, with sufficient office space for the purpose."

"I'd be inclined tae believe ye, Father, if it wasn't for the bed in there. A bed recently slept in, too…a locker beside it containing *your* effects. Such would indicate tae me that ye *were* sleepin' there and therefore were party to what was goin' on."

Cassidy waved a hand dismissively. "Sometimes one of the lads would use it. If a meeting went on late and they were tired or—"

Ranfurley guffawed. "D'ye hear that, Johnston?"

Johnston smirked.

"And how d'ye explain these?" The sergeant pushed the packet of Durex across the table. "Thought you Taigs—and most especially you Taig priests—were vast against contraception. What method is it ye preach from your high, papish pulpit?"

Cassidy glared at him.

"Johnston, would you know?"

"I believe it's called the rhythm method, sir."

Ranfurley threw back his head and laughed heartily. Johnston relaxed a bit and joined in.

"That's the very one, Johnston: the rhythm method. What's that mean, Father? That ye do it tae bong-bong drums or what?"

The priest's face remained impassive. Ranfurley picked up the pack of Durex and thrust it under Cassidy's nose.

"So, what are these johnnies for…eh?"

No answer.

"In *your* quarters, as ye call them. In *your* desk…huh?" Ranfurley sat back in the chair. "Not unless…not unless ye were havin' it off with one of the lads? Wouldn't be the first time a priest turned out tae be a shirt-lifter. Can't be too careful these days, what with clap and what have ye…the Divil might come lookin' his pound of rotten flesh later on."

Cassidy's face was a mask of disdain.

Ranfurley got up and stretched. "We'll be in this room for as long as it takes, Father, me and Johnston. So ye better start talkin'." He leaned across the table. "A couple of my men are roundin' up the shower of cretins ye entertained in that room, even as we speak. All of them have 'form,' by the way…not the holy-teetotaling-Joes ye're tryin' tae make out. But ye knew that already. That's why ye chose them, isn't it? Well, let me assure you, we have ways of makin' them talk. And believe me, Father, when they start grassin' on you, that collar will be no protection."

"This is ridiculous!" Cassidy jumped to his feet. "I demand a solicitor. I've nothing to hide. I've tried to reason with you but it isn't working. I will not be bullied by the likes of you. You think that uniform gives you the right to insult me. Well, let me tell you, Sergeant, no one bullies *me*. Mrs. Halstone had access to that room as well as those lads—or are you conveniently forgetting that? Why aren't you interrogating *her*?"

"Oh, tryin' to drop that poor woman in it again, are ye? Ye've pulled that one before. We checked her out. The husband was a hoodlum, but not her. Maybe that's why ye give her the job in the first place. Stranger from Belfast, tryin' tae start over, desperate for a wage. Could use her as a stooge later on, if things got rocky." Ranfurley shook his head slowly and tut-tutted. "And you a man of the cloth. Who could—"

A timid knock on the door.

The newcomer, a young woman in uniform, spoke in low tones to Constable Johnston.

"Sarge, there's a call for ye."

"Not now, Johnston!"

"I think you should take it, sir. The chief super's on the phone. Says it's urgent."

Ranfurley, reluctantly, thrust back his chair, eyes still on Cassidy. "Keep an eye on him till I get back. This isn't over yet—not by a long shot."

At Rosehip Cottage, Lorcan was guiding a fire engine into the yard. An ambulance was already standing by.

"Ma, would the Dentist be in China now?" Herkie at the window, looking out.

"Listen, son, how many times have I to tell you, stop lookin' out that bloody window." She pulled him away and marched him into the living room. "Now sit down there."

She switched on the television. "Watch something on that. And I'm warnin' ye, son, if ye move again, ye'll go upstairs tae the bedroom and I'll lock ye in for the rest of the day." She began flicking through the channels.

"Stop, Ma! There's Basil Brush!"

"Good, now you watch that crazy fox and give my head peace. I've been through enough this mornin'."

She shut the door on one of Basil's silly jokes: "*Hey, get me a crocodile sandwich, buddy, and make it snappy. Boom, boom!*" She allowed herself a brief smile. It must have been the first time ever that she'd had to *order* the boy to watch television.

At the kitchen window she lit a cigarette and gazed out at the unreal activity beyond the glass.

The fire brigade was lowering a long ladder into the well. The team worked wordlessly, as though obeying unspoken commands.

The ladder was hooked over the side and anchored in place. A rope was secured to a tow hook at the rear of the engine and coiled around the waist of one of the crew. He donned a miner's helmet and switched on the light. Having checked his gear, he gave the thumbs-up sign, stepped onto the ladder, and began his descent into the well.

Bessie drew hard on the cigarette as she watched the beam of the miner's lamp fade from view. She was torn with indecision. Would she bear witness to the ignominious retrieval of the monster who'd caused her so much anguish? Or avert her eyes, thereby sparing herself a final—and unnecessary—trauma?

She stayed put. She had to be sure he was gone. Gone for good.

Lorcan was conversing with one of the fire crew. As if sensing her turmoil, he looked her way and gave a reassuring nod. She raised her hand self-consciously, suddenly ashamed of her earlier outburst.

"Here he comes!" a man by the well shouted.

Two paramedics pulled open the ambulance doors, slid out a gurney, and wheeled it into position.

A signal to the fire truck had the winch turning.

The rope was being hauled up.

Bessie flinched as the Dentist's head came into view. Then, bit by cumbersome bit, the bulky, waterlogged corpse emerged from the well, trailing a nylon cord. It took four men to lift it.

Finally the body was laid out on the ground and a firefighter was disentangling the cord.

A medic felt for a pulse—procedures had to be followed. Bessie's heart did a somersault. *Jesus, what if he's still alive? Impossible!* She checked her watch. It had taken the emergency services nearly half an hour to arrive. Could anyone survive in the water that long?

Oh, Jesus, he has to be dead. Oh, please, God, please!

She couldn't stand it. She looked away. When she turned back it was to see the ogre of her nightmares being zipped into a body bag and lifted into the ambulance.

Her torment was at an end.

She gripped the windowsill hard and sobbed with relief.

Chapter forty-four

Ranfurley picked up the phone in his office in buoyant mood. He couldn't wait to tell his superior the news regarding Cassidy, and what he and Johnston had turned up during their search of the parochial house.

"Chief Superintendent Ross, to what do I owe the pleasure?"

"Good afternoon, Sergeant. You've arrested Cassidy, I take it?"

"Too right I have, sir. We—"

"I'll come straight to the point then. I—"

"Sorry tae cut across ye, sir. Yes, we have the good priest bang to rights. Caught him red-handed. Not only is he runnin' a bomb factory right under our noses, out of the parochial house, but it transpires he was behind the theft of the bingo money *as well*."

"I'm aware of all that—"

"What?" Ranfurley was nonplussed. "Pardon me, sir, but am I missing something here? How could ye be aware of any of it? Johnston and me have just been to the parochial house and seen it with our own eyes."

"You have him in custody then?" The superintendent's tone sounded disapproving.

Ranfurley was not a little incensed. Where were the congratulations, the well-deserved pat on the back?

"Well of course he's in custody! Or would you rather I'd said, 'Father, this doesn't look very good for ye now but I'll tell ye what: You say another Mass, 'ave yerself a good night's sleep, and we'll be back tae collect ye in the mornin'?"

"I don't like your tone, Sergeant."

"Well, that's good, for I don't bloody well like yours, either."

He heard Ross sighing. "Look, I'm sorry for keeping you in the dark. But this is a dirty war we're fighting."

"Damned right it is."

"Cassidy has been on the radar for some time. Those robberies—the break-in at the parochial house, and the bingo theft—were the tip of the iceberg. We have reason to believe the money was being used to fund terrorist activities."

"*Pardon me?*" The sergeant couldn't believe his ears.

"We have an informer on the inside, a very useful lad…has saved many lives in the past few months."

"Have ye, now?" Ranfurley's grip tightened on the receiver. The import was clear: You're only a plod. A sergeant, bottom rung of the ladder of command. We don't entrust the finer details to the like of you. "Would be mannerly to keep me abreast of things from time to time."

"Now, hold on, Sergeant, I'm—"

"Would it be presumptuous of me to ask who this fine, upstandin' lad is, *Chief Superintendent?*"

Ranfurley heard a sigh of resignation down the line.

"Sproule…Charlie. Gets 'Chuck' for short."

He had to digest this. Chuck bloody Sproule. He couldn't get his head around it. "That drunken ass! MI6 is really scrapin' the barrel, employin' the likes of him."

"That's just it, Sergeant. Dirty war, dirty tactics—depending on where you're standing. This is a dangerous game. You don't need me to tell you that. We needed to be sure Sproule was passing us the correct information. There were insufficient grounds for searching the parochial house until we received that call on the confidential line. It was traced to the Crowing Cock pub on High Street. Voice analysis matched it with the owner's son: Lorcan Strong. We checked him out…entirely aboveboard. Not a blemish on his character. D'ye think that search warrant would have been granted on the say-so of just any Tom, Dick, or Harriet?"

"So what are ye sayin', exactly?"

"You have to release the priest. We have our evidence. He's a liability we can do without."

"You must be jokin'."

Ranfurley loosened his tie. He was sweating. The golden chance of a promotion to inspector disappearing in a fog of fury and resentment.

"Release him. Immediately. That's an order."

He could not bring himself to answer. Too angry for words, he retorted with a blatantly hate-filled silence.

"If it's any consolation, Sergeant, I'm as appalled as you are. But it's way over our heads. We can't risk arresting him. Especially not now, with the hunger strikers dying by the day. The whole nationalist population would join the IRA in revolt. It would be all-out war. No, the Church have assured us they'll deal with him. And we must be satisfied with that."

"Oh, will they now? A law onto themselves, are they, the Roman Catholic Church?"

"More or less. He'll be moved over the border. We have the assurance of the bishop. A parish in Donegal—out of harm's way."

"Ye mean he'll still get to practice?!" Ranfurley could barely contain himself.

"Probably. But that's their problem, not ours. And on their conscience be it. The important thing is that he'll be moved out of harm's way. We've got Sproule and Lorcan Strong to thank for that. And of course the Lawless woman. Her curiosity was his undoing."

"I see." The sergeant, still very, very angry, prepared to hang up. "Right, I'll go now and do the dirty work of releasing the bastard for ye."

"Just a minute, Mervyn."

"I'm listening."

"You've done well—you and Johnston. I'll put in a good word for you. Have no fear of that."

Ranfurley grunted. He put the phone down very slowly and sat staring at it for a long while. He was still staring at it, his mind in turmoil, when Constable Johnston rapped on the door.

"Coming, Constable."

Slowly he made his way back to the interrogation suite.

Cassidy, seated at the table in the same position he'd left him in, did not stir when the sergeant entered. He had opened his breviary and appeared to be praying.

Ranfurley contemplated the bizarre tableau—the prayer book opened alongside the bomb-making effects—and shook his head. The priest, eyes cast down, was studying the page, lips moving over the words with a look of reflective reverence. Convincing, thought the sergeant—convincing enough to rival the acting skills of a Spencer bloody Tracy.

"Get out of my sight!" he barked. "You *disgust* me."

Cassidy didn't flinch. Instead, he smoothed down the silk bookmark and carefully closed the prayer book. Only then did he feel moved to push back his chair and stand up.

"Are you addressing me, Sergeant?"

"Damned right I am."

"I take it I'm free to go."

Ranfurley, outraged by the clergyman's insouciance, reached out, grasped him by the dog collar, and thrust him up against the wall. The breviary fell to the floor.

"Now, you listen tae me, ye goddamned hypocrite. You're the worst kind—absolutely the worst kind—I've ever come across in all my entire workin' life. And I've met many's the psycho in my twenty-three years on this patch, believe you me. You make Ted Bundy look like Mary friggin' Poppins. Takin' holy orders so ye can skulk in the dark and bomb the life out of innocent people, while stupid young lads take the rap. Have ye ever seen what a bomb can do to a human being?" He shook him. "Have ye? I thought I'd seen it all in this job, but you, you take the bloody—"

"Sergeant." Johnston had a hand on his shoulder, pulling him back. "Sarge, don't waste your energy."

"Aye, yer right, Johnston. He's not worth the bloody energy." He released his grip. "Get the hell outta here."

Cassidy righted his collar, bent down, and retrieved the missal. He straightened himself and smoothed his hair into place.

"May God forgive you, Sergeant," he said.

With that, Father Connor Cassidy walked—a free man—from the room.

Chapter forty-five

Bessie had just finished setting the table when she saw the emergency services depart. She'd remained by the kitchen window, not allowing herself the luxury of relaxing—of immersing herself in the tried-and-trusted ritual of setting out the china, cutting slices of cake, arranging biscuits on a plate—until she'd seen the last of Blennerhassett with her very own eyes.

It was only when the body bag had been zipped over his face and his carcass shoved into the ambulance that she could finally breathe more easily. The villain who'd made her life hell—the accursed IRA enforcer who'd terrorized her weak-willed husband and, as a sorry consequence, herself—was no more.

It was over.

She'd never have to hear his horrid name again, set eyes on his horrid face.

The back door opened and Lorcan came in.

They stared at each other. He shrugged, his look unreadable.

"I'm sure you need a cup of tea after all that," Bessie said, teapot in hand.

"Yes, please." He took in the beautifully laid table, the sugary fare he certainly had no stomach for.

He sat down. She poured the tea. An air of sadness hung over the room.

"This could be the wake," he said.

Bessie laughed mirthlessly. "I doubt many will be mourning him. Celebratin' more like."

Lorcan ignored the comment. "Where's Herkie?"

"Watching TV."

"He didn't see anything?"

"No…not that he didn't want to, mind. Wanted to know if the—" She couldn't bring herself to utter the nickname. "If he'd be in China by now."

Lorcan gave a small smile. She offered him a cigarette. To her surprise, he took it.

"No, I can't eat, either," she said, surveying the spread. "Don't know why I bothered putting all this stuff out."

"Force of habit." He drew on the cigarette. "We all have our ways of coping."

"You're…you're not sorry he's dead, are you?"

He shook his head.

"What I can't understand is, how the—" She was going to use the B-word but checked herself in time. "What I mean is, how on earth did he find me? Here, of all places."

"My fault, I'm afraid. All my fault. I didn't want to tell you because I didn't want to worry you. It was the wrong decision. I'm sorry. I thought I was protecting you and Herkie."

"But how?"

He went on to explain his involvement with Blennerhassett, beginning with his abduction on the Antrim Road, being coerced into replicating the portrait of the Countess; the threats against his mother. And finally the misfortune of being made to take a leave of absence by his supervisor at the museum, thus affording Blennerhassett the opportunity of visiting Tailorstown.

"When he came to the pub I wanted to tell you, to warn you. It was on my mind to tell you not to park your car at the front of the cottage, but..."

"My God!" Bessie was gobsmacked. "I had no idea." She got up, went to the window to gaze out at the well. The well that had ended their troubles—both hers and Lorcan's—so neatly. "And... and after all that...what he put you through, you...you wanted to *save* him."

"Save him, yes. But, only so he could be held to account. I would have turned him in—have no fear of that. I'd had enough of the blackmail."

"What are the chances, huh?" Her smile was grim. "I leave Belfast to get away from him, and end up running into him 'cos of you. Ye couldn't make it up."

She paced the room, arms folded tight. "God, what about the RUC? They'll be wanting to question me again. I can't face Ranfurley. Once was bad enough."

"Don't worry. I'll deal with that. I'm sure they know all about him. They'll be glad he's been taken out—to use the vernacular."

Lorcan leaned across the table and extinguished the half-smoked cigarette. "What will you do now?"

"Well, I can't stay here...my sister, Joan, in Sligo, I s'ppose... till I get meself a job. Don't want to—we don't really get on—but it's somewhere to stay till we get back on our feet. Don't have the money to rent another place. Gusty was very kind to let me rent this place so cheap."

"You wouldn't stay on here?"

She jerked a thumb at the window. "Knowin' that psycho met his end in that yard? Don't think so. Every time I looked out there I'd see him. Even sitting here in this kitchen gives me the creeps. I could've met me death in that chair you're sitting on."

A door opened and there was Herkie, bounding into the room and swooping down on the cake stand.

"Where's your manners, son?" Bessie grasped the cake-laden hand before it reached his mouth.

"Sorry, Ma. Aye…hello, Mr. Lorcan. I finished the pitcher last night. Canna get me money now?"

Lorcan ruffled his curls. "The hero of the hour! Of course you can, Herkie."

Herkie beamed with pride. Bessie pinched his cheek.

"Did I kill the Dentist, Ma?"

"No, you did not indeed, son. And for God's sake, don't go round sayin' that to anybody or you'll get the pair of us arrested. D'ye hear me?"

"Ma, mind when you were in the chair…all bleedin' 'n' all… and I was cuttin' the rope?"

"How could I forget it?"

"Well, you said ye'd buy me a new Action Man *and* a hundred Nicky Bocker glories."

Bessie sighed. She wanted desperately to lie down. "Tomorrow, son. Yer ma's tired."

Lorcan stood up. "*I'll* take you for your well-deserved reward, Herkie. No time like the present. A hero can't be kept waiting."

Herkie looked up at Lorcan. Bessie mouthed a "thank you" over the boy's head.

"God, canna, Ma?"

There was a knock on the door.

"Coo-ee, Mrs. Hailstone! It's only me: Rose McFadden."

"Oh, God!" Flustered, Lorcan threw Bessie a warning look and took Herkie by the hand. "See you later."

With that, he and the boy dashed out the back door, leaving Bessie to her fate.

Bessie opened the front door on a panting Rose weighed down by carrier bags.

"God-blissus, Mrs. Hailstone, are ye all right? Gusty said he saw the amb'lance earlier and I thought something terrible had happened to ye."

"No, nothing like that," said Bessie, shutting the door behind her, and wondering how on earth she was going to explain the ambulance. "Come in and sit down. I've just made a pot of tea."

Rose eyed the inviting table of goodies. "Well, I wouldn't mind a wee cup atall, Mrs. Hailstone." She eased herself into a chair with a sigh. "God, me back. I feel like Barkin' Bob's mule, truth be told." Her eyes roamed over the table. "What a lovely spread. Did ye bake all this yerself?"

"Oh, it's just simple stuff," said Bessie, making light of the complicated marble cake, the dainty Viennese whirls. She refreshed the teapot and poured a cup. "I enjoy making my own things."

"I agree with ye entirely, Mrs. Hailstone." She shed an Aran cardigan and hung it on the back of the chair. "There's nothing like yer own bitta bakin'. As I always say tae my Paddy: You don't know the Divil what's in any of that shop-bought stuff, or what kinda durty kitchens they've come outta. A friend of mine worked in a bakery once, and she tolt me she wouldn't ate a crumb of anything she made, for the man runnin' it was inclined tae stick his fingers into every bowl of stuff she was mixin', and accordin' tae her, his hands neither seen soap or watter from one end of the week tae the next."

Bessie nodded in understanding. Mrs. McFadden could have been describing her former boss, Scottie "Butler" Yeats from *My Lovely Buns.*

Rose drew a breath and dived into a shopping bag. "And on that very subject of bakin' and the like, Mrs. Hailstone, I brought ye a wee gift."

"Oh!"

She produced a cake tin and took off the lid. "Me toffee tipsy Irish whiskey layer cake with crushed nuts and touch-o'-mint," Rose announced proudly. "The one—" She stopped abruptly and pressed a hand to her bosom at the very memory of it. "God, I still get the palpitations even thinkin' about that day. Ye were so good to sort it all out. That's why I thought I'd make ye the wee cake as a present, like."

Bessie took the tin. "Oh, you shouldn't have, Mrs. McFadden… but thank you very much. It looks delicious."

"I'm glad ye like it. A lot of work went intae it. Wouldn't be a cake I'd make very often." She reached for a Viennese whirl. "Only for special occasions, if ye get me meanin'. And what was the amb'lance doin' here did ye say?"

Bessie, unused to Mrs. McFadden's tendency to skip from topic to topic, was caught off guard. She took a mouthful of tea to buy time.

"What ambulance was that?"

"Oh, the one Gusty saw comin' outta the backyard there this mornin'. He thought he saw a fire engine, too. But since he didn't see no flames comin' outta the roof, he thought maybe it was just a red van. 'Cos ye know, Freddie Dabbs, the butcher, drives a red van, and maybe he was leavin' off a bitta beef with ye. Dora used tae buy a pound-a mince steak and a bag-a chicken giblets off him every Monday, for a drop-o' soup tae take her through the week. But…" Rose reached for the teacup.

Bessie, sitting there nodding politely, wisely decided to let Rose ramble on. Now she understood completely why Lorcan was always so eager to get out of the woman's way.

"…and anyway, as I was sayin', Mrs. Hailstone—and I said this tae me Uncle Ned, too, when I was makin' his bed this mornin' and gettin' him intae a clean set of drawers: 'That amb'lance,' sez

I...'that amb'lance maybe broke down and pulled intae Dora's yard for tae—'"

"Gosh, you're spot-on," said Bessie with relief, offering Rose a slice of marble cake. "The engine was overheatin' and he called in here for some water."

"There ye go!" Rose smiled broadly. "God, I just knew I was right. Wait tae I tell Uncle Ned that."

Bessie eyed the clock and tried not to yawn.

Rose coughed politely. Then: "Now, there's another wee thing of a delicate nature I need tae straighten out with ye." She rummaged in her handbag and brought out a small brown paper bag. She pushed it across the table.

Bessie was nonplussed. It had been an extraordinary day so far. She'd nearly lost her life at the hands of the Dentist, but instead, he had lost *his* at the bottom of a well not ten yards from where they were sitting.

Her thoughts raced. She opened the bag with a sense of foreboding, and drew forth her missing panties.

"My goodness, how did you come across these?"

"Well, tae cut a long story short, I was ridin' me bike along the county road out there on me way intae the town last week, when I saw them lyin' on the roadside."

Rose felt bad about telling the lie to cover up for Gusty. She fully intended to confess the sin to Father Cassidy the following Saturday evening.

"Now, I had an idea they might-a been yours when I saw them, and not the underwear of any of the wimmin livin' round these parts. For most of the wimmin in these parts—meself included— would be wearin' the full brief 'cos we wouldn't be able tae get intae a pair of wee skimpy things like that. Not that I'm sayin' there's anything wrong with them, mind you. It's just that when a wommin gets up in years, like meself, she gets a wee bit broader of the beam, if ye get me meanin'."

"Can't understand how they made their way all the way out to the road. I had them pinned on the line."

"Well, ye know, Mrs. Hailstone, maybe the wind blew them off." A force-twelve hurricane couldn't carry them that far, Bessie thought. "Or maybe a magpie caught a-holt of them."

Rose saw Bessie's look of incredulity. "Oh, d'ye see them black-beaked scissortails? They'd take the food outta yer mouth if ye forgot tae shut it when ye were eatin'. But of course a city wommin like yourself wouldn't be expected to know the like of that."

Bessie's eyelids were beginning to droop, but she clung on, prepared to learn the thieving habits of every magpie in the vicinity of Tailorstown. Then, mercifully—

"God, is that the time? I have tae get my Paddy his tea. If he doesn't have it on the dot of three he gets that old acid influx, so he does."

Bessie helped Rose to her feet.

"Thanks very much for the lovely cake, Mrs. McFadden." She held up the lingerie. "And these."

"That's no bother atall. Now, there's just one more wee thing, Mrs. Hailstone." Her voice dropped to a confessional whisper. Bessie, suddenly fearful she might decide to sit down again, moved to the door. "Now, that lovely wee boy of yours, wee Herkie...ye wouldn't mind sendin' him down to Uncle Ned's the morra in the forenoon? Ned has a few wee jobs that need doin' round the place. And he's been so good so far."

"No problem, Mrs. McFadden. I could use the hour of peace."

"Oh, and another wee thing, Mrs. Hailstone. This is just for your ears, mind, but I think it's good tae warn ye, 'cos tae be forewarned is tae have four arms, or whatever it is they say.

"I was talkin' tae Betty Beard the other day and she tolt me her mother is very well mended. She'd come down with a Baker's cyst, don't ye know. Betty sez she'll be comin' back tae her job next week. Now, I'm sure Father Cassidy will be tellin' ye that the morra anyway. But it's good tae be a couple-a steps ahead, is it not?"

Little does she know, thought Bessie, as she finally—and with immense relief—shut the door on Mrs. McFadden. With a bit of luck, Father Cassidy wouldn't even have the luxury of telling her that her job was finished. If there was any justice in the world, he was in the clink by this stage, counting the bars on his cell window, as opposed to counting his priestly blessings.

Chapter forty-six

Can anything be sadder than work left unfinished? Yes: work never begun.

Lorcan Strong stared at the unfinished portrait of the Countess, turning over in his mind the aptness of the observation. Yet he felt certain that Christina Rossetti had not been pondering the whole sorry field of reproduction painting and counterfeit art when she coined those words.

Sir Joshua Reynolds's portrait had indeed been a thing of beauty—but no more. The villainous had forced the guiltless to misappropriate its beauty for the purpose of duping the unsuspecting. Lorcan's hand—his right hand, which had brought so many things of beauty into the world, whether by breathing new life into an Old Master or deepening the mystery of reality through his own work—had created *that*: an exact replica of a masterpiece.

Esthetic desecration should be alien to an artist's hands. Those hands are for giving, not taking; for creating and sharing, not grasping and amassing for oneself.

With that in mind he crossed to the portrait, took a steadying breath, raised a craft knife, and prepared to commit his first act of vandalism against—but for the sake of—true art.

And so the blade went through the Countess of Clanwilliam: through the flesh tints of her plain visage, the muted hues of her pale bosom, into the rich fabric of the magenta dress, the delicate leaves of the book she held.

He sliced through the Van Dyke browns, the Prussian greens, the indigo sky, the carmine roses, the glossy black of her abundant hair, until the fruits of the hours and days of his forced labor behind locked doors hung in tatters, unrecognizable in the wooden frame.

The assault over, he lifted the ruined work off the easel, ripped the shreds from the stretcher, levered the staples from the frame, broke it up, and tossed the lot into a garbage bag.

He would not be saving the stretcher for another canvas. Every trace of the painting had to go. As with Blennerhassett himself, he wanted the thing out of his life for good. He understood Bessie's need to get away from the cottage. The ill-starred well would always be a reminder. He, on the other hand, need not be party to such reminders. He could destroy the object. Burn it. Bury it. Throw it into the nearest river and hope to forget it.

He heard the phone ring as he was securing the bag. A few seconds later, his mother's voice, calling up to him. "Lorcan, dear... one of your colleagues...Stanley from the museum."

He went down the stairs, gripping the garbage bag.

"Stanley, to what do I owe the pleasure?"

"How ye, Lorcan...Some good news and bad. Which d'ye want first?"

"Now, let me guess...The Empire's been bombed, but luckily you weren't in it at the time."

"Not funny! No, oul' Feel-the-Pain's in hospital...Isn't expected tae last."

"That *is* bad news." Lorcan was recalling that his last conversation with Fielding-Payne had been less than cordial, with a heated exchange on the finer points of ladies' corsets. "He seemed in rude good health when I last saw him."

"Aye, it happened only a couple of days ago. They say it's a stroke. There's word that the powers that be are gonna ask *you* tac take his place."

"Don't know why they'd want *me*." He was aware that Stanley liked a bit of gossip. He guessed it came from isolation, of a working life spent handling fossils in a darkened room for most of the day.

"Well ye see, his niece is doin' your job now. Nice bitta skirt she is, too. Would suit you down to the ground. I'm sure they wouldn't want till be sendin' her away just 'cos you're comin' back. Well I hope they're not, anyway, 'cos—"

"Get to the point, Stanley. Is this one of your inventions?"

"No, it's true! Catherine at reception said she'd typed the letter till ye yesterday. Just thought I'd let ye know in advance, like. You'll soon be back anyway."

"I'll believe it when I see it. Well, thanks for letting me know, Stanley."

"No bother."

"See ye soon then. Regards to Catherine."

"Will do…Oh, Lorcan, hold on a wee minute."

"Yes?"

"See, when ye take over…ye wouldn't do a mate a favor and get me moved out of them bloody fossils, would yeh?"

Lorcan grinned. Stanley looking after his own interests, as usual.

"Yes," he said, "it's high time you moved on from there. I'm told there's a vacancy in Stone Age Artifacts."

"But…but…"

"Not modern enough? Right you be, Stanley: Bronze Age Implements it is then. I'll make it a priority."

"Now, come down here to the kitchen, Herkie," Rose said kindly. "The work ye're gonna be doing for Uncle Ned might take a lot outta a wee boy like you. So a wee bite tae eat first, tae keep yer strength up."

Herkie struggled up onto a high stool, eyes widening at the feast laid out on the table. There was a hefty slice of sponge cake, a Wagon Wheel, two bourbon creams, and a jam tart. Rose had provided the banquet as a salve to ease Herkie's pain. For what she had to say to him would be discomforting at best.

"Now, you and me's gonna have a wee talk while ye eat that," she said, pouring Herkie a glass of fizzy orange and sitting down opposite.

"How much are ye gonna pay me?" asked the bold Herkie— never one to mince his words when it came to the subject of money. A childhood spent hearing his mother complain about not having enough of it, and his jobless father concocting ways of relieving other people of theirs, had him believing that theft was the speediest and most painless method of acquiring it.

He took the slice of sponge cake in both hands.

"Now, Herkie, I think ye have a wee confession tae make?"

"I said me confession last Sa'rday." He well remembered the embarrassment he'd caused his mother and the resulting drubbing he'd taken on the backs of the legs.

"Aye, so ye did, but did ye tell Father Cassidy about the pension money ye stole outta me handbag, son?"

Herkie took a gulp of orange and gaped at Rose over the rim of the glass, cheeks going pink.

She waited for his shame to subside and for an explanation to be offered. When none was forthcoming, she said, "Now, I know it was you, so don't deny it."

Herkie had a sudden brainwave. Through the open door he heard Veronica snuffling about the yard. "Maybe the pig took it."

Rose tried not to smile. "Well, ye see, Veronica wouldn't be able to open the big clip on my handbag. And before ye blame Gusty…"

She reached into her apron pocket and drew out the tell-tale Milky Way wrapper. Rose had held on to the evidence, fully intending to report the theft to Sergeant Ranfurley. But the bomb scare had intervened, and while it had created unprecedented upset in her life, God-blissus-and-savus, it had nonetheless solved the riddle of the stolen pension.

"I found that outside there on the doorstep and neither Gusty nor Veronica eat choclit bars, truth be told."

Herkie knew the game was up. Two fat tears rolled out of his baby-blue eyes and traveled all the way down his cheeks, to fall off his chin and onto the plate.

"Don't tell me ma! She'll kill me, so she will."

"No, I'm not gonna tell yer ma. That's why I brought ye down here. Ye're gonna do a bit of tidying up round the place, tae make up for the money ye stole. 'Cos ye have tae do penance for breaking the Eighth Commandment. Ye get nothing in life for free, Herkie. Is that all right now?"

Herkie nodded, mollified that his sin would be kept secret. The backs of his legs would remain pain free, and his ma would never know about all the lies he'd told her regarding his expeditions to Kilfeckin Manor.

He could live with that.

Chapter forty-seven

Are you looking for something, dear?" asked Etta Strong, coming into the living room.

She had entered through the door that led from the bar to their living quarters. Lorcan had not been expecting that.

He quickly stuffed the wad of Aunt Bronagh's international money orders into his trouser pocket and turned to face his mother. He noted she'd been to the hairdresser.

"No...no, just...just seem to have mislaid one of my cuff links," he said, abashed. "You're not back at your station already, are you? I'm surprised."

"Oh, my legs are fine now. And, if I'm honest, I missed the banter...Chatting to customers keeps me occupied."

"Can I get you anything?"

"No, no, son. You carry on. Brother Brendan is out there, counting the takings from his charity boxes. You know how long it takes him. His eyesight isn't the best. I thought I'd get him a cup of tea."

"Wouldn't a pair of glasses be more appropriate?"

"Away on with *you*." She headed in the direction of the kitchen but paused. "Oh, before I forget. Socrates says he lost his dentures on Saturday night. You didn't come across them, did you?"

Lorcan, bemused: "No. I don't believe I did."

"Are you sure?"

"Well, I think I'd remember something like that. How on earth do you mislay a set of dentures?"

"They're a new set, you see, and he had them wrapped in a hankie in his pocket."

"What stunning logic! They don't call him Socrates for nothing, do they?"

"Now, don't be cruel, dear. He was keeping them out until he got used to them."

"I don't really see, but—"

"Oh, another thing, now that I've got your ear." Etta came closer to him, her voice a whisper. "It's about Gusty."

"Why are you whispering? There's no one around, and you're not in the confessional."

"Shush!" She cast a look at the open door. She heard Brother Brendan coughing softly and the chink of coins. She caught Lorcan's arm. "I'm worried about Gusty."

"Er, right. Why?"

"Well, when he was leaning over to change one of the beer kegs yesterday, I'll swear I saw the strap of a lady's slip sticking out from under his shirt."

Lorcan exploded with laughter. "That's ridiculous!"

"I know."

"You were just imagining it, Mother. The light can play tricks."

Etta's lips formed an *O* of pained disapproval. "Well, I hope so." She glanced back at Lorcan. "You look as if you're going somewhere."

"Yes, I have a bit of business to attend to in Killoran. I won't be long."

She continued on into the kitchen—but returned a moment later. "D'you know what Brother Brendan told me?"

"No, tell me."

"He said that Father Cassidy left the parish yesterday."

"Oh…" Lorcan was astonished by the speed with which events had moved, but very glad they had. *Little does she know.* "That's a bit sudden, isn't it?"

"Well, that's what I said to Brother Brendan. But apparently he's got bronchitis. He'll have to have treatment, and then he's off to recuperate in Donegal with the nuns, poor man."

"I see."

"You know, I never liked the sound of his cough," Etta said, her features scrunching up with concern. She decided to sit down after all, as if the move might lighten the great burden of injustice dealt the priest. "And all those cigarettes can't have helped him. I expect he'll be given a parish over there when he's better. Well, the air's cleaner for a start. Do him good."

"Hmm." There was really nothing more Lorcan could add. Cassidy had fooled them all.

He was gone, though, to that foreign land across the border— out of reach of the authorities. But, more important, he was rendered powerless. Powerless to destroy the blameless in the pursuit of some fatally delusional, flag-waving cause.

Chapter forty-eight

Bessie Halstone had come to the end of her sojourn.

She sat on a bench at the front of Rosehip Cottage, taking the sun on her bare arms and legs, eyes shut, thinking her own thoughts—thoughts that rarely focused on the present, but fluctuated between past and future, between regret and the torment of not knowing what lay ahead.

The relief she'd allowed herself, following the priest's removal and the Dentist's demise, was short-lived. Finally she could stop running, but like a harried deer, the fear of capture was snapping at her heels once more.

It had been a turbulent week, starting out with her harassment at the hands of the RUC and ending with Father Cassidy turning out to be a terror suspect. What could possibly happen next?

Her thoughts returned to Ranfurley. A week was time enough for him to have checked her out and alerted social services that Herkie was a truant. Oh, God! Lorcan's assurances that he wouldn't bother her were all but forgotten. Soon the sergeant's angry features were morphing into those of her sister, Joan.

Bessie shifted uneasily on the sunseat, anxiety rising, blind to the beauty that lay all around her—the flower-filled garden, the rolling fields, the serenity and calm of the distant mountains. She

recalled the dream she'd had at the table in the parochial kitchen—
a prophetic one, as it turned out.

No, she wouldn't be welcome in Joan's home. But Joan was the
only family she had. They'd never been close as children, lost to each
other through their parents' lovelessness. Why should adulthood be
any different? Joan the sanctimonious one, Bessie the rebel. Born
opposites, with traits as ingrained as lettering through seaside rock;
Bessie inheriting the genes of one parent, Joan the genes of the other.

Yes, she'd make her way to Joan's unwelcoming door, suffer
the indignation, eat humble pie. There were plenty of hotels in
Sligo. She'd pick up some seasonal work. She sighed, tried to con-
tent herself with the thought. It was summer, after all.

But time was marching on. She wouldn't make any money sitting in the sun. They had to hit the road. And fast. Ranfurley could
be on his way to the cottage right this minute. She'd go indoors
and make an immediate start on the packing. The cottage needed a
clean as well. Gusty Grant had to be told of her plans.

She opened her eyes and checked her watch. It was two fifteen.
Herkie was taking his blessed time. Mrs. McFadden was clearly
making him work for his money.

She got up to go in, seized now by the need to get things done.

But…a sound at the garden gate had her turning round again.
She was surprised to see Lorcan coming up the path. He had something in his hand.

"Not a bad time, I hope?"

"No…no, not at all."

"I decided to walk. Such a lovely day…couldn't bear to sit in
a stuffy car."

He sat down on the sunseat. He seemed composed. Perhaps
too composed. A sudden fear gripped her. *God, he's come here with bad
news.* She could *feel* it. Lorcan's calm was all an act.

She was truly anxious now. A question had been preying on her mind. She had to know.

"Did you tell Ranfurley?" She tried to keep her voice even. "I mean...does he know about...about the..."

"About Blennerhassett? Don't worry. Everything's taken care of on that score. They'll not be pursuing any lines of inquiry—to use police speak."

"A-are you sure?"

He nodded firmly. "Positive. Please, sit down. I've got something for you."

She joined him on the seat. He handed her an envelope. Nerved for bad news, she accepted it with mounting dread. Ranfurley *had* alerted social services. They *were* taking Herkie into care. They'd asked Lorcan to break it to her gently.

"W-what is it?"

"Open it and see."

"It's bad news, isn't it?"

He smiled. "I don't think so, but I'll let you be the judge of that, Bessie."

She tore open the envelope, slid out the contents.

She found herself holding two tickets: plane tickets. Her lips moved silently over the words. She could barely credit what she was reading.

Bessie Lawless née Halstone
Aer Lingus Flight number AL 88620
Depart Dublin International Airport 17:15, May 26, 1981
Arrive Miami International Airport 18:29, May 26, 1981
(flight duration 6 hrs 14 mins)

Disbelieving, she glanced at the second ticket. It contained the same details but was made out in the name of "Hercules Conan Lawless."

"My God!" She clamped a hand over her mouth. She wasn't going to Sligo; she was going to Amerikay! She would be doing what her erstwhile employer and role model, Mrs. Lesley Lloyd-Peacock, had done before her. And not on a dirty old steamship, but on an *airplane*! She'd never been on a plane in her life. But...

"I...I don't understand."

"I take it you approve, though?"

She could not speak. Tears welled up. She nodded.

He patted her knee, reached into his jacket pocket, drew out a photograph, and passed it to her.

An attractive, elderly lady was grinning out at her. She was lounging by a swimming pool, toasting the photographer with a cocktail glass the size of a fishbowl.

"My Aunt Bronagh. Your new employer."

Bessie, overcome with emotion, saw a woman not unlike Mrs. Peacock.

"She's in need of a 'darned good live-in cook,'" Lorcan said, imitating his aunt's American accent. "So I told her about you. She's looking forward to meeting you...and Herkie as well, of course." He checked his watch. "So, if all goes according to plan, this time tomorrow you'll be boarding that flight. I'll take you there in the car, of course. To the airport, that is. You...wouldn't have to bother with the bus...or anything like that."

She made no reply.

He glanced over at her.

She just sat with her head bowed, staring down at the tickets.

He patted her knee. "I know it's a shock. It's a lot to take in, after all you've been through. So, you have a think about it and I'll call you later. Okay?"

He got up.

"Okay?"

She still could not look at him. Could not give an answer.

He donned his hat and headed back down the path. She heard him break his stride, briefly. Hesitate. She didn't know what to do. Was he playing games with her? Was there a catch? The old, familiar tape began to whirr, the ribbon worn thin by negativity and mistrust. He was a *man*, after all. Men did not gift airline tickets to women they hardly knew. There was always a price to pay, a favor to be returned "in kind." That, at least, was how things had always been.

But, maybe...maybe...

Her mind was in freefall. She looked up, saw that he was out on the main road, heading back toward the town. He did not seem too concerned. Panic gripped her. If she didn't hurry up she'd have to run all the way to High Street.

She sprinted after him.

"Lorcan, wait a minute...Lorcan!"

He turned.

"I...I don't need to think about it." She held up the plane tickets. Not...not even for a minute."

"That's wonderful! My aunt will be pleased."

"Why...why are you doing this?"

He shrugged. Gave her a reassuring smile. "Because...well, because, Bessie, you deserve it. Another chance. A better life." He waved a hand. "Better than what's gone before...better than this. You and Herkie deserve it all."

She looked down at the tickets, abashed by the compliment. "He's...he's all I have. Herkie, I mean. Don't know where I'd be without him."

She recalled what he'd told her just a few days earlier. "Dreams come true if you hold on to them."

He read her thoughts. "Besides, I had to make good on that promise about—"

"Dreams?"

"Yes, dreams. A man can't bear to be wrong, you know." His grin was lost on her. She was staring in disbelief at the tickets. Finally, she looked up.

"I-I can't...I can't pay you back. Not now, but I promise I will...later on, when..."

"I don't want payment. The plane tickets are a gift. Can't vouch for my aunt—"

"But, I've nothing to *give* you." Timid. Hesitant. Waiting for the ax to fall. It just seemed too good to be true.

Lorcan saw her predicament. He took a couple of steps toward her. "Come to think of it, there is something you could give me."

She frowned.

"It'll cost you nothing and make you even more beautiful."

"That's a riddle. I'm no good at riddles."

"A smile, Bessie. Just a smile."

She laughed.

"That's all?"

"That's all."

There was nothing to fear. The ax had not fallen. Lorcan Strong did not carry one. Unlike her father, her husband, he didn't *need* to carry one. She'd sensed it the first time she met him. But all the old fears had kept her prisoner. Unwilling to trust, unwilling to turn the page that might have shown her a better way.

"Oh, and you could promise to write to me, too," he added.

She threw her arms around him, hugging him tight. "I'll write every day. God, how...how can I ever thank you?"

A warm breeze riffled her hair. She *heard* it rustle in the trees behind her. Truly *heard* it. Felt the beauty in its voice. Understood, right then, that there was no need to judge. There were good people in the world. Genuinely good people, like Lorcan. Perhaps all the years of suffering had been necessary to bring her to this juncture: this realization, so simple, so natural, and yet costing not less than everything in its gain.

He thought he understood. Planted a kiss on her cheek. Looked into her tear-stained face, into the eyes that had seen so much sadness: gatekeepers to the heart that had endured so much pain. "All right?"

She nodded. He released her. "Tomorrow's going to be a busy day. Better—"

She held on to his arm. He needed to know her heart. "We... we'll...n-never...never forget you for this. Herkie...Herkie and me...not for a moment, ever. We...we love you...*we always will... always.*" The precious words, so sincerely meant, were all she had to give him.

Lorcan smiled. "Thank you," he said and looked away toward the mountains, holding dear the moment.

And he wished, truly wished, that Bessie, the disenchanted widow, whom he'd met for the first time in church grounds on a windy Sunday morning not so very long before, would know happiness, true happiness, far away from war-torn Ulster, in another land, where bombs did not explode and the past could no longer hurt her.

He turned back to her.

"And I love you, too...both of you," he said, not realizing until that moment how much he cared for the two of them. "I love you both truly...in the highest, purest, most beautiful kind of way."

Chapter forty-nine

The day of departure was to be a hectic one.

Bessie Halstone woke early, letting go of a dream state that she hoped would never end. In the night, she'd floated along the boulevards of downtown Miami. Had splashed through the waters of South Beach, felt the sun on her face and the breeze in her hair—and joy. Oh, the joy of Herkie's hand in hers, the excitement on his face as he gazed in awe at the towering skyscrapers shimmering in the midday sun!

Oh, God, maybe it *was* only a dream.

She sat up in bed, beset by panic. Gazed about the room. Checked the clock and...

The tickets! She snapped them up from the bedside locker. Her dream a reality once more. *There* was her name and Herkie's, the snapshot of her new employer, Bronagh Valdez-Murphy.

She hugged her knees, reassured and ecstatic. Lorcan's gift—this lifeline—was like a second baptism. She felt light-headed, free, as if the burdens of the past had slipped away in the night.

She heard the cockerel crow down at Kilfeckin Manor. It was going on for seven.

"Herkie, are ye awake?"

Herkie stirred in his couch bed in the corner.

"It's time tae get up, son. We've a big day ahead of us."

She rose, went and gave him a good shake. "Herkie, wake up!"

He turned over and yawned widely, rubbed his eyes.

"Wha...?"

"D'ye remember where we're goin' today?"

"Aye...we're goin' tae...we're goin' tae Amerikay tae see the Statue of Liberry!"

She lifted him from the bed and swung him around the room. "Yes, son. Amerikay, here we come!"

Herkie giggled. "Och, Ma, you're makin' me dizzy."

She set him down.

"Now, first things first: We get dressed, clean this place up, then start packin'."

There was lots to do. Apart from the cleaning, several of Aunt Dora's ornaments—which had suffered Herkie's curiosity when they moved in—needed to be repaired. There was also the question of the broken picture of St. Clare. But she'd already thought of a good way of repaying Gusty, to compensate him for the vandalism.

By late afternoon, Aunt Dora's cottage was looking about as clean as a nun's conscience. Mother and son had the floors and windows washed, the carpets beaten, the linen aired, and every piece of bric-a-brac and ornament dusted, the damaged ones repaired.

The rattle of a truck in the lane had Herkie running in through the front door, poker in hand and fresh from his flailing of the dusty rugs.

"Ma, there's Mr. Grant!"

"So it is. I told Lorcan tae tell him tae call for the keys. And another thing, son: Ye have tae give him back something ye stole off him."

She rushed upstairs and found the purloined wallet. Into it she placed the two five-pound notes she'd pinched to cover the fan belt and the rent all those weeks ago.

"Herkie, come here." She thrust the wallet into his hand. "Now, you give that back tae Mr. Grant, since you were the one who took it from him."

A look of fright came into Herkie's eyes.

"It's all right, son. Tell him ye found it out there on the path."

"Hello there, Mrs. Hailstone," said Gusty, darkening the open door. "So ye're goin' tae Amerikay I hear. Lorcan tolt me."

"Yes, Gusty, time to move on. We only knew yesterday. I was goin' to ring you when we'd finished cleanin'. Hope you didn't think we were gonna go off without—"

"Nah, I know ye wouldn't do the like-a that, Mrs. Hailstone." He looked about the spotless living room. "The place is lookin' terrible well. But I knew you'd be a wommin that'd look after things. Me aunt was the same, God rest her; always kept a tidy house."

"Mr. Grant," Herkie piped up. "I found yer wallet out in the lane yesterday." He handed it to him.

"God, that's a good 'un!" Gusty took the wallet and checked the contents. "I wundered where it'd went. I can tell ye when I lost it, too…It was the very day I took yins here…Couldn't find it anywhere after that day. Looked everywhere, begod."

Bessie hoped her blushes weren't showing through her Max Factored cheeks. "Well, better late than never…Gusty, there's something I'd like to give you."

Gusty's eyebrows shot above his spectacles.

"You've been very kind to us and I'd like to repay you." She went outside to the Morris Traveller. "Maybe you'd like the car."

"God, I'd love the car, right enough!" He couldn't believe his luck. Saw it already jacked-up at Grant Auto Repairs—a week's pleasant tinkering at least.

"Well, we can't fit it in the suitcase. Maybe you could do it up and sell it."

"Aye, I could do that...or maybe, ye know, I could keep it for ye, if ye ever decided tae come back."

Come back? Bessie doubted that, but just to please him said, "Well, you never know." She handed him the car keys. They returned indoors. "It's been really lovely here. Everybody's been so good to us—and you especially. Isn't that right, Herkie?"

Herkie, playing marbles on the table, looked up. "Aye, Ma," he said mechanically, not really paying attention to what the grownups were nattering about.

"Well, I'll tell ye what." Gusty pushed his big glasses up on his nose, stuck a finger in his ear and wiggled it. "If ye do decide tae come back, ye can write and tell me. I'll not be sellin' this house, 'cos me aunt nivver wanted it sold...so it'll be here for yeh and the wee boy, if things don't work out."

Bessie held out a hand. "That's really good to know. Thank you so much...for everything, Gusty."

"That's no bother atall."

"Herkie, come over here and say thank you to Mr. Grant."

Herkie got down off the chair. He shook Gusty's hand. "Thank you, Mr. Grant."

"That's all right, son. Thanks for findin' me wallet." Gusty reached into it and pulled out one of the fivers. "That's for you, for the journey."

"Gee! Thank you, Mr. Grant." Herkie was delighted. No one had ever given him so much money. He looked up at his mother. "Ma, can I buy me Action Man now?"

"I don't know. Maybe you should ask Mr. Grant."

"Oh, buy whatever ye want, son," Gusty said. He patted Herkie's head. "Ye're a very honest wee lad, so ye are...a credit tae yer mammy." He turned to Bessie. "Well, I must be goin', Mrs. Hailstone."

She saw him to the front door. "I'll not check anything, Mrs. Hailstone, for I know ye looked after everything very well."

Bessie thought of all the reconstructive work she'd just carried out on several items in Dora's collection. The fishy smell of Copydex adhesive still hung on the air. She hoped the landlord hadn't a keen nose. She doubted it somehow. All the same, she *had* noted a faint whiff of scent coming off him. Odd.

"Aye, just leave the keys under that gnome there, afore ye go," he said.

"I will indeed," said Bessie, eyeing the gnome, which Herkie had relieved of its pointy ears on their first day in the cottage. She'd managed to glue them back on again in a rough, lopsided kind of way.

"Well, be seein' ye, Mrs. Hailstone."

Bessie extended a hand. "Thanks...thanks for everything."

The hand, she noted, felt much softer than the one she'd shaken on that first meeting. Interesting.

She saw him eye her tweed suit, the Mrs. Peacock cast-off.

"That's a fine costume you've got on," he said. "Would that blouse be the silk or the satin? Hard tae tell the diff'rence between them."

Bessie, taken aback, fingered her collar. "It's silk. Satin, ye see, is much shinier."

"Oh, I'm with ye now, begod. Satin's the shiny boy. I wundered about that, so I did."

He turned and climbed into his truck.

"Well, good luck, Mrs. Hailstone. Have a safe journey."

In seconds he was gone, leaving behind him a trail of dust and a very bemused Bessie.

She went back indoors, chuckling to herself.

Gusty's brief career as landlord might have ended, but Mrs. Hailstone would have been stunned to learn what seismic shifts her breakdown near the village had wrought in the mechanic's life. He would miss his glamorous tenant—that was certain. But such heartache was tempered by the fact that behind the locked doors of a room in Kilfeckin Manor, an altogether different Gusty had been born. As he roared away in the truck, richer by another vehicle, his spirits high and fancies free, he pressed down harder on the gas.

Satin, he thought. Aye, satin is the *shiny* one! Maybe, just maybe, if he hurried up, he could grab a half hour in the Turret Room before his bar shift at three.

Bessie pulled out her suitcase. Inside was Herkie's bag: the Dunnes Stores shopper. She thought back to the last time they'd packed up their things, in the old house in Valencia Terrace, and how panic-stricken she'd been.

No such panic on this occasion.

What a wonderful, serendipitous move breaking down outside Tailorstown had proved to be!

The packing didn't take long. They'd be traveling light.

"Right," Bessie said, when everything was safely zipped up, "I'll just take another wee look round…make sure we haven't forgot anything, son. You take the bags out tae the sunseat. Lorcan will be here soon."

"Ma, look!" Herkie was pointing at a chest of drawers in the corner.

"What is it, son?"

"The record player, Ma."

"God, you're right. What am I gonna do with that? We can't take it on the plane."

At that moment, there came the sound of clip-clopping out on the road. Herkie ran outside.

"It's Barkin' Bob, Ma."

"God, the very one. We'll give it tae *him*."

Herkie waved, and in under a minute the traveling junk collector was reining in Brenda at the front of Rosehip Cottage. He immediately launched into his spiel.

"Wid yer mammy want to boy a bucket?" he began, trotting out the words in his customary, knife-grinder's drawl. "A basin, a froyin'-pan for tae froy her sausages of a marnin'. Or some turf for the foyer, tae keep her warm of a long winter's noyt. Well, whaddya say, boy?"

"D'ye want a record player?" Herkie asked, looking up at the primordial chaos that was Bob's face.

"A *what?*"

"Here it is!" Bessie called out.

Through the front door she came, bearing the final endowment from her doomed marriage to Packie.

Bob scrambled from his perch and began making room on the cart. He shifted a shadeless table lamp, a chamber pot, and a sun-bleached portrait of John F. Kennedy to one side and relieved Bessie of her burden.

"It was a wedding present," she said. "My husband's dead now, and we're goin' till Amerikay, so can't take it with us. It's workin' all right, so you should get a bit for it."

"God bless ye, daughtur!"

"And the records...not much good without them." She handed over her prized album collection with a twinge of sadness. Gloria Gaynor, Tammy Wynette, and Dolly Parton had taken her through many a rough patch.

She'd miss the music.

Bob eyed Dolly's generous cleavage on the cover of *Heartbreaker* and stuck her on the cart within kissing distance of the slain US president.

"God bless ye, daughtur!" he said again.

"Ye can take that, too," said Herkie, proffering his Action Man. "I'm gonna be gettin' a new one."

"God bless ye, son!" said Bob. The headless Action Man joined the one-armed Barbie, and Bob swung himself back onto the cart.

A car horn sounded—and there was Lorcan turning in off the main road. The yard was small, and with Lorcan's arrival old Bob was blocked in.

"It's all right, Bob," Bessie said. "We'll only be a minute."

She ran back into the cottage. There was no time to delay. She grabbed up her handbag, pulled the door behind her, turned the key, and, following Gusty's instructions, stowed it under the garden gnome.

"All set?" Lorcan took her suitcase and opened the trunk.

"All set!"

"Lorcan, I'm gettin' a new Action Man, so I am."

"Excellent, Herkie...now you get in the back there. We can't keep this gentleman waiting."

Bob raised his hat in acknowledgment. "Good luck tae ye now and God bless ye!" he shouted. "May the wind alwa's blow at yer back!"

Lorcan put the car in gear and they moved off.

Bob and Brenda followed behind.

At the end of the lane Lorcan turned left. Bob turned right.

Herkie clambered up on the backseat and waved goodbye to Bob and his mare, to the cottage, the dwellings and fields of Tailorstown.

The car crested a hill.

Bob fell away from view.

Herkie sat back down again.

Soon Bob was turning down his own lane on the outskirts of town. At the far end of the lane, across a field, stood his old shack.

He bumped his way down the familiar route.

Without warning, a fox shot across Brenda's path.

She reared with a startled whinny, hooves flailing the air.

The cart lurched sideways, upsetting its load. Several items ended up in the ditch.

"Holy God!" Bob sighed and dismounted.

He stood, surveying the mess; some of the items were now even more damaged than before.

With resignation he got down on his knees. His most recent acquisition, Mrs. Halstone's record player, lay upside down. Luckily, it was still in one piece. He pulled it toward him. As he did so, the back panel came away in his hands.

"Ah, Jezsis! But you're aisy enough tae fix." He began shoving the panel back into place.

It would not go all the way, however. Something was jamming it.

Bob fumbled inside the record player. He frowned. There was what felt like wads of paper stuffed inside. He tugged one out and held it up.

"Oh, holy God!"

He was looking at the printed face of H.R.H. Queen Elizabeth II.

A wad of twenty-pound notes fanned beneath his blackened fingertips.

A thousand in the bundle, easy.

He upended the record player and shook it.

Immediately, obediently, unleashed, unfettered, out they came: sheaf upon sheaf, bundle upon bundle, the secreted spoils of Packie's heist.

The plunder, the hoard, the ill-gotten gains that Packie had died for, that the Dentist had drowned for, and for which Bessie Halstone-Lawless had very nearly given *her* life.

"Oh, holy jumpin' Jesus God!"

Barkin' Bob fell upon the scattered booty, eyes wide with ecstasy. He counted ten bundles in all. Ten thousand pounds lay strewn about him! He gazed in wonder. His heart on fire.

He could not see—or even begin to imagine—the pain the loot had caused, the lives it had ruined, the blood spilled in the pursuit of its gain, its loss, and its retrieval.

Bob saw only God's rich reward for a lifetime of hardship.

He lay on his back, opened his arms wide and burst into riotous song.

"Oh, Jesus' blood never failed me yet,
Never failed me yet, failed me yet.
Oh, Jesus' blood never..."

A flock of starlings flew from the trees. A breeze riffled the leaves. Brenda pranced in excited dance. But Barkin' Bob sang on and on, deaf to the strum and strang of nature's shifts.

He sang in celebration, in thanksgiving, in the undeniable knowledge that, after years of poverty, living off scraps and distant dreams, his prayers had been answered.

Finally.

The sun came out. Bob took it as a sign. God was smiling down upon him. The horrid past—all gone.

He gathered up the bills and headed homeward: a spirit freed, a man reborn, his life changed for good by the evil and the wronged.

Author's Note

Even though this is a work of fiction, the occurrences and situations involving the priest, Father Cassidy, are based on real events.

Acknowledgments

My sincere thanks to everyone on the Amazon team, most especially to senior editor Alan Turkus, editor David Downing, and copyeditor Elise Marton.

To my sister Ann and brother William, for encouraging me every step of the way.

To my special friends Catherine Lynch and Elizabeth Jean Hunter, for always being there for me.

To Anne and Robert Keogh, for providing me with a lovely setting where I could finally finish the book.

And last but not least to my husband, David, for his never-faltering faith in me.

About the Author

Christina McKenna is a graduate of Belfast College of Art, where she gained an honors degree in fine art, and later a postgraduate degree in English from the University of Ulster. An accomplished painter and novelist, McKenna has exhibited her art internationally and in Ireland, and taught art and English for ten years. She is the author of the highly praised memoir *My Mother Wore a Yellow Dress*, as well as the nonfiction books *The Dark Sacrament* and *Ireland's Haunted Women*, and a previous Tailorstown novel, *The Misremembered Man*. She currently lives in Northern Ireland with her husband, the author David M. Kiely, with whom she collaborates on occasion.